SWEET TEA & NECROMANCY
by
R.W. Badger

Same Old Story Publishing
A Same Old Story Productions Company

Copyright 2021 – R.W. Badger
Cover Artwork Copyright 2021 Essi Matthews
Edited by Stevie Chandler
ISBN: 978-1-945450-99-0

SAME OLD STORY PUBLISHING 2021
Amelia, Ohio, 45102
Sameoldstorypublishing.com

This book is dedicated to Allison, who is directly to blame for pushing me forward, and to Lizzie and Josh, whose personalities inspired a morbid but smiling world.

It's all your fault, so thank you.

Sweet Tea & Necromancy

Chapter 1. The Woman With Four Right Arms

Even for grave robbers, the two made an unusual pair. One complained about the work he had to do; one was resting in the shade. One hated the summer heat, one unpacked a little lunch they had brought to the midday heist. The two had made it this far without anyone spotting them. In spite of Karao's numerous assurances, Nika wasn't entirely sure that any of this was legal.

"I'm just saying." Nika scooped out another shovelful of dirt. "This probably doesn't look good." He took a breath before plunging back into the soil. The coffin they were at was, as Karao insisted, only two or three feet deep. He was sure that was supposed to be encouraging, but three feet of dirt was still a lot for one scrawny kid to unearth on his own.

Nika didn't remember Karao bringing a hammock, yet there she was, comfortably swaying in the cool breeze. "It's the first rule of necromancy, 'get used to looking suspicious.'"

This was the fifth or sixth 'first rule of necromancy' he had been taught since she had taken him in a few weeks before; they were getting hard to keep track of. Still, she had a point. Necromancy, otherwise called The magic of the dead, reanimation, black magic, etc., had optics... issues, to say the least.

Karao was an imposing figure. She was tall for sure, though nobody was sure just how tall since she never stood quite upright. She always seemed to be either relaxed or focused; neither mood lent itself to good posture. She had dark skin and bright clothes, a killing glare, and a warm smile.

Her second most defining feature would be her missing right arm. She refused to buy special clothes and would chop the sleeves off of what she wanted to wear anyways. This was fine since her single most defining feature was the four skeletal arms hanging off the right half of her body, each rooted in a different place in the spine. Each was the arm of some long-dead mage, capable of calling on the spells they had used in life. Karao had called it, "practical necromancy."

The way she moved and used these deadarms, her name, made them seem effortless and natural like they were a part of her that had always been there. Maybe it was the confidence that led Nika to agree to this.

It was curious, being comfortable with a 'gi' like necromancy. She promised to teach him how to do it, and he obliged—all for the price of working in her tea shop with the other necromancers. In spite of this shoveling, it was a good deal.

He struck something. "I found it! Wait, no, that's a rock. Wait, it's. Um. Karao?"

She dismounted from the hammock with the grace of a startled cat. Nika thought it was funny but kept it to himself. Karao's deadarms swayed as she walked. The fingers in one of them, the second from the top, twitched and writhed a bit. Karao's pitch black hammock receded into the ground. That deadarm could twist shadows into any number of things.

Characters in books Nika read might have used those powers to go on exciting adventures and fight off evil; Karao seemed more interested in grabbing things from across the teashop without getting up.

"No, you were right. This is it." She knelt down and placed her left hand on the casket's surface. "You may want to be, well, not here."

Nika took the hint and hopped out of the grave. For good measure, he made sure two headstones were between himself and Karao. The ground was moving below him, no, not the ground, just his shadow. And the tombstones. And the trees.

Every shadow within the entire cemetery was being pulled in towards Karao. She stood and stepped slowly back from the grave. The shadows amassed into a viscous ooze, swirling into the grave plot and kicking up dirt. Within a minute, the casket had been laid from the ground and deposited on the ground next to the cleanly excavated hole.

Nika couldn't speak. To most people, magic was just another part of life. Displays like this still unnerved him in a good sense, somehow. It was one thing to read about magic; these past few weeks living in the teashop was still something he was getting used to.

Awe only lasts so long, and he had a problem. "Why didn't you just-well, nevermind." He had picked up on the pattern pretty quickly. If Karao ever had him do something bizarre or nonsensical, there was usually some 'reason' for it. He waited to hear what the reason behind him exhausting himself on this project was.

Karao played along with a whimsical smile. "And take your sense of accomplishment? I wouldn't dream," she waved her hand dismissively. "It wouldn't have worked without you digging in first. I have my limits, you know."

Karao laid the lid open to the casket, and in an instant, Nika was assaulted by some unholy beast: the stench. "That's awful."

"You get used to it. Here, take a look. I promise it's fine."

Seeing a fully clothed skeleton was new, and he didn't quite know how to process it. Still, there she was. Dressed in what must have been fancy hundreds of years ago. It didn't look all that different than what he wore, now that he thought about it. This was his last chance to tackle that doubt rooting in the back of his mind.

"Are you sure this is ok?"

Karao ruffled his already messy hair. She always made him feel so short. She flicked the wrist of her living hand. Nika expected something magical or incredible; really, she was shaking a small black book loose from her long sleeve. She flipped through pages and pages of tally marks. Eventually, she found what she was looking for and showed it to him. A list of names, some crossed out in red ink, some faded by the aging ink.

"Melody Ton. Agreed to volunteer her body to advance necromancy. See?" Karao reached into her pocket and looked quizzically at something he couldn't see. "We still have a bit of time, but we need to hurry."

Squinting, he could sort of see the name on the tombstone. "Hurry for what?"

Karao's eyes anticipated his excitement. "I want you to try making your own deadarm." He nearly jumped. Talking was never his strong suit, so he nodded feverishly. "Or, I wanted you to, but we're out of time. So I'll just have you watch, ok?"

She knelt down by the casket and put her hand on the skeleton's hand in reverence. Nika took every mental note that he could. He watched the way her fingers hovered just above the body, the way her back stiffened a bit before the spell began. Purple sparks, the sign of necromancy, jumped down her neck and arm before darting between her fingertips and, finally, the body of the girl in the casket.

Threads of violet magic wove between the bones like the muscle fibers that once kept it together. It jittered and shook, the once disconnected bones reunited by a now invisible thread. As the sparks made their way up to her shoulder, Karao pulled the arm out.

"And just like that, you have a deadarm. Any questions?"

She had been talking the entire time, and he hadn't been listening. He shook his head.

Two startling sounds beckoned for his attention; a ringing and a shout. One had caused him to jump a bit, and the other just added to the height. He yelped and looked towards the cemetery gate. A man in a brown coat as frayed as his wispy white hair was charging at them from the gate.

Karao placed something in his hand. "Do you know what this is?" She continued on, ignoring the man closing in on them.

In Nika's hand was a small gold coin with an hourglass embedded in its center. The sand was flowing up instead of down. No matter which way he twisted it, the sand followed the same path. It was buzzing a bit. "There are two of these coins. One here, and one back at the shop and, well, tell me, have you ever teleported before?"

He shook his head and peered behind his mentor; the grizzled man had tripped but was still very much on his way. "Um, are we-"

"Nika, hold your breath. Now." She grabbed his shoulder. The last of the sand dripped through, and he obeyed.

The cemetery faded from view in a hazy blink, like a blanket had enveloped them slowly at first and then quickly finished the job. Even with his eyes open, the world became darker than Nika had ever known for one eternal second. The world went from dusty to freezing and back to a comfortable summer heat faster than Nika could fully register it. Every organ in his body felt like it was turning inside out in protest. His stomach, in particular, was staging a full-scale coup to prevent

Nika from ever teleporting anywhere ever again. It was a compelling argument.

The part he hadn't expected was the water.

The two were back in Karao's teashop, The Pale Garden, for certain. Specifically, they were standing where customers were out to be, in the front of the house, should one ever show up. It was filled with a chaotic catalog of different tables and chairs 'borrowed' from places all over the city. Behind that was a kitchen clearly not meant for commercial use and a door that leads either up or downstairs, depending on which direction the switch was flipped.

Karao was vocally upset about the water. It did not take long for her to figure out what had happened. They weren't alone in the room; the other two necromancers-in-training were in the middle of something that they themselves wound up in the middle of.

Nils was the oldest of the trainees and one of the oddest but most charming people Nika had ever met. They were tall, with ash-grey skin with no hair to speak of, and they seemed to be stuck referring to themself in the third person a lot. Nils was a homunculus, an artificial person, who had moved into the shop long before taking up necromancy. They were usually upbeat and happy and not the panicky, startled teenager in front of them.

Catherine was on the other side of them, and she was fuming. She was an unfortunate combination of being someone who you didn't want to get into a fight with and easily set off. She was sixteen, only a year younger than Nils, but substantially shorter. Normally, her hair was curly, brown, and unreasonably lengthy.

Presumably, her hair still looked like that somewhere under that utterly ludicrous hat. It was flat with little birds and faeries on the ends of springs bouncing around the top. One of them held a sign that read 'idiot' with an arrow pointing right down to Catherine. Nika's smile fought its way onto his previously shocked face.

"What-" Karao shook her hair loose. "-is going on?"

Nils stammered. "Nils was, um, cleaning when-" They were hiding a recently-emptied bucket behind their back. "yeah."

Karao sighed. "It's 'I,' Nils, 'I was cleaning.'" She turned to Catherine. "And the hat?" Catherine struggled for a moment, then came clean. "This is Nils's, and it won't come off."

Catherine had re-sparked whatever fight the two were in beforehand. "Well, maybe don't take Nils's things without asking."

"I just wanted to try it on! I wasn't going to wear it out or anything!"

Karao tried to intervene. "Look, I know-"

Nika had to ask. "That's cute? Even with the, er- springy bits?"

Karao tried again. "Look. I know-"

"Springy bits?" Catherine twitched a bit. "What springy bits?" Nils started laughing. "Look! I-"

Catherine had run out of the room in search of a mirror.

"Aren't you supposed to be the older one, Nils?" Karao slumped into a chair, nearly collapsing onto the table itself. "I get that it's hard for you two to share a room now, but that's just something we have to deal with for now. Also, no throwing the cleaning bucket at people."

Nils sat across from her, their face fixed on the floor. "The water was clean, at least. Sorry. Nils didn't really plan for things to get this out of hand."

A banshee, or more likely Catherine, wailed from the other room.

"I think you should apologize to her first. Nils. You do know how to get that hat off?"

"Nils- er- I think so." They got up and went to go and deal with their fuming sister.

"Was it always like this?" Nika asked.

"You've never had a sibling, have you?" Karao flipped the 'open' sign over. She regretted the words after seeing his face. "Sorry, I didn't mean to pry."

"It's fine." Life here was way different than the one he had; there was a lot about the world he didn't know, and how 'families interact' was just another one of those things, he supposed.

"I'm going to get something set up. We'll meet in the kitchen in about an hour. You should rest up, maybe take a shower."

Nika did exactly those things. His definition of resting was finding the most comfortable chair in the front room and reading a book Nils had lent him. It wasn't what he usually liked to read; there wasn't a lot of action, just day-to-day activities. Still, a book was better than no book, and he had run out of other options. The hour went by pretty quickly.

Karao called them into the kitchen with a devilish grin. There were two tables, a small round one to eat and one that, in theory, was for food preparation. In a rare change of pace, today, they seemed to be using it to prepare food. There were three bowls, each on a different side of the table.

"Wash your hands and pick a bowl," she commanded. They obeyed. "I wasn't planning on having you do this for a few more months, Nika." She shrugged with all five arms. "Oh well."

Nika looked into his wooden bowl. There was a very moist-looking ball of dough in its base. The three were confused.

"This dough needs to rise for 1 hour before we can bake it." Karao took the coin trinket and twisted the glass methodically. "Unfortunately, for that, we need yeast."

"You didn't put any in?" Nils asked.

"Oh, I did. Dead yeast," Karao answered, sipping tea.

"What?" Catherine and Nika asked at the same time.

"Yeast is a living thing that helps make bread. The yeast in those bowls is dead. Yeast is tricky, too. You can't just bring it back, you have to constantly refuel it, or it'll just shut right back down." Karao looked smug, setting the coin down in front of them. "You have one hour. Whoever ends up making the best bread gets the easy chores tomorrow."

The three perked up a bit. "I thought this was a punishment," Nika said.

Karao grabbed her favorite cup, the teapot, a book, and a chair from the dining table. She opened the door to the small backyard, intent on enjoying a peaceful evening. "Oh." She waved to them. "It is."

Nika gulped. Since coming to live at the house, he had only practiced necromancy a few times. He was still struggling with using it on command. He closed his eyes and tried to focus, but the crackling to his right was too much of a distraction.

Catherine was on full blast. Her hair, hands, and jacket rippled with lightning. The entire day's frustrations were being vented into this ball of dough. Her jaw clenched, her eyes glowed faintly, she made it a personal goal to ignite every bit of yeast in the bowl. If she was alone or lacked a little bit more restraint, she would be shouting at this dough to rise faster. Her hands being above the bowl soon proved to be too slow; she plunged her hand directly into it.

She said nothing, but her face screamed, 'I regret that immediately.'

Nils was holding the bowl from the base, their energy slowly pulsing up and into the dough. Their eyes were closed, sweat forming for a few minutes on their forehead. It was difficult for Nils to generate that much magic at once, but on a specific, metered pace, it was possible.

Nika's fingers shot individual sparks into the bowl, but that wasn't getting him anywhere fast. He kept pushing himself to do more. Two fingers. The palm of his hand. His right forearm. All became sources of this morbid magic.

"I don't think you two have it in you to finish this," Catherine taunted, she caught her breath. After half-an-hour, they had barely spoken and drained themselves. Nils didn't open their eyes but was certainly annoyed.

"Nils begs to differ. You can't just pour everything you've got into it," Nils said.

"It's 'I' Nils," Catherine corrected.

"What's burning?" Nika asked. He opened his eyes. Smoke was coming from Catherine's bowl.

"Mine's almost done cooking. Yours still looks moist, ha!" Catherine laughed.

"Cooking?" Nils asked. "Ok, one, it's baking, and two, we're just supposed to make the dough rise. It shouldn't be baking yet."

"What do you mean?" Catherine asked, nervous. Her lightning died down a bit.

"It's supposed to rise for an hour, and then you bake it," Nils responded.

Catherine looked at Nika. He nodded. That was, at least as far as he understood, what they were supposed to be doing. She put the bowl down, frustrated. For a moment, she started laughing.

"What's so funny?" Nils asked.

Catherine pointed to Nils's bowl. All of their energy had gone into the wooden bowl instead of the dough. It was sprouting some new twigs and a leaf. Nils hadn't looked once since beginning this exercise.

"Nothing, Nils, you're doing a great job." She nudged Nika's shoulder before grabbing a chair and leaving to join Karao out back. She couldn't really screw up worse than she already had. Effectively, she handed Nika the win.

Karao, at the end of it all, was disappointed. Nika's bread was lopsided, lumpy, and half-risen. Worse, that was the best of the bunch. Nils's tasted fine but critically failed the 'yeast-o-mancy' part of the challenge. Meanwhile, Catherine submitted a charred puck with two fist-shaped holes in it.

They ate a decent dinner that evening, save for the bread. They laughed and talked about the day, the fight completely forgotten. Nika had read and heard about family dinner tables. The concept always seemed so calming. It was his favorite part of living here now.

He had a lot to learn, and not just about necromancy. His old family almost never spoke to him. Most of what he knew of the world came from books he wasn't supposed to read. Fantastic adventures and more muted dramas. He knew what he wanted; a simple life with simpler problems. He didn't want to be alone anymore, even if that meant interacting with people. Maybe if...

Catherine caught him staring into space and tapped him on the head to get him back into the conversation. Nika decided it wasn't so bad to have people to look out for him, either way.

Chapter 1- End

Intermission- The Regulars

There are exactly four regulars that visit the tea shop more or less every day, as far as Nika could tell. They'd come in the same times each day, stay the same amounts of time, then move onto their respective lives.

The first two, who arrived early every morning, were a pair of elderly women. They had known each other long enough that they communicated with grunts, scowls, and the passive-aggressive use of napkins. They always 'ordered' the same thing, or, rather, it was already ready for them at the same time each morning. Karao would always prepare their tea first thing before leaving for a chunk of the day.

"If it isn't exactly perfect, we will never hear the end of it," she would say. "Although, to be perfectly honest, I doubt they can taste the difference between tea and rainwater."

The third would come in at the end of the workday, around three, and talk to Karao for a while. The two were always loud and argued politics and life for the half-hour he spent in the same chair by the window. He was middle-aged, highly opinionated, and always angry about something or other.

The last regular, Daniel, had absolutely nothing to do with Karao. According to Catherine, he didn't even like tea, to begin with. He always showed up around noon. He was here again, chatting with Nils.

Nika asked the obvious follow-up to the fact Catherine shared. "Then why is he here?"

"He's from our class." Catherine sounded exasperated even starting. "He's got a thing for Nils, I guess. Not that Nils has any idea." Catherine stopped wiping off the dirty table from the two earlier customers and glowered. "I'm deciding which one I want to feel bad for."

The two were laughing a lot and seemed to enjoy talking. "They both look happy."

"Nils is always happy, Nika." Catherine was cynical but not necessarily wrong. "They've known each other for years. I'm betting Nils doesn't want to change that."

Nika wasn't sure about Catherine's read on the room, but he didn't know any better, so it would stand for the time being. There was this strange sadness in Nils's eyes, a deep and suppressed shadow of something inside them.

If the regulars kept coming back, he'd have plenty of time to figure more out if he wanted. There really wasn't a rush for anything anymore.

Chapter 2. Beware of Moths That are Bigger Than Dogs

Nika's bedroom was the exact sort of unbearable silence that he couldn't stand. This quiet road in the city fell asleep all at once, and in these hours, he finally felt like he could just exist. He needed to explore. It was a twitching compulsion that he had to learn what this city was like, and waiting until night let him do that while not interacting with other people. It was less awkward for everyone.

Well, technically, it used to be Nils's room.

He couldn't remember the last time he had gone for a walk at night. He had the idea to do this a few nights before, and it had stewed in his mind ever since. Back at his old home, the punishment was too steep, but here he might get some extra chores. He changed back into the clothes he wore for the day and tiptoed down the stairs. Either Catherine or Nils was snoring from their room. He couldn't tell which it was.

He made it into the kitchen with only a few unavoidable creaky steps. When the light turned on behind him, his body gave him the choice to scream and run away or to stand completely still and hope that whatever had flipped the light switch would leave him alone.

He chose the second.

"Evening," Karao said, soft and measured. She was as unsurprised to see him as she was unprepared for a conversation. Nika was beginning to wonder if she had ever been caught off guard.

"Hey," he said.

She eyed his clothes. "Going somewhere?"

Lying made him uncomfortable, so he didn't. "I couldn't sleep."

"I see." Her deadarms were busy preparing another cup of tea as she leaned into the table. "The streets are very safe, in case you were worried."

Nika looked up. Karao's eyes were desperately covering anxiety. Her resolve was creaking behind her stable voice. He was peering into a ship that had sprung a leak.

"I was going to come back," he said.

She smiled. She straightened herself up a bit. Her hands busied themselves with her hair. "I know," she said, not entirely certain. "I just want you to know that you can talk with us if something is bothering you." Her tone shifted back to her usual matter-of-fact voice. "Not that I need to remind you again."

Nika smiled. "I have no idea what to say." He gestured to the room, "This is all-" good, excellent, scary, too fast, intimidating, too much, "-new."

"I understand." She whistled for his attention and tossed an apple to him. "The path to the park is nice; just head left down the street. Don't be out too long, moody." He turned to leave. "Oh, and Nika. I fully intend to keep my promise."

"Thanks, Karao." With that, he left.

As he walked, he thought about why conversations like that were so hard for him. He could have put her mind to ease a lot easier if he could go into more detail or elaborate at all. Fourteen years on this planet hadn't been enough for the first few times someone asked him how he felt about things.

During the day, the street was a few dozen people short of bustling, but the shops did just fine. Each was in a similar situation to the tea shop, business on the ground floor, and a family living up above. Even the smallest aspects of life had some magical component he was still getting used to. Water was heated, the darkest rooms could be lit with magical glass bulbs. Apparently, nobody outside of the teashop could see Karao's deadarms. It was a lot to learn all at once, and he had barely scratched the surface.

The ghostly moon lorded over the brick streets casting a deathly blue pallor over the colorful signs and expressive bits of graffiti awaiting their cleaning day.

For a summer night, it was weirdly cold. The streetlights hanging overhead lit up one by one as he walked beneath them. At any time, only three would be active, one ahead, one behind, and the one above. The heads would swerve and contort on their stems to track his footsteps. He preferred the moonlight, to be honest.

A lot of this night reminded him of when Karao introduced him to the house. Before meeting Nils or Catherine, Karao had promised him that he'd be welcomed, a part of the family from the first day. Safe, secure, and happy. She promised to turn his curse into a gift, that she would teach him to be proud of what he was.

She hadn't lied yet, though he felt he trusted people maybe a bit too easily.

He had been homeless and forsaken less than a month ago and suppressed in a lot of ways before that. Exploring new territory had this suspenseful excitement to it. The next lamp swung in to keep the spotlight on him as he walked out of the previous lamp's range.

Someone yelped. It wasn't him.

Something attached to the top of the lamp swung down and bashed him in the head. He stumbled back and hit his head a second time on the ground. He looked at the mysterious bludgeoner.

A girl was hanging upside down, hands clutching her forehead. Her maple hair hung in a ponytail under her head.

Other than that, she seemed to be wearing a hiking outfit and gloves. She had a rope wrapped around her waist, keeping her shirt in place. He couldn't quite see how she was sticking to the post, but it looked like a giant wad of glue.

"Gaah!" She shouted under her breath. "What was that for?"

"Wait, me?" Nika was indignant. "You're the one that hit me!"

"Shhh" She put her finger to her lips. The gesture seemed odd when upside down. "Ok, ok, ok." She patted around her shoulder and hips, looking for something. On the ground beneath her was what looked like a brown messenger bag, worn out and slightly rugged. He snapped it up from under her. "Give it back!" she insisted.

Nika shook his head. "What are you doing?"

"Hiding! Quick!" Nika looked behind her, the faint glow of streetlights down and around the corner. Someone was walking their way. He almost handed it back but pulled away as she swung for it, frustrated. She grunted.

"Wait, how are you doing that?" he asked, pointing to her feet, anchored firmly on the streetlight above her. She was effortlessly clung to the metal pole, not even wrapped around it, simply standing.

She sighed. "Nevermind." She curled up a bit and put her hand on her ankle. She whispered, "Luna." A faint green glow started and finished with a flash between her fingers. Nothing happened that he could see. The girl fell back down, arms swaying underneath her head. Her smug smirk was clear even in the bizarre lighting. The lamp creaked. She pointed up. Nika's eyes followed and immediately regretted the decision.

A butterfly, no, a moth with vibrant green wings which were probably taller than him had perched above this girl and was chewing at the lamppost around her feet. Its fur and body were the size and texture of a dog, which was unsettling in its own way. Its charcoal eyes put the night sky's deep blue to shame.

A voice called out from down the road: "Morgan!" The lights encroached as they approached. She stiffened up a bit, then reached for the ground. She was bracing for impact like she would fall at any moment. Something above her snapped, and her feet were free. She was probably planning on catching herself in a handstand and gracefully leaning back to her feet. Instead, she crumpled on the ground almost immediately.

"Ow." She was fine.

"You're Morgan, then?" Nika held her bag out for her. He had a newfound policy not to aggravate girls that are friends with sixty-pound moths. She snapped it from him, slinging it around her shoulder with a slight hint of dramatic flair. Everything about her seemed like she was putting on an act.

Her pose was calculated, her voice deeper than it was a moment ago. "And don't you forget it. Next time, you-" she stopped. "Wait." She stepped closer to him. He tried to back away, but his foot bumped into what could only have been the moth. He'd rather take his chances with the girl.

She reached out and touched the side of his head. He recoiled a bit, but the focus on her face was strangely relaxing. She wasn't looking at him, per se. It was something she needed him to stand still for. Either way, he was counting the seconds until he could go back to his walk.

"You're bleeding," she announced, pointing to the side of his head where he had hit the ground. She stepped back and clapped her hands softly, thinking. The lights had almost caught up. "Hey, one second." Her finger swiped up, and for a moment, Nika was curious what was happening.

That was before the moth had wrapped its legs around him from the back. He essentially melted into a puddle of spineless nerves. He didn't have time to object, question, or even scream before the moth's wings began to flap. His feet left the ground, but not willingly. He wasn't the kind to scream when afraid; he was more of a 'graven-silence-waiting-for-death' type.

The streetlights returned to their normal, upright positions. Morgan was hiding under a fruit display outside a shop while Nika was being carried off into the night. Well, specifically on top of a nearby building. The moth released him onto a flat, stable roof. It landed next to him, watching.

"Where is she?" The voice from before asked. Nika peeked over the gutters. They smelled awful.

Below, two people, a man and a woman were walking side by side through the street. The woman was the more vocal of the two. They were both tall, though the man was slightly taller. She looked like she was teetering at the edge of wit and patience while he seemed ready to go back to bed.

He yawned. "She's probably back home sleeping somewhere weird, again."

"You and I both know that's not true," she said. They stopped. "I'm not being unreasonable, right?"

"I don't think so."

"Like, I don't want to keep her locked up or anything."

"No, of course not."

"But is it so unreasonable for a parent to want her daughter to stay in at night?"

"It isn't."

"Then why do I feel like I'm being the bad guy here, Ben?"

The man, Ben, apparently, thought for a moment. "Morgan's a good kid. Unfortunately, she knows it. She knows we can trust her and doesn't understand why you're worried about her leaving at night." He put his arm around her. "We're in Eldes. She isn't in any danger. If anything, she's the scariest thing roaming the streets at night."

The moment lulled before spiking again. "What is that! Oh, great. Now there's fruit. I'm losing my mind." she asked. Nika realized he had dropped his apple when Morgan had accidentally ambushed him.

"Must have rolled over from that shop," he said. "There's a stand, see?"

"Gross, don't put it back in," she said.

"I'm pretty sure they have a drop bucket for animals." He paused at the stand Morgan was hiding beneath. Nika wanted badly to breathe, but the suspense gripped his chest. The stakes weren't even really that high. He was just rooting for the weird bug girl.

Mainly so he could get down from the roof.

The man broke the silence. "Well, I don't see it. I'm sure Morgan will be home at a reasonable time. Say, before one?"

The couple began walking back the way they came. "How is that reasonable?"

"You're always up that late anyways," he pointed out.

They bickered away into the dark, continuing the search. Nika took a moment to breathe. The moth leaped over him, deftly diving down to the road below. By the time he looked down, Morgan was being lifted up the same way he had been. Well, he had been dragged up. The way she arched her back, kept her feet level and arms balanced suggested she had way more control over herself and the moth. She looked a bit like a gigantic storybook fairy, just creepier.

She hung adrift, lingering in the moonlight. She was absolutely just showing off. She drifted forwards, landing on the lip of a chimney. The wings came to a stop, and she nearly lost her balance and fell off. The turnaround from graceful flight to botched landing was, in short, hilarious.

"Sorry about that."

"Your parents?" he asked. There were a thousand questions he could have asked, but for some reason, that was the only one to come to mind.

"Yeah, my mom can be a real pain," she said. Nika wasn't sure if he agreed. "Dad saw me, so I guess I'll head back soon. Eh! Hold up, you've still got that cut to deal with."

He had forgotten about that. "Fine."

"What's your name?"

He faced a new sort of dilemma. If he could get away with flipping a coin for it, he would have. He had enough trouble talking to people who walked through the front door, let alone strangers with bizarre spells who captured him and tossed him on rooftops. In the end, he remembered that he was a horrible liar. "Nika."

"Kind of a weird name, Nika, doncha think?" She started rummaging through her pockets, turning them inside out, searching for something.

"Thanks," he said.

"I'm kidding," she said he wasn't sure about that. After some feverish rummaging, she found what she was looking for, a bandage buried deep in her coat pocket. "What? I like to be ready." He sat down, she glared at the side of his forehead. "I can't see, hang on."

What Nika had thought was a messenger bag, the kind with a shoulder strap and a fold-over lid, was actually a weathered book with a shoulder strap and a loose-fitting cover.

The wrinkled pages and frayed notes sticking out of the side like petals on a flower, a very unkempt, ugly flower. She felt around the edge for a certain page marker and flipped to it.

The page was filled with elaborately decorative circles and sketches of insects that Nika could barely make out in the moonlight.

The green glow and flash returned while her hand hovered over the corner of the page. Nika flinched. Nothing. When he opened his eyes, Morgan was surrounded by a small and lazy swarm of fireflies. They circled and hovered around her, shimmering out of rhythm.

She seemed to be underwater, illuminated by the moving, tinted light. With a flick of the wrist, the swarm congealed into a single ball next to her head. The flashing synced up into a single, flickering ball of light.

"Hold on," she said. She slapped the bandage on his head. It hurt almost as much as the initial collision. "Got it!"

"Ow."

"Sorry, not sorry," she said. "It's my thanks for keeping quiet and my payback for causing that in the first place." She laid back onto the roof. "It was spider silk, by the way."

"What?"

"The way I stuck myself to the lamppost. I couldn't go slipping off after finding such a good hiding spot. Pretty cool, huh?"

"That's really weird," he thought then said. His mind was sort of on autopilot. "Also, it wasn't that good of a hiding spot."

"I forgot that they move. Hush." She stood. "Were you going somewhere?"

"Home, now, I guess." He had decided that the quiet bedroom wasn't so bad after all. "Tell you what, Nika. I'll walk with ya if you answer some questions."

"Questions?"

She proudly proclaimed: "I'm investigating!" Nika began to realize the patterns of her conversation. She says something cryptic, he asks for a simple clarification. She gets to deliver a dramatic line.

"Uh-huh." He already lived with the most cryptic person he cared to deal with.

"Hm. Fine. Let's say we take turns, then?" She asked. He shrugged. "C'mon, when I'm famous, you'll get to say you were my very first ever fan." she laughed but appeared to be completely sincere.

Nika had maybe a hundred questions that all began with 'why.' Curiosity supposedly killed the cat; the detail they leave out is the horse-sized moth and controllable fireflies. There are some curious topics too bizarre to not be questioned.

The moth lifted both down to the road one at a time. Morgan insisted that it could carry both at once if he was willing to hold onto its back. He declined. With a wave of her hand, it slowly vanished into the green light it came from.

The first volley of questions was fairly benign. He didn't know what school he would be going to if he went to any at all. She snuck out pretty frequently but usually stayed in her own neighborhood. The outfit was a potential dueling costume. She was supposed to look like an explorer. They covered all the basic introductory topics, like the name of a pet moth, Luna, or Nika's favorite book, *Hadrei*.

It was unnaturally easy for Nika. He was always thrown off when she asked for his thoughts or expected an answer to a bizarre hypothetical, like if a two-foot-tall spider could take a basilisk in a fight. He wasn't even entirely sure what a basilisk was. When the pauses grew long, she always had another point to add, trying to give him an out to keep the conversation up. He was enjoying himself and even laughed. It felt good.

"So." There were only a few houses left, and she decided she needed to start her 'interrogation.' "I've heard rumors, and by rumors, I mean Mom and Dad talking, about a dangerous person that lives around here."

Nika had a sinking feeling in his stomach. There was no way she was talking about Karao or even Catherine, right?

"She's supposed to be over a thousand years old, she's ended entire wars by herself."

He relaxed a bit. He didn't know exactly how old either of them were, but neither of them were a thousand years old, certainly. Karao's stark anti-violence rants made her seem ineffective on a battlefield. She taught peaceful, practical necromancy to those who were able to learn from her.

"They say that the reason the crime rate is so low here is because everyone is terrified of bumping into her."

"That's a weirdly specific claim," Nika said. The city was supposed to be absurdly safe.

She shrugged. "I just want to know what you know. Everyone who's grown up here has heard of her. She hides in the shadows, is smarter than anyone else on the continent. She has the strength of a beast and soars through the night sky. Some even say she dabbles in dark, evil magic."

He had checked out. "I just moved here."

"Boo."

"Sorry, not sorry." Nika grinned. They were outside The Pale Garden. "I'm going to go to bed." He paused at the door, his last question on his mind. "What did you mean by the 'when I'm famous' thing?"

She sprouted a chaotic smile. "You're looking at the future pro duelist, Morgan Farvue!" She struck a pose meant to show off her biceps. They weren't that impressive looking. "As my first ever fan, I'd be more than happy to sign an autograph."

Yep. She was crazy. "Maybe another time." He yawned.

"Hey!" she called.

"Hmm?"

She had lowered her own voice again. "I'd like to enlist you to aid my investigation."

"Huh?"

She gave up. "You wanna hang out and help me look?"

He thought about this for a moment. Over the past half an hour, he had felt confused, entertained, annoyed, terrified, thrilled, and content. He'd always been around people that either were older than him or acted like it. This had been a fun change of pace.

"Another day, sure."

She looked delighted. She stood the way a conquering explorer takes their first step onto unknown soil. The stage voice was back. "We will get to the bottom of this mystery, so swears I, the Magnificent Queen Bee."

Maybe not. "What?"

She sighed. "You won't know if a stage name is any good until you say it out loud. That one's real lame." She began to walk away, waving as she left. "Ask around, will ya?"

"I will," Nika said.

"Thursday, Library, 4." She leaped further ahead, not waiting to see if that time worked for him. His biggest takeaway was the existence of a library.

"Sure."

Her last words dropped like an axe. "We're coming for you, Necromancer!"

He wondered how he was supposed to sleep after hearing that.

Chapter 2- End

Intermission- Duel of the Ages

A lot of the previous night bugged him. First of all, seven people he saw on a daily basis asked him what happened to his head. Every time someone asked, he would think up the most outlandish possible answer; something absurd and funny sure to make them laugh. In the end, he would always just say that he tripped.

Beyond that, he couldn't stop thinking about these apparent rumors surrounding Karao. He knew that the tea shop was not super successful due to some kind of word-of-mouth issue. Of the specific rumors, the one about her age bothered him most. She seemed relatively young, in her thirties, maybe.

Lastly, Morgan has stated her intention to be a duelist without actually explaining what that was. Nika had a general idea that it was a sport where people fought each other, but that was it.

He brought all of these questions to Catherine and Nils during their 'lunch' break, otherwise known as the afternoon.

"Duelling is super popular in the city." Catherine seemed to be excited talking about it. "It's a sport. There's all these huge personalities using crazy spells in ridiculous costumes; it's awesome. Some people say it's all fake, but who cares? It's all about the show anyways."

"Thanks, but what about Karao?" Nika wasn't as interested in the sport.

"I don't know how old she is, now that you ask," Nils thought. "Nils has known her the longest, and it's never come up."

"I, Nils." Catherine kicked their shin.

"Sorry!" Nils laughed it off.

The three argued for a while. Catherine said she was in her forties. Nika really wasn't sure. Nils initially said twenty-five until Catherine pointed out that they were awful at telling ages. They decided to write down a guess for each and ask Karao straight up. Whoever was closest got the first crack at the shower for a week.

"Why do you need to know?" Karao asked, suspicious of their question. She spotted a bit of paper sticking out of Nika's hand. "Did you write down your guesses or something? Let me see." She read them for a moment, then laughed. "Not even close. I'd say better luck next time, but sadly, you only get one. Sorry, I don't make the rules," she said, making the rules. "Oh well."

Chapter 3. The Ones in the Suits

In any other shop, customers would not be surprising, and yet, three people in impeccable suits standing in the doorway was something Nika wasn't prepared for when he stepped into the front room. There were two men and one woman, each fiercely scanning the room. The man on the left had a briefcase in hand.

The suits themselves looked fancier than anything he had seen in his entire life. They had sharp corners, silver buttons, and green ties. They all wore the same gloves and shoes. It must have been a uniform. Nika had been told to welcome any customer who comes in, then get someone else to come to take their order. He was nervous. His throat didn't seem to want to give up his voice.

The man in the middle spoke first. His head was shaved, his eyes narrow and focused. "You're new," he said. His voice lacked any energy.

Nika pointed to himself, the man nodded.

"Is Karao in?" he asked.

Nika stammered, "I think so."

"There should be a bell in the top drawer back there." The man pointed at the counter. "Mind ringing it for me?"

He was right; the bell looked harmless. Cheap, even. Ringing it, someone in the basement very clearly dropped a lot of loud, heavy things. Nika threw the bell back in the drawer and shut it, worrying that he had caused that. The four in the room listened to the rapid footsteps climbing up the stairs, a rattling of metal from the kitchen, and finally, the door being flung open.

Karao strode in with the gusto of a woman who hadn't just emptied three cabinets looking for the small metal infuser in her left hand. She tried to look more confident than usual, but it really just looked more nervous than anything.

"Cruise," she said. "How are you?"

The man looked more and more intimidating with each step he and his partners took. "No time. Are we doing this or not?"

"There's a pot coming to a boil right now."

With a bit of dramatic flair, the two of them sat down opposite each other. The other two suits stood behind him; with the snap of a finger, the man brought the briefcase to the table and cracked it open.

Cruise pulled a tea set out from the case along with an infuser identical to the one Karao was still holding. He carefully placed plates, cups, napkins, and a bowl of sugar for the two of them around the table. He moved slowly like this was some ceremony to him. They sat, staring one another down until the teapot whistled.

Nils carried the pot in. Their quiet composure was strikingly different.

Two cups of scalding water were poured. Karao and Cruise handed each other their infusers. All of this elaborate setup was, apparently, for them to give each other a cup of tea.

"I noticed your newest," Cruise paused to choose a word, "recruit." He smiled for the first time since walking into the room. "Hello, there. I'm an old friend of Karao's. It's nice to meet you."

They talked for a while, almost every question ending in 'no.' Nika's takeaways from the situation were: Cruise hadn't met anyone special recently, Karao still hadn't gotten around to writing that book, everything got really quiet when the name Liz came up. The silence would probably have gone on forever if Karao hadn't picked up her cup and asked a bizarre question.

"How much this month, three? Four?" She leaned in a bit. "Five?"

Cruise chuckled or at least imitated what he seemed to think chuckling looked like. "Feeling confident?"

"Always." Karao flicked her wrist, and a small black book tumbled out of her sleeve. "Five is fine by me."

They both quickly drank, pondered, and paused. Karao groaned and threw her head back. Nika hadn't seen her look defeated before. It was pretty funny.

"You win." She admitted.

Cruise finished his drink. It was almost as if winning had flipped a switch. He leaped up from his chair, clenched fist raised high.

"Undefeated!" he yelled out. The man and woman beside him gave unenthusiastic applause. They had clearly been there for each of the previous wins and were definitely over the whole thing.

Nika's eyes narrowed. He recognized where he had seen them before. A few nights ago, he saw these two looking for their daughter in the street. Cruise's companions were Morgan's parents. If Morgan had overheard them talking about searching for necromancers, and now they were standing here, did that mean they knew?

Karao flipped up the small black book and scribbled a quick note into a page full of tally marks. "I can't believe I just gave up five favors."

"The bet was your idea, friend." Cruise pulled out his own book from his coat pocket. "I believe that makes it two-thirty-two to one-nineteen."

"Yeah, yeah." Karao was annoyed with herself. "You still have a ways to go there, pal."

"In time." He resumed his former composure. He noticed Nika trying hard not to make eye contact with any of them. "You ok, kid?"

He had zoned out; "Huh? Yeah. Just tired."

"Well, if you don't mind, we've come to talk shop, so to speak," he said.

Karao had recovered from the loss, likely with the help of the superior cup of tea. "Could you go check in the back to see if Catherine needs a hand with anything?"

He would've taken any excuse to leave the room; the air was weird. The two seated across from each other ignored the bizarre tension around their own words. He felt the eyes on his back as he entered the kitchen.

He was wondering what they wanted, how they knew each other, why they were so quiet and terrifying. Even for the curious, some things are best left alone.

Or he was too nervous to ask, whichever.

Catherine jumped as the door swung open. She and Nils were both pressed up against the wall next to the door, presumably listening in on the conversation he had just escaped.

"Oh, it's just you," she said, relieved.

"What are you-" Nils shushed him halfway through his question. "Nevermind."

They stayed up against the wall for a few minutes before Nils quit. "Nils gives up. I can't hear anything."

"I, Nils," Nika said.

"I said 'I,'" Nils said, oblivious.

Nika could have pushed harder on this but decided to move on. "That guy was... weird."

The other two nodded. "He stops by every month or so. Apparently, they go way back." Nils said.

"And the er, other, two?"

"They're called Suits. Well, technically, they're called something else, but really anyone just says Suits. Cruise is one as well."

Catherine tried listening in by holding an empty glass up to it. It didn't work. She Backed off of the wall. "She doesn't give a straight answer about this guy, ever. We've tried," she said, tapping anxiously. "Who knows what they talk about."

"You know that glass trick doesn't actually work, right?" Nika ripped a piece of parchment paper. Growing up, he learned almost no magic from his family, though this one trick he learned he could do with his eyes closed. He folded the paper into a sort of cone. "I cannot be caught," he whispered into it. It rustled and bent into a curved shape.

Whether or not saying 'I cannot be caught' actually did anything for this spell, he wasn't sure. Either way, this is how he always handled it. It was, until recently, the only magical thing he was able to do consistently.

"Where did you learn that?" Nils asked. Catherine just seemed impressed and amused.

"My," he began and then paused. He forced the words out of his mouth. "Brother taught me." It was clear from their reactions that Karao had told them not to ask about Nika's family.

Nils tried to play it off, "I didn't know you had a brother, Nika." They continued saying something, but Nika was up against the wall listening in to the other room.

"Thursday should be fine," Karao said. Her voice carried perfectly through the wall and into his makeshift spying tool. "I appreciate the extra work. Contracts are dwindling this time of year anyway."

"Right." Cruise responded.

"You seem off. Anything on your mind?"

"You were supposed to tell me before you took in any more students, Karao." He was annoyed. Nika's heart stopped beating, or so it seemed. "I'd like to think I've been lenient until now, but we both know how poorly this can go."

"I wasn't hiding anything, Cruise. He's only been here a few weeks." Karao said. "Well, either way. What do you think?"

Nika's breath stopped. Karao paused for a moment before answering.

"He's way behind for his age," Karao said. "It makes sense, given his situation, but he's been struggling with simple concepts."

"This is the part where you give me the spiel about his potential." There was a moment of silence. "No?"

Nika dropped the paper.

"What did they say?" Nils asked.

"Nothing." Nika handed the little makeshift contraption to Catherine. "Here. I'm going outside."

He leaned through the back door, leaving two confused teenagers in his wake. The backyard was a fenced-in, overrun slice of wilderness. The fruit on the one crooked tree was inedible and attracted hornets, the grass was tall and sliced at his shins, the small herb garden Nils had tried to start now served as a foster home to runaway weeds.

Still, it was quiet, and the shade under the tree was comfortable enough. This was too familiar a setting for him. Escaping the house to spend time away from, well, everything. Maybe this reaction was a reflex, but he had hoped that this new home would be different.

He sat curled up by the base of this twisted tree. His grip tightened around his own arms. He never wanted to have this 'talent' anyways. All it had done was destroy him. It was too much for his family to deal with and not good enough for where he was now.

Necromancy was bringing hope back into life just to dash it again.

Well, that was a bit dramatic. He had definitely felt himself improve over the first few weeks. He could finally use the power on command, even if it was weaker than the others. Maybe he had left that conversation too early and missed out on something, or maybe he shouldn't have been eavesdropping in the first place.

There was something by his foot. He had missed it when he first fell under the tree, but there was without question a tiny snake right next to him. Nika tensed up a bit, but it wasn't moving.

It was dead.

The snake was small and green with a bright orange head. It was only the length of his palm and the width of a string. They had these back at his old home. They were harmless little creatures. There was a bulge in its body by the head; its eyes were unfocused and dark. It was a little pathetic.

Nika thought about the yeast thing. To him, keeping his power up for an hour had felt like running a marathon. If he could do that, even to a meager level of success, surely he could do this too.

His hands sparked with the purple energy. It leaped from his fingertips into the snake, which jumped and writhed in reply. Its eyes closed, and tongue started flickering; It was back to life. Nika was ecstatic. He hadn't done this intentionally before.

This wasn't enough, though. Karao was able to control reanimated arms as effortlessly as if they were her own. Nils could borrow spells from fragments of the deceased's bones. Surely, he could make this tiny reptile obey his command.

"Move to the left," he said. The snake looked at him. Words wouldn't work. Why would a snake know what he's saying, obviously? He closed his eyes and visualized the snake moving to the left. He let more energy flow through him and out his hand.

He opened his eyes. The snake was in the same spot trying to cough out whatever was caught in its throat. It was an acorn.

Nika wasn't a biologist, yet this seemed outside of this animal's normal diet. It looked up at him and slithered onto his shoe. Nika was coming to terms with the fact that he had just brought a tiny idiot back to life, sorta. He scooped it up in his hand. At least it seemed like a friendly idiot.

Nils came out from the kitchen and joined him by the tree.

"So." They started, kicking a rock by their foot. "Overhear something?"

"You won't believe me if I say 'no,' huh," Nika said.

"Nope."

"Well, it wasn't really that bad. Just surprising, I guess."

"Wanna share?" they slid down, sitting next to him in the shade. He was probably somewhat tasteless to say to an artificial person, but Nils seemed like they were made to be an older sibling. Everything just came naturally to Nils.

"Not really, no." Nika put his head back. This part was what his old home was missing, someone actually caring what he was doing or thinking. He didn't know why he didn't want to talk but even having the option was nice.

"Well, that's ok too."

The wind kicked up, the grass swayed like a tiny section of a choppy ocean. The snake in his hand curled up. When it died down, it peeked out from between his fingers.

"What's that?" Nils asked.

"I found this snake dead. I tried bringing him back." Nika held it up for Nils to look at. The two stared at each other for a moment.

"Him?" Nils asked. "You can tell?"

"Nah, just guessing."

"He needs a name. Something cute and small." The snake curled up into a ring on his palm. Nils snapped their fingers. "I got it! Donut."

Donut felt appropriate. "I like it," Nika said.

"This isn't half bad, your first solo attempt too, right?"

Nika was a bit surprised by the compliment. He hadn't done much of anything. His first intentional reanimation was a success. "Thanks."

"It's so life-like! It's like you're not controlling it at all." They touched its head. Donut seemed to like that. "The tongue flipping a good touch."

"I'm not doing that," Nika said.

Nils drew their hand back. "What?"

"I'm not doing anything. Donut's just kinda doing his own thing."

Nils grabbed him by the shoulder and dragged him inside. Apparently, the others needed to see this. Catherine's reaction was a more muted version of Nils's. Nobody was explaining to Nika what was so incredible, just that Karao would tell him later.

They waited an hour for Cruise to leave. Karao looked ragged and worn out by an afternoon's worth of arguing and negotiation. Like everything that happened, he had stopped listening and had just escalated without stopping. She was not in the mood to be tackled by Nils.

But she was.

"It's a snake," Karao said, looking at Donut on the table. Catherine had put him under a glass bowl. He insisted that bumping the sides enough would reveal a secret exit. She was not impressed by this thing that Nils had to show her. "Just let it outside."

The other two filled her in on the details. It was dead. He brought it back. It was moving on its own. Apparently, this was somehow an impressive feat. Karao's eyes ignited.

"Now that. That's interesting." She took a closer look at Donut. Most people are intimidated by Karao's tall figure and deadarms. Donut was completely nonplussed. "I don't have them, well, anything, to approach this right now. I am going to take a nap."

Nils was frustrated that this didn't impress Karao as much.

"You three can close up early, as usual." Karao continued, throwing the switch by the stairs. "Oh, and Nika."

"Yes?" He had been relatively quiet throughout all this. She gestured for him to walk over. She took him in close and whispered to him.

"I take it this is something you did on your own, without the others?" she asked.

"Yes." He wasn't sure if he was in trouble or not.

"Good. There are things that only you can find out for yourself, and you're clearly ready to learn them. You're doing great." She smiled, then frowned. "But, as a general rule, don't bring reanimated bodies into the kitchen. Clean the table please."

Chapter 3- End

Intermission - Quirks

Karao opened the evening lesson with a simple, reassuring line: "There's nothing wrong with you."

Since the Pale Garden closes in the middle of the afternoon, there was always plenty of time for evening lessons in Necromancy. Nils was on the couch reading an ancient, hardly legible book over their head. Catherine, for her lesson, was trying to limit her output to non-table burning levels of energy. Karao was sitting next to him. Between the two of them, Donut was held in a covered wine glass that he was having an even harder time escaping from.

"What?" Nika asked.

"I'm sure you've noticed the difference between those two?" Karao tilted her head toward the others. "Catherine is practically erupting with energy that she can't control, and Nils has a hard time calling up enough to reanimate anything fully. Which do you think is better?"

He could see the pros and cons of each. With practice, Catherine could probably outdo Nils, but Nils's arm bracer was a perfect example of them using their limits to do something Catherine couldn't. These and a few other points rattled around in his head.

"Neither one is, strictly speaking, better," Karao answered before he could. "They will both be very talented one day, for different reasons. This isn't a necromancy thing, Nika. Everyone has a different relationship with their abilities; even the same kinds of magic can manifest in very unique ways inside of people."

"So. What's my thing?"

"Your quirk?" She thought. "At first, I thought you would be more like Nils." She tapped Donut's bowl. He didn't like that very much. "But this changes things. I'm not ready to explain this fully yet. Not until I've done a bit of research."

He was curious, as always, but didn't press it.

"For now," She continued, "I'll just say you're working on a different axis from the others. Things will feel more natural when you're in your proper element. Now, did you finish the reading for tonight?"

He nodded. She was surprised.

She pondered. "We're going to need more books."

Chapter 4. Leading The Investigation Into Yourself

It was, in hindsight, a mistake to volunteer to go to the library. He was planning on going anyways; there was a chance that Morgan would let the moth bite at him if he no-showed. He had also worked through the books he had wanted to read, both borrowed by Nils and had been forgotten to be returned, already and needed more fiction. No, the mistake came in volunteering out loud.

The list he was saddled with was long and erratic. Among the list of books were a few standout titles he was morbidly curious about:

The Frozen Heart and the Fire Magi

Necromancy: A Dark History

The Frozen Heart and the Lost Desire

And, lastly,

Cool It! Channeling Your Rage Into Productivity

The other books seemed much more mundane; famous stories that they needed to read for school, flavor profile recipe books, a book of simple household spells, stuff like that. Nils had added those *Frozen Heart* books as he left and asked him to sneak them in if he could.

Donut was still clinging to him, wrapped in and around the pockets of his shorts. If he left the snake alone, it became sluggish and started looking dead again. Whatever he had done to it, he was now stuck acting as a personal heat-lamp for his undead pet. At least he didn't need to eat. He grabbed the snake and slid it into the bag on his back. No matter how much he put into it, it wouldn't weigh him down too much, according to Karao anyways.

"Just stay put. I'm pretty sure they don't want anyone bringing in a live, er, well, a snake into their library." Nika said. Donut obeyed. Either that or he fell asleep in the dark bag.

When he arrived at the address described to him, he checked the directions two more times. He was standing in front of a small house with several revolving doors. There wasn't anything else to it. The space behind the doors looked smaller than their kitchen, and the stone bricks leading up to it seemed to be in better condition than the entrance itself.

A pair of people, father, and child, passed by him and walked into the building. They were laughing and chatting. The rotating doors leaked a bit of mist as they disappeared into the dark building.

He followed, each step more anxious than the last. The door hissed as he pushed against it. That was never a good sign. The air pushed back on him as he struggled to move the door.

Finally, finally, he had made it inside. He discovered that was a mistake. The wind pushing against him was an updraft from a bottomless pit which he now found himself standing on the lip of. The door had jammed behind him. He was led in the corner of the revolving door with nowhere to go but down, down, and then maybe a bit to the left as he would continue to fall. That did not seem like a great option.

A thunderous voice shook the ground around him. "Returns?" It asked.

"What?" Nika had backed away from the pit as far as he could.

"Please throw all returns into the void to be sorted."

Nils had given him a book to return, another of those *Frozen Heart* dramas they were into. Nika reached into the bag, nudged donut off the book, and threw it into the pit.

The voice grew more sinister. "Overdue." it was raspy and, although disembodied, still smelled like dusty shelves. "The penalty for this, Nils, is-"

"I'm not Nils." Nika objected.

"I beg your pardon?" the voice asked.

Someone walked in through another door, the one to his left. She stepped out into the void and vanished before uttering a single word. She didn't fall, didn't turn to mist; they were as gone as quickly as they had appeared.

"Nils is my friend. They asked me to return it."

"Is that so friend-of-Nils. What is your name?" the voice asked.

"Nika," he said.

"How alliterative. Tell me, Nika, do you intend to pay Nils's fine?"

"No?" Even if he had money, he had never thought to carry it around.

"Very well. Tell them to pay us back as soon as they're able. You may enter," the voice spoke as if it was revealing the grand entrance to this horrifying library. Nothing changed. "What is the matter?"

"Where do I go?" he asked.

"Do you not see the entrance?"

"Nope."

"Everyone with a library card should be able to see this, I don't understand..." the voice trailed off, muttering.

Someone had clearly forgotten to explain some very important details to him. "I don't have a library card."

"Ah, that makes- wait- How did you even find this place?"

"Directions?"

"Ugh." The mist began shimmering, dissolving as it was burned away by a bright yellow light. The void beneath him disappeared, and in its place, a humongous spiraling hall opened in front of him. A central winding staircase slowly rotated around the circular room's perimeter, each floor filled to the brim in every direction with books. "It is strictly against library policy to disclose the location to non-card carriers. This way, boy."

He took in more details as he approached the central desk. Books whose covers flapped like birds flung themselves around the library in flocks, perching and placing themselves back onto shelves. Tables at the ground level were full of people reading, studying, playing games, or just having coffee.

The building was ludicrously tall. He couldn't even see the top floor from the base. The sand-tinted tile floor was polished to a mirror shine so perfect he felt guilty stepping all over it. Behind the central desk, also immaculate, was an intimidating statue, a creature with a beast's body, feathered wings, and a human head and neck. Its arrogant posture confirmed what Nika had suspected; this was a marble statue of a sphinx.

It made sense, really. Sphinxes in stories were always wise, riddle-laden keepers of knowledge. It made a perfect mascot for a mysterious library like this one. It had made sense, that is until the face turned toward him and spoke. That was new, but he felt that absolutely nothing could catch him off guard at this point. The perfect mindset to be in when preparing to deal with Morgan.

"You'll be needing a library card, I take it?" It asked with the same voice that had scolded him in the entrance. He had been talking to this sphinx the entire time. It stepped down from its pedestal onto the desk and began to circle him. He was taller than the statue, at least when it was on all fours. "What do you seek?"

"Uhh, these?" Nika held up the list. Something sharp skewered it from his hands. He jumped a bit. One of the sphinx's claws had stretched into a thin spear and snatched it from him. This library had tried to kill him twice now. "I was also, um, looking for 'transfer exams,' if you have those?"

"Yes, this will take some time to put together." The sphinx leaped over the counter as if it wasn't a monstrous cat made of at least a ton of stone. After a few moments of clattering drawers and rustling stone feathers, she reappeared, sitting fully upright behind the desk. Nika no longer held a height advantage. She shoved a paper from her wing into his hand.

"Fill this out and feel free to look around." Her wings spread out as she stepped up onto the desk. "I shall find you when I have everything. There's a pen on the desk." With one thunderous flap, the sphinx flung herself into the spiraling labyrinth of books.

Nika sighed. That would probably be the second weirdest person he encountered today. Come to think of it, he had no idea how to find Morgan here, either. There was a bell on the desk he could ring, so he had at least one now. Ringing it caused the sphinx to reappear directly in front of him.

"Yes?" she asked.

"Oh, sorry, I thought there might be someone else nearby. I just wanted to ask-" Nika said.

"There is only me."

There was a strange sound behind him, like nails being tapped down on the pristine floors. There was also another, identical sphinx-statue behind him. She carried a pile of documents in her mouth behind the desk. They were very nearly identical but seemed to keep their hair- mane? - hair differently. Come to think of it, the one that answered the bell looked slightly different than the one that took off anyways.

"Though I do have bodies to spare," she said. "You had a question for me?" "Is there a section for books about duelists? Or mysteries? Or-"

"Stop." She held up a paw to silence him. There was a bookmark in it with tiny text scrawled on both sides. "This will tell you where to find any subject. The stairs will take you where you want to go. Is there anything else?"

"No." Nika had wanted to stop bothering the librarians before even meeting her - them? Was there only one, or was there a bunch? Either way, he didn't want to pry. "Thanks. Sorry. I won't bother you again. Thanks again. Um." He backed away with each step, every word more awkward than the last. Talking to people was hard enough; genius-lion-clone-librarians were somehow worse.

The stairs were thankfully easy to figure out. You say what section number you want, and in a matter of moments, you've been led up to it. The 'stairs' were really just an elaborate rail system with people standing on their own private platforms. Whenever two platforms should collide, one would go over and the other under. The people on them hardly even seemed to notice when it happened.

The first three sections he looked in were a bust. No worries. So what if she wasn't in the dueling, mystery, or summoning-studies sections? That just meant more time for him to fill out the library card form. It asked some weird questions. Along with his name, address, and legal guardian, it wanted to know his preferred forms of magic, reading preferences, level of education, citizenship, and his exact height. Some of these he even knew the answers to.

He figured he should go down to the ground floor and wait. She would eventually come to find him, anyways. Better to be in an obvious spot. He studied the bookmark for any other obvious places that she might be. None of the sections besides what he visited stood out, really.

Something had joined him on his platform, which was odd since he was traveling between floors. He looked over and saw a spider as tall as his knee.

Surprisingly, the immediate reaction to seeing a ten-pound spider is not screaming and nearly falling hundreds of feet to the ground. No, that's second. First is a moment of good old-fashioned denial. The mere concept of being suspended in the air with a spider that would probably eat his shoe if he tried to step on it was just too outlandish to believe.

Unfortunately, denial is a very brief phenomenon in the grand scheme of things.

Nika wasn't really much of a screamer. In moments like this, he was more of a 'white-knuckled-while-waiting-to-die' kinda guy. It was looking at him, and no, he didn't like that very much at all, thank you. Its leg twitched in a gross and uncomfortable-looking way.

Just one of them.

It made no movement towards him. In fact, the only sign that it was alive was the single appendage pointed skyward.

Wait.

He looked up where the bug was pointing. Yup. Morgan was waving frantically, apparently not worried she might topple over the very slim railing separating her and the very far-off ground.

He sighed and requested the platform go up and join her. This was the floor with the duelist section, but he was sure he had checked it thoroughly.

There are a lot of ways to greet a new friend, one of the first people to speak to him without disgust in their voice in his entire life. A normal, healthy relationship with someone he had read about but never quite seemed to get for himself. Today, Nika opened with:

"Don't ever do that again. Please." Nika said.

"Sorry, if it helps, you weren't really in trouble," she said. She sounded sincere. The spider dissolved into nothing- another of her conjured bugs.

"What are you talking about? I almost fell!" he said.

"What? Oh, no. Watch." She stood on the platform he had just stepped off of, then dropped to the ground, nauseating, and yet she walked straight off. Fully confident, not a single ounce of hesitation in her blood.

A, and he really lacked better words for this, flock of books rocketed off the shelf behind him, fluttering around him like a swarm. They formed a platform beneath the falling lunatic and caught her before she had even dropped beneath the level they were on. The books flung her back where she had leaped from, sending her rolling into a small local art display. The books nestled themselves back into their places on the shelves.

"Ow, ok, that ... hurt... more than I -ow- remember." She grinned. "No danger, see?" She was dressed much less like a lunatic adventurer now. She looked like your average kid in the summer. Nika was actually a little disappointed she didn't always dress in the giant hat and vest. Though, it did mean fewer people would stare if they were walking around.

"Yeah... ok. Where were you? I thought I checked this section."

She leaped up and hurriedly shuffled, the way one who isn't allowed to run does, off in a specific direction. "This way!" They stopped before a section on 3rd-century duelists, alphabetical. There were indents in a strange vertical pattern going up one of the sections.

"Morgan?" The sphinx's voice called out from behind them. For a cold, moving statue, she sure sounded agitated. "How many times do I have to-," her thought trailed off as the pounding of heavy feet picked up into a gallop.

Morgan had no intention of sticking around. She quickly scuttled up the bookshelves, her hands and feet grabbing the worn-in places on the shelves. This was either rehearsed or routine; her execution was flawless.

"Ah, Mr. Erring." The sphinx was talking to him. Nika hadn't heard anyone use his last name in a long time. Even before he had met Karao and the others, he had avoided association with it. His stomach knotted. It took him a moment to even question how she learned his name in the first place. "I see you've found the section you're looking for. Have you seen a girl, around your height, wandering through this section?"

"No, and Nika is fine." He had so far seen Morgan a total of twice, and both times she was being tracked down for some silly reason. She eyed him for a lingering, suspicious moment. Then she turned, taking the entire weight of the scene with her on folded wings.

Morgan popped out from the top of the bookshelf.

"What did you do?' he asked.

"Nothing, technically." She answered, patting the top of the shelf next to her. "Hop up! Oh, and try to do it the same way I did."

"Why?"

"Wanna find out?"

He did not. He dutifully followed her path, if less efficiently. He hoisted himself onto the top of the bookshelf. The space was surprisingly spacious. There was plenty of room for him to sit or even stretch, though he probably couldn't stand up without hitting the ceiling. There were a lot of opened books sprawled out around the top of the bookshelf, each one tabbed with scraps of paper and little notes. There was even a crate being used as a small table that Morgan had sat by herself.

"What do ya think?" she asked. "Not a bad secret base, huh?" She seemed oddly proud of a crate in a hiding spot.

"You hide a lot, don't you?" he said, thinking back to the roof.

She grunted, "Rude."

"What are we doing up here anyway?" Nika asked.

"Research!" She gestured for him to sit across the crate from her, turning one of the books to him. "There's a whole section on local myths and legends. Naturally, I borrowed some of them."

Nika tried to act nonchalantly reading the book. In truth, he was excited to figure this out. Morgan hadn't given a lot of detail the other night, but it sounded like this person was, in fact, Karao. He didn't expect to know everything about his new adoptive family right away, but something like this he needed to confirm for himself. Her mysteriousness and the details of this legend just happened to match up a little too well.

The book disagreed.

In this book, the 'Guardian of Eldes' was described as a terrifying beast who roamed the streets at night. Its gaze turned onlookers into dust, its howl would deafen all who stood too close, and any who attempted to harm the residents of its city would meet a swift end. An illustration depicted a multi-headed wolf walking the streets in the moonlight.

"Cool, right?" Morgan thrust another, smaller book into his hands. "But that's just one version. This one says that it wasn't a beast but a wise old man who watched the city from the rooftops and burned all evil with his holy flame."

"Okay..." Nika was following, but it seemed like none of these books had any idea what was going on. He listened to Morgan describe the three other common versions of the story. A bird, The roads themselves, a spider that lived in the moon. None of them sounded like Karao or, in fact, a necromancer. "I thought I heard you s-"

"There are three things that the stories have in common." She cut him off. He would just ask her later. "First, the guardian is active at night. Second, the guardian is wicked smart." She paused, snapping a book shut. "Third, the guardian died and was brought back to life."

Well, that's where necromancy came into play. Apparently, enough of the versions of the story mentioned that 'the guardian' died and came back. Morgan had been talking for a few minutes straight, barely registering his presence.

"Morgan," He said, tapping the table. He finally got her attention.

"Hm?"

"Why?"

"You're gonna have to be more specific than that."

"Why are you looking into this, exactly?" Nika asked.

She thought for a moment. "Isn't it exciting? The idea that there's something around us that powerful and heroic? I want to meet him." She looked like there was more to say, but she moved along to the next piece of 'evidence' she had uncovered.

"You know, these could just be stories," Nika said.

Morgan's eyes turned distant for a moment; she seemed outside her own body. "I know, but where's the fun in that?" She unfolded a map. "Besides, my parents are looking for him, too."

This surprised him. Cruise didn't seem like the kind of person that would chase urban legends, let alone send his subordinates to go on a wild goose chase.

The map she laid out on the table was covered in X's, notes, and haphazard doodles along the sides. Of the unmarked sections, Nika nearly physically groaned when he noticed there were no notes around his street. Which could only mean...

"You live here, right?" She pointed almost directly at the tea shop.

"Yeah," Nika said.

"That should be the next place to check! If we find the necromancer, we can figure out what happened. Now, Nika, think: is there anyone out by you who looks both unspeakably old and a little evil?"

"Evil?"

"Well, I mean, bringing a giant monster back from the dead has got to be some sort of dark magic." She hunched over like a haggard old witch. "Is there anyone with warts and a glass eye? Or an evil cackle with some missing teeth? Someone who sends a chill down your spine whenever you see him."

Nika shook his head. "You're the scariest person I've met." It wasn't really a surprise that she thought of people like him that way. Still, he was hoping that the people in the city wouldn't be as scared of him as out in the villages.

She hit him with a book.

"Ow."

"Serves you right," She said.

The two talked for a while longer. Nika kept trying to push the subject away from Morgan's investigation, but she was too eager to share what she had found. She had basically been keeping it all to herself and was relishing the chance to show off her work. Even when the words and places became nonsense, her energy kept the very one-sided conversation engaging.

Eventually, they decided to leave. It had been a few hours, at least. Nils would want to spend their time off this afternoon reading for sure. Before Morgan let him down, she had to check to make sure one of the sphinx statues wasn't watching.

"You always have to be careful with Gladys," she said, shining to another vantage point.

"Gladys?"

"The librarian. She lives deep below the building and controls those statues like puppets. She also really hates people climbing on her stuff."

Nika hadn't thought to ask her name. Considering that she took the time to collect that list of books for him, he felt awkward. Great, another failed social interaction. Add it to the pile.

Morgan grabbed the book she had been carrying the night they met from under the crate and clambered off of the bookshelf, "Quick!" She gestured for him to jump down with him. The two made their way to the moving platform and asked it to take them to the ground floor.

"Morgan," Nika said.

"Sup?"

"Aren't you scared of seeing a necromancer?" He asked. His throat got a little cold.

"Not really. Why?"

"Well, they're creepy, I guess. Just the whole idea is gross," He was now just pulling up comments he had heard growing up in memories, "And I mean, you said they were evil, too, right? Should you be messing with anything like that? Dark magic, I mean."

Morgan sat down on the platform and fanned open the book. He got a much better look at it now. Leather bound with a spine holding together through sheer force-of-will, the pages were ragged and slipping from their binding. As she flipped through them, Nika noticed more details about the pages of summoning circles.

All the creatures, circles, and notes were handwritten. Not by her, based on what he had seen, but by someone else. This was uniquely hers.

"I'm maybe not a great judge for what is and isn't creepy. This used to be my Grandpa's book. He was an ento-, enta-? He studied bugs, is my point." Her smile was sort of sad, "I'm used to being lumped in with creepy things. I think it would be fun talking to someone like that. Maybe I'm just weird."

The platform reached the ground. Gladys was waiting for him at the central desk with a pile of books that would have absolutely snapped his spine in two if he didn't have this bag. Morgan said good-bye with tentative plans to stop by at the tea shop sometime soon once she had a more concrete plan of attack.

"Wait," Nika said, ready to make a mistake.

"Hm?" Morgan asked.

"About necromancers." his voice was starting to shake a bit.

"What's the matter, scared?" She gave an exaggerated laugh. "Fear not, little one. I, the impeccable queen of the bugs, will not- ergh. That name was awful, too." She gave up her monologue partway through.

"No," He didn't really want to waste time playing cat and mouse with anybody. His voice lowered, "I am one."

Chapter 4- End

Intermission - The Test

For the first test he had ever taken in his life, Nika didn't really know what to expect of the results. The math and reading portions went pretty quickly, but the history, magic, and science were all just a bunch of guesses and blank answers.

Nils and Karao also seemed conflicted. They would read a few answers, look at him, then back to the sheet. They repeated this with a range of faces from 'impressed' to 'utterly bewildered.' Whatever grade he would start school depended on this test. Up until now, he had been homeschooled with little regard to what should be learned when. He was basically expected to read books and solve equations.

"You're fourteen, Nika?" Karao asked, barely trying to hide the concern in her voice.

"Yeah."

"What grade is he supposed to be in?" Karao turned to Nils. His informal education before never had anything like a 'grade,' though he was vaguely familiar with the concept.

"Well," Nils started, "Most kids his age are eighth grade."

"That doesn't help," Karao said. Nils nodded.

None of this was helping his already building anxiety. "What did I get?"

She folded up the papers. "In reading, tenth grade. In math, seventh," She circled up some numbers on the results page and tossed them to him.

Science, History, and Magic were all fourth grade. His forehead hit the table hard, "Oh."

"You told me your education was, well, limited," Karao pulled on her hair. "I know I told you that you didn't need to talk about your home until you were ready, but," she struggled to finish the thought.

Nils sat down quietly. They were curious, naturally.

"It would make it easier to help, you know," Nils finished for Karao. She agreed.

He thought about it for a moment. He thought about his nights locked away and his days spent hidden from the world. He thought about how much better things were now and how much he just wanted to move on with his life. Whatever had happened didn't matter. He needed to make himself someone new.

Chapter 5. Nika's History

"No," he said.

Chapter 5 - End

Intermission- The City

Eldes was a pretty boring city, all things considered. Unlike the capital or a few of the more prominent business centers, Eldes was a city only by population density. No breath-taking spires, no marvelous art institutions. The thing they had in common with a city was the public transit, something called a Tram, and even that was mostly on the north side of town. Primarily, it was just row after organized row of small houses and businesses scraping by.

There were a few defining features that Nika had wanted to explore for himself over the course of the summer. The library, likely the most well-known landmark of the city, was as spectacular as he was hoping. There were various parks and forests scattered throughout the winding suburban roads he wanted to spend time in. The largest of these was up near where Morgan lived in the center of the city; it housed an outdoor music hall and a lot of ground to play lots of different sports.

Including, as his very eager friend had pointed out, dueling rings. A river dissected the town into a north and south side connected by a different cobblestone bridge on every other street. This cut through that park, pooling up into a small man-made lake where they kept fish stocked.

A few blocks south of that park, the Pale Garden tea shop ground out its very meager existence. The two teenagers running the place were constantly cleaning and tidying as the
the owner, the elusive Karao, took odd jobs to pay the bills.

This wasn't really all that uncommon. There were only a few booming businesses in the whole town. Most of the labor traveled to busier cities through a portal station on the north side of town. Most of the businesses left behind were families and school kids. The schools were probably the selling point of Eldes. They were safe, competent, and, most importantly, affordable for families trying to get their little mages into the world.

Eldes South covered grades 6-12. Soon, they would be taking Nika's application and deciding where to place him. The building was squat but spacious. It covered a lot of acreage with historic architecture and lovingly kept gardens. Even in the summer, the air of the halls smelled like books and ink.

"Ready?" Karao asked Nika. She was dressed more business-like than usual, leaving her deadarms back at the tea shop. She didn't want to scare anyone away today. They were sitting outside the principal's office; his eager foot wouldn't stop tapping. They had just finished going over the results of the test and were meeting with him today to talk about school in the fall.

"Nope," He stood up, "Let's go, though."

Chapter 6. The Things You Have To Do To Get Into Eldes South

"Karao!" The man in the gaudy purple suit bellowed. In a word, he looked weird; in many words, his slicked orange hair and mountainous upper body made him look a bit like a color-blind lion on his way to work. His smile seemed to be bolted permanently and painfully to his face. "What a surprise! What brings you here?"

Nika wondered how exhausting it was to put that much energy into every word.

"It's been a while, Phineas." They shook hands then followed the principal into the office.

"Now, now, Karao, that's Principal Arcs in front of the students."

His office was less organized than Nika was expecting. Files were on tables, counters, propping up other files, etc. It was a mess. Phineas tiptoed carefully around a few stacks of loose papers to get to his seat on the other side of his desk.

"I'm not a student yet," Nika pointed out as he took the seat next to Karao's. "Also, Phineas, you don't need to keep that up." Karao looked pretty relaxed in her chair.

Phineas Arcs looked out the window and around the room. He asked Nika a question: "Can I trust you to keep a secret then?"

A cold chill shot down his spine. The other day he had told Morgan about him and the tea shop. When Karao found out, she sentenced him to clean the kitchen every night for the entire week. It was a grueling fate.

"Yes," he said, he had no intention of letting information like that slip again. Karao agreed.

Phineas sort of deflated in front of him. His posture sank, his eyes darkened, his tight forehead wrinkled. His once well-fitted suit now dangled loosely as he moved his arms around. His hair greyed and became frazzled.

"Thank you. You have no idea how exhausting that is," Even his voice grew tired and weary, "So, what's your name, young man?"

"Nika," He answered.

"Pick up another stray, Karao?" Phineas chuckled. "Only joking, kid. She's a good person. Now, I'm assuming you want to enroll?"

"Yeah," Nika answered.

Principal Arcs cleared his throat. A pen buried in paperwork behind him shot into his right hand, a piece of paper slipped out of a drawer, and gingerly landed in front of him. A pair of glasses unfolded themselves and perched on his flat nose.

"All right, I'm going to get this started and have Karao fill out the rest later. Now." He eyed Nika for a bit. "What grade were you in your last school?"

"He wasn't," Karao answered for him.

"Oh? Hm. Have you taken the-"

Karao produced the test Nika took and handed it to the shriveled principal, "Right here, Phineas."

His already wrinkled brow curled up more as he read through the results. "This is," He stopped fully, rereading the entire document. "Vexing." He put the paper down and turned to Nika again. "How old are you?"

"Fourteen," Nika said.

"Hm. A bit older than I thought. Ok. Well, that should land you in either the seventh or eighth year. But, well, these results are fairly polarizing."

"Right, that's why we came to you." Karao leaned forward, "What do you make of this?"

"Well, we have remedial classes, but those don't seem much like a good fit either. It seems like we would have to build up your magic and history understanding from the very beginning. Most of these seem like guesses at best." He squinted at the sheet. "Here, question thirty-two."

"Yes?" Nika asked.

"This is a fairly obscure question about the history of alchemy and transmutation. You wouldn't ever be able to guess 'copper, iron, calcium' unless you had experience with that. You got that one right. But if you go to question twelve, a much more basic question, "what is aether?", you were completely off base. Care to explain?"

He remembered the alchemy question. It was one of the few he had any confidence in. "Well, they mentioned in it," the two adults were confused. "In a book."

"What book?" Karao asked.

Nika blushed. It was one of his brother's adventure books. In this room filled with textbooks and reference material, it felt childish to mention. "Hex Ryder," he answered.

A chuckled built up somewhere in Phineas and rampaged through his chest, bursting out. Nika looked up and saw that he had gotten his energy back. The wrinkles, grey hair, all signs of weariness were gone. "That's incredible. I love those books!"

"Really?" He was excited. He had never been able to talk about it with anyone before.

"It's a great series. I love the way the more subtle down-to-earth drama and huge fights keep you turning pages. There's always something happening!"

"Yeah!" Nika stood up without realizing it. "And when Mauricio turns out to be working for the good guys and steps in front of the-" He had just realized something about Phineas's last sentence. "Wait, did you say series?"

Principal Arcs nodded.

"There's more than one!?"

He nodded but faster.

"Can we focus, please?" Karao was amused but ultimately busy. "There's still a pretty major problem. We don't really have time to talk about kids' books."

"Young adult!" objected Phineas, "And they're well written!"

"Uh-huh." Karao tapped Nika's chair. He took the hint and took his seat. "But, what are we going to do for Nika?"

Phineas thought for a moment. "Well, as it currently stands, we don't really have the resources to meet his needs."

Nika sank deep into the chair. He didn't want to hear that.

"I'm sorry. I think finding a tutor for him would be best. Maybe we can try again next year if his test results improve enough," He started to get up. "I might know some people. Let me give you their contacts."

"That makes sense," Karao agreed. Nika's mind started racing. The two were going over various retired teachers and recent graduates who were looking to get some tutoring hours in once the school year started. It was like a done deal, a finalized decision he didn't have a say in. It ate at him. Karao eventually turned to him and asked, "How does that sound, Nika?"

He was lost in thought. He was getting pulled around again. His life continued to be out of his own control.

"No," he said. He hadn't meant to, it just sort of came out.

"No?" Phineas's eyebrow shot up. "No what?"

"Is there a way I can just go to school?" He was pleading now. He had spent his entire life being taught one on one. He just wanted to go to classes, meet people, laugh. He wanted everything he had read about in those books. "Please, what do I have to do?"

Karao smiled. Phineas did not. Instead, he repeated what he had said before. "With what you've been taught, it would be impossible to catch you up to even our lower classes for someone your age. At least, by the fall semester."

"I can do it." Nika's eyes couldn't leave the floor. "Please, I just need a chance."

"There's no precedence for this." Phineas reclaimed his seat, fingers tugging on his hair. "There are other students who have been turned away from this school for similar reasons, Nika. It wouldn't be fair to them if-"

Karao cleared her throat and waved something in the air. It took both a moment to realize what it was. Phineas Arcs shriveled up again at the sight of the small black book. Nika had only recalled seeing it when Cruise came to visit.

"I believe," Karao had somehow found a way to make her walk as smug as her face. "That you still owe me a favor or two, Phineas. I'm cashing one in."

He thought for a moment. "There's no point in getting him into the school if he's doomed to fail. If these grades are reflective of his knowledge, he will fail half of his classes. I can't accept that."

"But-" Nika began to object, Karao silenced him.

"I don't want him accepted in; I want you to give him a chance to earn it." The principal looked over the sheets again. He was warming up to the idea.

"Very well, Nika. In 'history' and 'magic,' you scored around the same as a fourth-grader. Truthfully, it looks like you got some lucky guesses, so I'd say it was closer to the second-third grade level. You get those up to sixth by August, and we will be glad to have you."

Nika nodded. This sounded slightly impossible, but he was more than willing to give it a shot. Karao made a note in her black book and snapped it shut. The two worked out a few last details like the exact date of the second test and things Nika could do to study for it.

Phineas stopped Karao on their way out of the office.

"Oh, Karao, I nearly forgot. It's good that I have you in person," he started. "About Nils's locker, er, situation. I'm afraid the school's decision to just not give them one this year."

"I understand," Karao said. She wasn't thrilled.

"I'm sorry, but it was the simplest solution. If they have anything they need to carry around through the day, tell Nils they can use my office as much as they'd like."

"That's very generous, Phineas. Thank you." With that, they left.

The air outside made him realize just how dusty that office must have been. June always had the best weather.

"Think you can make it back on your own?" Karao was going over a list of materials Phineas had handed her for Nika's studying. "I'm going to see what I can dig up for this." They were only a few blocks away from the tea shop.

"Yeah, I'll be fine," he said. "What was that about Nils?"

She exhaled. "I'll tell you later." Her eyes perked up a bit. "Speaking of..."

Nika turned around. Nils was across the street, walking with that boy from the tea shop. Nika struggled to remember his name. He was a regular that Catherine had a grudge against for some reason. Daniel! That was it. They were talking and laughing about something. Nils spotted them and waved. They were dressed differently than usual, their clothes looked nice, though still sort of fancy and the way they walked seemed to be more purposeful.

Karao smiled, "Ah, that's why Nils wanted the afternoon off. Ok Nika, you need to go see if Catherine needs a hand with anything."

Well, she did. It wasn't anything to do with her job; no, there was nothing to do there. Catherine needed saving from Morgan's unending conversations.

Catherine's first words when Nika walked into the shop were, through grinding teeth and desperate eyes, "Nika! Your friend is here." Translated from 'threat' into English, this meant: 'occupy her time, or I will drop you in a lake while you sleep.' It turned out 'threat' is a very effective language to speak.

Before he could say anything to either of them, Catherine threw a towel over her shoulder, raised her chin, and headed for the kitchen. She was well past done.

"I don't think that witness was very cooperative," Morgan commented to him. Ever since he had let the secret slip to her a few days ago, she had been by the tea shop twice and asked roughly eight-hundred-thirty-thousand questions. Almost all of them were about necromancy. Karao's tolerance for those questions was astonishing, and Nika learned a lot just by listening while the two talked.

"Doesn't there need to be a crime for there to be a witness?" Nika sat across from her and her untouched cup of tea. It was probably cold. "Also, please stop bugging them about this. I wasn't supposed to tell you in the first place." Morgan was too busy taking notes on scattered papers to look up.

She took a swing at his forehead with a pen. She missed. "I didn't even talk about that. We were just talking about dueling for the past- hey, what time is it?"

He glanced at the clock behind her. "Half-past three?"

"Three hours, then. Wow, time flies, huh. Anywho, we don't need to jump right into that stuff anyway."

He wasn't exactly looking forward to this 'investigation' anyways. "Sounds good to me, although." He was still uncomfortable with someone knowing about him. "You really don't mind hanging out with, well, us?" He gestured to the kitchen, where Catherine was likely enjoying a well-deserved break.

"Nah, you said they're cool, so what's the worst that could happen." She tapped her papers on the table, organizing them. "So I've been trying-"

"What, just because I said so?" He was saying whatever he could to move the conversation along. "You trust me that much, huh?"

"Yup."

"What?"

"So, I've been trying to come up with a few new duelist names. Let me know which of these strikes you as being 'cool' but not 'trying too hard'. Ok, first up-"

"No, no, no, wait." He stopped her again. The difference being he actually wanted to know something this time.

"What's up?"

"I... I'm just confused. Why?" Nika struggled with phrasing, "I haven't known you that long and, well, I mean we're necr-"

"Oh, that? Easy. You're my friend now. Sorry, not your choice!"

Nika hadn't really made friends before. He wondered if it was usually coerced like this. "Huh. ok."

"And friends answer each others' burning questions about choosing one from many awesome names," The pen was now pointing accusingly at him. "Although now I'm curious why you're so... down. Something up?"

The looming test had been on his mind from the minute he left the school building. "Not really. I guess. I'm just curious. What is school like?"

"School? What about it?"

"It all just seems like a lot. I mean, the building was huge and people kept talking about grades and I'm just completely lost. 'Schooling' used to just be us going to the neighbors to learn how to read and do long division."

She didn't have the material prepared to answer this question. It would have been weirder if she did. "Well, it's basically that, but you get shuffled between professors and classrooms every day, and there are long study periods where they make you write and do homework."

"That sounds stressful."

"Yup." She thought, murmured, then scratched out about half of her list of names completely unprompted. "I've changed my mind about some, these are all terrible, but I still want your opinion on-"

He was trying his best to read the crossed-off titles Morgan was trying to give herself. One caught his eyes. "Oblit?"

"You know, like Obliterate?" Morgan sighed, "There's a reason I crossed it out, you know." She covered the paper, blushing a bit, "Are you even a real necromancer?"

She may have crossed it out, but a minute before, she had toted it as being an 'awesome name' and a 'real contender.' He wasn't buying it at this point. She was changing the subject. "Uh-huh."

Something fell over behind the counter, and he went to check it out. It was Donut, who had escaped from his box upstairs to menace every available cup in the shop. He had knocked something down and fallen with it. He looked about as guilty as a snake could.

Donut was curled up like his namesake. He was out of energy and lethargic, barely able to flick his tongue out. Nika brought it over to Morgan. The snake had impeccable timing. Donut stared at Morgan as Nika placed him on the table.

"Well, I'm not ordering off this menu again," she joked. She was pretty pleased with herself.

"This is Donut. Donut is dead. He choked to death on an Acorn." Nika had gotten better at channeling his magic through his body and out his fingertips. Small, controlled bursts of necrotic energy left his body and coursed through Donut's. The snake jolted up a bit. He was now full of life, ready to collide into any number of wondrous things like the dumb snake he was. "He's my pet now, sorta."

Morgan's eyes lit up. She was brought to life just as much as Donut. She spent the next twenty minutes observing and taking notes about the snake while Nika read for a bit. After some more interrogations, the topic of school finally came back up.

"What grade?" Morgan asked.

"No idea," Nika answered, still unclear what that meant. "If I study enough, I think they said eighth. It's going to be close, though."

"What do you mean?" Morgan asked. She brought her voice down to a whisper, in case some invisible person was listening in on their conversation in this empty room. "Are you getting held back?"

"No!" Nika didn't really want to delve into his life story. He'd had enough of that recently. Morgan would be fine just knowing the broad strokes. "I just have to do well on a test in August. I haven't exactly had the best education up to now."

She thought for a moment. "I mean, you seem smart, in a way."

"You're really good at saying nice things in a mean way."

"I think it's how you talk," she added, more sure of herself. "Most kids I know stutter and, like, add, um, words to their, er, every sentence."

Nika chuckled. "I read a lot," he said.

"Well!" She slapped the table, nearly knocking Donut off the side. "You have to get into the eighth grade. No negotiating!"

Nika had this cold feeling he already knew the answer to his impending question, but it was worth asking anyway, "Why?"

She grinned. Yep. She was going into the eighth grade.

"Ah," he said.

"I can help you!" Morgan leaned back, arms folded behind her head. "For the record, I'm a straight 'A' student."

Nika considered this for a moment. "No," he said. Her jaw dropped a bit. "No, you aren't. I don't believe that."

"That's mean!" Morgan said.

"What do they call it... an alt- no, an ultr- hm, ah! You have an ulterior motive," He pointed at her. "What are you getting out of this deal?"

"Well," She looked down, rebuilt her resolve, then returned with eye contact way too fierce for him to deal with. "If you get in, I'd have a favor to ask."

Nika could only picture Karao's black book. He had already turned his life completely around on the basis of a favor, but the stress and potential of writing a blank check were still too much for him. "What happens if I don't get in?"

"Nothing! On the house!" She shrugged. She had shaken off whatever had possessed her a moment ago.

"What's the favor, then?"

"I won't tell you." She seemed more serious now. This was a touchy subject, whatever it was. "Not until it's necessary."

Nika took a minute to mull it over. "Straight 'A's? That's good, right?" characters sometimes talked about grades, but he had never actually seen the scale himself. 'A' made sense to be the best grade, though.

"Well," Morgan said, her eyes avoiding direct contact again, "It's the best, and I would absolutely have that grade but, er, um, like." She sighed. "Ok. I get almost every question right, but sometimes I forget to, well, turn my homework in."

Of course. "I'm not doing your homework," Nika said, guessing the favor.

"No! That's not it." Morgan started packing up her stuff. She had just realized how much time had passed. Nika was a bit surprised too. The conversations with this girl were time sinks, but it wasn't like he was going to be using that time better anyways. "Tell you what, I'll bring you some of my tests, and if they're good, you have to agree!"

Favors are not to be taken lightly. That was the first and maybe most important lesson Karao had taught him so far. Committing yourself to unknown variables can be devastating.

Nils walked in the door, alone. They were smiling like always. Catherine called out to them, and they rushed into the kitchen. Without taking a leap like that, he wouldn't have been around for a small moment like that. He liked being here.

What's a little risk? "Deal, Morgan."

"Be ready to hit the books!" Her energy was probably the thing he liked most about hanging around her, not that he'd ever admit that. She didn't need help inflating that ego.

Chapter 6- End

Intermission- Fixing Things

Catherine had dropped a teapot. As far as disasters go, it was pretty tame. The handle had slipped from her hand and crashed around her foot. She wasn't burned or at least didn't look like it. Regardless, Nils insisted that she sit with her foot wrapped in a cold towel.

"Sorry, sorry, I didn't mean to-" Catherine was on her fifth or sixth round of apologizing for Nils, who had cleaned up most of the mess by the time Nika had walked back. Morgan had just left when the loud crash rang from the kitchen.

"It's fine!" Nils was almost mechanically repeating the words at this point. "It wasn't your fault!" Nils opened a drawer and pulled out their bracer. They had explained it to Nika a while ago, but the gist was that Nils was able to use little bits of necromancy on smaller bits of bone inside each of its four fake gems to call on a particular spell that those bones used to be familiar with.

One of those was, apparently, repairing broken things. The bracer hummed a bit as they channeled their energy through the foggy yellow gem. The teapot shards tumbled their way back into place. The whole thing looked like an accident playing in reverse.

This was, in fact, an example of necromancy being used in the tea shop while Karao was gone. Nils held up a finger to Nika. He knew to keep this as yet another secret.

"How'd your date go?" Catherine asked, drying her foot.

"Oh? It was fine," Nils's smile weakened as they put away the bracer again. "I think he took it well."

"Oh," Catherine didn't seem that upset. "I'm sorry."

"It is what it is," Nils shrugged their smile back in full force. "Nils is a homunculus and a necromancer! No need to drag someone else down with me!" Nils laughed alone. "Ah, come on, guys, it's not that bad."

Nika didn't have the details but understood the gist of it. Catherine was frustrated that she couldn't have done more to convince Daniel to stay away. It was just a hunch, but she seemed like she was furious with herself.

"I don't think he'll be around for a couple of weeks, so we can sleep in!" Nils said. Their inflection hinted at a levity that their eyes didn't share. Nils had found a way to make a zero-effort joke into a way to make them all sad.

Chapter 7. Deadarm Initiation

The rest of the week leading up to the weekend had been quiet. He would be getting help from Morgan starting Monday, his usual training had been progressing smoothly, and when he wasn't doing something around the shop, he was reading. It was pretty much a perfect week for him, but Nils and Catherine had been bored out of their skulls.

Nika assumed that boredom was the reason Karao had taken the three of them out this mid-June Saturday. The four of them were seated on a questionably clean bench in the Eldes Portal Station, a public transit hub on the Northside of the city.

Nils and Catherine were melting in the heat. In Nils's case, it was because they were wearing layers in the summer. Form over function, he guessed. Karao, meanwhile, was dressed comfortably for the heat. While in public, her skeletal deadarms were concealed away by illusionary magic; she didn't really need people staring at a five-armed, six-foot-seven woman.

Nika didn't have a wardrobe to work with, but even he was wearing the 'nicer' of his three shirts. Having to do manual laundry wasn't the worst part of living his former magic-free life, but Nils knowing a spell that cleaned clothes automatically helped so much that he didn't want to go back.

He was more taken by the portal station than any of that. Even for a late Saturday morning, this place was packed wall to wall with winding lines of people. The lines were sectioned off to make a walking path down the middle where they were sitting, but besides that, there was barely room to breathe. It was loud, too. A thousand annoying scrapes and conversations fought to dominate the air. The building looked newer than the ones around it, too. The stone walls and glass roof were clean and well illuminated.

"So. How does this work?" Nika asked anyone willing to answer.

"You stand in line until one of the station workers zaps you where you wanna go," Catherine had given up trying to figure it out herself. "Why aren't we in line, Karao?"

"We're waiting," she answered, barely looking up from the wrinkled newspaper she was skimming.

"Waiting for what?" Nika looked closer at the lines. Each section was color-coded and marked with where the different station workers could send you. Towards the front of each line, there was a frantic ticket booth with someone inside desperately keeping up with the orders.

Karao held four tickets up. "Patience is an extremely useful life skill. How lucky for us all that we have this extra chance to practice."

Nils had pieced something together and was excited; they had figured out where the group was going. Before they had a chance to ruin Karao's surprise, a bell rang directly above them. It was shockingly clear for a room cluttered with irritating sounds. Turns out that was because of proximity. The bell had appeared in a puff of noxious smoke above them. Nika only caught a short glimpse of this floating bell before it faded back into the air it came from.

"That's us, then!" Karao picked up her large and obnoxious brown bag and began walking to the other end of the station. "See?"

They followed though none of the lines seemed to start where she was headed. Nils was enthusiastically trailing them. The other two were just curious. As they approached the wall, Karao's pace refused to slow down. The bricks turned and folded outwards as she got closer, eventually forming a Karao-sized gate in the wall that she sauntered through easily.

Nobody else seemed to notice or care. Nika was annoyed that his hole in the wall was visibly shorter than any of the others. Even facts were out to put him down. Beyond the wall was a simple room that was clearly never meant to hold four people, let alone four people and an oversized canvas bag.

On the far end, a small window let them see into a somehow smaller office where a very bored employee tapped his cluttered desk.

"Where to?" They asked.

"Hello again, it's been a while." Karao handed him the tickets. "Also, we'd like to go here." She handed him another slip of paper.

"These are one-way tickets. Would you like to upgrade to a there-and-recall package for an upcharge of five-fifty per-"

"No thanks," She flashed the hourglass coin. "We'll be fine."

"Uh-huh," He gestured to the wall on Nika's right. "Please close your eyes and breathe normally. Teleportation begins in five, four, three, two, have a nice trip."

Even with his eyes closed, the world became darker than Nika had ever known for one eternal second. The world went from dusty to freezing and back to a comfortable summer heat faster than Nika could fully register it. Every organ in his body felt like it was turning inside out in protest. His stomach, in particular, was staging a full-scale coup to prevent Nika from ever teleporting anywhere ever again. It was a compelling argument. He kept his eyes closed until Catherine tapped his shoulder.

"You gonna be ok there?" she teased.

Nika would have thought they had arrived, but usually, that meant you went somewhere. They were standing in an apple-green field, knee-high grass scratching at them in the cool breeze. The four were in the center of a large clearing with verdant trees making up ninety-eight percent of the horizon, save for one boulder stalking them in the distance. They were standing in the middle of nowhere. The fresher air did help calm down his stomach.

Karao let down her bag gently, taking a deep breath of fresh air. Nils had already tumbled willingly into the grass with a soft yet satisfying crunching sound. Catherine looked just as confused as Nika did.

"So," Karao turned back to them, a confident smirk spreading across her face. "You three ready?" She reached into the bag and pulled out three separate, long objects wrapped in cloth.

"No?" Catherine answered.

"I disagree," Karao tossed each of them one of the three mysterious cloth packages. Nika's rattled as he caught it. The sound was unsettling. The shape seemed familiar now that he was holding it. It was a stick that was heavier on one end and bent in the middle. Sort of like an arm. "You've been ready for a while, Catherine."

Exactly like an arm, in fact.

It was an arm. Nika didn't need to fully unwrap his to understand that. Karao shouted at him as he first spotted bone. "Stop that! There's nothing holding it together. If you do that, I'm not putting it back for you!"

Nils stopped themselves cold from opening their new gift. "You could have said so!"

Karao held her own four deadarms out prominently. She looked sort of like the right half of the worlds' most macabre peacock. Deadarms was a name she had made up. It was just easier than explaining the intricate reanimation magic involved in constantly having the right arms of four long-dead mages at your beck and call at all times. 'Deadarms' was snappy, descriptive, and discouraged follow-up questions.

Nika dreaded what this gift meant for him: expectations. She was hoping to see results out of him, the same necromancer-in-training who couldn't figure out the yeast thing or how to un-reanimate an annoying pet snake. The other two would probably do great, but there was no way he could tackle something like this.

"To use a deadarm," Karao began, "is you borrowing a portion of a former wizard's abilities. Properly done, you can cast the spells a mage used so often it is ingrained into their very body. It's kinda like muscle memory, but for casting spells. Yes, Nils?"

Nils had patiently had their hand raised for a while. They had clearly been to this field before and was loving it. "Why did we have to come out here? Are these... illegally... obtained... bones?" Nils had no idea where that question was going when they started it but were not super happy with how it ended.

Karao's second deadarm, the second from the top, twitched briefly. The signature purple electricity started at its base, eventually becoming a glowing blue wisp in the deadarms's fingertips. Magic curled between the bones, slithering its way into her palm, forming a small, translucent marble. She haphazardly tossed the ghostly ball behind her.

A column of blue light erupted behind Karao. It rocketed into the sky, dissipating more and more as it continued on its warpath towards the sun. Each of their jaws would have dropped if Catherine hadn't been petrified at that moment.

A smoking crater was all that was left of the once vibrant grass where the wisp had hit. The grass burnt with a horrific stench, but only briefly. The land started to recover its color, from barren ash to life-filled soil. It only took a moment for the entire patch to be completely back to normal, grass and all.

"Because this might be the only place you three can't blow up by mistake," Karao said.

"Huh," Catherine said.

"Neat." Nika was impressed.

"Now," Karao was excited. "Who wants to get started?"

Bones, under normal circumstances, are held together with muscle fiber and bagged up inside of living things. Without the surrounding tissue, they would have no reason to stay connected. Nika had wondered how Karao's deadarms had always seemed to act like cohesive limbs without anything attached. The simple answer is necromancy; the complicated answer was a ten-page packet she threw at her three students. To be studied later, of course.

Catherine went first. Karao had her place the arm on the ground and then lay back onto it. She had never looked less comfortable. She was supposed to take all the energy she usually focused into her hands and try to force it into her spine. It took a few minutes of her focusing and roasting in the summer sun for the process to start. The cloth began to twitch, the arm beneath her curling and getting used to moving again. Where there was once muscle fiber, invisible fibers were now weaving their way through the intricate bones.

The whole process took nearly fifteen minutes. When Catherine finally stood up, her back hurt. Hunched over like an old hag, Her new extraneous skeleton arm dangled loosely from her spine down by her ankle. Karao removed the cloth, and the whole thing was sticking together pretty well.

Nika and Nils followed suit, each taking longer than the last to do what Catherine had done. Catherine and Nika had new right deadarms, Nils a new left.

"Whenever you use any type of magic," Karao began lecturing, her favorite part of these lessons. "It needs some kind of structure to form itself in. Has anyone ever seen a magic wand?" she asked with no intention of waiting for an answer. "Of course not; they're stupid, outdated tools for conducting magic from inside your body into tangible spells. But! Magic still needs a converter, from energy to spells. Anyone care to guess where that is?"

Nils raised their deadarm, ready to answer the question.

"Exactly, thank you, Nils." Two of Karaos deadarms plucked the fourth from its place on her back. Watching her wave it around, was a little unsettling. "Every time you cast a spell, your bones are converting that energy into, well, whatever you're trying to make happen. Meaning, your body is a pretty impeccable record keeper. Lucky for us, we get to use that record to call on spells that these bones remember casting." She sent energy into the deadarm she was holding, and it sprang back to life. The fingertips splayed themselves, sparked for a bit, and then fumed smoke into the air around Karao. It wrapped around her into an impenetrable cocoon.

Her three students crept towards the pillar of smoke that was formerly their teacher. They could just wait for the smoke to clear, but Catherine clearly had no interest in Karao's theatrics. Nils yelped. Karao had been behind them, watching them cautiously tiptoe at the smoke. She had earned a smug 'gotcha.'

"For example, I believe that this was once the arm of a moderately successful thief. Smoke shields, short-range teleportation, telekinesis, silencing, and muffling." She paused, counting off spells on her many, many fingers. "Paralysis, concealing, walking through walls, the list goes on. I can only think of so many 'jobs' where these are useful skills." She reattached it to her back and, with a few flexes, it seemed to be back to normal.

Nika was floored. Having all of that from one of her four deadarms was astounding. He was still getting used to the presence of the pile of bones suspended magically outside his spine.

"Of course, most people have a go-to sort of magic. When you first start using a deadarm, I expect that you'd find the spell they cast most. Yes, Catherine?"

"You never said where you, er, got, these." Catherine looked a bit worried.

"A museum. The curator owes me quite a bit," she answered.

"What kind of museum has a bunch of spare arms laying around?" Nika asked, sharing her concerns.

"Well, it's more of a touristy mausoleum," Karao said. "For famous historical-"

"What do you mean famous!" Catherine shouted.

Karao shook her head. "Calm down, these were just gathering dust in the back-"

"That's not better!" Catherine insisted.

The argument went on for a while. Catherine and Nika eventually conceded that necromancers needed something to work with if they were going to do anything at all.

"What you need to do is respect the person whose powers you are borrowing. Treat their history well. A body is just a pile of parts."

Nils was the first one to try out their new powers. Karao refused to say what sort of magic each one would produce, but she had come prepared with props from the bag. For Nils, she poured a glass of water and propped it up on a wooden block.

Nils stood a good twenty feet away from the glass. Karao stood directly behind Nils, helping them adjust and talking about methods. Catherine and Nika were standing way, way back. The earlier comment about 'being the only place they can't blow up' made the two of them think this could go very wrong.

Watching Nils try to call up enough energy to trigger their deadarms's new power was sort of like watching a fish hit a wall repeatedly trying to get into demolition. Every inch of progress took so much effort from them that it hardly seemed worth the time.

Karao wouldn't give up on Nils, though. She kept repositioning and encouraging her student; with each successive attempt, Nils took the smallest steps forward. Finally, with a victorious, stressed howl Nils's deadarm surrounded itself with a white mist. Its finger was pointed at the glass of water, but nothing changed. Nils fell over.

Nika and Catherine ran up to them. Nils was shivering.

"Nils is so cold. Why is it so cold? Ni- er, I don't get it. What happened?" Nils was completely out of it.

"Oh, dear," Karao reached down and helped Nils sit up. "Well, the idea was that the glass of water would freeze over not, well, you. All right, you go sit in the sun for a bit. You did a good job today Nils." Karao handed her the warm, definitely-liquid filled glass of water.

Nils nodded, walked a few feet, and collapsed again.

"They'll be fine. Nika, you're up," she said.

He was suddenly more nervous than he had ever been in his life. Nils was always talented with the execution of things like this. Even if he had more of an output than they did, the number of ways this mysterious arm on his back might backfire on him were being tallied up one by one in his head.

Explosion, Acid, Fire, Flying a thousand feet in the air, launching himself into the woods, being buried alive. Yep. All were ways he could die right then and there. Catherine was over by Nils as Karao walked away with Nika.

"So, what you're going to want to do is just let the arm do its thing," Karao said.

"I don't understand," Nika said.

"The bone remembers what it needs to do. You just need to fuel it." She held up a metal ball and chucked it as far as she could.

"What if it does something I don't want it to?" he asked, thinking about Nils nearly freezing themself on the spot.

"Hold up three fingers," Karao commanded. He did, she shook her head. "No, on the deadarm."

It took a little more focus. It was similar to moving his hands, just more forced. It was like manually controlling one's breath. Being cognizant of it was making it more difficult than it should have been. In spite of the hurdle, he was able to hold them up.

"You're the one in charge," Karao smiled. "So give it a shot, focus on the ball. Call it back."

He followed her orders. It was a strange sensation; watching something he controlled, but could not feel, move felt like swimming in a dream. The fingers twitched a bit and sparked purple. The solitary moment of stillness was shattered by the ball rocketing back to him.

He hadn't even considered being annihilated by a palm-sized chunk of steel, but that was another way that he could have died that day, apparently. He flinched, arms held up to reduce the incoming damage.

There was no damage. The palm of the deadarm hummed quietly a few inches away from the now harmless, hovering-metal-death-sphere. It was convenient his hands were already shielding his face since he now wanted to bury his blushed head as far away from any human being as possible, but especially Karao.

She was laughing, obviously.

Before she could say whatever was on her mind, an overwhelming wind nearly knocked both of them down from behind. Catherine couldn't wait to try hers out, apparently, and she was now trying to shake a hurricane off of her hand like it was a bug. Nils was holding onto the grass for dear life. Karao vanished into smoke before appearing behind Catherine and attempting to solve the problem.

His near non-death experience had left him jittery, but this was undoubtedly a win. He had never picked up anything as fast as this, and of the three junior necromancers, he was the only one whose first attempt hadn't ended in complete disaster; it was a miniature catastrophe at best. It was weird feeling good about it, but not unpleasant.

They spent the rest of the morning practicing and running drills with their borrowed abilities. Nils's final range for freezing things was a full two feet in front of them. It wasn't up to Karao's expectations, but it was certainly better than the first shot, certainly. Catherine's handheld tempests were an intentional choice by Karao. It was a way for her to exhaust huge amounts of energy without being overly destructive, provided that it was pointed in the right direction. She spent the entire time trying to limit the eruptions of wind conjured from her fingertips.

In the end, Catherine managed to restrict a hurricane into a mere violent wind. She would still need work.

Nika's practice couldn't have gone better. He was getting used to picking up and dragging things with his magnetic power. He could make things hover, turn them over, fling them and, most importantly, stop them from hitting people in the head when he threw them too fast. He was delighted the entire time.

"All right," Karao announced to her exhausted trainees. "We're about to head back, so I'm going to show you how to take these off," She helped Nils first. It took some sharp breathing and focus, but eventually, it slipped right off into Karao's hands. She wrapped it back up in cloth and handed it to Nils. "This is yours now. Take care of it. It's more fragile than you think."

Nika was next. He listened as Karao gave him directions. It didn't work. She repeated the steps; same results. Catherine managed to do it on her own while waiting for him.

"Ok, Nika." She grabbed his shoulder. "This might hurt a little bit, but I have to pull it off."

"Ok," he said. He was getting nervous. Nils had explained what they had done. Even Catherine was starting to be concerned. None of the things he was supposed to be feeling were happening. No easing of muscles in the back, no slight tingle in the fingertips, no sense of release in the spine, nothing was happening the way it was supposed to be.

Karao pulled, but he went with it. Though it wasn't physically attached to his body or shirt, it had tied itself to him some other way. It wasn't moving. It did hurt. He screamed for her to stop. Karao kept pulling.

The metal ball lunged at Karaos face, directed by the deadarm. She snagged it before it landed, but she wasn't happy.

"That wasn't me, I didn-"

"Shh, Nika, I know. Catherine, give me a hand." Catherine grabbed Nika's wrists. "Get it, hand?"

"Ugh," Catherine groaned before helping to rip the two apart. Nothing happened.

"What's happening?" Nika asked. Nils shook their head. Karao's mind was sifting through options trying to figure it out.

"I had you wrong," Karao said. "I thought I understood your quirk, but I have no idea what's happening here."

Nika's pulse became erratic and feverish. The arm was twitching without his input. The idea that he hadn't been in control made him sick. Who was there with him, doing these things?

"I'm sorry, Nika," she said. She looked frustrated. Her eyes were burning towards her own chest. He saw her defeated once, with Cruise, but her face was entirely desolate. She was pummeling herself inside. "I'm going to look into this, I promise. For now, you'll just have to keep that deadarm on."

He nodded, then thought about sporting a skeleton hand in public. "Wait, what?"

Chapter 7- End

Intermission - Payday

"We get paid?" Nika asked. He was in disbelief of the envelope despite the fact that it was in his hand.

"Well, yeah, we work, don't we?" Catherine had already counted hers out and seemed satisfied.

"Sorta," Nika said. The envelopes were labeled and left on the kitchen table by Karao before she left for the morning. Nils had gotten to them first and had disappeared, leaving just Catherine and Nika to sort through the cash.

The currency in Eldes, and most major cities across the world, was called gemslips. Each piece of paper currency was backed by a percentage of some precious stone. One full sapphire, for instance, was a one-hundred slip, a ten was ten percent, et cetera. He had just recently read about it in one of Morgan's old social textbooks.

"I guess it's been a month, huh." Nika hadn't even noticed how much time had gone by with all the nonsense that's happened. The few hours he had put in had come out to one-hundred-eighty Gs, as Catherine called them.

"You should save some of that, you know. I usually put most of mine away." Catherine was definitely in good spirits as she prepared to open.

"Save it for what?" Nika asked.

She shrugged. "In case."

Nils burst through the kitchen with a huge paper bag from one of the shops down the road. They noticed Catherine and hid the bag behind their back. "Catherine! Don't look!"

Catherine rolled her eyes and turned away from Nils. "What did you do?"

"You'll find out tomorrow, birthday girl." Nils tiptoed to the staircase then abandoned all pretense of being quiet as they sprinted up the steps.

"The best money advice I can give you, Nika." Catherine slid her deadarm into place on her back. She'd been using the extra hand to help with prep and cleaning, with a strict caveat banning any amount of its power being used within a mile of the building, or the city for that matter. "Don't be Nils."

Chapter 8. The Cost of Consideration

It was, in fact, Catherine's seventeenth birthday the following day. Nils couldn't have been more excited to celebrate, and Karao was happy to go along for the ride. All Nika could figure out from bits of overheard conversations was that Catherine would get to pick dinner and that Nils and Karao were getting her gifts.

In flattering terms, Catherine told Nika not to worry about wasting his money on a present. More accurately, she told him that if he bought something for her, she would return it and put his money on the roof for him to go and get.

The main thing Nika learned about Catherine's birthday was that she didn't care for it. She went along because Nils was excited, and Karao liked the excuse to do something a little fancy. She didn't like the fuss and didn't really want the extra attention. She wouldn't turn down a chance to pick dinner, though.

Karao had taken Catherine out after work to pick out a present which gave Nils and Nika time to set up the rest of the night. They had only a few hours to go shopping for ingredients and clean up after an unusually busy day at the tea shop. The tasks were simple enough: buy groceries, tidy up, set up a single nice table, and cook the food. Karao had added: 'not forgetting any of the above' as a final step. It was an important step. Nika's more immediate concern as they walked back with the food was the eyes. To hide the stubborn deadarm stuck to his back, he had been wearing a super baggy hand-me-down sweatshirt out in public. He was getting quite a few weird looks, and he hated that above most other things. It wouldn't have been too noticeable if it hadn't been boiling hot. Nika was ready to topple over at the first opportunity.

A cool jet of water struck him in the face. He was, in order: shocked, enraged, and relieved. Nils was smiling at him, their bracer still glowing a bit from use. Apparently, Nils had thought he had needed a bit of a splash. Whichever long-dead wizard specialized in tiny, useless jets of water was likely rolling in their grave.

"Anyone home?" Nils knocked on his head.

"Sorry."

Nils laughed. "Let's just hurry back, ok?"

Nika eventually asked, "Were you saying something?"

"Yeah, you were zoning out," Nils said. "I was asking about your little friend."

"Donut? I finally found a box he can't escape from. I think he-"

"No, no, not Donut." Nils nudged him with a bag of food. "Megan!"

"Oh, Morgan?"

"Oops, I guess." Nils shook their head. "She talks kinda fast. I must've misheard." Nika nodded. That sounded about right. "She's helping you study, right? How's that going?"

"We've only met up once for studying, and she ended up talking about dueling for most of it," Nika said. "Her notes are really good though, I've gotten a lot from the books too."

"Feel good about it?" Nils asked. "The test, I mean."

Nika answered by reflex. "No." He didn't stop to think about it until after the fact. "Well, maybe, I guess. I don't know."

"I believe in you, kid." Nils had this obnoxious, infectious optimism to them. They were also the oldest of the three, which wouldn't be obvious to anyone looking in. He wondered what Nils was like before anyone else lived with Karao.

"Hey, Nils?"

"Sup?"

"What was it like when Catherine moved in?" he asked.

He could almost see the nostalgia wash over Nils's eyes. Nostalgia is both happy and watery, then it snaps back into a lukewarm reality. "I just remember her yelling at me for saying 'Nils' instead of 'I' a bunch," Nils answered.

Nika had practically forgotten about that. They had been doing a really good job at remembering it recently. "Oh yeah, huh."

"Yup! It was-" Nils hunted for a word. "New. I haven't had anyone be so aggressively friendly to me. She pretty much accepted us immediately." They were rounding the final corner. "You too, you know. Once Catherine's decided she cares about you, she won't let you be sad for even a-"

Nils stopped. Their eyes were quivering, horrified.

"What is it?" Nika asked. He turned to see what had trapped their gaze.

It was the Pale Garden tea shop, just as he remembered, with one key difference. The front windows and doors were plastered with papers. They clung to every imperfection and crevice in the wooden storefront. Each of them had writing scrawled in frantic red ink.

The two ran up to the building to check more closely. Nika could finally read what they said if he made a few assumptions with the awful handwriting.

BEWARE OF INHUMAN FREAK- MAY BITE

BROKEN DOLL

ROT, FREAK

He couldn't bring himself to read more of them. He worried if the word had gotten out about the tea shop if this is how people in the city treated necromancers. This wasn't better than before; this might be worse. His chest started collapsing. He turned to Nils.

Nils ripped one down from the window and sort of just stared at it. Searing tears started quietly falling down their face, but Nils wasn't crying. Rather, they weren't breathing the way one would when they cry. Their eyes didn't redden. Nils cried without emotion, and yet, their eyes looked devastated. The paper they held read:

LOST: TRASH- RESPONDS TO 'NILS'

"What happened?" Nika asked.

Nils wiped their face on their sleeve. "Nils is sorry, Nika. Nil- no, I need you to bring the stuff inside. I- I will clean this up. Go get a drink."

He followed most of Nils's instructions. He technically had a drink, but it was just a gulp of tap water on his way back out to help Nils clean the front of the shop. When he stepped back outside, Nils was standing on a barrel, reaching as high as they could to rip more of the papers down. The tears were gone, replaced by a resentful determination to clean the mess up.

Nika said nothing. He just started helping in areas Nils wouldn't have gotten to for a while. Nils objected and told him to go back inside and follow their checklist. He just stubbornly stayed to help, and Nils had no further objections.

"Thank you," they said.

"Don't mention it."

"It's not always this bad, you know," Nils was speaking softly, but the street obediently stayed quiet enough for Nika to hear what they had today. "Usually, it's just my locker. I guess they heard I won't be getting one this year."

"'They'?" Nika asked

"You know what Nils is, right?" Nils asked. They gestured at their ash-grey skin, the creases in their joints, the hairless head. "I was never born. I was made. I was made for a job I couldn't do and was thrown away. I didn't even have a name until Karao came along." Nils wasn't crying, but their eyes were fighting. "There are people who hate me for it, and nothing I can say will change what I am to them." They swiped at a whole row of the papers, flinging them into the breeze. "Just a freak they have to sit with in school, a gross unnatural *thing*, they're mad because Nils-er-I- will be one of the first homunculi to graduate. They can't stand it."

"I'm sorry." Nika didn't know what else to say. "You're not like that, Nils."

"I know." Nils was weirdly optimistic. "I know they're wrong. But that doesn't mean they don't scare me." The store was looking mostly cleaned up by now. A few stragglers were shot down by Nils's water jet. "Don't tell the others about this, ok? Nils wants to find the right time to bring it up."

"I-, Nils," Nika said. They paused.

The two shared a sad chuckle.

"Oh shush. We can't let Catherine's birthday be ruined by this." They both went inside again. Nika was ecstatic to be free from the sun. "I know she doesn't really care, but I do."

"Wait, when's your birthday, Nils?" Nika asked.

"Nika. I don't have one. Wherever Nils was made didn't even write down the day they made me."

"I'm sorry."

"It's ok. You're coming from the right place. Appreciated!" Nils had clearly had this exact conversation with other people before. "Have I ever told you about when Karao named me? No, probably not." They were quietly zoning out, almost talking to themselves. Nika was listening. "People used to call me nothing. It was always 'you' and 'freak.' They seemed to think I could read their minds and just know when they were talking to me."

"When did Karao find you?"

"I was like you. I ran away. Honestly, I don't even remember much of my old life. I was pretty small. She asked me what my name was. I said it was nothing. She came up with Nils. It took me about ten years to learn that 'nil' means nothing. If I was going to be nothing, she said I might as well own it."

The rest of their work went relatively smoothly, though there was absolutely no way to cook the food all the way before Catherine and Karao got back home. Nils talked more about the time since Catherine had been living with them as they cooked vegetables and threw the meat into the oven. All that was left was to wait.

Donut liked playing on the pair of candle holders they had on the table, especially the molten wax that would drip onto his tiny forehead. The snake would coat itself in one wax hairstyle after the other, each time turning back to Nika to pull it off his head.

Nils's expression grew more serious in the quiet. "Nika."

"Yeah?" he asked through sips of tea.

"What would you say if I told you I was thinking of moving out?"

He coughed up what had been some very tasty tea.

"Wait, wait, wait, easy there." Nils was smiling again, so that was good. "I haven't decided yet." They waited for Nika to finish hacking up the rest of the drink he had breathed in. "I just, when it was just Nils's locker, er, my locker, it was just me. Y'know? I could handle it all myself." They put their arm around Nika. "I don't want to drag anyone else down with my problems."

"You're not-" Nika said.

"Besides!" Nils interrupted. "Lots of my classmates moved out last year. You gotta strike out on your own eventually."

"But, Nils-"

"I would still be at the tea shop most days. I'd basically just be eating and sleeping somewhere else. Things wouldn't change that much. And-"

"Nils!" Nika shouted.

Nils looked at him with large, surprised eyes.

"Stop." Nika wanted to get his thoughts in. "I, well, I left once because people were threatening my family. I thought it was all I could do. They were scared, Nils. They were scared of the town. They were scared about the future. They were scared of me."

Nils grabbed his shoulders and looked him in the eye. "That's why I want to step away."

"But I'm not scared!" Nika shouted, his voice cracking. Nils's grip loosened, their face reset to a blank expression from the surprise. "You all have been nothing but great to me, I don't think I want any of this to change." A lot of the thoughts he had kept to himself were pouring out. Internally, he cursed how easy it was to talk to Nils. "Whatever those cowards want to say, they wouldn't say to your face, let alone Catherine or Karao."

"Nika." Nils had nothing to add.

"We can't help you if you leave, you know?" Nika said.

Nils ruffled his hair. "It was just a question. I'm in no shape to move out just yet." Nils started laughing.

"What's funny?"

"I thought you'd be the easy one to convince." Nils shook their head. "If you can talk me out of it, then there's no chance I'd get past Catherine."

"What about Karao?" Nika asked.

"She'd let me do it even if it was a bad idea just for 'the learning experience.'"

"You're not wrong."

"But Catherine would fight me tooth and nail. She's basically my sister. I would be crazy to try to think about this without talking to her. I couldn't do that to her. What kind of family would I be?"

"She'd probably toss you over the building," Nika said. Nils laughed.

Nils spent the next few minutes listing reasons moving would be a horrible idea. The list started with, but was not limited to:

    * Nils has no money

    * Nils doesn't know the cost of living

    * Nils has trouble waking up on time and needs someone to check on them

    * Nika might catch up to Nils if he gets impromptu -- lessons from Karao

    * Catherine wouldn't help Nils with homework as much

    * Free tea is the best tea

By the end, there were enough reasons in the CON column that they needed to borrow space from the mostly empty PRO column to put it all down. Nils looked a little dismayed. Even though Nika had said that he wasn't scared, Nils would rightly still worry about things getting worse at the tea shop.

Nils had the brilliant idea to hide and wait to ambush Catherine when she came back. Nika objected, saying that it sounded like a great way to get punched as a reflex. Regardless, arguing against one of Nils's 'fun' ideas is like politely asking a river to stop, so that's what they did.

"Hey," Nika whispered from beneath his table.

"Yeah?" Nils answered from the drapes. He was going to ask what the present was, but he didn't get the chance. "They're here! Shh!"

The room was dead silent. Appropriately, two necromancers livened things up by entering. They had been arguing about something, and now Nika and Nils would have to hear the tail end of it. "I'm tired of being treated like a kid, Karao. I don't need you to constantly keep an eye on me."

"I only watch you like that in the shop, Catherine, and that's mostly to protect my property."

"I'm tired of those jokes, too," Catherine's voice sank a bit. "I'm not like that all the time. I'm not some reckless, angry jerk."

"You aren't. I'm sorry," Karao said. "I know you're frustrated, but-"

"Wait, Karao, stop." Catherine's voice was shaking. "Let me just say one thing."

Nika peeked out to see Nils. Their feet were shuffling under the drapes, unable to stand still. They hated arguments like this. Catherine had her back to the window, but Karao definitely noticed the moving curtain. Nils decided to leap out and try to stop the fighting. Karao saw them and tried to stop Catherine. Nils didn't even get to make a noise.

With a steady voice, Catherine destroyed Nils in three words: "I'm moving out."

Chapter 8- End

Intermission - Opening Up

Good Morning, Nika!

Thanks for stepping up to this. Catherine is still getting settled in, and, well, with how Nils has been, I decided to give them a few days off. Either Catherine or I will be in by eight every day, but we need you to get things set up. Typically we're dead before ten, so you should be fine, but the recipes are in the back if you need to prepare anything. Here's a checklist of everything you need to do before opening up:

_____ Wipe off the tables

_____ Find Donut (he's been hanging around the broom cupboard lately)

_____ Fill water pots and put them on the stove, do NOT start the oven

_____ Reanimate the flowers in the flower box (don't overdo it, please)

_____ Turn on the lights (the switch will tickle a bit, it uses a bit of your energy for the whole day)

_____ Help yourself to a pastry, they're in the kitchen

_____ Flip the sign to 'Open'

Thanks again, Nika. We appreciate it a lot. If Nils tries to help, you send them back to bed or shove a dessert in their face until they take it easy.

- Karao

Chapter 9. A Moment in the Replay Box

For most people, an unmarked envelope containing nothing but their name, an address, and a time would be suspicious and a worrisome thing to find under the door in the morning. Nika considered himself a part of this inclusive group until he saw the name 'Morgan' written on the back in elaborate letters. Now it just made plain sense, somehow.

She probably spent more time on the calligraphy than she did on the contents of her vague letter.

Precisely ten minutes after the appointed time, Nika caught himself checking the letter for the twentieth time. He had gotten lost once or twice along the way, but he had made it. This cute little suburban house, with its dusty blue siding and perfect black roof, was the place Morgan wanted to meet up with him to study today.

He was still uncomfortable walking around in public with this baggy sweatshirt. He thought that the overcast sky would help, but really that just meant it was miserably hot with bonus humidity. He fanned himself with the letter as he walked up to the door. He went to knock, and a window flung itself open from the second floor. Morgan's head popped out, glaring down at him.

"You're late!" She shouted down to him.

He had suspected this was her house. One theory confirmed, one hundred to go. "Sorry!"

"What on earth are you wearing?" She shook her head. "I'll be right down!" The window slammed shut.

"A sweatshirt," he answered to himself quietly. "Thanks for asking."

The door opened faster than Nika expected. Likely, because Morgan wasn't the one answering it. Instead, he was looking at what he assumed was her dad, the man standing by Cruise's side a few weeks ago. When he was wearing the suit, he looked polished, well put together. His posture and expression were focused and attentive. He was the picture of a good soldier that came with the uniform.

Now, in an ill-fitted tee-shirt and pajama pants, he looked like he hadn't worked a day in his life and was much, much happier for it.

Nika hadn't considered that they would be here. His mind went into high gear deciding if this was weird, should he introduce himself again, since they knew he was a necromancer would they let him in the house, would there be-

"You're Morgan's friend?" He said, his lax expression changed to a leer. Her dad's chest puffed up a bit. It was a cheap and stupid intimidation tactic. It worked.

"Yeah," Nika said.

"Yeah, what?"

"Yeah, sir?" Nika guessed.

"I don't like your attitude, boy. Drop and give me twenty!" He barked. His face was straining and reddening.

"Twenty what?" Nika was quickly losing control of the situation.

"Oh, so you think you're funny?"

Nika was panicking. He was hot. The world started spinning around him. Then the man started laughing.

"I'm just messing with ya, kid." He patted Nika's shoulder. "I can't keep the 'tough guy' act for that long. Sorry for bustin' your chops a bit there. I couldn't resist. Say, isn't it a bit hot out to be-"

"Dad!" Morgan screamed from somewhere behind them. Nika had never been happier to have Morgan intervene

in his life than that exact moment. She tackled her dad from the side, and the two slammed into a wall. "Knock it off!"

Morgan rebounded first and came to the door. "Sorry about that, come on in!"

Despite the risks to his physical and mental well-being, Nika entered the house. "Dad, this is Nika. He's new, so I'm helping him with school stuff."

Something clicked in his head. "Nika, that's an unusual name. I'm Ben, Ben Farvue. Mr. Farvue, the incredible, impeccable Benjamin, if you will." He extended his hand. "But you won't. It's nice to meet ya." Ben seemed to be scrutinizing his face. The sweatshirt was probably a better disguise than he had expected since Nika's face was getting redder by the second.

Nika gulped. Right then and there, he decided to lock-in to the 'never tell him that we had met before' plan.

"Ah, well, sorry again. If either of you needs anything, just holler. I'll be downstairs. Oh, Nika! Have you eaten yet?" It was, as Morgan was about to point out to him, just after lunch. "Plenty of leftovers for you two. And don't forget Morgan, I know all the best places to hide a body!"

"Thanks, Dad." She sighed and started up the stairs next to the door. The house was as quaint and considerate inside as it was outside. Every inch of hardwood floor was polished. The teal wallpaper matched the brassy aesthetic of picture frames hanging from the wall. The sunlight entered in just the right places to keep the entire floor illuminated. "He thinks he's really funny."

Nika suppressed the urge to say 'that makes two of you,' but he sure did think it. "Where are we going?"

"My room, duh," she said, "I've got a stack of stuff for you to take home today, and I don't feel like carrying it. So I figured, let's just study at my place and save me the work."

"How-" he didn't have a word that encapsulated that level of laziness and generosity. "-kind of you. Thanks."

"You're welcome!" She stopped by the door at the end of the hall. Her hand lingered at the doorknob before she threw it open.

Right. Morgan's room. It was a complete disaster. Her bed was buried under chaotic stacks of dueling magazines, her desk was cluttered with small cards and wax figures, and sketches of costume ideas covered every inch of the wall that wasn't already occupied by a fight poster. The scent of paper, which Nika didn't know had a scent, tainted the breathing air. As stuffy as the world outside was, this room was probably worse on principle alone.

"I tidied it up a bit so we'd have room to sit," she said, gesturing to a spot on the floor about the size of the doorway he was standing in. She claimed her spot. Between her and the pile of books, Nika was looking at about two square feet of space to claim as his own.

"You did?"

She didn't respond. Instead, she slammed a book of sixth-grade level history in front of him. "First. You have to answer a question."

"That's nothing new," he said.

"What's with the sweatshirt?" she asked.

"Not much, really." He lied poorly. "It was cold in the tea shop."

"So then why are you wearing shorts?" She was probably more excited that she caught the lie than actually finding out the answer.

Nika considered a few options. All of them sounded desperate. There was no way to walk himself back on this one. He was well and truly caught. "Fine, I have to. But I can't tell you why."

That was where Nika learned one of the most important lessons about Morgan; telling her, she can't know something is the only surefire way to make her want to learn it. Her eyebrows creased, and her chin curled up, but only for one passing second. "Would you like some water?"

Nika, usually was the sort of person that would suffer through all sorts of things to avoid inconveniencing anyone, even if that inconvenience was an errand as trivial as getting a glass of water. The heat was too much, and the sweat forming on his face raised a compelling counterargument, so he agreed to it. Morgan left him alone to truly take in the dire situation of her room.

Well, one part of it anyways. The clutter was causing some mild sensory overload, and he really didn't care to snoop through Morgan's things. Her desk did have one interesting object. It was a small, ringed platform made from a cool, brown metal. There were two slots opposing each other on the top and one on the side of the device, though he couldn't tell what was supposed to go in them. Coins, perhaps? Compared to everything else in the room, this was given its own private space on the table, which was kept clean.

Morgan entered carrying two things. The glass of water that she handed to a very grateful Nika and a translucent blue ball. It looked like an overinflated marble with scratches on its glassy surface. "Here, catch." She tossed the crystal ball to him even though he was already holding the glass. Luckily, he caught it. He may have spilled about a fifth of the water on himself to do it, but he caught it.

"What is it?" he asked.

"Is there something under that sweatshirt?" she answered. Her eyes were fixed on the ball in his hand.

"No," he said. The ball flashed red in his hand. "Wait, what? What's happening?"

"I knew it! Liar!" she yelled, triumphant. "That's my dad's. He uses it to catch bad guys. When do you think it blinks?"

It wasn't a complicated riddle. "When someone lies."

"When someone lies!" She snatched it back from him, holding it in her hands. "How am I supposed to help you when you don't tell me the truth?" She was mocking him now.

"What does this have to do with studying?" he asked.

"Well," She thought, "Not much." She sat in her spot on the ground gripping the ball like she was about to throw it. "But what about the investigation? How can I trust my partner-detective if you don't talk to me?" She was on about finding that 'guardian' or whatever it was again. "It's very important to me that we find it."

The ball blinked red, and Morgan's face followed.

"You didn't see that! Nope!" She threw the ball into the piles of dueling magazines, where it continued to blink. "It was just a joke. It blinks randomly!" the blinking got brighter.

Nika had to take this one thing at a time. "Uh, Morgan? I think your bed is smoking." The Orb of Dumb Nonsense, as he had internally named it, got hotter as it grew brighter, apparently. Morgan leaped in and dug it out, smothering the source of the smoke before a fire could start. She hit the stacks of magazines a few more times than was necessary and then collapsed face down into her spot on the floor again.

"What I meant to say was that it was all a joke, this thing is, um, just a, um." She sighed. "There's no chance you'll forget that, huh." Morgan's muffled voice weakly rose from the ground.

"None." Nika was smiling. It was rare for him to have the upper hand in these back and forths. "How about a deal?"

"I like deals," she said.

"You tell me what that was about, and I'll tell you why I'm baking like a potato right now."

She thought. "You first."

Nika explained the deadarms, Karao's training, and how he was stuck with an uncooperative one hovering just above his back. The way Karao had control of four simultaneously seemed impossible to him, given how much trouble this one was giving him. Morgan was fascinated. The only reason she wasn't jotting down notes about the possible dueling applications of necromancy was that Nika threatened to leave if she did. Nika had the arm pop out from under the shirt and wave to her. He could do that much.

"So you can just use whatever kind of magic you want?" Morgan asked, missing the entire point. "That's awesome! You could be unstoppable with that. People would have no idea what to do against someone who could do, well, anything."

"I can't do everything." Nika stopped her before she spun out of control. "In fact, right now, I can't do anything. I can't get it to use magic ever since we tried to rip it off."

"Lame."

"Yep." It was quiet as Nika waited for Morgan to take her turn to fess up.

"Hey!" Morgan jumped up and ran to her desk. "Wanna try this?" She was clearly deflecting, stalling for time.

"What about-" Nika couldn't object before the round metal object was thrust in his hands. Morgan was digging through piles of cards, ignoring him. He flipped it over. The bottom had an inscription. 'Property of the Duelist Appreciation Society.'

"It's called a 'Replayer'" She had a small pile of small, rectangular cards in her hand. Each had a costumed duelist prominently posing on the front and a pile of statistics, and a miniature biography on the back. She handed him the whole stack. "Pick one, whichever is your favorite."

The cards were absolutely wild. There was a woman dressed as a bear wielding an ax. A man in a full jester's outfit had two cards from two separate years. A card with a golden frame and the word 'champion' at the top depicted what could only be described as a pile of fabric with a person underneath it all. In the end, Nika picked the one he thought looked the funniest.

Molten Phoenix - Age 31 - Height 6'6" - Weight 280 lbs. - Signature Spells: Conjured Phoenix, Molten Fist, Pillars of Lava. His pose was absolutely hilarious like he was trying to flex every muscle in his giant body at once. His costume depicted a bright orange bird in the center of a purple jumpsuit. Nika noted one last statistic on his card. Wins: 263 Losses: 37

"I love Molten! He has this great stage presence, and he always puts on a good show. He was always the runner-up and would lose in the finals, though. Oh! I know just the fight." She pulled another card out of the deck. It was that cloth-covered champion.

"Now what?" He asked.

"Put it in the Replayer." Morgan slid her card into the slot nearest her, Nika did the same. "Then, hold onto this." Morgan handed him a blank card, or rather, had him hold it at the same time. She led both their hands to the slot on the side and inserted the blank card. "Ready?"

"No?"

"Too bad!" She hit a button on the side of the device, and the two vanished from the disastrous bedroom. Well, Nika assumed that anyone watching from outside would have seen it that way. To him, the room had shifted around their feet.

The world changed one small, spinning tile at a time. It started with a square in the ceiling that Nika hadn't noticed before fluttering like paper in the wind. Soon one square became twenty, one hundred, a thousand, and by the time the scene around him had settled down, he was somewhere entirely different. It wasn't a cramped, cluttered bedroom but an open and roaring stadium. There couldn't have been a single unsold seat. The crowd hollered and howled like animals as colored lights circled around them.

Nika and Morgan were in the middle of a particularly rowdy crowd, only a few rows away from the main feature of this stadium; a sandy pit framed by a shimmering metal ring. Nika checked himself for any changes, none. He was exactly the same as he had been the moment before. He didn't know if he was relieved or disappointed. He definitely seemed out of place next to the crazy body paint and graphic shirts around him.

Morgan took the seat. The only seat. The last one left in the row. The one that, like the others, was way too big for her. "This is the replayer! You can watch any match you want, as long as you have the cards. Waddaya think?"

Nika was speechless. Not unusual in and of itself, but this time it was a good thing. No detail was fudged. He could see stubble growing on the neck of one of the audience members. He didn't need to imagine; he was physically standing in the audience on whatever night this happened to be.

"This is amazing," he said. Someone below them had accidentally chucked a drink behind them. Nika didn't notice it heading toward him until it was far too late to move. He braced for an impact that never reached him. The recreated drink passed through him like he wasn't even there and struck someone behind him. They weren't actually there. They couldn't interact with anything for real.

The crowd's already feverish volume strained itself laughing, Morgan and Nika included.

"I like this," Nika said.

"I don't think I've seen you this happy." Morgan was patting herself on the back. "Well, it is pretty cool."

"You've only known me for a couple of weeks," he argued.

"Yeah yeah, you going to sit down or what?" she asked, pushing herself against the side of the chair. "The replay doesn't start until the viewer is seated."

"Oh, uh." He felt weird about it, especially with the deadarm quietly moving behind his back. "Ok." It wasn't as tight a fit as he had expected, not that it mattered much. Whatever he had been worried about melted away in an instant as the lights went out the moment he sat down. The lights that had been rounding the stadium had now focused in the center of the circle. A woman in a suit held a stick up to her throat. It looked like it anyways. Her voice shook the entire stadium, drowning out the rabble in the seats.

"Welcome, One and all!" The crowd roared to fight this woman's volume. "We've got a thrilling lineup for you all tonight! The up-and-coming champion is here to lay claim to one final bout before the playoffs. Can our unstoppable challengers tackle this stalwart legend?!"

Morgan shouted out so loud Nika thought she might have damaged his hearing permanently. She looked like she had completely forgotten about him. The arena was just way too distracting. Wait. This whole thing was just one big distraction.

Morgan was just trying to avoid holding up her end of the deal. He wasn't going to let her forget. He couldn't shout out over the announcer, so he waited for her to finish. Something about tonight's performers, a giveaway they were doing for one lucky ticket holder, and where they were selling cards of tonight's match after it was all over.

"So," he said, as the crowd and announcer died down. She was still focused on the ring, so he nudged her.

"Hm?" She nudged back.

"That truth-ball-thing?"

"Oh, right." She sat way back. Her stare now had no fixed address. She looked lost a bit.

"You forgot?"

"I didn't forget! Just a little sad you didn't." She took a deep breath. "Can it wait until after the match?"

He had already nearly forgotten once. "No."

"Ok." She looked like she was bracing herself to open the floodgates. It all came out in a blur. "It's all made up, and I don't care about that urban legend at all. I get curious about what my parents investigate and wanted to check those things out for myself. I just happened to bump into you, and it's important to keep your story straight, so I've just been rolling with it."

"That's an elaborate lie."

"I'm an elaborate person, now shush! It's starting!"

He felt like there was more, but he had no time to push on that point. When they got back to the room, he could just use the Sphere of Convenience or whatever it was called to determine if that was true.

The announcer was calling out the fighters. Molten Phoenix was the first one in the ring, and he lived up to his absurd card. He was a gigantic, muscular man in some kind of purple get-up who would do nothing but strike poses to thunderous applause. The announcer asked if he had any words for the audience, just two.

"Stand back." Molten Phoenix flexed again, this time accompanied by pillars of flame searing the ground behind him. He was a crowd-pleaser for sure. His mask captured his entire persona. He was more of a ham than any character he had ever read about.

It was amazing.

"And his opponent!" The announcer called out. "Tragic with the fabric, The Cloth!"

The Cloth, as his stage name implied, looked like an overcrowded coat rack had gotten lost and found its way in the ring. The opinion of the crowd was mixed with this one. His cold lack of presence garnered booing and heckling. It was impossible to read any kind of facial expression or even know if there was a face to read. The Cloth seemed like he was there to do a job and nothing more.

He couldn't quite hear the swishing fabric but could almost feel it rubbing up against his skin. He didn't seem weighed down by the mismatched coats, pants, and scarves even slightly. It was intimidating in its own weird way. Comparing fire to fabric, it seemed obvious who should win to Nika.

"Wait," Nika realized. "He's not going to try to burn the other guy, is he?" As cool as this was, Nika didn't want to watch someone burn alive.

Morgan shook her head. "Nothing inside the ring can hurt you, remember?"

"No?" Nika answered. He found himself saying that a lot.

The match started with the two combatants standing opposite each other in the middle of the giant metal circle. The announcer started a countdown from ten, but the crowd was more than happy to finish for her. In the final moments, the Phoenix saluted them for one final uproar of approval. Then, the bell. It was perfectly obnoxious.

If Nika had blinked when the bell rang, he would have missed the first move. A flurry of cloth, tendrils of fabric jetted from the shorter duelist. It flowed like the waves of raging rapids towards various targets. Some buried themselves in the ground beneath him, some curled around his own chest and head, but most importantly, an entire wardrobe's worth of fabric lashed out at the Phoenix.

The announcer called out: "The bird has been bound! The Cloth plans to rip another five-second duel with this furious flinging fabric!"

If the goal was to knock the other duelist out of the ring, this seemed surefire. Molten Phoenix was completely bound, completely covered head to toe in coats, jeans, and a good number of thick-looking wool blankets. Everything, save for his face, was being restrained, including Molten Phoenix's unchanged grin.

"Bwahahahahaha!" he forced. "This again? I'll burn through as many pairs of pants as you want to throw at me." As effortless as his bizarre flexes, the fabric started smoking, snapping one article at a time.

The Cloth pulled on one of the lines of fabric. The tendrils between the two began twisting into a single, taught rope. With some elaborate arm waving, the rope began to fling Phoenix towards the edge of the ring. He had no desire to hear what his opponent had to say. Next, he just wanted this over with.

Molten's purple glove broke through its barricade. It was shimmering with heat. The entire stadium was warming up with it, uncomfortably so. Morgan didn't seem to mind. She loved every minute of this, cheering and shouting along with everyone else. She had probably seen this fight before, possibly a few times, but she was just as excited as ever.

She shook him by the shoulder without taking her eyes off the ring. "Nika! Nika Nika Nika watch watch watch! This part is just so- ugh. It's so cool!" He was already watching and didn't need the reminder but felt that anything he said would be ignored anyway.

The two duelists looked like they were in the middle of an incredibly tense, horribly dressed tug-of-war. There was something wrong. As the one commanding the bundled line of clothes, the Cloth should have easily finished throwing Phoenix out of the ring. Instead, the two seemed deadlocked.

The Cloth stepped back. His extraneous clothing arms were sagging and falling apart. He seemed to be smoking. Nika didn't think fabric conducted heat that well, but then again, this was a magical duel, not the science textbooks he was supposed to be pouring through.

Molten Phoenix began to pull the Cloth in by their own rope, one armful at a time. Each piece he let go of turned to ash, crumbling unceremoniously onto the floor. He lifted the frail man from the piles of discarded clothes and blankets. He wore just his athletic gear beneath it all. The Cloth was dropped from above Molten Phoenix's head, and a punch was trained directly on his chest. If they could be hurt inside the ring, that man might have died from a hit that brutal. In the end, the bombastic Phoenix won out. That one punch was enough to rocket the smaller man into the magic barrier around the ring. He unfurled and then collapsed outside of it. The crowd was silent for a moment. Even under the assurance that he couldn't be hurt, he looked like he was about to curl up and die like a spider. He certainly wanted to, but no, he was fine.

Nika began to wonder what the Phoenix would be like if he wasn't followed around by scores of applause. He wouldn't find out anytime soon. It was only striking him now, but the voice seemed to be a bit familiar. That didn't seem possible since he could count the people he knew outside his old hometown on two hands. It was definitely there, though. Something about it was just scratching at the back of his brain.

The stadium dissolved as Molten Phoenix took a victory lap, displaying a terrifying amount of literal firepower in the palm of his hand. Showboating to the crowd, he faded, shimmering and morphing until eventually becoming Morgan's desk. The crowd vanished too, replaced by the toppled stacks of magazines. Before too long, they were back in Morgan's room. She had an expectant smile on her face like she was waiting for him to gush about how amazing it was. Granted, it was.

"No." He held up his hand. "First." He Ball of Minor Inconvenience out from where Morgan had thrown it. It was still glowing blue. She looked nervous. "That wasn't all, and you know it."

"I have no idea what you're talking about," she said, snatching the ball with confidence.

"If you made that up to tell your parents, why did you pull me into it?"

"I don't have that many friends, you know. Most people kinda stop with the whole, well, everything. The whole 'keep the story straight thing' was true, but eventually, it just actually started being fun. Plus, it's a good excuse to hang out."

"We don't need an excuse to hang out," Nika said. For once, he felt like the reassuring one. It felt good. "Can we use the Replayer again?" Inside her happy eyes Nika could see her combing through hundreds if not thousands of duels archived in her head, searching for the perfect matches.

Chapter 9- End

Intermission- Tricks and Toys

As he left Morgan's house, Nika went through the mental checklist of topics he was supposed to study today. They had covered, in total, three of the eight. After watching that first bout in the Replayer, Morgan had wanted to show him fight after fight after fight. Each one was more exciting than the last. Some were over in a moment, some dragged on for minutes. He was having fun watching, even if he didn't get some of the nuances that Morgan rattled on about.

Morgan and her dad saw him out, with numerous offers for him to stay for dinner. Karao wouldn't be home tonight, and he didn't want to leave Nils alone, so he declined.

"Ok, Nika. See ya!" Morgan left, but her dad stayed still a moment like he had just recalled something important.

"Oh. Wait a minute." He leaned on the doorway as if it was helping him recall whatever it was that was so important. "I do know you!" He snapped. "You're that necromancer kid, right? We met a few days ago in the tea shop! I'm sorry, you probably didn't recognize me out of uniform."

He was throwing Nika a lifeline, and out to the awkward 'pretending not to know you' game, he had played earlier. Nika gladly accepted.

"Oh yeah, sorry."

"Well, Cruise says you lot are trustworthy, so no worries here, pal." He was a warm person when he wasn't purposely looking scary. "By the way, did Morgan borrow that 'Truth-Teller' of mine?"

Nika decided it wasn't wise to lie in the house with that thing in it. "Yeah, we were using it for a bit."

"Well, don't worry too much about it. That old thing barely works, it's a toy from when I was a kid. Got it in a cereal box. It popped up once you added the milk."

"What?" It wasn't as much a question as it was an exasperated groan in word form.

"Yeah, this old thing got me in a lot of trouble back at school. There's a trick to it. Next time she tries to use it, just think of the word 'strawberry' over and over. Always worked for me." He held a finger to his lips. "Don't tell Morgan, alright?"

Nika wasn't sure how he'd use this information, but he very badly wanted to. "Got it."

Chapter 10. Cruise Causes More Problems

Saying that the final weekend of June got off to a rocky start would have been putting it lightly. Catherine and Nils still weren't talking to each other. One from feeling betrayed, the other from feeling unfairly cold-shouldered. There was no progress to be made there, so Nika just went about his usual morning routines to open the Pale Garden for business.

Karao was painting by the door. She claimed that she used to paint a lot, but Nika was waiting to see the results before coming to any sort of conclusion. Each of her deadarms was participating; two held brushes, one palette of paints, and the final was the designated 'tea-hand.'

Oh, yes. Deadarms. Nika's was still acting up, almost worse now. He would be in the middle of something, and it would spasm, reaching out and hitting whatever was in reach. It hadn't been too much of an issue, but feeling he was losing control more and more terrified him. Karao was waiting on a book to be returned to the library so she could try to solve the problem.

This was all before the main disrupting factor of this otherwise normal weekend: Cruise. He hadn't even announced himself before entering the tea shop. Nika had tried to walk out the front to tidy it up but was pushed back by some translucent yellow barrier outside the door. Not just the door, actually. The front windows, out the kitchen, the entire tea shop. Just because he couldn't leave didn't prevent Cruise and company from entering uncontested.

"Morning, Karao." He droned.

"Morning, Cruise." She painted. "Not just stopping by to visit, I guess?"

"I wish."

Morgan's parents looked much more relaxed than on the previous visit. Ben whispered something to his wife and pointed at Nika. Her face didn't change, but of the two, she was the more somber looking. Well, whatever was being said, he was probably going to hear about it sooner or later.

"There's been a few reported, er, incidents." The man in the cleanest, sharpest suit continued. He walked like every step had been rehearsed a hundred times and that no ounce of energy was wasted. Cruise had a sort of calculated efficiency that was eerie in and of itself. "Out in Morrenson, there's been some attacks. Nothing fatal yet, but we do have a missing person."

"Morrenson?" Catherine butted in, "That's like a hundred miles away!"

"Two hundred and thirty-five, actually," Cruise said. "And having gone through your travel records, I'm certain you've not been there before. I'm aware. I know that none of you had anything to do with it."

"How?" Nils asked. It wasn't meant to be antagonistic. They seemed genuinely curious. Cruise, for his part, wasn't much bothered by it. He walked up to Nils and held the palm of his hand a fraction of an inch away from their face.

"Like this." The hand began to glow a soft blue. "Are you guilty?" Nothing changed, and he was satisfied.

"I like the curiosity Nils," Karao said, finally putting down the painting. "But you're asking the wrong question. If there was a crime in Morrenson, why would they come here?"

Nils was lost. Catherine was pretending to be busy with something else. She had stopped paying attention.

"Necromancy?" Nika guessed.

"You got it." Cruise took a seat. "I know there's no chance Karao's involved in this, but I'm not the one calling the shots here. The Suits in Morrenson want me to interrogate you about this. You're their prime suspect."

"They've heard of me all the way out there?" Karao said, impressed with herself. "I must be the most poorly kept secret in the country."

"Only rumors, but rumors of a prominent necromancer are still worth keeping track of. We have six recorded necromancers in this country. We know the one in the desert, and the other five are in this room. Naturally, any crime involving necromancy means I have to come to you."

Nika nodded, counted, and then was confused. He didn't know the one they were talking about in a desert somewhere, but that still didn't explain the 'five.' He, Nils, Catherine, and Karao made four. He doubled and triple-checked in his mind, then waited for Karao to correct him.

She didn't. They just continued their conversation. Nobody else seemed to think it was weird, either.

"I'm sorry," Nika said. "Who is the fifth?"

They all looked at each other, the people in on some secret that only Nika didn't know. With a simple nodding of heads, Karao and Cruise decided to share.

"Nika." Karao knelt down next to him. "Cruise is one of my oldest students."

"Was," Cruise said. "I gave it up."

"He's chosen not to play to his own strengths," Karao said, daggers in her eyes.

"And yet I'm doing just fine, don't you think?" He shot back. "The point, Nika, is that I am legally speaking a necromancer. I'm a bit out of practice, but labels like that tend to follow you around. That's one of a few lessons she won't teach you."

"It's not a label if you're proud of it, Cruise," Karao said.

"It's a label if it makes you the leading suspect of a crime a hundred miles away from you," He retorted. Karao said nothing in return. "We're going to ask some questions of you four. Mostly a formality, like I said, I'm doing this because my arm's twisted on this one."

Of the three interrogators, Nika would take Ben first, Cruise second, and Morgan's mom last. A conversation with her was probably going to be awkward since they had heard about one another but never directly talked before. She also seemed irritated. Unfortunately, the universe rarely takes requests, and so Nika sat across from her in the kitchen.

"My name," she started professionally. "Is Lisa Farvue. I'm an investigator with the Royal Suits." Her gloves were different from the others. A thick plate of golden metal covered the back of each hand. With a silent spell, the metal glowed and seemed to melt a bit. It didn't burn. It wasn't even hot. A drop of liquid metal drifted up, dragging more behind it. She snapped it off with her other hand and shook it. She had made a pen for taking notes. "I would like to ask you a few questions."

"Ok," Nika said.

"Where were you two days ago between two and six in the afternoon?" she asked.

There was no way to say this that wasn't weird. "Your house, ma'am."

She wasn't surprised but visibly agitated by the answer. "Ben can verify this, I trust?" She jotted down notes. Nika wasn't sure of what. These questions seemed unnecessary, considering one of the investigators knew where he was that day.

"Morgan, too."

"I see. And how do you know Morgan? I've checked the school records, and 'Nika Erring' never came up. Additionally, there wasn't any record of you in this city until you made a library card a few weeks ago. When did you two meet?"

"I'm sorry, I just don't see what this has to do with, um, whatever happened."

"An investigator is permitted to ask questions she thinks are relevant to the case at hand."

That didn't sound right, but Nika's knowledge of criminal justice came entirely from mystery books with elaborate plots and campy detectives, so he deferred to her judgment.

"We just sorta bumped into each other on the road." He left out the detail that they were hiding from her. "She's very, um, energetic."

"That's true," She conceded.

"I don't know. We started hanging out after that. She wanted help with something."

"Oh no, not that 'investigation' thing of hers? You don't buy into that stuff, do you?"

"No," Nika said. "Not really. It sounded like fun, though."

"That's a relief. I'm flattered she wants to play detective like us, but it's still a bit childish."

Nika was struggling to see the family resemblance. Morgan really took after her father with the maple hair and relaxed attitude. The only thing she had in common with her mom was her height, and that was likely going to change over the next few years.

"I have one last question for you," she said. Nika wondered if it was about the crime she was supposed to be investigating. "You're not into that dueling stuff, are you?"

So much for that. "No," Nika said. "Well, I wasn't. Morgan's been showing me more of it recently, and it seems-"

"Stop it. She needs to cut that out." Whatever amount Lisa had relaxed had snapped back tenfold. The pen strained in her hand. "The longer she thinks all that fighting is cool, the harder it will be to pull her out of it. Don't encourage it, please."

"Oh, um, ok." Nika didn't really know what to think of it. He wasn't really encouraging her. He was basically a punching bag she got to vent all her excitement against...

"I think they're still going in the other room," she said. "Why don't you tell me more about you? For the investigation, of course."

He gave her the truncated version of his life story. He was from a small town that abhorred magic, discovered he was a necromancer by mistake, he was ostracized, ran away, taken in by Karao, and had been living there for about a month. Lisa nodded along and wrote nothing down. She thanked him for sharing and instructed him to go back into the main room with the others.

"What did they ask you about?" Nika asked Nils.

"Same as you."

"I doubt that. A lot," Nika answered.

"It was mostly about Karao," Catherine said.

"There are two pods of three whisperings about me right now, and I think I hate it," Karao announced, sitting in the same spot in the middle of the room. Somehow even a compulsory interrogation was not enough to phase that woman. "You're making it quite hard to listen in."

"Well, then what I have to say will only be a half a surprise." Cruise walked up to her. "I'm sorry, but I'm afraid there are only two ways forward. House arrest until another lead is discovered, or-" he took a small dark ring out of his pocket. It was too large to fit around anyone's finger and brought this ominous air with its presence. Karao stiffened at the sight of it. She would never back away from, well, anything, but she certainly wasn't happy to see it.

"No. Never," Karao said. "I could, in theory, choose to resist arrest."

"You wouldn't," Cruise said.

"It's more likely than that," Karao said.

Nika whispered to Nils, asking what it was.

Nils leaned in and whispered back, "It stops you from using magic. At all. It's awful, what it does to you."

Cruise already knew the answer but had to make that offer as a formality. "House arrest it is, then."

"How many favors?" Karao asked.

Cruise shook his head. "Not this time. But, I do have a proposal."

Karao was annoyed but interested. "What is that?"

"If you actually follow the rules, I'll have you consult on this case. Which means, of course, you'd have access to as much information as you need."

"So I obey, or I won't know anything about this possible necromancer?" She was smiling. "I raised you too well. What a wicked choice."

"It wasn't my call to remove you from the picture, but I'm not turning down a great opportunity like that."

"Good boy."

"Don't call me boy."

"All right, deal." They shook on it. "But if I can't leave, you'd better believe I'm cashing in some of those favors for errands." Cruise winced for a single, glorious moment. Even when completely defeated, Karao wasn't going down without taking blood.

"Hey, I said this wasn't my call, right?" He tried to object.

"What was that you mentioned about great opportunities?" Karao said. Going just by her face, she had just won a battle at a great cost. The war would rage on, but today she would walk away with her head held high.

The rest of the visit went without any incidents. Karao was given a small red mark just above the wrist that would let Cruise know if she ever left the property without permission. The barrier around the shop faded into the morning air, and the barely functioning tea shop was now open for business. Ben saluted Nika as he left, leaving everyone but his wife confused; she rolled her eyes.

"Well," Nils said.

"This sucks." Karao had slumped down into the chair. The painting was no longer important. "I shouldn't be getting blindsided like this."

"You ok?" Catherine asked.

"I'll be fine. I'm just trying to think. I won't be able to work for a while, I can't run errands, and we will have to put the deadarm training on hold. Especially you, Catherine. I can't really afford to have the walls blown out right now."

"Is there anything we can do, Karao?" Nils asked.

"Yes, actually. I was going to run out and pick up some things. Grab the cash box from the back, and I'll tell you what you need to get." Karao began scribbling a list on a napkin, adding costs in her head. "Nika, how do you know the Farvues?"

"The who?" he asked.

"Cruise's lieutenants, the husband, and wife." Karao had picked up her brushes again and started eyeing the painting. It was a still life of Donut sleeping in a fallen cup. The snake was more than happy to lie still for her. It was his greatest talent, after all.

"Oh, yeah. They're Morgan's parents."

Catherine groaned. She still saw Morgan as the annoying kid who wouldn't stop talking and did nothing else. "Of course. That guy was ticking me off. Of course, they're related. He even looks like her, ugh."

"Mean, Catherine." Nils carried the metal box into the room.

"Oh, shut up."

"Nils doesn't have to," Nils said. Catherine didn't correct them. "Nils is just saying not to run your mouth so much."

Catherine dropped the broom she was toting around. "You'll be around today, Karao. You don't need me here. I'm going home early. Bye."

"Bye!" Nils shouted.

Karao yelled at the closing door, "Wait, Catherine, don't-" She sighed, thinking. "Nika, would you mind running this errand instead? I want to talk to Nils."

He nodded. Nils said nothing. They just stood against the wall, clutching the sleeve of their shirt like they wanted to tear it up.

"Or." Karao looked into the cashbox. "We have a bigger problem, Nika. Go flip the sign. We're closed today."

"What?" Nils's eyes were tearing up still. The others didn't mention it.

She snapped the box, and her eyes shut again. "What day is it?"

"The twenty-sixth," Nika answered. He had a few library books due back tomorrow, and that twenty-nine in the corner was hanging over him.

"That means the mortgage is due Tuesday."

"Can we afford it?" Nils asked.

"Barely." She tossed the box on the table. Donut was shocked awake, briefly. "And I can't work until this whole thing blows over."

"So we need money," Nils said.

"It seems that way," Karao answered. "I just have no idea how to do that. We haven't earned a single cent through this place, it's barely paying for its own ingredients."

"So, we change that." Nils was determined. "We fix it up and get people in here!"

"What, in five days?"

"Nils isn't losing this place." They looked like they wanted to say another word but stopped themselves. "I won't."

"I have sort of run this into the ground, haven't I?" Karao said, proud. "Very well, Nils. As of now, I'm naming you the manager, and I'm stepping back. Let me know what I need to do."

Nils smiled at Nika. They had needed something to work on, something to take their focus off of things. "We need ingredients."

Chapter 10- End

Intermission- Breaking

The first time the noise had woken Nika up, he ignored it. The second time, he looked out the window to see what was making it. The fifth, he got up to do something about it. There are only so many times you can hear a glass pitcher get smashed against a brick wall before wanting to stop it, even without knowing how.

From the kitchen, the view was better. Nils hadn't noticed him yet, so he watched a few more times, just to be sure. They held the glass pitcher up in the moonlight, head slunk down with a dispassionate glower. Their hand shook, then dashed the innocent pitcher against the wall once again. The shower of glass nicked their hand, and they recoiled a bit. But Nils didn't regret it. Magic coursed through their armband of corpse bits. That was a bizarre way to phrase it. A spell was cast to repair the pitcher yet again. Hand bleeding, they picked the pitcher up yet again.

Nika had never seen Nils glare until he opened the door. "Go to bed, Nika."

"I've tried, but-" He gestured to the wall, "I keep waking up for some reason."

"Oh." Nils collapsed under their burdens, gripping their knees as they buried their head in them. "Nils is sorry, Nils keeps getting in the way."

"It's 'I,' and no, you don't." Nika sat down. "Maybe just this once, though." His attempt to lighten the mood fell flat. There was no response. "Catherine?" Still nothing. "Have you talked to her about it?"

"No. Why bother?"

"I'm not sure." Somewhere in the distance, trees rustled. Bats tumbled through the air and leaves rolled down the road. Somewhere, these two mages in training sat silently through all the things that happen at night. "Is it because she left or because she didn't talk to you first?"

"All of it." Nils curled up tighter. "It all hurts."

"Nils-" Nika said, but he couldn't finish.

"Nils can't talk to her because Nils doesn't know why Nils is mad!" Nils had been emotional in Nika's time here, but this was different. The tears seemed unbound. A rushing river had cut through their face and poured to the ground via their cheeks. "What does Nils do?"

"I don't know," Nika said. Nils's crying was contagious, at least a bit. Nils stood, grabbed the pitcher, and threw it one more time.

Chapter 11. Cheering for the death of D.A.S.

When thinking back to what Lisa Farvue had said about not encouraging Morgan's hobby, this certainly would have counted as a violation. He didn't really intend to follow through on her mother's request, anyways. Morgan seemed happy doing this stuff, so why get in the way? Anyways, Morgan had asked him nicely to go with her to her tryouts. Nika could have asked why her parents wouldn't go with her, but he felt he knew the answer already.

Her costume was a last-minute change and, according to her, entirely optional. Nika felt that she would be the only one taking them up on the offer. She had an ill-fitted brown leather coat, a pair of goggles slung helplessly around her neck, thin gloves, boots that went up past her shins. She looked like she had blindly grabbed at her wardrobe and ran out the door without checking. Still, it fit her. Naturally, the book was slung around her shoulder by its strap.

As they waited in the hallways of Eldes High School, Morgan traced summoning circles from the book onto her forearm and shins. Nika had time to really take in the school's hallways. He wasn't expecting everything to feel so plain. The sand-colored stone walls, the overly polished tile floor, everything about the school was devoted to looking and feeling plain.

"It makes summoning faster if people expect me to open the book, bam! I can get the drop on em'!" she was proudly explaining scheme after scheme to him. They ranged from clever, like using the moth as a distracting shield, to stupid, like trying to creep them out with a swarm of grasshoppers.

"Why don't you just draw them on all the time?"

"Mom won't let me get a tattoo, so they're single-use."
That seemed like a smart call on her mom's part. "Besides, what
if I find better things to summon?"

"Better than bugs? Wow. Hard to imagine."

She hit him, rightfully so. "Shush."

"So." He joined her on the bench outside the gym.
There were other would-be-duelists sitting around, waiting to
be called into the gymnasium. Most of them looked like they
were in athletic clothes, a few were dressed casually. Exactly
two others were in costume, standing at the far end of the
hallway. "How exactly does this work?"

"You get called in!" She responded automatically,
"Afterwards, the three-team leaders will let you choose which
one of them you will face off against. Depending on how you
do, they decide if you make the team or not!"

"That's very specific." Nika thought. "Have you done this
before?"

Morgan got very quiet. "Maybe."

"Ah." She didn't make it. "Sorry. Well, at least you're not
the only one dressed up."

Morgan looked confused for a minute, then excited. She
whipped around and saw the two waiting by the far end. "Guys!
Over here!" They recognized her immediately, with polar
opposite reactions. The first seemed thrilled to see her; the
second didn't really care one way or the other. Regardless, they
both made their way over.

"Well, well, guess who decided to show up!" The first
taunted. He looked like what would have happened if you took
a twig and stretched it to its breaking point. His leather helmet
strapped under his chin, but even through that, the golden
stubbly rumblings of a soon-to-be-beard were announcing
themselves. His clothes were super loose and baggy, tightening

around a belt in the waist. A pair of shoddily repaired glasses were mounted on his nose, clinging for dear life.

"You were almost late. Again." The other said. He seemed much more reserved, his costume a simple robe which parted in the middle and athletic gear underneath. His hair was short, black, and as lacking in enthusiasm as the rest of his general demeanor.

"Nika, these are Sam and Michal. They're in my club!" The two were clearly upperclassmen. They couldn't have a year or more left in the school.

"Your club?" he asked.

"It's a school club, and it's dead now," Sam, the drearier of the two, said.

"We hope, anyway!" Michal chimed in.

"This year for sure!" Morgan added.

"I'm completely lost," Nika said.

"I'm the president of the D.A.S. - the Dueling Appreciation Society," Michal said.

"We're the ones that love the sport but had things to do so we couldn't practice enough to-" Sam was cut off by Michal.

"In short, we didn't make the cut last year but wanted a club to talk about dueling anyways!" he said, smiling from ear to ear. Morgan and Sam were sulking in the wake of that unintentional gut-punch.

"Yeah, pretty much what he said," Morgan said with what sounded like her dying breath.

"But if we all make the team, then we won't need the club anymore!"

"Yeah, yeah, yeah," Morgan said, eager to redirect the conversation. "When do you guys go up?"

"Oh, we already went," Sam said.

"And!" Morgan said.

"And what? Of course, we lost. Nobody's going to beat those three."

Michal turned to Nika. "You just have to put up a good fight, and the coach picks based on what he sees. Hi, I don't think we've met. Nika, was it?" the two shook hands.

"I didn't know Morgan had any friends. Ow. OW!" Sam received simultaneous comeuppance from her fellow club members. "What's with the sweater? Isn't it boiling outside? Let me guess, you're trying out too."

"Me? No. I'm just here for moral support? I guess," he said.

"Who did you go up against?" Morgan asked.

"Well, going against the third seat makes the most sense, plus it's a great matchup." Sam seemed proud of his reasoning.

"Matchup?" Nika asked.

Michal rolled his eyes. "He means that his strategy was going to be good against hers."

"Are you still on that counting thing?" Morgan asked.

"It's counter, as in counter-magic, and it's the most consistent performing magic in the pro leagues. She uses pretty basic magic; I figured it would be easier. I tweaked my spells a bit to fit my abilities-"

"And that's why it doesn't work anymore," Michal finished. "I fought the second; he's a friend of mine, so I thought it would be fun. Of course, that didn't end up working out so well. He ended up wiping the floor with me, eventually, but he usually one-shots people, so I'm ok with that."

"That's the meteor guy, right?" Morgan asked.

"I'm sorry, what?" Nika went unheard.

"Yup! I kicked the first one right back at him!"

"I'm sorry. What?" Nika was ignored.

"Oh yeah!" Michal rolled up the legs of his pants to his knees. "Check it out." He breathed in and out and hopped a bit. He was mentally preparing himself for something. With a grunt that melded into a shout, his twig-like legs nearly exploded. His legs ended up looking like an extreme bodybuilder's. Each leg looked like it weighed the same as the upper half of his body.

"You can do both now!" Morgan was excited. Michal nodded enthusiastically. Nika began to see where her energy came from. The implied image of only one limb at a time being supercharged was even worse.

"I'm sorry wh-nevermind." Nika gave up. "So if you do well enough, you make the team, right?"

"Well, it's only a team of six, and the top three seats are already chosen, so," Michal said.

"Which means there's only one more slot for Morgan," Sam said.

"Wait, you already know?" Morgan yelled.

"No, we don't. But it's a safe assumption."

"Oh, shut up," Morgan leaped up. "You'd better hope that you weren't third on the list, Sam."

A man in a tracksuit came through the door to the main gym and called out: "Morgan Farvue!"

"Here!" She replied. "See you two at practice."

Nika was not asked to join her in the other room, but he was curious. For all her talk and technical knowledge, he hadn't actually seen her put any of it into practice before. He was curious and a little bit excited. With a wave goodbye to her friends, he pushed through the double doors into the gymnasium.

There were a lot of books set in schools, and one thing they all had in common was important scenes set in a gymnasium that the author didn't think to describe. They just assumed that everyone knew what one looked like, and so Nika had always imagined them to be this fantastic jungles-filled equipment and games. Inside it was possible to play any sport imaginable; a stadium with different arenas for each sport, all surrounded by bleachers. A lap around a gymnasium, from his understanding in books, was a horrible task to undertake.

In reality, it was a larger-than-average room with hardwood floors with lines taped into them. He knew he had a vivid imagination, but he was still audibly disappointed. Morgan turned to him, confused. Before she could ask any of the questions she had, like 'what was that' or 'why are you here,' the man with the clipboard in the middle of the room called out to her again.

"You've done this before, yes?" he asked. She nodded. "And, who is this? Spectator?"

"He's just here to watch, I guess," Morgan said.

"So, spectator. Got it. That's fine. You want a spot on the bleachers?" He pointed Nika to the rising benches, which were yet another disappointment to go on the list. Still, Nika took his spot. The man raised his voice as if he were talking to a crowd that wasn't there. "All right, last try out on the day, Morgan Farvue. What sort of magic do you use?"

"Summoning, sir!" she answered, saluting.

"That's- stop that- that's an... interesting choice, and who would you like to challenge?" He gestured to the three standing at the other end of the gym from Nika's spot on the sidelines. They were all wearing what must have been a school uniform. They were dark green with gold trim. They had black gloves and boots, but other than that, they were very minimally dressed compared to Morgan's weird attire.

"The number one, of course," Morgan answered.

Eyebrows around the room raised like a band heeding its conductor. The boy in the middle, who had until now looked bored out of his mind, walked with a stride that screamed, 'I have been waiting all day for this. You have no idea.' Nika hadn't noticed the circle of bells clasped to his right ankle until their chiming tolled every footfall.

"Are you sure?" the coach asked. "Remember, you're not trying to win. We're trying to gauge how well you do in a fight, for that you'd need to-"

"Yup," Morgan said. "I'm taking that spot someday, Emil!" Her botched dramatic posing made even Nika cringe a bit.

"Are you now?" the upperclassmen, Emil, asked. He stepped into the dueling ring marked in blue tape. Compared to the shimmering silver ring in the replay box, this was quaint. The barrier shimmered around him as he crossed its threshold. "Well, I'm all for it. Come on, then!"

Morgan entered the ring with him. She was different; the carefree girl had left her mind to be replaced by a stern, focused spirit. At least, that was the only way Nika could explain the look in her eyes. No smile, no fear, just determination. Admirable, in a sense, but different than the dueling they had watched. Those fighters were able to keep their personalities in the ring. Morgan had to choose to be upbeat or to beat down.

Still, it was exciting to get to see her in action.

The man with the clipboard counted down from five, and then the tryouts began.

What happened next happened in a matter of seconds, albeit very memorable ones. Before anything else, Morgan began to summon Luna, the giant moth. Emil crashed his foot into the ground. The air around the bells chimed a cacophonic toll.

Each rhythmic pounding of the foot shook the air more and more until the air in the arena started quaking. Dust from the gym floor swirled around the first seat until he was dead-center in a wheel of dust and tornado-like winds. Somewhere inside, his silhouette started moving. Nothing menacing, his arms swayed, his hips twisted, his leg kicked.

Emil was dancing with the wind.

Luna had finished latching onto Morgan's back, wings folded forward to shield her from the wind. From the bleachers, two uninteresting defensive pods were standing across from one another. Emil arched his back and flung his arm like he was hurling a disc. The dust shield broke, and a torrent of wind crashed into Luna. The moth was ripped into the barrier, wings shredded, and antenna blown apart. It dissolved into the green magic it had come from.

Morgan stood, unmoved.

Everyone in the room was surprised. Morgan was too. She just didn't look like it if you didn't know her. Her scheme had worked so far. Nika noticed it right away, but it took the other duelists a few noticeable seconds to see it, a spiderweb keeping her feet cemented into the arena.

Being unmoved did not mean she was unharmed. She looked ragged and ready to fall over at a moment's notice. Still, she wasn't giving up. With each hand, she tried to summon something with a circle she had drawn on the sides of her knees. From the summoning circle on her left, that freaky spider emerged again. From the right, a swarm of bugs too small for Nika to tell. He hadn't seen them before, though.

Emil had recovered from the initial surprise and had already kicked up another storm. The swarm had been sucked in and eviscerated without accomplishing much of anything. The spider had tried to ground itself with its webbing, but even it wasn't strong enough to not get pulled apart by the wind.

Step by elaborate step, Emil's tempest swept closer to Morgan.

"Well," he said, his voice cutting through the wind. "You've found a way to not lose."

Morgan was tapped out; one hand weakly shook over the last circle on the back of her other. It glowed faintly, briefly, and then gave up. Her hair whipped behind her. She threw her goggles off to stop them from choking her.

"But," Emil lunged forward, his spine twisted back. His hands seemed to be holding back an inevitable tide, the ocean itself formed at his fingertips, and he alone chose when and where it would crash. "That's not the same as winning, is it?"

At his command, everything fell on Morgan. Nika told himself over and over that none of it hurt that none of it was real. Her scream calmed him, strangely. It wasn't pain. It wasn't agony. It was frustration. She was mad at herself. She was mad when she collapsed. She was mad when she couldn't convince her body to get back up. She was mad when the man in the tracksuit called the final results.

He was relieved for a moment and then crushed. The webbing around her feet dissipated into the air, but for a moment, she didn't get up. She wallowed in her defeat for a second—just one.

"Ah, dang! I thought I had you there. I was hoping the surprise would get ya!" she said, desperately trying to fix her windswept hair. "Man, ah well."

Morgan and Nika were escorted out of the gymnasium through the other door, where Sam and Michal were standing at first. She held her head up high, hair looking it had gotten permanently stuck up in the air. Nika, on the other hand, wondered how all the other hopefuls they walked past in the hall did in their tryouts.

Without saying a word, her fellow members of D.A.S. knew exactly what had happened to her, and they were mad. They began demanding from her reasons why she would willingly try out against Emil, why she would throw away her chances, why she would give up such a favorable matchup against the other two. Still, none of it bothered Morgan. She laughed it off with the same bravado and showmanship that she would have boasted about a crushing victory. Just like her invincibility in the ring, she hadn't even been touched by this defeat.

"Guys, guys. It's fine!" her ear-to-ear smile put them at ease a bit. "Everything worked out perfectly. Just like I planned." The two others turned to him, waiting to see if he'd validate the statement.

That was a lie, but Nika let her have it. He nodded.

"I'm gonna miss the old club room," she said.

"I'm not," Sam countered. "That dusty old place can rot away for all I care."

"What? No! C'mon, man, we've been in the place for three years now," Michal feigned being hurt. "We're on a first-name basis with all the spiders and just finally got those cobwebs organized."

"You mean she is on a first-name basis with the spiders."

"Hey, if it weren't for me, you guys wouldn't even have the room!" Morgan said. "You're welcome."

"Yeah, yeah. Thanks, oh mighty beekeeper," Sam said.

The bickering continued for a while, and Nika was content just to watch. He had never been good with interacting with people, clearly, but just watching these three friends jeer and prod each other was fun in its own right. It helped that he knew Morgan and how it was easy to set her off, but this was very entertaining.

Eventually, the fire to fight died down, and the three waited anxiously for the results by the door. Apparently, Emil would come out and announce who he wanted on 'his' team. He was some kind of prodigy at the school, and the coach deferred to his judgment about almost everything.

"Arcs barely does anything anymore. He's a coach by name alone," Sam said.

"Arcs?" Nika asked. "Like the principal?" He pictured that towering man trying to wear a tracksuit and carry a clipboard like a teacher that was already in the gym. It was funny. Even funnier if it was his 'deflated' body.

"Yeah." Sam pointed out a picture of a previous dueling team on the wall. Even though he was with a group of teenagers, Phineas Arcs stood out as a ludicrously tall person. "He says he loves the sport, but he won't go anywhere near it. He just likes touting winners around, I think."

Nika didn't know enough to argue, but his impression of the man was different. Still, impressions were certainly never always right. There was probably much more to the man who tried to keep up appearances than he first suspected. Phrasing it like that made it seem obvious.

"Can I have your attention, please!" The clipboard man said. His voice turned every neck in the hallway. Murmuring died. The air felt thicker than it had a moment before. Two of Nika's three arms were shaking with anticipation. The deadarm couldn't be bothered to follow along. "We would like to announce who made the cut. Emil, would you mind?"

The three-team members walked out side by side in the same order they had been sitting on the bench. Nika wondered if it was intentional.

"We will be taking Michal, Helen, and Yu." Emil made no attempt to add frills or cushion his announcement. He stated the facts and was ready to turn around. The room was shocked. Even the people who made the team were expecting a longer explanation.

"Wait."

Many people in the room likely wondered for a moment who said that. Nika was not one of them. Morgan's face was stoic, the way she had approached the fight itself. The show was over, her demeanor serious. She was rejecting this decision.

"Why?" Morgan asked again, the eyes of the room on her.

One of the duelists looked indignant, like her questioning their decision had crossed some sort of line. Emil gestured that he calm down.

"Why what?" Emil asked her. "Why them or why not you?"

Morgan couldn't answer. It was, in itself, her answer. Nika could practically read every objection she had in her eyes. How she had cleverly fought someone stronger than her and done something no one expected. How she had the ambition, the look, the drive. So much of her had been working to become this.

"The reason we didn't pick you, Morgan, is that we need people who win, not people who, at best, lose slower." Emil's words cut through the hallway as harsh as any of the gales Nika had seen him unleash.

Morgan's invincibility shattered, but her face gave no ground. She had treated Emil like a friendly rival, someone who would push her to be stronger but was within her abilities to one day beat. He would disagree.

It was a subtle change, mostly in her posture. Somewhere in her, beating Emil was no longer a goal; it was a necessity. But for now, she said nothing.

"Anyone else have a question?" Emil asked. "Alright, See you three next week."

Sam was too busy sulking to notice what had happened. Michal, trying to dodge as many half-hearted congratulations as possible, made his way to Morgan.

"Hey, you ok?" he asked. Something about his face reminded Nika of Nils for some reason.

Morgan turned around. "You made it! Ah! I'm so happy! I mean, I'm not surprised or anything, but it finally happened!" She hugged him. "Don't go slacking, or I'm gonna take your spot, ok?"

He looked relieved. "I can't believe it yet, finally! Gah! It finally happened!" All the concern washed over his face again as he turned to Sam. Sam seemed lost in his own gloomy world. It was probably best to leave him be, yet Michal went off to talk to his fellow group member.

"For the rest of you; you know what that means!" The clipboard man continued. "We have doubles tryouts in August. Get a partner and see you there." He retreated back into the gymnasium, and the rejected duelists began to disperse.

Morgan stood in front of Sam. "Hey, brainiac, you know what this means?"

"That we can't burn the club room," he said, staring into space.

"It means we're just going to have to make the doubles team!" Morgan said. She held out her hand. "Partner?"

Sam thought for a moment, then pushed her hand away. "Morgan, if I was going to do this, I wanted to do this alone. I'm sorry." He finally seemed to be seriously considering what Michal and Morgan were thinking. It was a rare glimpse into what Sam was thinking about under all the quips. "Frankly, I thought I'd be disappointed, but I'm not. I think I realized that I don't need to be on the team. I'm happy with where I'm at right now. I'm happy with D.A.S."

"He always gets weirdly philosophical after a loss like that," Michal said.

"It's ok." Morgan's words were losing credibility. "I'll figure something out."

"You'll need a third," Michal said. "School rule: A minimum of three club members for any given club."

"We have that," Morgan said. The other two were confused. Nika had seen this coming from a mile away. She pointed to him, conscripting him to join her club against his will. "Long live D.A.S.!"

"Not if you make doubles," Sam pointed out. "I didn't peg you as the type to just give up."

Morgan wasn't in the mood to be toyed with. "I mean, I'm obviously going to try, but you said no, and Michal can't do both, I don't. Um. Hm." She stopped.

Nika was already weary of the writing on the wall and had crept towards the door while they talked. He made his excuses, quietly, and to himself, and bolted for the door. They chased.

Chapter 11- End

Intermission- Games and Rain

Karao was afraid of rain. No, she would never say why. When it rained, she usually just tried to occupy herself, though she tensed up a lot when she saw lightning or heard thunder. Catherine had other important things to say to Nika on this rainy day, but he would rather wait and see them for himself.

The tea shop was already starting to look like an entirely new place. Nils had forced Karao to painstakingly get rid of half the tables and chairs in the main room. They were all special to her, but Nils's argument that there was no route to the counter without moving them was too solid. The room looked cleaner, the menu was cut in half, several of Karao's more creative paintings were moved into the cellar.

The work on the revamp was done for the day and trapped in by the rain, Karao was showing her three mages-in-training a favorite board game of hers. It came in a weird box and folded out in four directions. There were flat tiles, slopes, holes, and a large black throne in the middle. After a never-ending lecture on pieces and how they traversed the board, how to claim the throne, and at least three egregious but accidental cheats by Nika, the game had come to a turning point.

Karao was in a terrible position. She had only two of her originally twenty-piece army standing; a monarch and a peasant. The peasant was surrounded by Nils's impenetrable cavalry, and Nika was about to knock the Monarch out for good.

"You'd really shift the delicate balance of power?" Karao asked. She seemed to be bluffing.

Nika shrugged. "Well, if you hadn't killed my archbishop-" He didn't finish the thought, just the execution of the Green Monarch. The board rumbled a bit. It wasn't the first time. Sometimes pieces would shift or change based on magically bound rules in the board. Karao pointed to where they should be watching: The last green peasant. It rattled and spun, eventually becoming a new, towering monarch. Several of the cavalries around it shifted from blue to green. Karao was back in the game.

"I feel like you should have told us about that, Karao," Catherine said, thankful it wasn't her army that had just been gutted.

"I did. I just don't repeat myself. This way, you won't ever forget. It's my turn, I believe." She used her monarch to eliminate yet another member of the formerly impenetrable cavalry. Thunder roared, Karao nearly fell out of her chair. The universe had become balanced once again.

Chapter 12. The Storm, Bringer

The rain never stopped. Each day it continued, Karao became more visibly stressed until she just couldn't take it. She had contacted Cruise again and asked that she be taken to investigate the scene of this other necromancer's crimes. It was a reasonable excuse, but an excuse is what it was at the end of the day. She really just needed to be somewhere else.

That, unfortunately, meant fewer people were around to help with the relaunch of the tea shop. With only three days left, Nils's plan was really a last-ditch effort to keep them on a shoestring budget. They never earned anything on rainy days anyways, according to Nils, so they had sent Nika and Catherine out on some errands.

They had divided, conquered, and returned to the meeting point outside the Eldes Library, where Nika had spent a lot of free time. Catherine had approached him with a bag of ingredients as he wondered whether or not he had some kind of unhealthy addiction to books.

"Find it?" she asked, hair dripping from what was now a downpour. They stood under the slight overhang right next to the library entrance, not daring to set a single toe outside the canopy.

The spoils of his search were three books:
Prone To Scones: Tricks of the Tea Trade
Exa Necro Ifthla
Basics of Dueling
He only showed Catherine the first two. The first was Nils's request. The latter was the book Karao said she needed to help fix the deadarm still stuck to Nika's back. It seemed to know it, too. Under his sweatshirt, it twitched and writhed in protest. He was considering tying the thing down.

"What happened to your umbrella?" Nika asked. She had had one when they walked together to the library.

"It blew away! I'm lucky I still have the vegetables." The wind gusted past the two almost on queue.

"We'll probably just have to run," Nika said. He had heard that the books were enchanted to not get water damage, but he didn't really want to test the limits of that.

"Not happening. We'll just wait for it to die down." Catherine and Nika listened to the rain a bit.

"Excuse me," A voice from the other door called to them. "Two questions, actually." The speaker poked his head out a bit before retreating from the rain. "Actually, mind stepping back inside?"

The two had nothing better to do, so they listened. The library was also pretty much dead on a day like this anyways. A little conversation in the door would probably not draw the Sphinx's ire.

The man with two questions was a vagrant, a traveler. No one would ever need to ask if this was true. His general appearance and demeanor did an excellent job introducing him. His hair was at one point likely blond, but not anymore. He had shaved recently, but clearly not in a day or so. His Green coat was clean but patched in a few places. He carried an overstuffed suitcase and looked like he hadn't slept in about a week. Still, somehow his most noteworthy feature was the giant sack slung around his back by a number of shoulder straps. Well, either that or the massive umbrella hanging loosely in a loop on his coat. Well, come again, it could have been the metal band strapped around his ankle. His pant leg was rolled up on top of it. Even looking at it made him feel uncomfortable.

A lot was vying for attention with this stranger, but he seemed friendly enough.

"Sorry, first off, do you two need an umbrella?" he asked.

"We can figure-" Catherine was cautious by nature. She didn't get to finish her deflection. Nika appreciated the attempt.

"I have spares, please, I insist." He tore a patch in his gigantic satchel off. He pulled what looked like a miniature duplicate of his giant black umbrella. Catherine had no objection to a free gift. "I carve the handles in my spare time. Seems everyone always forgets their umbrellas." The bag rattled on his back. It was either full of umbrellas or loose pieces of wood and tarp.

The umbrella handle seemed lovingly crafted to his credit, depicting a bird's wing mid-flight while still being comfortable to hold. Nika wasn't by any stretch an umbrella-handle connoisseur, though by simply thinking about things like ease-of-holding and style, he might have just become the world's first. That was a weird, if funny, thought.

"Thank you," Nika said. Gladys, the librarian, was keeping a distant eye on them in the door. Having someone he trusted around was helpful. He was both soothed and distressed that she didn't seem to think it was worth intervening. His read on the guy could have just been too negative.

"Not at all! Consider it yours." He chuckled a bit to himself. "Although that's no way to run a business, is it? Ah well."

Catherine's protective suspicion flared up again. "What, you sell umbrellas?"

"Man's gotta eat, no?" He unsheathed the umbrella from the loop in his coat. The handle of his had worn into the shape of his hand. It seemed unspeakably old. "No matter where I go, people always seem to forget their umbrella." He stopped himself in the doorframe, swiveling on the umbrella he was using as a cane. "Speaking of forgetting! I almost forgot just now, the whole reason I stopped you two. Sorry for that, the old noggin isn't what it used to be."

"Uh-huh," Catherine said.

"Yes?" Nika asked.

He laughed at his own absent-mindedness. "Call it a hunch. You two know Karao, don't you?"

Someone who hadn't been living with the family of necromancers for a while would not have noticed Catherine's reaction. She didn't blink. She didn't reel back. Her breath remained steady. Nils had told Nika what Catherine's 'tell' was when he should be looking to put distance between himself and her. Her heels lifted slightly, ready, in the event she needed to pounce.

"Who?" Denial was her first line of defense.

"Karao? Scary looking, super tall, dark skin, black hair, usually commanding the undead to do her bidding? Likes painting?" He was convinced they knew. "Look, I can spot a necromancer when I see one, and you two dabble at the very least."

"Even if we know her," Nika said. "We have no clue who you are."

"Shoot, see, I knew I forgot something. My name is Bringer." Bringer seemed to turn his attention to Nika. He had made the correct assumption that Catherine wasn't going to help him much. "Karao's never told you about me? Well, she told me to come to the city. See, I owe her a favor. I guess it's time to pay the piper."

Catherine relaxed a bit. This was a familiar, plausible story in her eyes. "Oh, yeah. She does that. Didn't she tell you where to go?"

"She did, but, well, I've forgotten." Bringer's memory seemed frail at best. "All I know is that she told me what city she's been in these days."

"Right, well." Catherine hummed and hawed for a minute. She was rightly skeptical; the idea of turning away someone who might help them out of this situation was enough to scare her into wanting to help the guy out. "She might be back by now. We can take you there if you can answer one question. Just so we know you're not up to something."

"A little caution never hurt anyone," Bringer said. "Fire away, miss!"

"How old is Karao?" Catherine asked. The question nobody knew the answer to. It was a devious trap.

"That's not fair," he said, "I don't remember what I guessed. It's been too many years. I remember she said my guess was far too low. I think it was ninety-something? She really doesn't look it, though."

That was about as good an answer as they could ever hope to get. Sheltered under two umbrellas, the three left the library and marched into the unforgiving rainstorm. The patter of rain on the umbrella canvas and sloshing of shoes in brick-laid puddles made each step, breath, and thought drag out for an eternity or two.

"So," Nika said, trying to break the unbearable awkwardness. "Why do you owe Karao a favor?" Catherine elbowed him. He didn't understand. She was probably wondering too.

Bringer laughed. "Straight to the point with you, huh. Ouch. ok then."

Nika realized it was probably a rude question. He decided to try and avoid that in the future. However, he started wondering where the line between rude and acceptable was.

Figuring out people was mentally taxing. Doing something rude usually had only one correct follow-up if he didn't want another lecture from Nils and Karao about human interaction: apologies. "Sorry, I didn't mean to pry."

"No, no, it's ok. I'd have even more questions if I were you," Bringer said. Nika did have more questions, but that no longer seemed like a great idea. "It's honestly just a funny story. A long time ago, I asked her to help me find someone important. He stole something very precious to me, so she was helping me get it back. Of course, even after we found the guy, he managed to sneak away! Still, a deal is a deal, and she did track the man down for me. So, favor."

If that was the sort of thing Karao did during her 'contract work,' Nika thought it was cool. Karao was always finding new ways to help people, even if she got something out of it. Especially if she got something out of it, in fact. Maybe that wasn't as altruistic as it could have been, but in the end, people got help. He imagined Karao dressed as a private investigator conducting a stake-out of this thief's house. She probably would dress up for something like that, knowing her.

"You're wondering what he stole, right?" Bringer said. Nika realized he had become secluded for a full minute or more. What's more, he hadn't been wondering that until right then. Now it was all he could think about.

Nika didn't even know where to start narrowing down the list of all possible things Bringer could have owned. A particularly fancy umbrella, maybe. A better coat, the key to the metal clasp on his ankle; there were a number of options. He was lost in thought, and Bringer took the silence as a signal of defeat.

"No?" Bringer asked. "Not even a guess? That's disappointing."

"What was it?" Catherine asked. She was slightly less tense.

"My name," he said. Under his ridiculous umbrella, he seemed like a kid that was messing with them. "You seem surprised!"

"How do you steal a name?" Catherine's grip on the umbrella grew tighter.

"Very carefully." Bringer had clearly done this same routine before. It was a bit. "You don't think my mum named me Bringer, do you? It's a bit ominous."

Nika had recently read a story about someone who had assumed identities as a double agent to some far-off kingdom. He imagined something similar happened to Bringer. "So, did they frame you for something?"

"Nope. He stole my name, my face, my whole darn body," Bringer said. "Well, I think. It's been a long time, I remember not being like this before, but that's about all."

"Before what?" Nika asked.

Bringer just smiled.

"Sorry," Nika said. "Again."

"That." Bringer was pointing at the Pale Garden tea shop. "Seems like the sort of place Karao would own."

"You know her pretty well." Catherine had, at some point, grabbed Nika's sleeve. It wasn't for her safety, but his. She was ready to pull him back at a moment's notice. Bringer didn't seem too intimidating to him. His only friend in the world was someone who had command of a spider the size and approximate weight of a pumpkin, so maybe his scale for what constitutes a scary person needed adjusting.

"Yeah, well, we've bumped into each other a few times since then."

"I see," Catherine answered. "Well, last I saw, she had stepped out for the day." The three stopped at the door—Nika and Catherine in the doorframe, Bringer in the road in front. "I'll see if she's around, but we're closed today. You can try coming back tomorrow if you want. We open around eight." She stuck the handle of the umbrella to him, trying to return it. He refused.

"Well, that's no fun." Bringer tapped his foot. "Well, if you do see her-"

The door behind them opened. If a stopped heart produced a sound, Nika would have heard Catherine make it. Their eyes shot back to see which of the two people it could have been had just opened the door.

On a positive note, Nils had just opened the door. Catherine was relieved.

On a slightly less positive note, they looked awash in terror.

"You-You're-What-" Nils couldn't start a thought, let alone finish it.

"Long time no see, Nils," Bringer said. "You've grown so tall!"

At this point, Catherine would have pushed Nika through the door and out of the way and done the same to Nils, but she never got the chance. Nils had already grabbed both of them and pulled so hard that Nika only recalled seeing Bringer and then the floor.

"Stay back, Karao's not here!" Nils said. "They didn't do anything to you!"

"Neither did you. Calm down," Bringer said. "I guess Karao told you about this whole mess then, that's fine. I believe you." He sighed a bit. "Or, rather, I can see that for myself."

"What's going on? Who is this?" Catherine asked.

"Fill them in for me, would you, Nils?" Bringer turned back in the direction they had just come from. "Tell Karao that I would like to talk to her, and more importantly, to not get in the way. Well, specifically, I guess I want you to say this: I found him myself, without your help, and when this is through, we are going to have a chat."

The rain grew furious. The swirling sheets of water made everything but the man under the giant umbrella impossible to see. Still, it was safely outside the tea shop. They were safe. No matter how much the walls creaked, how much the windows moaned, Karao said it was completely stormproof.

Bringer waved goodbye, cheerful as he had been a moment before. "Oh, Nika, that book you have there. It was a good read. I learned a lot."

As he walked, his umbrella crackled and buzzed. Lightning struck it. There was no thunder. Bringer walked like nothing had happened. To him, nothing had. The man hadn't lost an ounce of his stride as the electrical current sparked and leaped down the wireframes in the umbrella. The redirected lightning carved a burning circle in the ground around him from each of its eight points. The smoking stone was quenched immediately by the pouring rain.

It was a chore to get the door closed, but a chore Nika needed to do to prevent Nils from getting drenched in the doorway. Locking it was the only way to keep the wind from ripping it open again.

"Nils?" Catherine asked.

Nils wouldn't move. Their normally ash-colored face glistened silver in the dim Pale Garden light. It was probably the rain responsible for that. They closed their eyes and breathed.

"Ok." They turned, thoughts organized. "Karao will answer your questions later. It's actually good that you guys are here."

"What's going on?" Nika asked.

Nils was pacing. "No time now. I need to think. What did she say, find her, find Cruise, um..."

"Nils!" The table Catherine hit had been fixed by Karao earlier that week; otherwise, it absolutely would have split from the blow. "I'm not doing anything until you tell us what is happening!"

Nika was on Catherine's side both in the conversation and in literal room space.

"Fine." Nils was defeated. "Back when I first met Karao, before I was 'Nils,' I used to play in the shop while she had visitors, clients, really. She'd take jobs from them, and then Cruise would watch me while she worked. There was one visitor that always made her really uncomfortable, but she never took a job from him."

"Bringer, we got it." Catherine had taken a seat at some point.

Nils nodded. "He stopped showing up after a while. Karao only told me more about him a few years ago. He's something else."

Ominous wording like that was never great. "Something else? Like, is he-" he didn't have an end to the question ready, so he dropped it.

"She wasn't really clear on that." Nils was anxiously checking the clock. Time was wasting. "She told me that if he ever shows up while she's not around, I have to do three things. I have to find her. I have to find Cruise." Nils counted on their fingers, pulling back the third one harder and harder as if trying to break their hand would jog their memory.

"Aren't they both-" Nika realized the problem. "-out of town."

"What's the third?" Catherine asked.

"We need to warn. We need to warn. We need to warn principal Arcs!" Nils leaped from the table to go prepare.

"The principal?" Catherine asked. "Like from the South?"

Nika was confused. Of all the people in the world that he knew, so about ten to twelve, the last one he expected to get involved was the principal of a school he wasn't even sure he was going to yet. If there was an obvious connecting thread between the ominous umbrella man and the showboating principal, he missed it.

All the questions he had were best condensed to a single word: "Why?"

"She never explained it. She just said that it was important."

"How do we get in touch with them?" Catherine was thinking aloud. "We don't have any messengers, and even if we did, we don't know where they are." He had seen them at Morgan's house before: small square papers that would fold into little birds and fly off with whatever you'd written on in. He wondered if the rain was a problem for them.

"Morgan might," Nika said. The others turned to him immediately, confused. "Her parents are the guys hanging around Cruise all the time."

"If they have one, we might be able to call them." Nils liked this option.

"Nika, you know where they live, right?"

"It's really close. I can get there in like fifteen minutes." Nika paused. "But it's the direction he was heading off in."

"Do you know the back roads?" Nils asked. He shook his head. He barely knew the main roads. "Then Catherine and I will go there, here, write down where it is."

As he scrawled out the address, he asked the next obvious question in his mind. "Why don't I just go with you two?"

"Because I need you to go to Mr. Arcs," Nils said. Nika knew it was a bad time to be noticing this, but Nils's use of the word 'I' had come back, and he was happy about that if nothing else. Maybe he was looking for a small solace, but he was happy to find one regardless. "He's in a small blue house directly across the street from the school, do you think you can get there?"

"That won't be a problem. Will I know the house when I see it?"

"It's comically small," Catherine said. "Should we wait for the rain to let up a bit?"

Nils shook their head. "It won't go away."

"Why?" Nika asked.

"Karao said that Bringer is tied to this storm. It follows him wherever he goes. This isn't normal; there's something up in those clouds. As long as he's in Eldes, it won't let up, not even for a second."

Suddenly, the idea of selling umbrellas seemed like a lot more of a tenable business strategy. What a worthless detail for him to latch onto.

"This is why Karao's afraid of the rain, isn't it," Nika said. Catherine had just realized it as well. Nils tossed each of them a raincoat from the closet. They nodded.

"You ready?"

"Be safe, you two."

"If he tries anything, I'm going to fry him."

"I'm not letting you do anything, hothead."

"I'm not bringing either of you back to life, for the record."

"Same goes for you, shortie."

"Stop talking like that. We're just the messengers. He doesn't care about us. I think."

The three ran into the rainy summer day. The rain physically drained them at each step, dragging them down ever so slightly en masse. There was a plan, and that plan was to find the people with the actual plan. It was a small role to play, but it was one they felt confident enough to do.

Nika shook. It was probably just the cold.

Chapter 12- End

Intermission-A Tragic Tale

Long ago, there lived a farmer. He had spent decades of his life on the same plot of fertile land, surrounded by his loving family and ample friendly neighbors. His life was not an easy one, but it was a satisfying one. His family steadily grew, and his bounty was so consistent and delicious that he felt beloved by all.

Time grew wary of this. It's nothing but a petty and fickle thing, and one by one, that man's boons became banes. The soil beneath his feet bore less and less food year after year. His neighbors left their already barren farms for better land, his family became an ever-increasing toll, mouths to feed. His wife died of disease, and with her, his motivation.

And when he had nothing left to give, time stole the rain.

The drought was brutal. Livestock died every day, his children were sent away to live where they could find water. At his absolute lowest, he wished to sell the land. He had never wondered why new neighbors had never moved in: nobody wanted his useless dirt.

"Please, gods, pity and bring me rain!" The man cried out, the last useless plea of a once secular mortal. There was no reply. Not from gods anyway.

A figure approached him, almost as if answering his plea. Each step this being took was accompanied by the small and magnificent pitter-patter of raindrops on a deserted land. The farmer dropped to his knees in thanks, head bowed and sobbing. He asked what the figure wished in return for this gift.

All it wanted was for the farmer to listen to a deal and make a choice.

"You wish for rain that badly?" it asked.

"Yes, I am old. I have nothing left. If another drought comes, I will die with nothing left for my children."

"I can give you the rain to command if you agree to carry the burden."

"Yes, anything, please!"

"It is not a duty to take lightly. You will carry it with you until it is time to put it down. You're still interested? Very well. I ask for only one thing in return. It is something I've never had before. I would like your name, Phineas Arcs."

Chapter 13. Cold Rain on a Hot Day

On any other day, Nika would probably have spent a good hour or two wondering how a man like Phineas Arcs could fit inside such a tiny house, let alone live in it. It was a farther sprint than Nika had expected, and he had definitely taken a wrong turn or two. He hoped that Nils and Catherine had found Morgan ok and that Morgan was taking this seriously.

The door seemed to get smaller as he got closer to the small porch. It must have been the rain messing with his vision. Stepping onto the porch suggested otherwise. Standing next to the door, it suddenly looked massive, like it would take several of him to push it open. He stepped back into the yard in front of the porch, and it looked small again. It was like the library, an illusion designed to make his head hurt, probably.

Just another thing that he didn't have time for. He knocked on the door.

Somehow, principal Arcs's voice overtook the stampeding rain. "Just a minute!" There was a shuffle and some mumbling about who would be out in a storm like this. Before long, Nika was staring at the man who had clearly planned for a cozy evening inside with a book. "Nika!" He boomed. They had only met once, but he remembered Nika's name, which was impressive. "What are you doing out there? Come in, come in."

"Thank you."

The house was, in spite of its manipulative door, very normal. It sort of looked like Morgan's, with a few bits of decor scattered on some tacky wallpaper. The small hallway fed into a kitchen and what he definitely called 'a study'. It was lined with bookshelves filled with things ranging from reference text to contemporary young adult literature. It seemed the clutter followed him from the office to the home.

"What brings you here, son?"

The word son bothered him, but he decided to leave it be for now. There really wasn't a way to easily break a life or death warning, at least it seemed like. "Bringer's here. I was supposed to warn you."

"I see."

Nika had expected more of a reaction. "I don't know anything else."

"Is Karao on her way?" he asked.

"Sort of. She's out of town. They're trying to call her back."

He reached for his drink. It looked like hot cocoa. His hand shook a bit as he brought it to his lips. It wasn't worth the effort; he burned himself. Phineas was slowly taking in the news piece by piece. "That. Isn't good."

"Nils didn't know much about it, can you tell me?"

His forced smile wasn't fooling even himself. "You can only run from your past for so long, I'm afraid." He steeled himself and stood from his well-worn chair. "Right. This was going to happen sooner or later. You stay here until the storm clears. If Karao comes here, tell her I went to deal with this myself. He'll probably be out looking for me, so I'll make myself ready to be found." With a clap of his hands, a purple coat loosened itself from the rack and wrapped itself around him. He didn't have a hat or umbrella, which seemed strange. "Also, Nika, tell her, thank you."

The guilt in his words hung heavily on Nika's ears. If Bringer's story was true, it sounded like Phineas Arcs, principal of the South Eldes Academy, was the one who stole the umbrella man's name.

He wasn't sure what to think but knew what he would do; "I will."

"The act ends today." Phineas Arcs flung the door open. From behind, with the purple coat, the size, the dramatic soliloquy, Nika felt a bizarre sense of deja vu. A nagging recent memory was exactly like this moment. He couldn't place it, though.

The rain was hitting his coat, but he stayed dry. Each drop evaporated on contact with the giant man. A tower of steam wafted off of him. Nika had seen this kind of shimmering before. It was the duelist, Molten Phoenix, who was also huge, loud, dressed in purple, and, come to think of it, Phineas was in charge of the school's dueling club.

"Oh. No. No, no, no-no." Nika checked again. Yup. It was definitely exactly the same man.

The pro-duelist turned principal turned back to him, completely unaware that his cover had been blown. He waved to Nika again from the road.

With a flash of harrowing light, Phineas Arcs was struck by lightning.

Well, it was hard to tell. One moment he was standing tall, the next, he was blinded, the third, his ears were being assaulted with shattering thunder, and finally, he saw the principal laying; a smoking heap on the ground. His ears were ringing.

Something was approaching, slowly drifting into view from the downpour.

"I knew following you was the right idea." Bringer was pleased with himself. "The other two ran off to who knows where, but I felt like you'd be the one to warn this filth."

Phineas coughed. He was alive but shriveled. All of his strength had gone into keeping a pulse going. Nika couldn't move. He couldn't move. The deadarm on his back twitched, useless as always. He ran into the street without thinking.

"Mr. Arcs!" He was in rough shape, obviously. The fact that he had survived something like that was incredible in and of itself.

"Nobody's told you anything, have they, kid?" Bringer asked. "He's not dead. Not even close."

"Shut up!" Nika had no idea what he was doing. He certainly didn't have a follow-up. He just hated how nonchalantly Bringer walked through the rain, umbrella held high, completely impervious to the small destruction around him. The big ones, too, it seemed.

"I know what it looks like." Bringer was standing over them. The umbrella-covered Phineas's legs, but not his face or Nika. "This has nothing to do with you. Back away."

Nika didn't know what to do. The only thing he sort of knew how to do was necromancy, and as injured as he was, Phineas was still very much alive. He was relatively certain that something being dead was a requirement of Necromancy.

Still, he was apparently weird. He was different from even the other necromancers. It was maybe the one thing he had felt confident in doing in his whole life. Still, he couldn't do anything with Bringer staring at him.

Bringer's expression dropped. "Move."

Nika's sweater ruffled, the deadarm was moving slightly. Its hand-twisted, a bit of Nika's energy sparked through its fingertips. The metal struts in the umbrella buckled a bit, the wind shoved it to the side. Bringer yelled and fought for control of the giant thing again. He was looking away.

He hadn't done that on purpose. The arm was still stubbornly refusing to do what he wanted, but this would work. He quickly shot as much necromantic magic into Phineas's crisped neck and shoulders as he could. He backed away quickly before Bringer could regain composure.

Bringer walked backward as Phineas reclaimed his full height. The intensity of the jet of steam lifting off from him grew more and more, A beacon of white smoke in the ominous clouds. Even with the cold rain, Nika needed to keep taking steps back. The principal's hands began glowing red, the air around him shimmered through the steam. It was like watching the replay, but without the promise that anyone would make it out alive.

"So what, you're going to kill me now?" Bringer's upbeat demeanor was, without question, the most terrifying thing about him. The way he talked about and treated death was so relaxed, so carefree. It was impossible to tell what mattered to him, other than this hatred. Hatred was shown through his smile.

"Of course not," Phineas said. The rain wasn't even reaching him now. As he walked forward, the steam swirled around each step. The ground sizzled under his foot. "But I won't let you hurt one of my students either." A jet of flame born from his palm tried desperately to reach its target. Through the rain and wind, it could barely manage to make it halfway there.

"I'm not really a fan of fireworks." Bringer hadn't even flinched. "Oh, wait, I had something prepared for this. What was it, right! I'm more of a light show guy." He pointed up.

There was another flash of light, another cataclysmic roar that shook Nika to the ground. The difference this time was that Phineas was completely untouched.

"You're standing under the lamppost. You did that on purpose." Bringer was impressed. "Very nice, but." The wind began to pick up, a horrible gale crashed in from behind the master of the storm. His umbrella tilted backwards, he laughed as he watched the results of his work.

Doors tore open. Windows shattered. Tree branches snapped and collapsed, Nika with them. He hoped desperately that the principal's doorway wouldn't give way because he couldn't stand anymore. Phineas had dug his molten hands into the road, the rock giving way beneath their immense heat. He held on for dear life, each second draining him more than the last.

It was unending. Even the deadarm was useless in the oppressive wind. Nika couldn't think, couldn't act, couldn't see. This was it. He had done what he could, but there was nothing left to be done.

It ended. Abruptly. In its place was a horrible scream, and Bringer, slanted and clutching an arm made limp. Two other people were standing between Phineas and Bringer. Nika prayed that they were Karao and Cruise. He couldn't hear what they said to one another over the rain. Still, one rushed Bringer, and the other knelt down next to Phineas before vanishing, taking the giant principal with him.

The one in Bringer's face wasn't Karao. For one thing, she was swinging what looked like a sword around. Bringer made no attempt to fight back, though not for lack of wanting to. He seemed too focused, trying to stay alive in the onslaught. Though every strike was blocked, evaded, or left just a small scratch, each one looked like it could be fatal.

"Gah, I love my wife. She's just awesome," the voice, unknown, called from behind. Nika had nearly killed him from shock. It was Ben Farvue, Morgan's father, Cruise's guard, and Lisa's husband. "Sorry there, you doing alright, bud?"

He had no idea when Ben got around him, but it had to be a good sign. Behind the suit, Phineas was lying on the ground, completely out of energy. He was no longer fried from his brush with lightning, at least not his body. His clothes must have been specially made to withstand heat because they had just charred, not burned.

"Yeah," Nika said. He had no idea if it was true or not. It was just the first word in his head.

"Karao and Cruise are on their way. We were home today while those two took their trip. They told us to meet at Arcs's place, so I guess we got lucky, eh?" Ben's cheeriness was somehow similar to and completely opposite Bringer's. There was a genuine warmth and optimism to it. He had this confidence that nothing could go wrong. "Oh, hang on." He touched his ear. "Could you repeat that? Right. Recalling."

A blue ring appeared around his wrist. He turned it the way one would turn a doorknob. With a sweeping blue light, Lisa Farvue was teleported from sixty feet away into the foyer with the rest of them, mid-swing.

Her hair was tied back, her sleeves rolled up, her eyes narrowed and focused, even away from the battle. The momentum she was carrying flung her hair, but her trained arm knew to stop short of ripping apart an innocent painting on Phineas's wall.

"What's up, dear?" Ben asked.

"Take this seriously. We're switching tactics. Three-speed, wind-resist, one strength." Lisa barely acknowledged Nika's existence, though she did seem slightly relieved he was alive. Her sword was the translucent, gold-ish material that she had made a pen out of during their interview.

Ben nodded and tapped at slowly rotating symbols on the blue ring around one wrist with the opposite hand. "Got it, got it, what's the plan?"

"Lightning doesn't hit under the umbrella; I stay under the umbrella." Lisa was fiddling with the hilt of her weapon. The gold material began melting, seeping over itself. It must not have been hot since she let it cover both of her hands. She clapped, then waited a moment for the transformation to finish. Spikes began swirling out from her knuckles before solidifying into a terrifying pair of spiked knuckles that covered her entire hand.

"You've been on a boxing kick recently." He waited for her to finish his thought.

"Was that a kick-boxing joke?" She smiled at him.

"You ready to go back in?" He didn't answer, but she did.

"I hate that, and I hate you." She nudged him with her elbow. Her hands were a little too dangerous for a shoulder punch.

"Love you too, don't break him too badly." With a dismissive hand wave, she was sent back out to fight the nervous and confused Bringer.

Nika hadn't seen a family interact like that before. He liked it. "What was all that with the numbers?" It was easy to see where Morgan got her, well, everything from. Lisa was a flurry of lethal strikes, and her father was a laid-back man cheering from the sides.

"So." Ben had clearly practiced this explanation before. His role in this tag-team was clearly to stand on the sidelines and make sure nobody tried to get involved who didn't have to. "Basically, I'm just her support. I majored in augmentation."

"Majored?"

"Er... focused? In university. I enchant things, including people! You can only enchant with a few things at a time, though, so we have to switch it up depending on what she decides would work best. Besides that, I have general medical spells, protective barriers, short-range teleportation-"

Nika had checked out. He was curious, but now was not the time for a full-on lecture on the life and studies of Benjamin Farvue. A man so confident in his partner's abilities that he sent her to punch a thunderstorm and didn't bat an eye.

The first time lightning struck in their fight signaled something. Bringer was willing to let her die. As long as she was underneath a lamppost or the umbrella, she was safe, but that was proving trickier than expected. As fast as her augmentations had made her, Bringer was keeping up with each swing. Each one that connected with the umbrella sparked and shocked her back. Electricity stored from captured lightning was released one jarring hit at a time. It hit both, indiscriminately, with only a fraction of its original potency.

A single full-force fist connected with his chest, and for a moment, the world seemed to stop. The rain came to a swift halt. Lisa backed out and was recalled once again by Ben. Slowly, the pair of them and Nika walked out to see what was happening to Bringer.

He was alive, bleeding, and muttering. The world seemed so quiet without the storm, though the shadowy clouds still reigned as tyrants over the sky. The umbrella dropped.

"No, I can still handle this," he said to nobody. "You'll get your old body back. Just give me more time."

"Is he talking?" Lisa asked. Nika stopped walking forward.

"By order of the crown and the authority of chief Cruise, I place you under arrest." Ben sounded just like the time he had tried to scare Nika after having just met. This time, it was backed up by something.

"I can take them. They're nothing," Bringer said.

Ben put a hand on Lisa and Nika's shoulders. Nika felt strange like his entire body was being suspended by strings. "Put your hands behind your back, Bringer."

"He's not getting away, not this time. It won't be the same."

"I don't think he's listening," Lisa said. "Cruise just said to make sure Arcs, and Nika are safe. We just have to wait."

"You aren't taking him anywhere!" Bringer's voice had changed. He stumbled forward, the first step nearly toppling him then and there. "I'm not done with him yet! Give him back!"

Before, he had an air of playful superiority. He felt invincible. He felt like there was nothing that could stop him. Now, Bringer seemed like a cornered animal fighting for its life. He had spared Nika and was regretting it. He had taunted Phineas and felt stupid for it. He didn't take this pair of suits seriously and was paying the price.

He seemed eager, no, compelled, to learn from these mistakes immediately. He clutched the sides of his head, recoiling from a noise the others couldn't hear. "Fine then! Do it already!"

People had been watching the windows, the lull in the storm drawing them out from wherever they had been hiding.

Once again, lightning descended on this one peaceful road. It hit its exact target: Bringer. The sky struck him once, five times, a continuous stream of electricity arced the clouds to his shoulders. Bit by bit, his skin burned, flaked, and fluttered away in the wind.

What remained was a man-shaped pile of cinders and grudges.

Ben had been tinkering with his augmentation ring time while the others watched, agog. "I'm switching you up. Full resistance, no speed or strength boosts. Don't do anything stupid."

"Same to you." The couple was, for the first time, actually concerned with the other's safety. "Get them out of here."

Lightning is a very problematic thing to be chasing you. Primarily, it's too fast to react to, but it's also just impossible to predict. Lisa Farvue wasn't concerned with whether or not the sky had it in for her. There wasn't anything she could do about it, either way, so she continued with the plan to stay up close and get in what she could.

Compared to her frantic assault before, she looked like she was moving underwater. A punch to the jaw missed and the time spent recovering the lost momentum felt exaggerated. Bringer was stumbling, his body cracking and screeching with each exhaustive movement. He couldn't talk or wasn't talking.

Again, a punch landed. Square in the forehead, the spikes certainly aiming for a fatal blow. Again, the world stood still. Again, Bringer survived something that absolutely ought to have killed him. The source of lightning was no longer the sky. It was coming from him. He had been storing the lightning inside his body, waiting for her to connect with the metal weapon.

Had Lisa not been augmented to be as resilient as she was, she would have been cooked through in an instant through sheer voltage. Whether or not she was alive was up for debate to Nika, but Ben hadn't made a move yet. He would know when the time to worry is.

"Calling you back, Lisa?" Ben said. "Lisa?"

Nika's heart stopped.

"Hm, sir! Right. Understood." Ben grabbed Nika's shoulder. A painful droning sound pierced his ear fairly. When he regathered his bearings, the two were on the other side of the road, behind Bringer and out of sight. They were also away from Phineas. Ben wasted no time calling his wife back from the fight.

She was conscious but physically spent. She wasn't able to stand. She was barely able to speak. "I told you to get away, idiot."

"You also said to wait until they get here. You were right, as usual." He gestured to the road. "The cavalry just arrived, so you're on break. Nika here is gonna watch out for you."

Karao looked disgusted with the mess standing in front of her.

Chapter 13- End

Intermission- A Sordid Story

All deals are, in essence, unfair.

The demon knew that fully well when the farmer begged and pleaded for rain. He did not know the farmer. He bore no grudge, no feelings at all one way or another. He didn't see a man begging and pleading; he saw an opportunity.

What Are You Doing? The storm asked its herald.

"I lead. You follow. That's how it's always worked," the demon said.

Then where are you leading us?

"To the end, my friend."

The demon removed the shackle and exchanged it for the farmer's name. Phineas was such an exciting name. For the first time since he could remember, the voice had stopped. There was no longer a storm bound to him until the bitter end; the end was here. He felt his skin. It was human, real. His hair, eyes, all of it. He was well and truly alive.

For the first time, he was free from the burden he never asked for.

Nothing is free for the free.

The storm would want its master, its real master, back under its eye soon enough. After all, what's half of a demon? The farmer would soon learn how awful a curse the rain at his heels would become. Both would try to find him, and as a mortal or demon, he would soon be forced to take the storm back whatever he was.

The demon never enjoyed his freedom. It became a tool for him to put distance between himself and the storm. When it rained, he hid. When it was clear, he ran. He talked to nobody. He lived a shell of a life. He lived this way for a hundred years, they say.

The demon was wasting the life he had bargained for.

"What's bothering you?" A woman asked him. She was confident, eerily so, and could see right through him. She seemed to know exactly what he was before exchanging a single word. She didn't know when to call it quits. "Let's make a deal."

Chapter 14. The Let Down

Contempt, disdain, abhorration. With each step, she took Karao's face embodied a distinct form of hatred for the monster in front of her. Her eyes were drowning in disappointment, her lips curled with tempered fury, her deadarms spread like the hood of a cobra. The only thing besides her that moved was the rain, and even that was letting up a bit.

If Bringer still had eyes under his charcoaled face, he would be staring directly at the deadly woman walking towards them. "You." Talking seemed too painful to continue, though he seemed satisfied with that. He begrudgingly dragged his body forward. With each effort-filled breath, thin lightning bolts arced out from his teeth and into his chest, arms, and the nearby lamp.

"I have nothing to say to you." Karao didn't seem to be getting wet in the rain. In fact, the rain seemed to be going right through her. One of her deadarms let her pass through things. It probably was hard at work, letting the rainfall through unobstructed. Bringer howled.

Her top-most deadarm curled in front of her, palm facing the demon. The lightning that struck Karao was silent. Nika wondered what dictated if there was thunder, not that now was the time to question these things. The air smelled again. Nika's hair stood on end. Karao remained unmoved. A ball of erratic electricity was crackling in the palm of her deadarm. She had caught the lightning.

In all likeliness, her invulnerability to things like rain and walls would have been enough. This seemed intentional. It swirled around her fingertips before slowly infusing the bones.

"If you're done." She pointed at him with the same deadarm. The stored power shot in a straight bolt hitting

Bringer in the chest. The former man stumbled a bit but didn't fall. "I'd like to talk to Bringer, please."

It, apparently no longer Bringer, hissed. She slung another bolt at it.

It strained to speak. The voice was not Bringer's. "He would die."

Karao bluffed. "That's not my problem." She walked up to the husk, placing her real hand on his shoulder. "I'll keep him alive long enough to talk. Unless you would like to go with him?"

There was no answer. Smoke seemed to pour out from Bringer's skin, spiraling up into the clouds.

"Nika, Ben. Over here."

Ben had been treating his wife's injuries. They didn't seem that bad, considering what she had been hit by. He left her head propped up on a bag of medical equipment he'd been toting around. Nika felt the strange wooziness that he had learned to associate with short-range teleportation very briefly. Then they were by Karao's side again. It was only a sixty-foot leap; it felt unnecessary.

Up close, Bringer was a horrifying sight. Nika had only seen that he had burnt himself. He had no idea the complete and utter annihilation his body had been put through. Without context, he would never have guessed that the smiling man he had met earlier that day would have become this. The thought made him sick. The question of whether or not he had done this to himself or if something else was at play stuck out in Nika's mind. It was a question for after the fact. The smoke spewing from his face, and the tear in his arm grew more intense.

"Mr. Farvue, would you mind tending to the wounds?" Karao asked.

"I don't think he can be saved," he said. "The burns are too deep. I wouldn't be surprised if he's charred bone tissue."

"I would be grateful if you tried. Healing isn't really my strongest suit, and I don't want him to fall under my area of expertise."

"Area of- oh. I see." Ben Farvue began using some of the same ephemeral magic he had been using on the other two back in Arcs's house.

"Nika." Karao dropped to a knee. Nika was bothered by the fact that she was about the same height as him despite this.

"Yes?" he asked.

She attacked him. It was a surprise hug that he could not have seen coming with a thousand years worth of training and preparation. "Are you ok?" she asked.

He hugged back. "I'm ok." He thought he was telling the truth, but he could always have been wrong. All things considered, not being a pile of ash on the ground was probably considered coming out on top.

"I was so worried. I didn't want any of this to happen to you." Karao never cried. Even her most brief acquaintances could have guessed that. Her voice cracked a bit, though. "Where are the others?"

"They're at Morgan's," he said. Karao was working out who had the brilliant idea to send Nika out on the more dangerous of the two missions. Ultimately, this was something that he would explain later. The list of things to talk about after Bringer was getting long.

"That's fine then. I want you to head back."

Nika thought about this. "No." He was safe, or felt safe, with everyone around him. He had taken too many things at face value and wanted to know how this ended for himself.

"Nika, please. I can handle this, but having you around is just another thing I need to worry about."

There were too many unanswered questions in his mind, the kind that Karao would usually sweep under the rug or stubbornly refuse to answer. Hanging around might be his only chance to learn who this guy was, what his connection to Karao was, and what she had done to him. He wouldn't say it to her face, but Nika wanted to know that his trust was in a good place.

He felt guilty harboring that thought. He felt worse after her face suggested that she understood. "Go back to the house, at least. Don't go outside no matter what."

Nika had every intention of following through with those directions. Given a chance, he would have locked the door and stayed by the window. Bringer's coughing changed that plan in an instant. One of Karao's deadarms grabbed Nika by the back of the neck. He realized, simultaneously, that the deadarm felt really uncomfortable, but he also couldn't feel the rain anymore. It was passing through him the way it had been going through Karao. She was making him invulnerable.

Karao, on the other hand, was finally exposed to the rain. Her hair weighed itself down more as Bringer finished his coughing fit.

"Can he talk?" she asked Ben.

"I doubt it. He's barely alive. Most of his body is completely shot."

Karao touched Bringer's chest with her left hand. One reviving jolt of necromantic magic later, he was fighting to sit up. Karao's eyes had a soft purple glow to them as she continued to support the dying man. Ben picked up and sheltered Bringer with the umbrella that had been cast aside.

Bringer sighed. "Hello, again. Miss me?" Nobody answered. "Figures. Well, I already knew that you know? Your eyes always looked so scared when I was around. You were terrified of me." He tried to stand, but his legs wouldn't allow it.

"I was scared," Karao said, looming over Bringer. "I was terrified that you would do something to hurt other people and yourself."

"You were terrified of me, don't lie. There's no point to it anymore."

Karao's annoyance was seeping into her voice. "You gave me eight years. I don't make deals with people that can get rid of me that easily."

"I guess not." The rain's volume stayed consistent. "Then tell me."

"Tell you what?" Karao asked.

"What? What!" Bringer laughed, coughed, and laughed again. "Tell me why, why you sided with that demon."

"Demon?" Nika whispered. He hadn't meant to say anything, but the thought sort of slipped out.

"Is that Nika?" Bringer asked. Nika's breathing stopped short. "I can't really see. Nika, she won't tell you what she did." He was beginning to sound desperate. "If you don't listen to me, then you can't be surprised when she stabs you in the back, too."

Karao didn't object. "Go on then, it sounds like you have something to say."

"That man, Phineas Arcs, is a demon," Bringer said. His cheeks cracked as he spoke, something inside his face was squeaking, and Nika didn't want to think about what that was. "He stole my name. He put me on the leash of this stupid storm. He's been running and hiding from me for decades." It seemed impossible for him to be doing so, but Bringer was standing. "He ruined my life, and for what? To play 'human' and waste his time on silly things."

Nika didn't know what to say. Karao hadn't argued a single point.

"And her. She's just as much to blame for this. She's spent all this time hiding him, but that's not the worst of it. Not by a long shot. She promised to help me and sent me running around this entire world while she kept him safely stashed away in this cursed city. You pride yourself on deals, do you, Karao? Hah. Your word means nothing to me."

Karao seethed, "I was trying to save you both, you idiot." Her grip on Nika's shoulder tightened. "I didn't want either of you to die. I just needed time to figure this out."

"You had time!" he snapped. "You had years. You had an actual decade to work something out! And if it takes that long, there's no answer. Not one I care about."

Karao's gaze could have frozen any other heart with fear. "How do you know what I tried?" There was silence for just a moment. Bringer refused to answer.

"I didn't want to believe her," Bringer said. "She said that you were going back on our deal to help out that demon. She said you were keeping me away from the city because you feared me. I wanted to believe you, and then when I came back." He pointed at Nika. "The first thing I see is this one run-off to warn that monster on your orders."

"Who?" Karao asked. "Who is 'she'?"

"Unlike you, I keep my promises." Bringer coughed. "She said to say 'hello.'"

"Useless, as always." Karao paused. Releasing her magic from him would mean he would die soon, but she couldn't keep him there forever.

Ben Farvue looked up. "What happens now?"

"If - when - he gives out, that storm won't be bound to anyone. That is unacceptable," Karao answered, the rain around them thinning.

"It's just a storm, won't it just do storm things? I don't know." Nika didn't understand why that was such an impending threat.

"It's not just a storm." Karao released her power over Bringer. He buckled a bit but stayed up. "He was correct. Phineas, well, our Phineas, is a demon. Half of a demon, to be exact. The storm and its herald. Bringer's job is to make sure it never rests, or else it-"

"Annihilates. Yeah, my other half is pretty ugly," Phineas said, startling the group. How someone of that size could approach them undetected was somehow the most mystical thing that had happened to Nika today.

Bringer tried to move, he was unable to.

"Phineas Arcs," Karao said, impressed with him. "How on earth are you standing right now?"

"You forget I work with a bunch of emotional teenage mages. This is only the third-worst thing that's ever hit me." He had this big, stupid smile.

"That's a lie." Karao turned to him. "We will need to talk later, but for now, we need to know how to deal with this."

"Is he dead?" His voice dropped. He sounded disappointed in himself more than anything.

"No. Mr. Farvue here is keeping him here, but who knows for how much longer."

"I've had enough, Karao." Phineas walked up to the charred man. Nika had only just noticed the limp. "I should never have brought you into this, any of you." He knelt next to the dying man. "Especially you. I am sorry."

"Rot," Bringer commanded. It was the most concise way he had to get his feelings across.

"I deserve that. I deserve worse. All I wanted was to live a normal life."

"Phineas, what are you doing?" Karao started to sound worried. Her fingers tensed.

Phineas ignored her. "And you've given me that, although our trade was not an even one, I hope that there was some substance to the cursed life you've taken on. I know you resent me. My, no, our time here has done nothing but bring sorrow and pain to others."

"Phineas, stop!" She reached for him. Phineas punched the ground, conjuring a ring of raging fire around himself and Bringer. Even Ben fell back as the ring expanded, leaving the two completely alone. Bringer's life support was gone, but the flames bothered neither of them. Nika had tripped on the way back. Released from Karao's grip, the rain was crashing on his skin again. It was cold.

"I've borrowed your name for long enough. You're suffering my death, and I won't stand for it any longer. I would like to offer you a trade. You will take the name Phineas Arcs, and I will take the burden of your body."

"No more of this!" Karao had walked through the flames. The brand of magic she was using to do this did not matter. "I've already failed one of you. I'm not letting you throw away your life for his stupid mistake!"

His shoulder pulsed a bit. A jet of flame shot out and cut through Karao. She was unharmed thanks to the ghostly invulnerability, but the message sent was clear. "I can't do this anymore. This is my burden to bear, and it's about time I took responsibility for it."

"I'm cashing in my favors, Phineas." She marched up to him, half of a terrifying demon, about to reunite with its other self, a fearless, indomitable necromancer. "All of them. You'll owe me nothing. One request." She reached out to him. "Don't do this. We can find another way."

"I'm sorry. We can't, and I won't." Phineas smiled at her. "I mean, I've always been a liar. Are you really so surprised that I won't return those favors?"

"Ok," Bringer choked out. Lightning struck one final time, the afterimage of a branching bolt carving a path from Bringer's chest into Phineas's burned into Nika's eyes. Ben had gotten close to him while he was watching the scene unfold, ready to jump in and protect Nika if the need arose.

Karao screamed. All of her deadarms billowed purple smoke, overflowing with reckless necromancy. She grabbed Bringer's hand, collapsed completely and entirely on the ground. There was no struggle, no fight to stay alive. He had died.

Phineas felt his face. "It's... back. I'm back!" he laughed. "The voice is gone, I don't hear that-"

"Shut up!" Karao's face snapped up. Her hate-twisted scowl was terrifying. "Shut your mouth! We are fixing him." She gestured for Ben to come over and repeat their previous necromancy-healing act.

"Karao, don't." Ben pointed up. "Look."

The clouds were very much still looming overhead, but they were quickly dissipating. Light punctured through a few holes, then some more. Through one egregious wound in the sky, Nika spotted the blue summer sky. The storm was dying, too. Whatever was in it, whatever entity was holding it together, dissolved before them.

Karao shielded her eyes from a freshly opened ray of light. One of her deadarms, the second from the top, snapped its fingers. Phineas yelped, startled. The black hands of his shadow had reached from their place in the ground and held down his ankles. Karao turned, her body swayed a bit, losing control.

"Not one word, Bringer," she said to Phineas.

They had successfully traded bodies. Bringer was now the school principal, the retired duelist, the towering figure fighting to keep his form.

"It's not 'Bringer' anymore. I have my name back, finally. Finally." He tried to kick the handoff from him. Instead, it reached up and grappled his knee, causing him to collapse.

"Wrong," Karao said. Ben was tinkering with the glyphs around his wrist. The way Karao lurched forward was unsettling, but Nika wasn't scared. He wasn't scared of her, he wasn't scared for him, he was sad. She looked completely broken. "Phineas is, and will always be, gone."

"He got what he deserved," Bringer choked out with curling of fingers. Bringer's shadow stirred again, this time in the chest. It swirled like water, pooling, and curling. It slowly spiraled out of the ground, and, quickly, A narrow spike pressed up against Bringer's neck. He didn't bleed. It hadn't connected yet.

"I've already made my peace with your death. Don't push me."

"Karao, stop!" Ben yelled. His hands were dripping in a shimmering blue aura. "That's enough." The spike retracted into the ground, and the shadowy hands released their prisoner. "Karao, I'm sorry. You can't save them all."

"I guess not." She looked up. Her stoic face-concealing something difficult to read. She turned to Nika. She seemed ready to leave. Ben's blue aura became a pair of handcuffs around Bringer's wrists. Lisa was hobbling over to her husband, eager to help clean up the mess and get whatever work needed to be done.

"Pretty rich that you'd get upset by someone dying." Bringer had to have the last word.

"Death is final. I'd suggest you take my word on that." Karao looked down the road. The idea of having to walk back taxed her. "Come on, Nika, I'm taking you home."

"Ok," his voice cracked.

Along the way, he thought of what to say. It wasn't the first death he had witnessed, but it was the first person he knew. His voice was frozen, his thoughts fuzzy. He unintentionally stepped in several deep puddles. Nika couldn't focus at all. All he wanted was time.

"Karao?" he said.

"Yes?" she answered.

"I'm sorry." He felt colder now, somehow.

"Me too."

Chapter 14- End

Intermission- A Pyrrhic Parable

Karao had called everyone into a circle to talk about what had happened earlier that day. The Pale Garden was even quieter than usual, which was an impressive feat in its own right. Nobody had any idea where to start, what to say, or what to do.

Karao reluctantly got the ball rolling. "Nils. I'm proud of you. Truth be told, I had completely forgotten what I had told you all those years ago. You really are one of a kind."

Nils smiled briefly.

"You should not have sent Nika alone." Karao raked her fingers through her hair. "I get that thought process that got you there, but your safety is my absolute highest priority. You should have stayed together." They listened to the silence together.

Catherine was the first one to challenge Karao. "How are you involved with this?"

Karao puffed her cheeks and blew. "I was in the middle of it all, I suppose. Phineas came to me first and asked for help. He told me he was being chased by some sort of half-demon and needed help hiding. Years and years later, I met Bringer, and he told me he had been tricked into trading away his name and body. Connecting the dots didn't take long."

Nils didn't like their thoughts. It was clear on their face. "It's principal Arcs fault, right?"

"Perhaps, but maybe not. Life isn't cut and dry like that, unfortunately. Bringer's life was a hard one, but Phineas didn't have much going for him either. He was desperate to be free, and I don't really blame him."

Nils balled their hands. They had liked the principal. This was a personal betrayal. "How could he just pass off his problem to someone else and pretend that he'd done nothing wrong?"

"Nils." Karao didn't have an answer. "I could have dedicated more time towards them. If I had a solution for the storm, then maybe- well, who can say. Maybe Bringer could have listened to reason; maybe he wouldn't have. Yeah." She was just thinking aloud. "You shouldn't dwell in your past, you three. Wallowing in things that could have been will destroy you. However, We, in particular, have to honor the past. Learn from it, take lessons, and forge ahead."

"Learn from it how?" Nika asked.

"The moral of today: violence will destroy more than it gives. The lesson for me is to not take this time for granted. I may not be able to save everyone, but I refuse to give up the goal." She closed her eyes and smiled. "Let's move forward with this in heart, shall we?"

Chapter 15. Business As Usual

Nils had collapsed. Not because of that whole business with a murderous umbrella salesman or the physically taxing goal of revamping the entire tea shop in under a week. No, Nils collapsed from knowledge. Specifically, learning that being late on a mortgage payment is not the end of the world and that they weren't about to be evicted.

Karao hadn't thought to explain how mortgages worked to Nils until the day the payment was supposed to be due. Nils had toiled day and night under the assumption that they were falling behind deadlines and were going to be immediately kicked out.

Nils had spent the first half-hour of slow business face down in a checkbook in the kitchen, processing. Karao had spent most of the time trying to make them feel better. It was an honest mistake, and she had a lot going through her mind in the days after the business with Phineas.

That left Nika in the front, alone. Despite the two people commenting on the decor over cups of tea, it was quiet. He was trying to get through the section of this study book before moving onto something more fun.

Catherine was the fourth person to walk through the front door. "Sorry, sorry. I slept in, I wasn't sure- oh, just you?"

Nika looked back down at his book. "Gee, thanks."

"You know what I mean." Catherine was in a better mood. Ever since she left, she had been harder to rile up and easier to get along with. She had considered taking another job to help cover her rent, but that was on hold until the relaunch went through. At least if business picked up, it would be a non-factor. She wrapped an apron around herself and started cleaning the one and only dirty table. "Where's Nils?"

"In the back, they needed to sit down for a while," he said.

"How come?" Catherine asked.

"Existential crisis."

"Ah." Catherine paused. "Wait, what?"

"Karao's taking care of it, I think." Nika closed the book.

The two went about their normal business, tending to a mostly empty shop for the rest of the morning. Nils eventually walked out dressed a bit too casually for work. Karao had given them the rest of the day off as thanks for all that they'd done. So, with a cheerful goodbye, Nils gleefully left to go and enjoy an afternoon alone.

Karao joined them in the front room shortly after. She looked exhausted, but that had been the norm for the past few days. She was trying not to let things get to her, but the combination of her house arrest and her perceived failing had dug her into dismal fun. Still, she refused to let it get in her way. She dropped the book of necromancy on the counter before Nika. The noise startled Donut, who was curled around a bit of the cash register. He went back to sleep like nothing had happened.

She sighed. "Good news, bad news."

"The bad news?" Nika asked.

"I'm no closer to explaining your, hm, particular let's say, brand of magic than when I picked up this stupid thing." She seemed ready to go into an entire tirade dedicated to the poor layout of the book. She thankfully restrained herself. "There's maybe a paragraph in here dedicated to 'bizarre and long-standing effects that warrant further research. That's what I got the book for you, ugh. Nevermind."

Nika wasn't disappointed or surprised. He really didn't expect much of anything from it. He wasn't in a hurry to understand his magic.

"But! I did find a way to get that deadarm off of you! So, that's something."

He hadn't even thought of it in awhile. Every day he had spent with it, he had grown more used to it being there. It was annoying that he had to sleep on his stomach, but that was pretty much the only thing that bothered him now.

"Oh, um." He was excited by the news, really he was. But the deadarm had worked for him again, begrudgingly, and he was hoping to get more time getting it to listen to him again. As if the arm could hear his thoughts, it flicked his ankle. "Ah! Yeah, let's do it."

The process probably looked painful to other people. Getting a deadarm connected to your spine by magic forcibly pulled. Simultaneously, very specific incantations severed its ties to you one invisible string at a time sounded like torture. Nika couldn't stop laughing; it tickled him a lot. His howling from the kitchen definitely frightened a customer or two and confused a few people walking by.

It had been a while since Nika had seen the full arm. Still, looking at it wiggling in Kara's hand, he realized how comically large it must have seen on his still relatively short body. Great, just what he needed.

He felt a bit cold, like something was missing now. Karao told him that was normal and pretty much exactly what the book described. He'd be like that for a few hours, and then everything should go back to normal.

"For now, we're going to forgo the deadarm training," she explained while wrapping the still squirming skeleton arm in a cloth. "Disconnecting should be as effortless and hooking up.

But, until we know more, I think it's a good idea that you stay away from this kind of necromancy. Or..."

Nika waited for her to finish the thought. "Or?"

"Or any at all, really."

Nikas's throat was now the coldest. "What?"

"I don't know, Nika. It's getting dangerous to be a necromancer around here. The investigations are going, well, poorly. I can't protect you three from inside this house, and there's no sign of things changing soon."

"What am I supposed to do?" he asked. He felt himself getting angry and tried to stifle it. His cracking voice gave it away.

"Study for the test, help Nils with the relaunch, hang out with Morgan." She smiled for the first time in days. "You have a lot of options right now, Nika. We can take a break from this stuff for a while." The fact that he wasn't fine with this was apparently obvious from his face. "At least until I have this figured out, ok?"

Nika considered it for a minute. "Ok, but in return, I get a favor."

Karao laughed. "You're devious. Alright, you got it."

Catherine popped in. "Karao, someone's here for you."

"Be right there. Come on, Catherine could use the help up front." She led him into the front room, where a vaguely familiar face was eyeing a teacup suspiciously. He was crouched by the window-side table, squinting as though that cup was somehow threatening everybody in the room.

He was definitely not dressed for the warm July weather. He wore a long-sleeved, brown sweater with a thick collar, polished shoes, and pants that could not be comfortable to crouch in. Nika hadn't seen him around for a while, ever since his date with Nils. It was Daniel, the regular who had been gone for a few weeks after their date had ended poorly.

"Nils's friend, right?" Karao said, unaware or apathetic of what had happened in June. He had seen her around enough to not be put off by the deadarms, or at least to grin and bear it.

"Yup!" He was as cheerful as ever. "Nils said you guys needed help."

Nika started cleaning after a table that had left, but he didn't have much better to do than listen in on the conversation.

"I appreciate it. A lot, actually. They mentioned you worked at a newspaper. Are you a journalist?"

"Photographer!" He grinned. "Well, for the summer anyway. My uncle owns the place and needed a hand. Is Nils here?"

"No, sorry. They're out of the day." Karao bent her knuckled back until she heard a satisfying cracking sound. "What can we do to help?"

"Nils asked me to take pictures of stuff from the menu to frame-up."

Karao led Nika and Daniel into the kitchen and began to mix tea for him. Nika was tasked with finding the nicest cup available. It wasn't hard, they were all resting on the drying rack, and only a few looked even remotely fancy. He went with a faux-stone mug with a copper handle.

Nika turned back to see Daniel sprinkling tea leaves onto a cutting board full of random trinkets and foods from around the kitchen. He was squinting at this pile of stuff he had accumulated; he would adjust something, take a step back, hold his hands out in front of him for some bizarre reason, and repeat. He seemed completely oblivious to anything happening around him.

Karao, on her third attempt to get Nika's attention, poked his face. "Mug, please."

"What are you doing, exactly?" Nika asked.

"I'm framing the shot. People like pictures of fresh ingredients, so I'm just trying to make it look nice." He opened his bag and placed a portfolio of blank sheets of paper and a small glass jar filled with blue gel onto the counter behind him. He dipped his finger into the jar and used the gel to paint a circle on the palm of his other hand. He tapped the center of the circle. His palm became a focused light source that he began swiveling around the cutting board.

After finding the angle he wanted and the lighting to match, he grabbed a piece of paper from the portfolio and placed it neatly on the table. He kept one hand on that paper, the light source hovering where he wanted it, and took a breath.

His eyes went white. Next to the glowing palm, the light emanating from them didn't seem like much, but any amount of glowing in the eyes was still weird. A humming sound was a clicking that synced up to a pronounced blink, and his eyes were back to normal. He tapped the circle in his palm again, and the light turned off.

"Check it out!" he said, swiveling the paper around to Nika.

The page was slowly filling itself out in his hand. A perfect copy of the image he saw in fine detail. He could see the creases in the leaves more clearly on the paper than directly in front of him.

"Woah."

Daniel took pictures of lots of things with the same meticulous method. Finished tea, furniture in specific lighting, Donut curled around the handle of a teapot. He ended up staying through the middle of the afternoon. After an hour or two, they had pretty much started ignoring him as he insisted on focusing on his job. The only time they really noticed him was when a tower of cutlery he had been stacking toppled repeatedly with increasingly agonized sighs.

Nils's return was awkward. Not overtly so, but the two weren't able to make much eye contact with one another. They both tried hard to keep the conversation centered on work, but neither wanted to end the tangents. Catherine couldn't stand the silent pauses between one answer and the next forced question and left the room.

"So." Nils was stretching for a topic. "Did you take all those?" They were pointing at the pile of photos and empty jars of photo-gel scattered haphazardly on a table.

"No, well, yeah, well, those are the rejects. The good ones are hanging to dry in the back."

"Oh." They kicked the back of their foot. "Thanks so much for helping out. It helps a lot. A lot, a lot."

"Don't mention it. We have some scrap paper stock I can mess with to blow up the pictures. Do you have frames?"

"I managed to dig some up."

Somewhere, Karao's teeth gritted. Her collection of older, ugly paintings in the basement had been unframed in the name of renovation. Nils had never liked them and was really happy to be moving the tea shop away from those abominations. Nika agreed with Nils.

"I should be heading back soon anyways." Daniel paused at the stack.

Nils helped him grab his stuff from the kitchen. Nika was not prepared for the spectacle that followed. Daniel's arms were gripped by dozens of coat hooks. A single photo dangled from each one from a small wooden clamp. Each step he took added to the accruing stress on his face. He kept his arms spread wide, his feet scraping along the floor as he dared not lift afoot.

"How exactly are you-" Catherine asked, without a chance to finish.

"It's fine, I'll be fine." He slipped and nearly dropped one of the fruits of his labor. "Yup. Definitely fine."

Nika swept the rest of Daniel's supplies into his shoulder bag. There was no way the photographer-in-training would be able to carry this with the rest he had to pointedly not juggle.

"Hey, how far is it?" Nika asked

Daniel was surprised. "How far is what?"

"The newspaper, er, place." He didn't know where they were written. Probably some kind of studio, although perhaps a grand hall filled with resources and magical technology. He was interested in seeing it first hand, whatever it was.

"The office?" Daniel gestured with his neck. "Bout two, two and a half miles that way."

It was disappointing, but taking back the offer would have been awkward. "Want me to carry some of those?"

With the photos more evenly distributed and Daniel carrying his own bag again, the two-headed out. Observers that peaceful evening would have seen a shorter boy growing increasingly frustrated as a taller one repeatedly thanked him for his help. Nika had never really explored south of the tea shop before. It was mostly more of the same.

"So, why'd you want to come with me?" Daniel eventually asked.

Nika was still coasting on autopilot. "Uh-huh."

"Sorry?"

"Huh? Oh, sorry. Um, what was the question?"

Daniel pretended that he wasn't slightly hurt by that. It must not have been new. "Oh, just wondering what made you want to help out?"

Nika shrugged. "It just looked like a lot to carry." He nearly tripped over a loose brick. "Besides, photo-magic looks fun. I wanted to see a bit more of it."

The walk was only another ten minutes, but Daniel's endless pitch for photo magic made it seem to go on longer. He wasn't boring or uninteresting, just repetitive. Every third sentence was him recapping what he had just said, followed by a quick 'are you following or something similar. Still, the basics of photo magic had been drilled into his head when they arrived at the news office.

The magical component is the gel, not the eye. After it's applied to the skin, there's a timer, and the image is based on the person's perspective and focus. There was other stuff, but by then, Nika's interest had wavered a bit.

"This is it!"

"Uh-huh- er, huh." Nika tried to recover. "I meant huh."

The building was weirder than he had imagined. It was three to four stories, but there were only windows on the top one. The most eye-catching detail was the lack of a door. The wood walls and stone corners seemed smooth and well kept.

A pair of long tables reached out into the road from the base of the building. Paper was streaming from two slots above them, curling and folding over itself into neat piles before being cut and pushed towards the end as a finished newspaper. Despite its minuscule size, a blackbird swooped and lifted a tied-up paper into the air for delivery. Well, presumably, it was for delivery.

"How do we get in, exactly?"

"I'm thinking." Daniel was trying to recall something. "It changes every day, oh! Today is 'press the stops!'" With a single blink of smokey light, Daniel was gone. Without having a better plan and not wanting to hold his arms out much longer, Nika tried saying the same phrase. The words had barely parted his lips when he felt the familiar tug of teleportation magic pulling him. He braced himself for the journey. It was never nice to him.

This time was no different. He had a single second to decide if he'd rather unleash the contents of his stomach on a mid-distance potted plant or a fairly overrun desk directly in front of him. He had chosen the plant, though he didn't end up needing it. His insides calmed themselves quickly and let him properly take in the room around him.

The office was a series of haphazardly laid-out desks, each buried under their own personalized mountains of notes, photos, and paperwork. The day must have been over, given the lack of people in all these uniform chairs.

"Oh good! You figured it out. I realized I forgot to-you know what, nevermind," Daniel said.

"Which desk is yours?" Nika stood on his toes, looking for any sign of a desk that would belong to either a newcomer or a student.

He laughed. "You think they'd give me one of those?" Daniel led them to the back corner. There was a coat rack, and a shelf blocked off by a thin wall from the main room's view. He hung the photos on the coat rack, then pulled a box out from underneath some cleaning supplies. He threw his bag into it. "Go ahead and hang those up wherever."

"This seems like a fun place to work." Nika was mostly serious.

"I wanted to ask you. Has Nils-" Daniel never got to finish his question.

They heard someone from the other end of the building. "Hello?"

Daniel looked confused. "Hi?" The two peeked out from the divider wall. Standing among the desks was a cautious-looking woman. The symmetry of her lightly colored hair was the first thing Nika noticed. The bizarre way it was fashioned, curving around her face neatly down to her chin, sort of demanded attention. She wore an impeccable brown jacket that seemed way too warm for July. Even beneath the thick sunglasses, she looked ready to leap out one of the windows if the place was being robbed.

"Oh, it's you." She righted herself. Her tone had completely reversed.

"Hey, Beth, Sorry about that." Daniel had also relaxed. The two seemed back in their default settings like they were repeating the same lines day in and day out. They did not like one another. "Just bringing stuff back to work on."

"First off, don't call me Beth. Second, I hope you're done with your actual work. Third, no guests. Whoever you are, out."

"He was just helping me carry stuff in. We were about to leave," Daniel said.

"Sorry," Nika added. He had only just realized he didn't know how to leave.

"Wait." Beth, a name he would not be saying aloud lest he be yelled at, walked up to him. She lowered her shades and squinted in his face. His reflection curved strangely in the downturned glass. "You're a necromancer." Her lips curled a bit.

Whoever had told Nika that necromancy was a secret had lied. "I, what? I'm just, um."

"A bad liar." She pulled a notebook out of her jacket. "I have questions about the recent string of attacks. What, specifically, does a necromancer gain when they steal a dead corpse? I assume they are adding a soldier to their army. What other benefits could they reap from that? Why would one target the graves of workers and artists instead of soldiers if they were making armies?"

"Beth!" Daniel snapped before Nika could even process the barrage of questions properly. "I thought you were on a different beat."

"Listen, squirt," she said. The nickname clearly bothered Daniel. "I am more than able to go after multiple stories at once. And I am very interested in this one." She reached her hand out to Nika. "I apologize. I am covering the recent string of necromancy attacks. You don't meet such a small necromancer every day. I would love to ask you some questions if you don't mind."

Nika wasn't sure if he should say he knew people who were investigating this same crime. For now, she didn't need to know that. He accepted the handshake. She slid a slip of paper into his hand. Maybe it was because of Bringer, but he couldn't bring himself to just trust this stranger. He wanted to ask about the slip, but his lips wouldn't move. His throat strained to ask what the blank card was, but no noise was made.

"How did you know?" Nika asked. It wasn't the most pressing issue, but it was one his body physically let him ask.

"Trade secret," she replied.

"She won't tell me, either," Daniel said. "Come on, I'll show you the exit."

"Until next time, friend of Daniel's." She waved.

Chapter 15- End

Intermission: Life In The Dorm

All Nika knew was that Catherine had gotten sick. She had missed a couple days of work now, though she had always tried to show up anyways. Karao wouldn't have that and sent her home with soup or something like that. Today she hadn't even bothered coming in, so it probably wasn't getting much better on its own. He had been sent out with some kind of nasty medical potion and a test item from the new menu to see how Catherine was doing.

She had moved into a dorm connected to the school not too long ago. It was a far cry from the independent apartment lifestyle Catherine had wanted. Still, there was only so much any of them could do with the state of the tea shop. The building, named Hearthstead by the engraved stone archway over the front door, was just one thin hallway. It didn't seem like it would be comfortable for anyone to live there. Still, Nika had stopped questioning the addresses people gave him.

"Who are you here to see?" A droning voice asked. It didn't seem like anyone was actually behind the door; the door itself speaking to him.

"Catherine -" he had either forgotten or had never learned Catherine's last name. He would have to fix that today, "-uh, who lives in 412."

Things fell silent, then the door began rattling. The shaking intensified, Nika took a step back. It ended with an abrupt stop and a bell chime.

"Come in." A familiar but broken voice called out to him from beyond the door. Nika entered.

Similar to the stairs in the tea shop, this door shifted depending on where it wanted to send you. There was no hallway, just Catherine's small dorm room. The door snapped shut behind him and locked. Catherine's room was mostly barren save for some boxes of clothes, a mattress on the floor, and a chair she had taken from Karao. Catherine had a plank of wood propped up on two slightly uneven boxes serving as a table. She was sitting, wrapped so completely in blankets that Nika had mistaken her for a pile of laundry at first. She was holding a paintbrush that, judging by the dry spot on the paper, hadn't moved in a good amount of time.

"Hi, Nika." She smiled. "Welcome to this grand estate."

It was a small space, but there was a tidy kitchen, a bathroom, and closets. Nika didn't know that she painted, but she had put some of her work around the room. It fit well.

"I like it," he said. She snatched the medicine from his hands, grinning.

Chapter 16. Powerful Soul Baring

Morgan had three fewer hands than Karao, yet her multitask ability was somehow even more impressive. She and Nika were in her usual hangout in the library, Nika on the ground with notebook and pen at the ready and surrounded by source material. Morgan, for her part, was hanging upside down again. Her spiderweb-bound feet held her in place on the top of the bookshelf, her body hung over the edge in the same aisle as Nika. She was, at that moment, quizzing Nika on material from her past tests, doing crunches, and maintaining control of her summoned bugs.

Sure, she was managing three crunches every few minutes, but Nika wasn't going to get on her case for that.

"Who won the battle of Lorregar?" she asked, staring at the aced history test her spider was holding in front of her.

"Queen Macius," Nika said, recalling one of the most bizarre paragraphs buried in a very boring "History of Eldes and You" packet she had given him.

"How?" she asked.

"Something about, no, she ended up drowning the enemy army by dropping them in the ocean."

"Close enough," she said. "What's the difference between Cryomancy and Frostblood magic?"

"Cryomancy is incantations and hand gestures. Frostblood is a hereditary thing." Nika didn't mention that he was staring directly at that page of the notes, but he probably didn't need to for that one.

"What sort of government does Eldes have?" The intent in her eye wasn't new. She was looking for a specific, pedantic answer.

"Eldes is just a region in Heirute, which is a constitutional monarchy. There's a congress and a king currently. The capital is Hadius, the king's name is Gregory, the congress consists of-"

"Bored. Yeah, you got it."

Nika smiled. He hadn't gone through one of these spontaneous quizzes without missing at least a few questions before.

"Last question." Her crooked smile suggested it was going to be an evil one. Nika braced himself. Before she could ask, the two heard the distinctive clack of a stone paw on the nearby tile floor. Morgan jolted back up onto the top of the shelf. She had either dismissed the spider and its silk to break free, or she had broken both of her legs to hide more efficiently. Either way, the approaching librarian would not see her.

Gladys rounded the corner. Well, one of Gladys's many stone bodies did. According to Morgan, she was able to patrol any number of hallways at once with the statue copies of her body. According to Morgan, using this ability to become the ultimate librarian was also a gigantic waste of potential. She was an army of Sphinx statues with a single shared consciousness. It was 'way too cool to work there.'

"There you are," Gladys said. She seemed perplexed. "We have open tables downstairs, you know."

She was clearly talking to Nika. "Yeah," he said, "I know. I'm comfy here though." It was the best lie he could come up with on short notice. Morgan had perfected staying silent. Somehow, Nika could hear her silently slapping her forehead.

"Ok then." The sphinx unfurled her wings upright in the small aisle. The statue shook the feathers a bit, causing a slip of paper to fall from between two of them. It landed on Nika's lap.

"I need you to bring that to Karao. She has overdue books and must pay the fee."

It was the most menacing threat Nika had ever heard. "I'll give it to her."

"Thank you." The sphinx eyed the shelves for a moment, then backed into the hallway and left.

Morgan was very cautious coming back down, but she eventually made it.

Nika switched books. "I'm amazed you haven't gotten caught yet."

"I will be if that's the best you got." She pulled out her field book of summoning circles and started flipping through pages next to him.

"Mean."

"And fair," she said.

"And fair," he said.

"So. Question."

"No," Nika said with confidence.

Morgan protested, "You don't even know what I was going to ask."

"Something about your doubles tryouts, right?"

"How did you guess?" she said.

"You kidding? I'm surprised you didn't ask me back when they announced it." Nika stopped himself from adding, 'who else were you going to ask?'. Morgan never mentioned any friends besides the two other Duelist Appreciation Club members, and neither of them seemed able or willing to team up with her. Nika just wasn't sure yet if he was interested in the sport as a whole.

"I didn't want to ask while you were worrying about the test." She seemed annoyed.

"You say that like I'm done worrying about the test," he said.

She glared. "Five-hundred-twelve divided by eight and a half."

Almost by instinct, he began scratching out the problem on paper. A few moments later, he had a question. "How many decimals?"

"Two."

"Sixty-four point two-four," he answered. "Is that right?"

"Probably, I don't know, but you're already better than most of the people in my class." She leaned in and checked. Nika was right.

"I feel like I don't actually remember much of this stuff."

"Well, you'll probably forget a bunch of this after." She shrugged. "That's just how cramming works. I'm not a teacher; just trying to help you get into the school."

"Thanks." Nika closed the book up. He thought he should reconsider the offer Morgan was about to ask. He had enjoyed everything up until that point. One issue was still pretty glaring. "What would I even do in the ring?"

Morgan was confused. "Necromancy. What do you mean?"

He wasn't sure how many corpses were in a regulation stadium. "How does that help?"

"Oh. Huh. You know, I didn't think about that," Morgan said. "I don't know much about it at all. I figured you had something up your sleeve. What about that skeleton hand?"

It had been a few days since Karao had taken the deadarm from his back. It still felt a little weird, like a piece of him, had dissolved into the air. She was almost ready to have him try it again, wanting him to practice attaching and detaching it on his own.

Nika shook his head. "Not an option. Besides, it never really listened to me anyway."

She thought for a moment. "We could find out."

"What do you mean?" Nika asked. Morgan stood and started climbing the bookshelf again.

"I think we've earned a break." She gestured for him to climb up too. He sighed and followed.

Morgan had brought the replay box to the library. It was perfectly squared between the two shelf tops that made up her hideaway. She handed him a blank card to put into the slot.

"What's this?" he asked. She didn't answer, sliding her own blank card in. Nika did the same, and the two were transported into the replay machine once again. It was just as psychedelic a transition as it was the first time. Nika really didn't like any form of magical movement. He was learning.

The stadium was physically the same, as always, but barren. The empty rows of expensive seats were a bit unsettling. Instead of the usual front row seats, they were square in the middle of the dueling ring. It was a completely different view. The seats seemed to go up and up forever, up to the glaring lights at the top of the arena. The bleachers' height made him feel as though he was staring up from the center of the earth, past the darkness in the tunnels and into the lights above.

"Woah." Nika hadn't meant to say that aloud, but he did. Morgan looked smug.

She smiled, closed her eyes, and punched him in the stomach as hard as she could manage.

The range of Nika's reactions began from shock and fear to pleasant confusion when nothing hurt. In fact, he couldn't even tell that she had done that. Morgan had mentioned that the ring is usually protected by some barrier that prevents people from actually being hurt. Getting sucker punched was uncomfortable, but that was the end of it.

Morgan was sure her message had gotten across. "It was faster than explaining." She stepped back to the other side of the ring. Her shoulders dropped a bit, her hand cradling her field guide. She was looking for a fight.

"What are you doing?" It wasn't Nika's most astute question, but it worked.

"Give it a shot. If you like dueling, great! If not, no worries." She paused. "What do you say?"

He wanted to. It sounded like it could be fun. Being in a club or team with Morgan sounded like a seamless way to make friends at a new school, to stop living alone. Everything he had seen looked thrilling and enjoyable. It was normal; he could be normal. It was a free invitation into everything he had come to Eldes to have, really.

"I can't," he said.

Nika couldn't stop thinking about Bringer. He felt so weak and powerless in the face of that monster. All he could do was quiver. His legs and voice failed him. If it hadn't been for a misbehaving deadarm and the Farvues, he would be dead. He had run away from conflict in his hometown when it threatened his life, and now he was about to do it again.

"Because of last week?" Morgan asked.

He telegraphed surprise too easily, and Morgan picked up on it.

"My dad told me." She walked back up to him and placed a hand on his shoulder. He hadn't been shaking before, but he still felt that small act was steadying him. "He told me how awesome my mom was, and you, too."

"Awesome?" he chuckled a bit. That was absurd.

"His word, not mine. He said that you didn't run, you didn't even look away—that guy who," she struggled. "Well, he wouldn't tell me no matter how much I asked. All he said was that it was terrifying. If Mom starts worrying, then it's a real problem, and she was scared."

"How-" Nika didn't know what to say, just that he wanted to say something.

"She always has ice cream after getting scared," Morgan laughed. "Dad had to run out and grab some before she could properly freak out. Still, They both thought you were braver than they were at our age."

Nika needed to correct her. "I was so scared I couldn't move."

"You can be scared and brave at the same time," Morgan said. "Can I tell you a secret?"

"Is anything not a secret with you?"

"I'm full of 'em." She stepped back and turned away. "I'm scared of heights."

"You. You're scared of heights."

"Mmhmm."

"The girl who willingly lets moths carry her around in the sky, who hides near the top of a towering library on a fifteen-foot bookshelf." He paused. "That girl is afraid of heights."

"Yup. Terrified," she said.

"Then why- no. Yeah. Why? Why?"

"One: I don't want to be afraid forever, and two: flying is just too cool!" She had been trying to take his feelings seriously by being calm and helpful. She wasn't able to keep a lid on that for long. Morgan coughed. "Um, right. I was kind of surprised, honestly. I thought you would've run."

The growing good feeling in him extinguished in an instant. "You're too kind."

"No- wait- I would've too. Who wouldn't?" she said.

It was a weird compliment, and it took a while to get there, but Nika was grateful nonetheless. "Is that why you want to team up?"

"Yes and no. I was thinking about it, but I couldn't think of a theme we could go with."

"We need a theme?"

"Technically no, but - nevermind." She was about to go another tangent about the importance of aesthetics in dueling. "But, hearing that did sell me on the idea." She was never subtle, but that was endearing in a way. Morgan was, somehow, the strangest person he had met since moving to Eldes. He wasn't upset about that.

Nobody had ever regretted a risky decision before. "I'll give it a shot."

Morgan bounced back to her place on the other side of the ring. "I was hoping to hear that."

He wasn't sure what he was going to do, but he might as well try something new. Catherine had somehow managed to burn off excess magic into some kind of blunt projectile for hitting things. He could probably do something similar on a smaller scale. Granted, he had never tried to do anything like it before, but just cutting loose looked like it didn't take too much thought.

"What are the exact rules, again?" he asked.

"For now, just try to knock them out of the ring." Morgan was flipping through pages. Nika looked around. The ring was a lot bigger than it seemed from the seats. He doubted he could throw anything more than a few pounds that far, let alone whatever 'knock' meant.

More importantly, he had focused on a keyword. "Them?"

She pulled a loose piece of paper that had been wedged in the book out. It was covered in scratched-out summoning circles. She put her hand over it and conjured. Nika was expecting some new, horrifying bug that was never meant to be the size she was making it. He was wrong.

A scarecrow, complete with straw-stuffed sleeves and a ragged hat, formed between the two of them. The smile carved into its pumpkin head looked both genuine and unsettling.

"What's that?" Nika asked, wary of approaching the hunched monstrosity.

"A training dummy," Morgan said, proud of her handiwork. This had clearly taken her a lot of effort to put together. "I copied the circle from a fairy tale book and made... adjustments."

"Adjustments?" He was more concerned than before.

"The face was creepy, so I fixed it. So! Try and punch it."

With cautious footsteps, he approached. It swayed without rhythm. It was possessed by something, but nothing about it seemed malicious. The pole running down the back of its shirt kept it in place.

Nika drew a breath, pulled back, and replicated Morgan's gut-punch on the dummy. Its arms flailed as it spun and whacked him onto the ground. Morgan stifled a snicker, the dummy pulled itself back up to its original position. Nika stood up, truly wanting to knock this thing over now.

Morgan couldn't hold back her roaring laugh at the second failed attempt. This one had sent him spinning back before tripping over his own feet.

The scarecrow wasn't just going to take hits lying down—a very annoying trait for a training dummy. Morgan was yelling some sort of advice or encouragement. He wasn't really listening. He did, however, focus on the pumpkin head of this stationary foe. The inside was straw, too, for that matter.

It readied itself as he stood up again. Ready to take some meager damage and dish it all back out at him. He charged again. It swayed as he prepared a punch. He pulled back his fist and instead slapped the pumpkin head with his left hand, filled with crackling, purple necromancy. He kept it in place on the pumpkin rather than let the slap carry through. It made a satisfying, hollow 'thunk' sound. With his other hand, he reached down the baggy shirt to bring some of the hay back to life, at least in some way.

Nika stepped back, waiting to see what happened next. The answer: very little. Mostly, the thing toppled over. Whatever enchantment was keeping it sentient didn't seem to work on a now living vegetable. The dummy slowly faded, dissipating as Morgan dismissed it.

"That was," Morgan said, unable to finish the thought.

"Pretty pointless, huh," Nika said. "Who's gonna bring food into the ring?"

"The Baker, but she hasn't dueled for years." Morgan had snapped off that name with no explanation, not that Nika was looking for one.

Ok, maybe he did want to know what a food-based duelist would do.

"It looks like electricity to me. Have you tried just shocking someone with it?"

"That sounds like a terrible idea," Nika said. She didn't blink. "No, I haven't."

Morgan flipped to another page. She was summoning some other magical object for him to beat up. It was the spider. It was still much, much too tall, even though a good portion of that was just its hairy, disgusting legs. As ugly as it was, it wasn't threatening him, and he had sort of gotten used to having it around. That didn't mean he wanted to look directly at it, but he didn't see a reason to start kicking it either.

Nika shuffled a bit. "I don't know how I feel about this."

"You coward." So much for her pep talk.

"No, not that. Well, a little that. It's just standing there. It would be like kicking a pet."

"Hm, well, one: summons aren't alive and don't feel pain even outside of the ring. And two: would it help if it was self-defense?" She looked devilish.

"Self-defense?" The cold portent shocked his spine. "You wouldn't."

She would. She did. With a dramatic wrist twirl, the spider accepted her command to take the offensive. Ugly was bad enough, ugly and skittering was too much.

Nika had felt some comfort in knowing how to hurt something shaped like a person. He didn't need a plan of attack since the head was usually a safe bet. He didn't realize how nice that familiarity was until he was being chased around the dueling ring by a relentless eight-legged hunter. He didn't even know where to begin if he wanted to hurt the thing. Strangely, even though it was faster than him, he managed to keep ahead of it.

Morgan was, again, yelling useless advice. It was probably all very practical, but unheard advice is the biggest waste of air. He was too busy trying to figure out how he would even react to that thing up close.

He nearly tripped. The ring was flat; Nika didn't know what possibly could have snared his foot, what was keeping it from moving still, why he was stuck. He checked around the ring. The spider had been spinning its thread onto the ground the entire time it had been chasing him.

Nika wasn't arachnophobic before. He considered taking up the fear.

With fumbling fingers, he pried his foot from a now-abandoned shoe. No version of any plan he had ended well. Try and punch the head? Get bit. Kick? Get grabbed. Headbutt? Die, hopefully. Rule number one, if he pursued dueling: be able to attack from a distance.

If he couldn't fight the spider, he did have one last option open to him. His eyes trained to the ground, he hopped and skipped between silky threads in a bull rush towards Morgan. If he could knock her out of the ring, maybe that would be enough.

"Wait, what are you-" She didn't finish the question, though she stepped up to the challenge with eager eyes. "Ok then!" Her hand rested on a page that seemed familiar to him. It was the moth, Luna. "Bring it!"

Nika had no quips, so he was glad she was talkative enough for the both of them. She had already done him the favor of standing only a few feet from the edge. He just needed one good shove.

Catherine had always thrown around necromancy like it was nothing. Karao had said she was taking delicate, intricate magic and smashing someone over the head with it like it was a bottle. Karao would be annoyed, Catherine delighted, and Nils moderating between the two. He focused every bit of magic he could muster, which wasn't much, into his hand.

Summoning was not instantaneous. The creatures manifest in a matter of seconds, but seconds in the ring are a precious currency. The detail Nika had always been unclear on was a period as it formed, where it seemed translucent and ethereal. At that moment, the wings of the moth were exactly that. They were wrapped around her the way they had during her tryout, cocooning her in a protective barrier that he really, really did not want to deal with.

He had at least some semblance of an answer as he passed directly through the shimmering green wings with a trajectory to hit Morgan right in the face. She had raised her arms quick enough to not get slapped in the forehead but still took the full brunt of the hit. He was aiming for the wings and hadn't intended on hitting her. Nika felt all the energy had intended to shock the moth with his hand.

The moth knocked him back. The wings that were taller than either of them hit him like a door. That wasn't the issue. Nika's head felt fuzzy. He felt like he was going to topple over at any moment. He heard ringing, his sight weakened. Even his hand felt blurry. The toppling hour arrived.

"Nika! Nika, are you ok?" Morgan said. It sounded like she was talking from inside a fishbowl right next to his head.

Nika looked up. He was already worried about his health, and using his eyes wasn't helping.

Morgan had explained numerous times that keeping summons active took a lot of magic. Her limit was Luna and one smaller one. Even then, that was usually so draining that she liked spreading her summons out throughout a duel.

Seeing six full-sized Lunas fluttering in the air around the ring confirmed it. Nika had lost it. That, and the faint glow Morgan was sporting herself. He felt that he should be more concerned and care more about what he was seeing, but he was too tired to manage.

"Yeah, I'm fine." He passed out.

Chapter 16- End

Intermission: The Weirdest Place To Wake Up

Karao, by all rights, should not have been able to sit comfortably on top of a library bookshelf. The ceilings of each level were so ludicrously tall that even with her dizzying height, she had plenty of room. How she got up, there was a mystery Nika was not going to pursue. He was still piecing together why he was waking up in the library with Morgan and Catherine. They were still hiding from the librarian.

"I hope you had a nice nap," Catherine said. She was relieved.

"What time is it?" he asked.

"Evening. The library's closing soon. Do you think you can walk?"

"Yeah." His answer was a reflex. He recalled the wooziness he felt earlier thanks to Morgan and her spider. He twitched his legs. They seemed to be responding well. "Yeah, I'll be fine."

Morgan apologized about a hundred times on their way down. Gladys glared at them as they left in a group. She had lost track of Nika for an entire day and had no idea where he could have gone, just that he had left a mess of books for her to clean. Nika tried not to look suspicious. The three parted ways outside. The moving streetlights kept Morgan company on her way up the street.

"So. Morgan said something interesting," Catherine said.

"Interesting good? Interesting bad?" Nika felt a sharp pain in his shoulder. He must have hit it after the fight. "Interesting weird?"

"All three!" she said. "You tried using necromancy on her?"

"No! I mean, yes, not on her, but I did hit her, and-" He gave up. "I'm sorry."

"Do you know what happened after?"

He couldn't recall much after getting hit by a giant green bug wing. "No."

"Wait, you have no idea? Hm." She seemed annoyed. "You have the absolute worst timing, by the way. Karao and I were just talking about you-er- not you, but your- ah, forget it. Tomorrow'll be fun, that's all."

Chapter 17. Confessions of a
Sun-Dried Necromancer

On their way to meet up with Cruise, some random person walking down the road intentionally ran into Nils for some unknown reason. Nika had been ahead of the other two and didn't see it happen, but Catherine looked ready to explode. If she had been taller, she would have lifted the woman up by the collar of her expensive sweater and stuck her up on the streetlight.

The stranger had whispered her insidious thoughts through a self-satisfied grin. Something about how she was sorry that she had bumped into 'your property and that it was 'gross to be walking around with that.'

Nils physically held Catherine back, begging her to just let it go. Nika told the woman that she had a tear in her sweater just below the forearm. She went into a panic, looking for it as the three necromancers went about their day in a much fouler mood than before. They'd told Nika about this sort of thing before, and even then, he wasn't ready for how awkward and awful it was to witness in person. It was pretty common when Nils left the house.

Cruise, impatient, and formal as always, asked them what was bothering them so much. Clearly, they were still trying to get over it. Nobody gave him a straight answer.

"It doesn't matter. Let's go," Cruise said. He noted that Nika was carrying the deadarms bundled up in a cloth slung over his shoulder. "Be careful with those. They're already questionably legal." He turned heel and set a quick pace into the scrambling portal station. The three of them struggled to keep up without breaking into a jog.

"Where are we going?" Nils asked, doing their best to swerve around people carrying towering boxes. Karao had been predictably silent when it came to the details of this little day trip. All that the three of them knew was that she had cashed in a few favors to get Cruise to take them out for some kind of lesson for the afternoon while she looked after the tea shop. Not that Karao had much of a choice, but if the four remaining regulars showed up, someone would have to serve them.

"Adruin. Hurry up, Catherine." He hadn't even looked back at them, yet he knew she had gotten caught up behind a line of kids traveling in a pack.

"What, the desert?" Nils said.

"Unless you know another one," he opened a door marked 'authorized personnel' and gestured for them to walk through, "then yes, the desert."

Nils had spent a non-insignificant amount of time complaining about the heat as they approached the middle of July. Their gray face grew pale; they were going to hate this.

The portal station's restricted access area was more or less the same as the other side, albeit less crowded. Nika was actually a bit disappointed it wasn't some fantastical secret lair. Some doors were better left unopened, at least for the mystery's sake.

Cruise showed the portal mage at one of the counters his credentials and explained that he was taking the three of them as guests. Nika wasn't really listening. He was bracing for yet another instance of teleporting. He skipped lunch just to avoid throwing it up on the other side of this portal. Without much further delay, the four were propelled into some desert unknown to Nika in a completely separate part of the world.

To add to the nausea, the transition from temperature-controlled portal room to frigid darkness to oppressive desert heat was making his head hurt. He could barely see, but seeing wasn't really the issue at the moment. He clutched his stomach.

The pain went away. He actually felt pretty good all over. Come to think of it, he didn't even feel that hot. With a moment to take in his surroundings, he saw that they had landed under some kind of tent on the top of a sand dune.

"Easy there!" another voice said. Nika turned to see Morgan's dad, Ben, tapping at the illusionary glyphs surrounding his wrist. He had apparently finished using his enhancing magic on Nika, which explained why he was comfortable in the sweltering heat. "Do you get sick every time? I have a pill for that if you want one."

"Thank you for coming on your day off." Cruise cracked open his canteen.

Ben moved on to Nils, who looked like they were melting. "My day off is just pushed back, not canceled. You've only been here thirty seconds. How are you sweating that much?"

Cruise stretched. "Nika, you brought the deadarms, right?"

He nodded and untied the knot on the poorly thrown-together parcel. They would be nearly identical to most, but each of the three could identify their own. Nils had practiced using their cryogenic magic on glasses of water to mixed results. Catherine had been banned from ever having hers attached indoors after one unfortunate accident involving a small typhoon in the backyard that took an entire day to fix. Nika could count on the deadarm's fingers how many times he got it to do what he wanted.

The other two hooked their arms up to their backs. It was almost second nature to them by this point, like putting on a jacket. It was the only thing that both of them were equally good at. Nika stared at the top of his deadarm, anxiety filling his lungs. That, or sand. Either way, he coughed a lot. The last time he had put the thing on, it had gotten stuck for weeks. He didn't really feel like reliving that.

Those thoughts went on the backburner as he really took in his surroundings. Their tent was set up on four poles on the top of the tallest dune for miles, it seemed. The desert sand had painted a beautiful abstract portrait below them, swirling and settling chaotic patterns that rose and fell in the dunes below. None of that was the focus of his attention, though. That was all set, dressing to the main feature in front of them.

Nika learned that they were actually on top of the second tallest hill from the southern side of the tent. The largest seemed unnatural. Where the others rose and collapsed with consistent curves, this largest hill seemed lopsided, curved to one side. It was abrupt, steep. Thinking about it only bore one practical answer: there was something underneath it. At the base of this huge hill, four smaller pegs stood out, each covered in sand. Miniscule pillars in the face of the behemoth sand 'dune.'

Cruise, of course, began walking towards the anomaly in the sand the moment Ben had finished imbuing them all with magical sun protection. All three of the necromancers nearly tripped in the sand on their way down. Ben had come prepared with a sled and tried to ride his way down with a goofy smile on his face. He frowned when it only made it halfway.

"Today." Cruise rolled his eyes, having just seen what Ben had tried to do. "Karao asked me to give you some no-spells-barred training in self-defense, so that's what we're going to do. Any questions?"

After a moment, Nika replied. "Lots?"

"Save them for the end. Now, can anyone tell me the first rule of self-defense?"

The absurdity of being lectured in the middle of the desert seemed to hit all three of them at once since nobody had answered. Catherine eventually threw a guess out.

"Hit them first?" she asked.

Cruise chuckled, "No, but I like the instinct. The first rule is to be aware." He turned his back to them. "If you suspect things are taking a turn for the worse, observe as many details as you can, they could make-" he spun quickly, bottle uncapped and held menacingly in his hand. In one swift motion, he splashed all three of them with water. Nika yelped, Nils jumped back, Catherine fumed.

The lecture moved on from there to cover Cruise's seven rules of self-defense. His main priority was teaching them how to remove themselves from a dangerous scenario rather than them trying to engage in a fight. Most of it made sense, and rules five and six were almost exactly the same. It was over in under half an hour, which led to the lesson's 'practical' section. As laid out before them, the plan was to have them try one at a time to escape an attack from either himself or Ben.

Nils went up first. Their deadarm hung nervously down by their ankles. Cruise took out a small metal rod.

"Pretend this is a knife," he said.

"Ok."

"You're walking alone at night, and you see me approach you like this." He crouched a bit, holding the knife out to intimidate. "Walk me through the steps."

"Nils probably can't get away. There's not really anywhere to go." Nils said, looking at the vast nothingness around them. Catherine bit her tongue, refusing to correct them in the middle of whatever practice this was supposed to be.

"Good. So, how are you going to ensure your own safety?" Cruise stepped forward. There was only about ten feet of space between the two.

"If I tell you, it isn't going to work," Nils argued.

"Well, let's try it then. Count us off, Ben."

Ben, for his part, had been reading a book while leaning on one of the pillars. It was slightly shorter than he was and had a divot at a nearly perfect height for his elbow. He counted down from three. Nils, taking the initiative, used their deadarm to shoot freezing magic at patches of sand between them. Patches of ice formed wherever the white pulses hit, each about the size of afoot. They tried to make the ground between the two difficult to cross. Even doing that much had drained Nils quite a bit. They started panting. They looked up to see how well their deterrent was doing.

Not very well, it turned out.

Cruise, without leaving his spot, held up a single hand with outstretched fingers. Golden ribbons streamed out from his palm, flowing and winding their way through the air like serpents. Nils batted away, one reaching their shoulder, but the one attacking their shin connected. It knotted itself tight and pulled Nils toward the 'attacker.' They tripped over their own ice trap.

"Please. People have magic, nobody is going to attack you with just a knife." Cruise released Nils. They stayed on the ground by choice.

"Rule 4. You don't know what the assailant can do," Nils said, contemplating every decision they'd ever made. "Got it."

"Exactly, nobody is coming at you with just a knife. Never make assumptions about what they can do and focus on the best way you could escape. All right, Catherine, you're up next."

Catherine's bout went quickly. The setup was almost the same. A moment before the countdown ended, she curled up a fist and, with a violent arm swing, conjured a brief but devastating wind between the two, kicking enough sand in Cruise's face that he wasn't able to follow her as she walked away.

"Yes, very good." He coughed, regaining composure. He stumbled back a bit. Catherine strutted back to her spot between the other two, chin raised proud and insufferable smugness spread across her face.

Nika had been cooking up his strategy since seeing Nils get dragged across the hot desert sand. He still hadn't attached his deadarm yet, but it wasn't like he was able to do anything without it. If he could get it to cooperate and pull the knife out, he could maybe send it back with its magnetic magic. Getting around the ribbons was going to be a problem. He probably wouldn't be able to predict where they were coming from, but if he kept track of himself and his immediate surroundings, he might be able to avoid them long enough for the knife to throw Cruise-

His thought process was cut off by Cruise calling for a break between coughs. Still, he was going to get ready. He started to hook the deadarm up to his back. Someone stopped him. Ben had pulled it away from him just as he was feeling sparks jump between bone and his spine.

"Hold up there, Nika. I'm not supposed to let you do that yet," Ben said.

"Hm? Why not?" Nika asked.

Cruise had stepped up to answer the question on queue, "Yeah, don't do that. Not yet."

"Nobody told me," Nika said. He felt like those words were the start of a thought that didn't really need an ending.

"I figured you wouldn't be so eager to jump back in after last time." Cruise said. Karao had obviously detailed how long he had gotten stuck to the thing the first time. "Pay attention, and you'll have your answers by the end of the day, sound fair?" He held out his hand for Nika to give him the deadarm.

Nika obliged. "Sure."

The water break didn't last long. Cruise had reassembled his small class in the middle of the four pillars, his back to the behemoth object covered in sand. The combination of sweat and sun glared off his shaved scalp terribly. It was hard to see his face. Fortunately, that was unnecessary. His stance gave away his intention to lecture at them for another considerable amount of time.

"Before we spend the rest of the afternoon practicing, would anyone like to guess why I brought you all here?" Cruise waited for an answer he wouldn't get.

"How are we supposed to know that?" Nils asked, still not fully recovered from using seemingly every ounce of magic they had on an ineffective trick.

"Asking your students questions is a way to engage them and get them invested in the lesson, I don't know," he admitted. "Look, I read it in a book. This clearly isn't my job. It doesn't matter. It doesn't matter. Nils, you would say you know Karao best, correct?"

"Probably," Nils said.

"Has she ever told you how we met?" The wind had been a constant, low rumbling throughout the day. It was silent now.

"No," Nils said. They would never admit their rising interest in what Cruise was saying, but it was clear from their tone.

Cruise closed his eyes and took a breath. He lifted Nika's deadarm into the air. His hands started crackling with the unmistakable violet lightning. The arm began to move, fingers spasming and settling. He was in control of it now, wielding the thing like some kind of macabre sword. He swung it Nika's direction, finger-pointing an unknown accusation.

"You three aren't Karao's first students, you know that," Cruise said. "You're not even the first trio, matter of fact. Karao has trained many groups before you, each necromancer a sparkling and unique gem in her eyes. She's mentioned something about quirks to you, Nika?"

"She mentioned it."

"Well, that's not special to necromancers, but our difference do tend to be a bit more pronounced than other magics." He dropped the deadarm into the sand. It fell limp on contact with the sand. "Catherine's sheer volume of energy, Nils's very pinpoint technicality, those are easy to observe and fairly common traits no matter what sort of magic you're using." He thought for a moment. "No less impressive, of course." He backpedaled his unintentional gaff.

"That doesn't- what does this have to do with the desert?" Ben asked. Everyone looked at him. They had forgotten he was also sitting in on this guest lecture. It was a good question, though, and the three turned back to Cruise for an answer.

"I'm building to that, be patient." Cruise was a lot more animated when he was off the clock. He gestured for the three to take a seat. They all did, Ben included. Cruise rolled his eyes a bit. "Karao used to be, well, different. She has always tried to look out for her students and did what she thought was best." He sighed. "She had a really poor sense of 'best' thirty years ago."

Nika had forgotten about Karao's age anomaly. It wasn't the biggest concern at the moment. Still, he hated being reminded that there was a nonconsequential mystery he would never get to know the answer to. Maybe it was like the door. He didn't really want to know what was behind it.

"Like what?" Catherine asked.

"She was reckless. Karao trained necromancers to fight for themselves and become stronger over almost anything else. She would praise the strongest more than the others while helping those lower on the ladder climb to the top." Cruise paused for a moment, struggling with words. "No quirk, no variant was too much to overcome. Your natural affinity for one aspect of magic could be worked and improved on. You could patch up weaker areas, hone your strengths; both. She wanted to be able to trust that, on our own, we'd be untouchable, and what we did with our power was up to us."

He had been bothered by a nagging thought of late. He wondered why he had trusted Karao, why that didn't change with Bringer, with this new information. There were multiple verbal warnings and more than a few red flags regarding whether she was a proper caretaker. The skeptic in him wanted to stop. He wanted to quit. He'd find another avenue to a normal life somewhere. When he talked to her, when he was in the tea shop, he saw people like him trying their best and enjoying their life when he was with the others. That was maybe more important. For now, he'd continue to trust Karao, the new Karao, and he didn't know what to do should that change.

That didn't mean he didn't want to know more. "What changed?"

"Ah." He looked back at the pile of sand. "Well, before that, Nika, I have good news for you. We have the specifics of

your peculiar magic worked out. You can thank Donut for that."
He reached into his pocket and tossed a glass ball containing the
reanimated snake to Nika. Donut seemed happy to see him
again, as happy as a snake can look anyways. Nika hadn't even
noticed he was missing. He felt a little bad about that and
promised himself to do better about it.

"Thanks," he said, though he wasn't sure he was
grateful.

"Don't mention it. It's good for all of you to know this,
too." Cruise sat down in front of them. "Nika, you have a
potentially potent skill on your hands there. See, when most
necromancers do their thing, whatever they're reanimating is
only active as long as they are directly controlling it. Donut here
isn't like that at all, Right?"

They nodded.

"Despite the name," Cruise continued, standing again.
"Necromancy isn't just death magic. Technically that's called
necrosis, which is its own thing. Yes, they're connected, no you
don't need to think about it for now. If this magic is a coin, then
necromancy is the 'life' side. The way a necromancer creates
more life varies from person to person." He reached out for
Donut.

Nika handed him over. Donut was oblivious.

"This snake was dead. Right?" Cruise held it up for the
three to observe. "This? It shouldn't be happening. Returning to
life is not a thing. It's still dead. It still doesn't need to eat or
breathe. So we ran a few tests on it. What did we find?"

He wasn't going to continue the thought until someone
bit. "What?"

"Nika's soul. Or at least, a part of it..." He seemed happy
that the payoff for his long-winded speech got a reaction. "Your
soul is bolstering what little was left of the snake when it passed

away. Donut is dead, there's no question, but you're giving him the strength to keep going, completely oblivious to that fact."

Nika's heartbeat tripled. He had felt faint after using necromancy on Morgan and Phineas. This explanation certainly explained why. He even passed out once, if he had gone further-

"Could he die?" Nils asked. "Does his soul come back?"

"It seems to, but I'm not sure. There's quite a bit we don't know, but based on what happened the other day, there's something I'd like you to try." He gestured Ben over. "Would you mind walking over here, you three?"

They were now standing in front of all the weird protrusions in the sand. Cruise grabbed Nils by the shoulder and walked to the back with Ben, leaving Catherine and Nika in the front. "All right, I'm sure you've figured out there's something under there by now. Catherine, would you mind trying to blow away the sand?"

She seemed really excited by the idea. She wanted to start with one of the pillars. It took thirty seconds of air-blasting while the others hid behind a barrier that Ben had put up against the sand. After the cloud settled, they were greeted by a statue of some kind of wizard, clad in robes and holding their hands close to their chest. His face was somber, downtrodden.

"Yeah, that'll never work for the big one," Cruise said.

"What is it?" Catherine asked, marveling at her discovery. The detail of the statue was incredible. The intricate carving of the face, knuckles, even the tiny divot between the fingernail and fingertip were all so excellently executed it was hard to believe it was a statue. The more he stared, the more he concluded it could not have been a statue.

"That is an amber mage," Cruise said, clearly hoping to end the discussion. Ben picked up the answer.

"Oh!" Ben started. "An amber mage is someone the kingdom uses during huge emergencies. Basically, they freeze themselves and something else in time, neither able to move until the life of the amber mage comes to an end." He looked at the other three pillars, turning pale. "Are all three-"

"Yes, Mr. Farvue, they are all amber mages," Cruise said, his dramatic retelling once again undercut. "Now, Nika, I want you to give Catherine a boost, understand?"

"No?" he said. The only context he could figure was to use necromancy on Catherine, a very much living person. It hadn't killed Morgan, so he could give it a shot, but it could also end horribly.

Ben spoke up again. He was pointing at the much larger sand pile. "Are you sure you aren't going to wake that up?"

"I know a lot about amber, Mr. Farvue. We are completely safe." Cruise nodded at Nika.

He was just going to try the first thing in his head. He reached his hand out to Catherine, she took it. He tried recreating exactly how he felt, putting everything into that unintentional slap. Sparks rippled across his neck and down his arm, striking Catherine's arm and hand. She jumped at first, then calmed.

"It doesn't hurt. It feels pretty good, actually." Her eyes seemed to be glowing purple; it was too late for him to stop. He was already woozy. The damage was done.

Nika let go, nearly falling over. He was saved from hitting the ground by the golden ribbons Cruise had used earlier, pulling him into a hasty retreat behind the shield.

Catherine roared, unleashing the largest maelstrom of hurricane wind Nika had ever seen. Well, wind could normally not be seen, but the sand standing between her and the dune was kicked up and spread in a chaotic frenzy. Even though the

tent was well behind them, it was pulled into the storm
Catherine had conjured. Cruise pulled her back into the shield
when he felt it was getting too risky to keep her out there.

It took a few minutes for the storm to completely settle.
It was, after all, a breeze amplified by two teenagers. On a
grand scale, that's still a fairly small tempest. Catherine's
deadarm was cracked and fractured, several fingers were
missing.

"Karao is going to kill me," Catherine said.

"And then bring you back and make you fix it," Ben
joked. The others didn't find it as funny as he apparently did.

Only Nika and Cruise were more focused on the object
appearing ahead of them than Catherine's impending
punishment for breaking a very difficult-to-find piece of
equipment. The blast had uncovered about three-quarters of it,
with the base still comfortably nestled in newly set sand. It
seemed like a greyish mass of stone, uneven and bumpy.

The barrier lowered, the two walked towards it. As Nika
approached, he realized more and more that he was not looking
at a rock, rather a mass of bones. Disjointed femurs, rib cages,
and skulls. There was no rhyme or reason for any placement. It
was larger than any building in Eldes, save for maybe the library.
The depth and texture of the thing were enthralling. Staring into
the gaps seemed to make time slip away. It whispered to him,
too quiet to make anything out, but it wanted to speak.

"Mortimer Cruise." He announced, catching the other's
attention. "Liz Ulstraine." He pointed up to the mass of bones.
"Hult Tinner."

Nils was the one to ask the question. "That's a person?"

Cruise shook his head. "Not anymore. These were
Karao's former students. Myself, Liz, and Hult." He had their full
attention, but this was no longer fun for him. "Hult was an

ambitious guy. He was convinced that he could just keep pushing past limits. Karao tried to warn him, and he didn't listen. Liz was the same. She was convinced she could possess her own corpse and become immortal."

Chapter 17- End

Intermission - Dinner

Dinner was awkward. It had been a long day, and they were all starving and careless by the time they made it back to the Pale Garden. Nika was the one who accidentally let slip the things Cruise had told them. The topic of the older students dominated the conversation for the rest of the night. How long ago, what they were like, who was better; the old or the new. Karao enjoyed reminiscing once she got over the initial shock. She intended to tell them later, but they've never really seemed like a good time to do so.

Nobody asked about what happened to Hult or Liz in the end; Karao danced around it as well. That question lingered over the table for the entire meal, and they all politely ignored it. It permeated their thoughts and followed each of them to their respective beds. Each time Nika attempted to drop into sleep, the skeletal mass appeared before him again. This continued until the next distraction: a tapping on his knuckles.

There was nobody in the room, just a small piece of paper floating around his hand. It seemed important like he had seen it before, but he had no idea from where. The paper flitted and twirled in front of him. He was too tired for critical thought; whatever this was, he would roll with it until he could mercifully go to sleep.

It stopped in front of his face. Words began to write themselves. The paper twitched and curled as the loveliest cursive he had seen formed in the dim light in shining, golden letters. 'Good Evening.'

"Good evening," he said, not expecting it to respond. The slip of paper, no bigger than the palm of his hand, shook off the golden ink and began to write again. A bit got onto Nika's hand and sank into his skin.

'You learned a lot today.' it read.

Nika didn't respond.

'I'm always here to listen.' it read.

Nika was feeling sleepier and more concerned than before. He had wanted this sensation of drifting off to sleep for hours now, though this felt forced. He couldn't speak again for some reason. He remembered he had, once before, handled something that prevented him from speaking. He couldn't remember where or when, though.

'You won't remember anyways.' it read. 'Tell me what you know.'

Chapter 18. Farewell to D.A.S.

Lisa Farvue was intimidating to sit across from. It should have been hard to feel threatened within a comfortable living room filled with little decorative touches and welcoming furniture. If Nika had to narrow it down to a single feature, it would be her eyes. They were the same brown color as Morgan's but sharper. They never wandered, and he wasn't entirely certain that she blinked.

Maybe it was that she wore her uniform even when she wasn't working.

The two waited for Morgan to wrap up a mandatory last-minute room cleaning. She had invited Nika to join her and her friends from the not-dueling club for a final goodbye to the club. Since the founding member had made the real team, he'd be too busy to spend time at the club. At least, that's how it was explained to Nika. Nika would have made for enough members, but Sam was not interested in being the president.

"Why" Lisa paused, considered the rest of her question, and continued, "did my husband leave the house with a sled the other day?"

"Cruise took us all to some desert. He kept trying to sled down the dunes," Nika said. He laughed a bit. "It didn't work."

To his surprise, she was laughing too. "He would. Of course, he would. That man." Her focus had been broken by a smile for the moment. With a final sigh, she returned to the focused state she was in before.

"You've been encouraging this dueling stuff." She cracked her knuckles and leaned forward, fingers folded, elbows on her knees. "Haven't you?"

He fidgeted a bit. "Uh... yes."

She tilted her head a bit. "Points for honesty, but do you remember the little conversation we had the first time we met? Good. Well, I want you to forget all that."

"I'm sorry?"

"You know, I worry about her sometimes. She used to just sit in her room alone, sorting cards and reading magazines. I wonder how many friends she made and why she doesn't seem to talk about anyone. It's been different lately. She's happier, and so am I. So, as thanks, I'll look over the direct order you disobeyed. Just this once."

If a normal conversation was anything to go off, the response to 'thank you was usually 'you're welcome' or something similar, but that didn't seem like a good fit. He nodded, thinking of what to say.

Morgan leaped into the room wearing a shirt and hat, both covered in logos and other various dueling symbols. "Wait, Nika! You don't have to incriminate yourself! You have the right to stay silent."

"Hey now." Lisa raised an eyebrow. "This isn't an inter-. This isn't an official interrogation." She rose and led them to the door. "All right, be back before dark, Morgan."

Morgan had kept their destination for the day a secret. Nika only knew a few key details.

1. They were heading into the north side of the city and taking a tram to get there
2. Sam and Michal were waiting for them.
3. She had brought a small drawstring bag that clattered as they walked.

She quizzed him for the still-looming test as they went. The date had been pushed back due to recent leadership changes in the school. Even with an extra week, it was a short amount of time to go over the material he had again and again.

Nika would have taken the tram over a portal station any day of the week. It only went through the main roads and was packed to a claustrophobia-inducing degree. Anything beat warp-sickness. There were other positives, too. They had managed to snag a window seat after the first stop, and the soft summer air softly flowing into the cabin felt really nice. The windows were more like a liquid, made of shimmering bubbles than solid panes of glass, and through them, the city seemed more vibrant and colorful than ever.

It was definitely a good distraction from the filthy floor of the thing.

Their final destination was marked by the two students standing in front of an indistinct building a block away from their stop. The shop, labeled 'Hogg & Windell's Games and Tradeables' in fading paint, was only remarkable by its lack of distinct features. Almost every other sign and storefront was vying for Nika's attention with gaudy lettering, flashing sale signs, and in the case of one very ambitious potionary, a fiddle quartet.

Michal was exactly as he had remembered him: carefree and upbeat. Sam seemed much more relaxed, likely because there were no stakes today. They both had small cardboard boxes with them that rattled with the same sound Morgan's bag had been making the entire trek.

It had been driving him just a little crazy.

In spite of his better judgment, Nika followed the others through the threshold and into the most cluttered store he had ever seen. His hometown housed primarily neat freaks. The Pale Garden had started as a mess. Still, it was getting better and better, with Nils single-handedly leading the cleaning effort. Before this, the most disorganized place he had ever seen was Morgan's room, and he was only half-sure there was even a bed in there. This store was an abomination. If there even was a floor, it had been caked in trampled sheets of paper and magazine covers; on closer look, they were waxed in. If they even were shelves and not just precarious stacks, the shelves were overflowing with stacks of cardboard. Posters were nailed to pillars of fliers, one of which looked like the primary structural support for whatever was up the make-shift staircase.

All of it was about dueling, he assumed.

"Hey, Hetra!" Michal called to an unseen person knelt behind a counter somewhere.

A woman shot up like a startled animal from her station, her multicolored hair catching up to the rest of her. She enthusiastically greeted her returning regulars.

"Hey, guys! Long time no-" She spotted Nika. "Aw, you brought a fourth?"

"I think you mean 'introduced a potential new customer,'" Sam said. He stepped over a pile of small empty boxes and approached the counter. "You guys head up and grab a table." He started a rigorous examination of the glass case that made up most of the back' wall'.

"The usual spot?" Hetra asked, making notes in a sticker-covered ledger.

"Oh yeah," Morgan said.

"Got it. Off of your store credit then, Michal?" She had already gone back to whatever task she was doing before they had gotten there.

"Works for me." He started up the stairs and called for Nika and Morgan to follow. Sam usually took a minute to stare at all the new stuff.

Nika seemed to think of a new worst-case-scenario with each step. If this was the room that customers were meant to see, the idea of an 'upstairs' was terrifying in-and-of-itself. To his relief, the upstairs was the polar opposite of the atrocity behind them. It was, and he couldn't believe this made him happy, acceptable. Sure, there were tears on some of the seats, and yes, looking at cobwebs in the corners gave him flashbacks to his run-in with the spider, but the floor and tables were spotless.

The tables were much more ornate than he had thought when they first walked in. They were small and square and looked completely unusable. Each side was angled towards its corresponding seat, with the center being a felt-lined pit. Each wall had its own color: red, blue, yellow, and green. Morgan grabbed the green seat as if there was some sort of race for it. That was fine. He sat at the red one and Michal the blue. The two of them giggled.

"Sam hates yellow," Michal explained to Nika, who was falling further and further behind what was actually happening.

Sam bounded up the stairs. His eager face drained after seeing which seat they had left for him. "I hate you all."

"It was Nika's idea," Michal said. Sam hit him.

Morgan laughed, opening a box from her bag. One of a few that, presumably, had made that perplexing sound on the way there. It was filled with a neat stack of cards, the same ones they had used in the Replay Box. She fanned them out and told Nika to pick one. The other two had selected their own cards from stacks they brought themselves. He grabbed one at random: The Captain, a somewhat stocky-looking man with the most out-of-control facial hair Nika had ever seen. His billowing coat and enormous hat sold the pirate motif. If that didn't do it, the giant steering wheel he was wielding did.

"Ok. What do I do with it?" he asked.

Sam answered, having selected his own duelist in secret. "You see that little square in front of you? Put it on there, like this." He slid his card into his yellow square.

Nika did the same. It snapped into a straight position when it was close to the center. The others were still picking but eventually caught up and placed their own cards into the table's lower part. The outer, upper part rumbled. His instinct told him to back away from the table immediately, and he tended to listen to them. In front of each of the four appeared a series of buttons and a stick.

"You see the stick?" Morgan asked, nodding when he pointed at the correct contraption. "You can use it to move around."

"Move what around?" Nika asked.

"Him!" she answered. He looked into the table. Standing on top of each of the cards was a miniature version of each of the duelists. Before Nika stood the captain, wheel vaulted neatly over his back. He swayed side to side, awaiting orders.

He moved the control to the left, and the miniature illusion followed. The irony of the captain taking orders was funny to him. Each of the buttons was a different action; a punch, a spell, or a grab. The others gave him a few minutes to mess around with the control panel to get used to it. By twirling the joystick and mashing buttons, he was able to pull off a few neat tricks. At least he thought they were cool.

He lined the little duelist back up on the starting tile for the miniature fight to begin. Michal started the countdown from five, though by the end, they were all chanting.

The Captain was wiped out in six seconds flat. He had been struck in the face by a wad of black sludge, buried under a pile of rocks, and put to sleep just for good measure. The card shot out of the table. Nika nearly fell out of his chair, trying to catch it as it flitted up, around, and down again. The rest of the match went on for some time.

Morgan's duelist looked more like a pile of molten tar than a human being and was taking hit after hit like it was nothing. It's a good thing it was that bulky since Sam's had put it to sleep. The duelist was wearing a thick nightgown and carrying a pillowcase that must have been stuffed with bricks for how hard it sent Michal's careening into the edge of the table. He was the next one eliminated.

"Sam is really good at this," Michal said, picking Morgan's card off the floor.

"He had to be good at something." Morgan taunted as she had shaken the molten heap awake again and lobbed another volley of molten projectiles.

"You should try it sometime." He shot back as he avoided the attack and landed his own. A blast of sand to the face and Morgan's fighter was asleep once again. As she frantically rattled the buttons, Michal suggested Nika try to pick out his next fighter. He shuffled through some of the cards Morgan had brought and grabbed one that seemed too wild not to try; a woman with a dragon's head where her right forearm was meant to be. There was a lot he wanted to try. This was a blast.

They had completely ignored the passage of time until the light in the window started to fade. Over the course of several hours, they had averaged one round every ten minutes, with breaks. The score was displayed on a little chalkboard suspended above the table that updated automatically every round. Sam had won seventeen, while Michal and Morgan had each won four. Nika stared at the zero next to his name with growing contempt after each passing bout.

So, the members of D.A.S. announced the final fight. Michal suggested that an appropriate sendoff was going to be around with something on the line.

"What does the winner get?" Nika asked.

"Get?" Sam wasn't on board. "They 'get' to win."

"No, I like that idea." Morgan sat back, searching for the perfect card for the evening's grand finale.

"Majority rules! Sorry, but not. What'll it be?" Michal stretched. He had just finished a successful war of attrition against Sam in the last round and needed a minute to relax.

"Fine, fine." Sam thought for a second. "Well, we still have to clean our old club room." The other two groaned. "So, the winner doesn't. How does that sound?"

"Wait, just, doesn't?" Michal asked, excited.

"The winner doesn't have to do anything!?" Morgan was standing with the most energy she had had since losing five rounds in a row. "Oh, you are on."

"Wait, what about me?" Nika asked.

"What about you?" Michal asked back.

"I'm not even in the club." If the clubhouse was anything even remotely like the store downstairs, he wanted nothing to do with it. "You can't make me do that."

"Would you like to join our club?" Morgan asked him.

"No?" he answered.

"I heard a 'yes. Guys?" Morgan looked to the other two club members to back up her stupid bit. They agreed.

Nika grumbled.

"I woulda asked for your help anyways," Morgan said. Nika shook his head. "You know you'd help out, too." She wasn't wrong, probably.

"Is it too late to back out?" Nika had already picked out his card for the last duel. It was the Captain again. He had used him a few times in the other rounds and liked the controls for him the best.

"Way too late." Sam held up a card with some bravado. It was hard to make out the picture from across the table, but the gold border and signature could have been seen across the room. "Besides, I have a new friend."

"When did you get that?" Morgan was nearly drooling over the fancy card.

"Today, It was in the case." Sam placed it on the table. "Couldn't help myself."

"Why, is it special?" Nika asked.

"Gold cards are championship cards. They're super hard to come by." Michal put his card on the table. "And expensive, so."

"I may have sold some cards to get it," Sam said. "Ok, a lot of them. It doesn't matter. Let's go."

It wasn't just the card that got the fancy treatment. While the other tiny duelists just appeared on top of their respective cards, the champion arrived with a small light show and some slight musical fanfare. The champion wore slatted green armor with red frills around the neck. She looked like a rose.

The battlefield filled with vines and thorns before anyone could act. Luckily, the captain's jump was always a little higher than Nika expected it to be. Morgan's favorite card, some sword-wielding duelist, was hacking at the exploding foliage with mixed success. Michal was already out, swallowed whole by the very first attack. Roots had snared his fighter's feet and dragged him 'into' the table.

Sam was tapping away at his controls like a crazed lunatic. Each action taken seemed to need some elaborate combination of button presses and small inputs. The Captain would have been flattened numerous times by collapsing walls of stems and spikes if it wasn't for Sam's mistakes ruining his own combos.

It was impossible to just keep fighting plants forever. The goal was to get through enough of it to land a hit or two on the champion, the simply named Rose.

Rose, for her part, didn't move much during the fight. The roots and vines stemmed from her body, primarily her legs. They burrowed into the table and allowed her to attack anywhere at all from under the stages. It also prevented her from moving.

He aimed a few projectile attacks her way, anchors and cannonballs made of conjured water. Still, they were batted away by swirling vines. That was a non-starter. Morgan was somewhere else in the tangle, complaining that she couldn't even see her own fighter.

The two seemed to make a breakthrough towards Rose at the same time. Figuring it had only gotten in the way so far, Nika decided to throw the weighted steering wheel full force at the target and hope that would work.

It didn't. She caught it with her hands. The momentum nearly uprooted her, but no visible damage was done, at least not from the wheel. Morgan took the chance to close the gap and get a good swing in. Her swordsman brought his only remaining blade down on Rose's forehead.

The rule that duelists couldn't be hurt in the ring applied to this game, too, thankfully. It was a sharp sword, clearly, but the protective magic prevented it from cutting into the skin at all. Her helmet was dented from the force, and getting hit that hard from any length of metal, sharp or not, was going to do something.

There was an unused button that Nika had been waiting to press the entire day. It hummed softly in the corner, taunting him. It read, simply, 'all cannons, fire!'. With his two remaining enemies being clumped up next to each other, now seemed like the perfect time for a haymaker.

The Captain brought his hands together and stomped the ground. With a slight rumbling, a comically large cannon burst from the table aimed directly at the other two. They had been too occupied trying to parry and attack each other at short range to notice. Michal was giddy.

A single shot ended the fight. Nika looked up to the scoreboard. The zero scratched itself out to be replaced with a solitary one. He was happy.

Morgan and Sam got over it, eventually. They had overstayed their welcome at the store by a good twenty minutes at that point. Hetra apparently trusted them enough to let them stay after closing for a bit. Still, eventually, she wanted to go home too.

The four stood outside for a bit. Leaving meant the official end of the club, and at least three were attached to the thing. They filled the awkward air with small talk about the upcoming year, what teachers they had, what Michal was doing to prepare for his season on the dueling team.

"We're still going to hang out, right?" Morgan asked.

"Nah," Sam joked. "I got so much going on, no time."

"If you two stop going to the meets just because I'm on the team, I will find out," Michal laughed.

"And do what?" Sam said.

"Cry, probably," he said. Nika thought it was funny.

They said their goodbyes. They found it appropriate that the club of people not good enough for the dueling team would be ousted by an outsider in the end. Nika shrugged and accepted his role in their finale. The two groups turned to leave in separate directions, then Sam remembered something he had wanted to say.

"Morgan, are you still doing doubles?" Sam asked.

"Hm?" She seemed tense.

"The doubles try-outs, do you still need a partner?" he asked. Nika remembered the dejected Sam in existential crisis after the last round of try-outs. Apparently, he had decided not to give up in the end. A day of mostly beating the three of them senseless in a game must have lifted his spirits.

"Oh, um." Morgan was stuttering a bit. She seemed hesitant to answer. "Well, you see-"

Nika cut in. "We were going to try out." Morgan rolled with it. She had asked him before, but he certainly hadn't answered. She nodded.

"Oh! Duh." Sam turned and waved. "Good luck, you guys!"

Things were quiet and a little awkward while they waited for the tram. The only conversation since the others had left had been about getting back, what time the tram would arrive, stuff like that.

The city was calm in the evening. Orange light looked beautiful off the brickwork.

"You didn't have to do that," Morgan said.

"Sorry?"

"I mean, he's not a bad guy, just." She slumped a bit. "He's the absolute last person I'd ever want to team up with."

"He seems," Nika tried and failed to come up with a good word for his thoughts, "control-ly."

"Oh yeah. Nitpick Express, all aboard." Morgan looked at Nika. He was confused. "I've been calling him that for years. It doesn't matter. Thanks, but you didn't need to try and cover for me."

Nika took a breath. The current thought dancing on his tongue was a bad idea, probably. "I mean, I wasn't just covering for you." She raised an eyebrow. "I may, possibly, potentially, be slightly interested in dueling."

If she wasn't sitting down, she would have leaped in the air. "So that's a 'yes!'"

"Catherine and Nils told me it was 'normal' to join a sport or a club-"

"So that's a yes?" Morgan pressed.

"It's a yes." Nika sighed.

Morgan tapped his shoulder for his attention. She was holding her hand up expectantly. After an awkward moment of staring, she taught him what a high-five was. It took a few attempts to get a good one, and Nika's palm hurt by the end of it, but she seemed happy with it, so he didn't worry too much about it.

The ride back was a lot more comfortable than the ride there. The tram was less cramped, the evening air lazier and more relaxed. Nika was mostly listening to Morgan talk about how doubles are different and what sorts of things they could practice. He was paying more attention than usual, distracted only occasionally when the setting sun peeked through a window directly into his eye.

Like the bricks, the orange light seemed to work well for him.

"Are you doing anything for Fete?" Morgan asked in the middle of their long-winded strategy talk.

"I have no idea what Fete is." He had learned too many things today already; he just wanted to take the stuff he already had in his brain to bed and let it rest.

"SummerFete! It's like a big party towards the end of July. No, nothing?"

"We didn't have parties, really." Nika had read about lots of holidays and celebrations. SummerFete did sound familiar. Usually, fiction books starring kids or teenagers had a chapter or two dedicated to a holiday. This must have been it.

"Fete's awesome! There's food, fireworks, we usually go downtown and watch a parade and-"

"Sorry, did you say fireworks?" Nika interrupted. He had read about them a lot, and they always bothered him. Authors made them out to be these life-changing emotional experiences, and everyone was always so excited in the books. None of them did a good job explaining what they were. All he knew was that fireworks were loud and colorful. He had no idea what that meant. Normally, he would just ask someone else to describe them. Not for fireworks. Nika needed to experience them for the first time going in blind as possible. He was excited.

"Yeah, there's a huge fireworks show. We usually go to the park to watch it."

"Shhh." He didn't want any more of it spoiled for him. "No details. When is it?"

"Fete? The twenty-fifth. A week from tomorrow, I think." Morgan grinned. "Wanna go?"

He hurt his neck, nodding. "Ow."

Morgan laughed. "My mom told me to ask ya." they were coming up on their stop. "The rest of your family, too!"

Nika thought about his mother, his brother, the village in the woods. "I don't think they want to."

"Really? Nils seems like they'd love it." Morgan sounded a bit disappointed.

Nika realized. This was his mistake. The faces of his past life slowly faded from his mind, replaced by the comforting smiles found in the Pale Garden tea shop. The nerves shook his lungs on the way up, nervous at first but gaining confidence as he finally said it.

"You're right. I didn't ask my family. I will!"

Chapter 18- End

Intermission- The Plan

Nils had way too much fun setting up the 'briefing room.' In reality, it was just their bedroom with all the furniture shoved to the side to make room for a large wooden board with paper bolted to it. Catherine had been curious what Nils had done to the room since she had moved out and was a bit off-putting.

Karao, for her part, was staving off the stir-craziness of house arrest by drawing. Nils had most of her attention even though her deadarms quietly scratched away at a notepad behind her back.

"So, we focus on a smaller menu and encourage people to take a cup to go. Not enough people have time to sit and enjoy it then and there, and we need to sell more tea." Nils had been reading from notes scrawled out on whatever scrap of paper they had left. "The book said that we should give people a specific reason to want to come to us, and that should be the quality tea."

The way Nils commanded the meeting was inspiring in a way, even when they fumbled over figures or forgot the next thing they wanted to say. The amount of work and research they had put into making the tea shop self-sufficient was incredible.

The plan explained painstakingly involved an opening day special, passing fliers around wherever they went, and hosting various events throughout the year. The new menu and kitchen system would only require one of them to be working in the back at a time and one in the front. They'd all have to practice a few simple spells to make things more efficient, but that wouldn't be a long-term issue.

During the grand reopening, they were going to advertise a 'Local Art Day' Nils had thought of hosting in August.

"Catherine, do you think you could help with that?" Nils asked.

"Help how?"

"You're so much better with a brush. I can't think of anyone better to run it." Nils smiled, Catherine blushed. "Better with a pen, too, for that matter. Really Nils will just be working."

Nika and Catherine corrected them in unison. "I, Nils."

Karao was proud of what they had done. "When do you propose we 'relaunch'?"

Nils was so excited. "Summerfete!"

Chapter 19. The Steps
Before The Leap

Breathing had never been harder. Volunteering to paint the four chairs that needed a touch-up sounded fun before Nika learned what the paint smelled like. The fumes were so unbearable that Karao insisted he set up out in the small backyard with a cloth before even touching the lid.

He thought she was just cautious. Clearly, that wasn't the case. No cautious person would keep something this noxious buried under her old winter coats in the basement. He stood as far from the can as he could and kept the lid over it to prevent the smell from spreading, but it wasn't much use. As long as he wore a magically-imbued paint mask, it wasn't supposed to affect him. Sure, the strap was broken, and he had to hold it in place, but surely that couldn't have been a problem.

Each chair would need two even coats. The first acted as a primer, and the other brought out the oaken color Nils was looking for. Luckily for him, the same odour can somehow acted as both, so he got to spend twice as much time with the thing.

Karao called him over to the kitchen window. Still unable to leave the house under Cruise's order, she looked silly, trying to talk with him while he was outside. To be by that window, she was definitely seated at least partially on the counter, probably wedged between bags of ingredients and stacks of dishes.

"How are things going out there?" she asked, sipping tea.

"I just finished the first coat. I think." He switched mask-holding-hands, realizing how tired his right arm had gotten. "Nils doesn't want me to paint the underside of the chair, right?"

"No, you're fine." Karao put the cup down somewhere out of sight. "I wanted to talk to you if you don't mind."

"I don't mind." He sat cross-legged in the dirt, the second-best option once the chairs were made unusable. "What about?"

"I wanted to check up on you." She seemed adrift. "We haven't gotten to talk much, with everything going on."

"I guess so." Nika had been thinking more about Bringer lately, but he wasn't sure what he should have thought.

"Are you still liking it here? You can be honest." She could have been more subtle about bracing herself for an answer.

"I love it here," Nika said. The relief seemed to carry through the screen between them. "A lot, yeah, a lot."

"You know you can always talk to me about anything, Nika. We've loved having you here these past few months."

Nika couldn't help but hear Cruise's words echo back from some deep corner he had buried them. Everything about the previous students, what had gone wrong. How that Karao seemed so distant from the warm, protective woman in front of him.

"Could you tell me about your old students?" Nika asked.

Her surprise was evident and immediately muted. "Of course."

Nika had time to kill before the paint dried enough to apply another coat, anyways. He spent it listening to stories of Cruise from his youth. He was, apparently, a bit like Nika in a few ways. Very studious and inquisitive but reserved in most things. Liz was extremely competitive; she couldn't stand being outperformed in anything, necromancy least of all. Thinking about it made Karao cackle since Hult tended to win most of her competitions. She had brief stories and anecdotes about them all, talking as if they were her own children.

"Karao?" He interrupted a fun but a predictable tale of some trial the three had undertaken together. Their life seemed full of adventure and danger. It made for a good story, but Nika couldn't imagine living a life like that. Having a roof over his head seemed better.

"Yes?" she said. The minutes lost recounting that seemed to catch up with her all at once.

"What happened?" Nika regretted asking before the words had even left his tongue.

The lively Karao slumped and lost all her gusto in one second flat. Her breathing seemed forced, like a chore she was forcing herself to do for other people's sake. "A lot," she said. "I don't want to hide anything from you, from any of you." She looked him in the eye. "Things were, no, I was different back then. I didn't think it, no, I didn't know-" She gave up and started again. "We used to be a lot more taboo. Now, most people don't think twice if they hear about a necromancer; it's just another type of magic to them. I used to think it was us against the world."

Nika nodded. He had nothing to add.

"That's how I raised my students. To win against the world." Karao looked at him. Her eyes broadcast a sad joy, plain as day to anyone who could see them. "I was an idiot. I trusted nobody, and they learned that from me, too."

"Cruise trusts people," Nika said. "I think."

She shook her head. "By the time I saw what I'd done, it was too late. Two of them were in an arms race against the others, while the third could do nothing but watch. Cruise was my wake-up call. He showed me that the madness needed to stop. I tried talking to them, I really did. But Hult and Liz wouldn't listen. It's my fault."

"What did you do?" Nika asked, growing more and more nervous about the answer.

"Something I'll never live down: I left." Karao fought, tearing up with the most stoic face he had ever seen. She looked like a portrait. "They were bent on self-destruction, and whatever I did only made things worse. Cruise asked me to leave it to him, and I did. It didn't work out, though that's not his fault." She righted herself in the window. "I was supposed to be talking about you, you little jerk." She smiled. "It was a long time ago. If you knew the whole story, I doubt anyone would trust me but thank you."

"I do trust you."

Nils's head popped through another window, the one above the sink, a few feet to Karao's left. Catherine had taught them how to tie bandanas around their forehead the day before, and now that was the 'hard at work' aesthetic for them. "Hey Nika, can I ask you a favor?"

"Yeah, sure. What's up?" He stood and stumbled, the paint having more impact on him than he thought.

"Hang on, I'll be right out." Nils slammed the window shut. Karao had left to do whatever was next on her list of chores. They nearly choked on the air in the yard. "Gah, it reeks."

"Yeah, it's, it's pretty awful," he said. "Need something?"

"A favor, yeah." Nils pulled their shirt over their nose. "Is that ok?"

"Probably," he answered.

"So," Nils paused. "I need you to ask Daniel something." Nils couldn't hide the red blush on their grey skin.

"Is he here?" Nika asked. He hadn't been inside for over an hour, the entire front half of the tea shop could have vanished, and he would never even know.

Nils nodded. "He finished up the prints we asked for. He's hanging them up now." They took a long, long breath. They could only manage to force out a few words at a time. Each fragment of a sentence felt like it needed to be wrestled out of their lungs. "I need you. To ask him. If he's interested in another date...still. The 'still' is important."

The idea of anyone in the world coming to him for relationship help was mind-boggling. He had spent most of his life devoid of any kind of social interaction. He was likely the least qualified person in the entire house to ask for help; come to think of it, Nils would be the one he would go to if he needed help with anything.

"Uh, yeah." He was processing. "I feel like Catherine would be better at this."

"I don't want to ask her right now."

"Ah." They were still upset with each other. The two walked into the kitchen.

"Thank you, thank you so much," Nils said.

Nika, for his part in all this, had no idea what to say. Nils didn't dare follow him past the kitchen and into the main area, but every step along the way, Nils gave more and more instructions for how this would go down. He needed to be subtle but certain. He should try to frame it as a casual conversation or even just have a conversation and try to nudge it in that direction.

Still suffering the punishment of nearly breaking her deadarm the other day, Catherine was stuck in front of an unconquerable mass of dishes. She chuckled at Nils's lack of courage and then coughed. She was still in the tail end of the sickness.

Going through the doors, he found that the new layout worked really well. The space was open and somehow brighter than ever before. The extra light might just have been from the lack of dust, though. Daniel was standing on one of the better chairs, trying to hang a large photo of cookies on the wall.

"Oh! Hey Nika, how are ya?" he said, turning only enough to see who had walked in.

They exchanged small talk. The job at the paper was going well, although Beth was showing up more and more and driving him nuts. He talked about her as though it was someone Nika knew, and the name was familiar, but he couldn't place a face to it. Luckily for Nika, Daniel was more than capable of carrying most of the conversation by himself.

Nika had spent a good five minutes trying to concoct some clunky transition to talking about Nils but gave up. "Hey, so, Catherine wanted me to ask you something." He was not a good liar, but this would have to do.

"Catherine?" He seemed confused.

"Yeah. What's up with you and Nils?" he said. He was now sure that Nils was not listening in on them, or else he would have heard someone collapse in the back room from how idiotic that attempt was. Still, the ambush worked. Daniel didn't really have time to prepare an answer.

"Dating-wise, you mean?" Daniel was really hoping Nika would let him off the hook.

He did not. "Yeah."

"Uhh, well, I asked them out, and they said yes, so we went out. After the date, Nils told me that they couldn't do this right now. They didn't say why, though."

That all sounded about right to Nika. He seemed to recall Nils having called off whatever relationship was starting back in June. It didn't seem a bit odd that they were the ones trying to get it going again.

"Right now?" Nika said. "Interesting."

"Yeah, it's just been a bit awkward since. Things will get better." He sat down for a second. "Hey, do you think Nils would ever want to try dating? Me, specifically, I mean."

He knew the answer was probably yes, but saying it would probably cause Nils to go into shock. "I'm not sure."

"Catherine might know, do you think you could ask? Oh, and it's ok if the answer is no, I just- well, it's nice to know for sure."

Nika nodded and compiled externally. Internally, he was screeching. Here he had been, minding his own business and painting chairs only to be pulled into the middle of some benign romantic subplot to his own life. This was awful.

Nils jumped on him the moment the kitchen door closed. They wanted to know all the details. It was only after they had calmed down that Nika realized he hadn't actually gotten an answer to the straightforward question.

"He... wanted to know what you thought," Nika said.

Catherine was laughing like it was the funniest thing she had ever heard in her life. Nils was more than a bit disappointed.

"You didn't tell him, did you?" Nils's horror was palpable.

"No, no, I said I'd ask Catherine."

"Don't drag me into that!" Catherine snapped from her cloud of suds.

"Sorry," he said. "The answer is 'yes, right? Should I just go-"

Nils held up a hand in his face. "No. No, do not say that."

"Why not?"

Nils didn't have an answer for that, but the idea was stressing them out enough that Nika decided to drop it. "What should I say, then?"

What happened was something Nika would never come to fully understand. He was sent back and forth as a messenger for a problem that he really didn't want to be involved in the first place. More incredible than the situation was both of their ability to dodge answering simple questions.

The eternal back and forth, omitting the middle man, could be summarized like this:

Nils - Nils isn't sure, what's your opinion?

Daniel - I don't want to make Nils uncomfortable, is there a specific way to bring it up?

Nils - Why don't you just ask Nils yourself?

Daniel - I did that once, and things have been weird. Do you think it would ruin things?

Nils - Aren't you scared you'll get caught up in Nils's problems?

Daniel - Like what?

That simple two-word question was the one that finally made Catherine snap. She had enjoyed the entertainment at first, but her frustration grew faster than Nika's somehow. She shoved whatever dish she was holding into the sink and spun around. She marched up to Nils, untying the soaked apron.

"Last chance. Are you going to go out there and ask him out?" The way she bunched up the apron in her fists was terrifying.

"I- I don't-" Nils stuttered. Their fate was sealed with the first balk. Catherine shoved the apron into Nils's chest and walked out into the main area. Nils protested until the door was open.

"I'm tired of you dancing around stuff," she said.

Normally, he would feel sympathy for Nils in this situation. Being in the middle of the absurd turnabout was enough to change that, just this once. He had wanted to do what Catherine just did for a while but couldn't bring himself to.

Nils's arms hung low, the apron draped over a clenched fist. Their breathing was heavy. The two stood still and silent while they waited. It wasn't long, shorter in fact than any of Nika's expeditions out into the main room.

Catherine reentered. Her face gave no indication whatsoever what had happened.

"Tired of me dancing around it?" Nils said. They refused to make eye contact with anyone but the floor. "Fine." Nika had never seen Nils mad before. It didn't look good on them. "Fine! I still hate you for leaving! Not even. I hate you for not talking about it first! That's all you had to do, and you couldn't even get that right! Is that 'to the point' enough for you!? You're basically my sister, and you think you can just walk away without even saying good-bye!"

Catherine wasn't expecting that. Nika was expecting her to fire back, to get mad again. The fight had been going on for too long, and Catherine agreed. She quietly walked up to Nil and gestured for a hand. She slipped a napkin covered in writing into it.

Her voice broke a bit. "You have a date on Sunday." She sort of fell into Nils, going for a hug. It wasn't reciprocated. "I know I was wrong. I know I should have talked to you." Catherine was buried in Nils's shoulder. "I wanted to, you know. But you would have talked me out of it."

Nils wrapped their arms around her back. "Nils would have tried."

"I, Nils."

"Yeah, yeah."

"I'm sorry."

"So am I."

Catherine stepped back. "Two things." She wiped her face on her sleeve. "First, if that boy ever hurts you, I will hurt him."

Nils laughed. "Got it."

"Second, if you let those creeps stop you from having fun again, I will dunk your head in this sink."

Nika was confused. "What creeps?"

The two had almost forgotten that he was there. "Like that woman on our way to the portal station."

She had meant the one who almost shoved them to the ground and belittled them for being artificial. Homunculi were, as he had found out, gross to some people. Maybe they didn't like the implication that they could be recreated. Whatever the reason, or lack thereof, they always seemed like wretched people.

Nils had said 'not yet' instead of 'no' when Daniel asked for another date initially. They had prepared themselves for weeks to want to try for it again. Catherine seemed to think this was because Nils didn't want people to harass Daniel, even though they wanted the relationship. It made sense to Nika, in a way. Nils seemed so happy.

Karao, who had entered the room at some point during the final exchange, made herself known. "Well, glad that's all sorted out. Honestly, you two bicker over the smallest things." She stepped up to the window and peered out into the back. "Nils, you've done an excellent job. I couldn't be prouder of you.

But." She let the word hang in there. She seemed to feed off suspense and tea alone. "I think you owe Nika for that little run-around. Grab a brush."

Nika and Nils finished the second coating of paint while the sun hung somewhere between setting and late afternoon. The sky was still blue, but a grainy blue, not that it mattered. They were too focused on getting the work done and getting back into breathable air.

Generally speaking, Nils had always seemed like the happiest person at the Pale Garden. They were almost always upbeat, pushed to improve things, a reliable person for support. Winding down a day where their big project was coming to an end, where they made up with a loved one, with a date to look forward to, and a fun story to tell from it all, Nils wasn't happy.

For the first time, they seemed truly content. It was contagious.

Chapter 19- End

Intermission- The Eldes Review:
Necromantic Crimewave Update

Beth G.

Grensburrow, Heirute: The recent rise in necromancy-based crime has finally swept its way into the small town of Grensburrow, located roughly ten miles from the northern gates of Eldes. Law enforcement and reporters alike had been following this unprecedented wave of grave-robbing and larceny that began in the capital and seemed to head straight towards Eldes. Although nothing is known officially about any potential perpetrators, experts believe that the recent upswing in violent crime stemming from this suggests that it will not stop before hitting the city.

Unlike general trends in crime reporting, which take aggregate data from cities and compare them to previous records, this appears to be the work of one actor or group of actors. Meteorologists have compared maps following these crimes to the shape of a growing storm. Though the comparison is, at best, superficial, it appears to be holding true in Obluit.

The town is perhaps best known for being the home to a state penitentiary, which found itself the target of a full-scale raid. Several people have been hospitalized by the necromancer(s) responsible for dozens of emptied prison cells. Law enforcement insists that the victim remain anonymous while they conduct the investigation. What we can say is that they are, in fact alive, but are currently in critical condition... (cont. p.6)

Chapter 20. SummerFete

It would be close, but he could fit everything into a single day if it all went according to plan. Well, not everything. Working at the relaunch took a higher priority than his first holiday, so he would miss the early festivities. With a lot of negotiating, he managed to work out a way to squeeze as much out of his day as humanly possible.

The rundown was this: He would work from opening until close, eight to five. He would get as much done as possible, then Lisa Farvue agreed to come to get him and take him to the parade a few blocks north. There he'd meet up with Morgan and anyone else who was going. After that was a street food dinner and a trip to the park for the fireworks show. When he got back, he'd have to do his chores, including getting the front room ready for opening the next day.

As for the actual day, Karao and Catherine were going to work in the back making the tea and the food while Nils worked the front. Nika would basically go wherever he was needed, the default being to keep the front organized and clean.

Nobody had any idea how busy the day was going to be. They had done their best to advertise and promote with their limited resources. Daniel had even managed to get them a cheap ad in the paper using one of Catherine's paintings. Fliers had been put up all over the place. Karao had called in a few favors to get local business people to spread the word throughout the holiday.

Donut, for his part in the relaunch, was locked away in a box upstairs. He, unfortunately, didn't fit with the new aesthetic of the place: clean.

Karao, tired and bracing herself for the first full day of work she'd have done in a long time, had a cup of tea in two deadarms and an apple in another. It would have been a bad day to skip breakfast.

"You ready?" she asked. She didn't seem to be listening for an answer, just making small talk while waiting for her morning cup to snap her awake.

"Yeah, think so." Nika had started trying to make the lobby perfect, and now the itch couldn't be scratched. Every time he finished adjusting a chair, he would notice another small thing in the room that needed fixing. Napkins, not full-on table three, table four not being centered with the window next to it, stuff like that.

"It looks good enough. You can take a seat." She yawned. "You'll be glad you did by the end of the day."

Catherine arrived at her usual time. She worked and left like clockwork every day, staying for dinner and to talk a bit in the evenings before heading off to her room in the dorms. 'Ownership' of that small space really meant a lot to her. She hadn't gotten in any pointless arguments with anyone since the change. Her hair was tied back, her sleeves were rolled up, and her stride showed the confidence of someone who could never trip over anything. She did, though, a pot handle sticking out in the kitchen.

Nils, the only one with enthusiasm before eight o'clock, greeted them all with cheer-filled "Happy Feet!" The other two responded in kind.

"Happy... fete," Nika said. He figured everyone else was used to it, but the phrase was really clunky to him.

"You're seeing the fireworks tonight, right?" Catherine asked him.

The words he thought were along the lines of 'yes, yes, and I am so excited, I've been looking forward to it all week. It's going to be like living in the chapter of a book. I've reread every chapter of every book I have with fireworks in them, so both of them, and honestly, it has been affecting my dreams all week. I just have no idea what to expect. How do you split the sky with light? I cannot wait."

The words he said were, "Yeah, I'm pretty excited."

"It was nice of the Farvues to invite us, too," Karao said. "Please tell them we're sorry we can't go. Very literally, in some cases."

"I'm sure they get it," he said. Karao's house arrest was much more pronounced on a day like this.

"Just because you're getting the night off doesn't mean you're getting out of working, though." Catherine jabbed him with her elbow. "If you're staring into space again, I'm putting you on dishes."

He knew he would have to work, but taking orders from Catherine was new to him. He had to ask Karao, "Can she do that?"

"I'll allow it," Karao smirked. Catherine had already started. The shop would open in under an hour, and there was still some work to be done.

The buildup to flipping the open/closed sign didn't pay off. None of the festivities started until later in the morning, so it made sense, but the first hour of service was pretty much the same as usual. A pair of elderly women commented on the new decorations, one of which liked it the way it was before. Nils kept their customer service smile through the whole exchange.

Slowly, almost one at a time, people decided to try out the Pale Garden. By an hour into service, they had matched an entire day's worth of customers, so eight. They were mostly people Nika had recognized from around the street; workers, students, and parents. A lot of them had always assumed the Pale Garden was either abandoned or some bizarre fortune-telling shop. One quiet man even said that he thought the place was some sort of criminal front since there's no way it could stay in business otherwise.

By noon things had gotten out of hand. They thought they had done a lot of advertising, but in the end, none of that really made much of a difference. People were trying out the tea shop because the leading reason people were trying out the tea shop was the increased, curious, and overheated foot traffic.

Nika hadn't worked so hard in his life, but it was enjoyable, in a way. There was always something to keep him occupied, whether it was a table that needed setting up or taking orders. At the same time, Nils had stepped back into the kitchen. The tasks themselves were tiring and boring. Wipe down one table. You've cleaned them all. The spell Nils had taught him made it even more trivial. Taken as a whole, though, maintaining the rapidly shifting room was a challenge. The idea of doing it every day frightened him, but for now, it was fun.

Catherine used her break to check out the art tents before they closed. Nils wanted to stay in the front, so Karao was having Nika run around mad in the back. Even with five hands at her disposal, she was adept at using them as little as possible. Whichever deadarm of hers could manipulate shadows was doing all the work in the kitchen. Black tendrils formed out the shadows from the windowsill, cast by the cupboard. Even her own shadow contributed to the autonomous kitchen. She was focusing on keeping it all together.

"I think it's going well." One of the shadows reached into a bowl but scooped nothing out. She stood up to investigate. "Green tea!"

"Got it!" Nika was reasonably sure he knew where it was. He was wrong, but only by a cupboard or three. The kitchen was an entirely different level of stress. "When does Catherine come back?"

"What time is it?" Karao ripped open the box and poured its content into the bowl. She continued prepping the next order. Each one required different base teas and ingredients, which Karao would crush up before sealing inside a diffuser.

Nika was absolutely sure that wasn't how tea was supposed to be prepared. "One... twelve."

"Thirty-eight minutes," she replied. The crawling passage of time annoyed them both.

Somehow, they trudged on through the afternoon. Nils's voice was getting rough from talking to every person who walked into the building. If Catherine burned her hand on another teapot, she was going to explode. While the others grew weary, Nika just got more and more excited. Once it hit five and they closed, he would be off to enjoy his evening.

The people coming in intrigued him, too. Some had their faces painted. Others had wreaths strewn around their heads. There were wacky shirts and festive dresses on nearly every patron, and they all added to the mystique. He struggled to imagine what sort of event would be appropriate for both a regal floral patterned skirt and a novelty oversized sun hat so massive it needed to be folded to fit through the door.

Five o'clock, closing time, came faster than expected.

The customers didn't stop.

A seemingly unending supply of festive holiday-goers kept the front door swinging. There was never a moment to cut off the line, and sending people away would have looked bad for a place trying to eke out a profit. Karao was the one to make the final decision: they stay open until the customers stop coming, then they close as fast as possible.

Lisa Farvue arrived about twenty minutes after closing to witness the fanfare. As always, she was in full uniform. She seemed lost and confused in the crowded room, which was true for any of them by that point. She eventually got Nika's attention between sweeping and bussing tables.

"This seems... hectic." She pressed against a wall to get out of the way of a chatty family that wasn't looking where they were going. "Are you sure you're ok to leave?"

He looked back to Nils, who was drowning behind the counter. Wave after wave of customers and questions crashed down on them, and still, they stood. Their bandana was coming loose, their eyes darted back and forth between tasks and people. Their smile never faltered. There was only a brief window where Nils looked back, not even a full second, but it was enough. Nils waved him away, telling him to go, have fun.

Nils wanted him to go and enjoy the holiday. The moment passed, and the maelstrom of tasks swept them up once again.

"I-" Nika took a breath. "Can't. Not yet, I'm so sorry."

"Hey, hey, it's ok. I get it. Think you can still swing the fireworks?"

"Yes! I will." He wrung out his cleaning rag before getting back into the fray. "Where are they?"

"We usually go to the park on Hill Street. Do you know where that is?"

"The one with the fountain?" It had always weirded him out, yet he couldn't stop staring at it whenever he walked past. It was a beast carrying a raven on its back. Their poses were dynamic and intimidating, but their goofy faces and eyes ruined the whole look.

"You got it. We'll be there at eight-thirty. It starts at nine!" Lisa was shouting through a crowd of teenagers that had left a giant mess on one of the tables that Nika would now have to clean. "Good luck!"

"Thanks! See you soon!" Nika hoped that shouting at the table would refract the sound from her since he could barely hear anyone's particular voice anymore. It was back to work. Nils was surprised, though relieved, to see him still working. They pretended to be upset that he didn't go with a paper-thin disguise.

The overworked, over-hours staff of the Pale Garden tea shop fought on, one order after the next until the stream mercifully started pittering out at around seven o'clock. By then, they were out of a lot of ingredients. Baked goods had run dry hours before, and the last of the black and green teas went out, much to Karao's dismay.

"You're the last cup until tomorrow." She murmured to a rejected blend from earlier, unaware Catherine and Nika could hear her. "We'll make this work." She went to take a sip, put the cup down in restraint, then took a sip anyways.

The people towards the end were a lot less festive. Many seemed tired, and their clothes were a lot less fun—fewer bright shirts and goofy hats, more long coats and, well, sensible hats. People seemed to be bundling up as the sun got lower in the sky. Nika hadn't set foot outside, but the air coming in did seem cooler than before.

Sometimes a genuinely chilling breeze would sneak in and catch him by surprise.

The last customer left at eight seventeen. The entire front had been cleaned around them. At this point, they really just wanted him to leave. Everyone, including Nika, was too tired to celebrate their accomplishment. Catherine had grabbed a bundle of food and walked out, wishing everyone a good night.

They had no idea how busy to expect it to be after that, so everyone was expected to work again tomorrow, though not nearly as hard as that.

Nils was slumped in a chair. If their shirt hadn't snagged on the back, they probably would have fallen off of the thing. "That was a lot."

"Too many. Too many people. Drinking my tea." Karao stared longingly at her empty cup.

"There's still plenty of the jasmine," Nils argued without inflection or emphasis.

"I think." Equally drained of emotion, Karao replied. "I'd rather die."

They all watched Donut struggle to choke down a sugar cube for a solid minute.

"I like the jasmine," Nils said.

Nika wanted to eat and knew that he probably needed to, but his body was too tired to stay awake and recognize that it was hungry. He had made it through enough of the day that giving up now would be a gigantic waste. He just needed to put his head down for a minute and imagine the fireworks.

Descriptions like 'flashing lights' or 'colorful bursts' were absolutely useless. He had read a lot of short novels. Usually, authors took stuff for granted. They assumed that some things were so universal that they could glaze over the descriptions like there was nothing to be gained by spelling them out. They never imagined someone in his situation would read them. He had to assume so much, and this one thing had always bugged him the most.

The idea was nice. The air was nice. He was tired. He just needed to shut his eyes for a minute.

Or twenty.

Karao was the one that noticed the time. She shook him awake, telling him it was eight-forty over and over. Nika yelped. He needed to run, so he did. He knocked over at least two pieces of furniture on his way out, barely stopping to secure his own shoes. His head felt like it was lagging several feet behind him as he sprinted up the road.

The wind was a lot colder than he was expecting. The sky was dark, the streetlights hurried to keep pace with him. He was cursing himself with every alternate step when he had a thought to spare. The park was only six blocks away. If he kept pace, he would make it in time.

The people walking the other way down the road were giving him odd looks, but he didn't care. There were a lot of them, all distributed around the road at random. What started as a straight sprint became a game of dodging oncoming foot traffic. Families huddled together, rowdy men and women took up way more space than was necessary. He involuntarily would apologize and excuse himself whenever he came within a foot of another person.

The closer he got to the park, the thicker the crowd got, and the more desperate his mad dash became.

Crossing under the gate to the park was like stepping into the night. There were no more lights, no more crowds. People were leaving the park still, but he didn't have time to pay attention to that. He needed to find the Farvues. The fountain was not far from the entrance.

He sprinted up the barren path. Each footfall echoed across the black grass and the distant shadowy trees. The quiet was back. It was unsettling. The only light around was an illuminated clock. It read two minutes to nine. He still had time.

The beast-statue stood in the center of a tiered stone podium. In the night, it was impossible to see its lighthearted faces. One person was sitting by the statue. No lights, nobody else around. Just one sitting quietly in the dark. The only sound he could hear was the trickling water.

"A little late, huh." It was Morgan, though he didn't need that confirmed, really.

Nika could barely speak. His whole body seemed to be punishing him for waking back up. It couldn't have picked a worse day to protest, in his opinion. Still, he heaved out what could have been his last words as he found the most comfortable stone to lay on and did so.

"Sorry, sorry."

Morgan didn't seem mad or even upset. Someone was bothering her, but it wasn't that he was late to the show.

Nobody was around, come to think of it. Even her parents were gone.

"Where... where are yo- where is-" He mouthed the word everyone, but he couldn't get any breath to come out.

"Going home." Morgan curled her knees up and wrapped her arms around them. "The show was canceled."

"What!" His breath was finally starting to settle. "How come?"

Morgan pointed up. Nika was confused. There was nothing to see, nothing at all. The entire sky was overtaken by low, dark clouds. Not even the moon could reach them where they sat.

"Weather. They called it off a few minutes ago."

"Oh."

'Oh' was, remarkably, an accurate summary of every feeling and thought he had condensed into a single syllable. 'Oh' represented his understanding that fireworks were somehow weather-dependent. 'Oh' captured the moment he lost the motivating force that got him through that rough day. 'Oh' was his entire being in a two-letter word.

"Are you ok?" Morgan had moved, but he wasn't sure when. Maybe he had zoned out for a minute, navigating his newfound understanding of his world. Her tone was much more sedated compared to usual, or maybe he was just that tired.

He responded more out of a guttural reflex than an actual self-evaluation. "Yes."

He drank in the silence. His eyes hurt a bit, though he only realized that after a soft, green glow sparked in front of him. He'd seen it before. Morgan's summoned swarm of fireflies. It was a small group that slowly twirled and fluttered around her hand. He wasn't about to count them. He guessed there were a couple dozen of them at best.

"You." She squinted in the dim light. The fireflies were doing a better job of illuminating her face than it was his. "Are crying."

"Huh?" He felt his eyes. Yup. It wasn't much. Maybe a trailblazing tear streak marked that there was at least one before and one on the way. He wasn't sure why. He had felt sad and broken before, but not now. The only thing he felt was done.

That was probably enough, on second thought. If he said he wasn't disappointed, he would be lying. He was, clearly. The stress of everything was folding in on him from all sides. No, that couldn't have been it, either. Today had been a huge success, and he felt good enough about his entrance test. This couldn't have been the setback. Not getting to watch fireworks was way too normal of a problem-

Ah. There it was.

He had felt like a regular kid, like one from the books. Not some social pariah who went from one crappy home to a makeshift one off the back of his weird, creepy magic. His favorite stories were never the grandiose adventures but the small views into normal life and problems. Even just for a few days, he had gotten caught up in the fantasy of normalcy; life wasn't a book. It wasn't a story. Even if rushing to see the fireworks was normal, missing it was normal.

But it hurt.

Diagnosing himself was half the problem. Sharing his findings with Morgan would be the next. He couldn't say nothing. He had clearly been in deep thought for a significant amount of time. Besides, lying and hiding things had been causing enough problems around the tea shop lately without him adding to anything.

"I was just, I was really looking forward to it. That's all." He shook his head. "Wait, wait, that's not all. Not even close, but I don't know how to say the rest. I really don't."

Morgan pushed him, making him sit up. She sat across from him, legs crossed. The fireflies circled the two of them. As she walked back, shimmering, flowing green light felt once again like she was floating underwater.

She was balancing on the lip of the fountain. "Well, try. Just say words until something sticks. That usually works for me."

"I'm bad with words," he said.

"That's a lie. You're bad with talking," she said. "I saw your test scores, remember?"

"Oh, right." He took a breath. If he could sum up his conversational prowess in one word, it would be inept. 'Just saying what was on his mind was not his forte. "I just want to be normal." He smiled, then repeated it. "I just want to be normal."

Morgan put her hands to her chin. "What do you think normal is?"

It was a cruel follow-up, but a good one. "Normal is." He watched the fireflies cross paths, collecting his thoughts. "Normal is going to school, coming home to a family, having friends. It's not having people run away when they know about you."

Morgan hit him with her book. She had done this before. It was usually a lot more playful; she was upset. "So what's the problem!"

"Huh?"

"You have all of that! You want to be normal so bad? Well, look around, you got there. Family? You like yours. School? Gonna happen soon enough. Do you see anyone running away?" She gestured to the empty field. "Ugh. Nevermind. You have a problem with me or something?"

"No." Nika had nothing to add.

"Then you're going to moan that you have no friends?"

"I didn't mean that."

"Is your family too weird to be normal for you?" She had stepped back, still facing him. "How about me?"

"Wait, stop, stop." Nika realized what he had said.

"What's wrong with weird?" Morgan slammed her fist into her chest. "You think I don't know how weird I am? You're going to daydream about normal because weird isn't good enough?"

"Wait, please," Nika pleaded. She listened. "If you weren't weird, we wouldn't be friends. I wouldn't want you to be different. Normal is just an idea, I guess."

"You weren't describing normal," she said. "You were describing belonging. Weird belongs, too, you know. And more importantly, you belong with the weird. The shoe just fits."

He was too tired to argue philosophy. She was clearly trying to help in her own assertive way. She didn't know how long he had wanted a routine life and how close he was getting to having it. He wouldn't be able to put it into words, so he dropped it. "You may have a point," he said. He wasn't lying.

She stepped away. "You've never seen it before, right?" She was trying to balance on the edge of a bench but couldn't get steady enough footing to commit to the stunt. "The fireworks?"

"Never."

She pointed to the dark skies. "Look up."

The fireflies went dark. The swarm still made this soft sound which melted away into the cool night air. Nika didn't know what to look for in the clouds.

Around fifteen feet in the air, the fireflies started blinking on again. They had congealed into one large ball of light and dispersed, each bug carving its own individual trail of faint light into the darkness. As they got further away, the lights started going out for good until they reunited at another random point in the air and did it again.

"What are you doing?" Nika asked.

"Fireworks," she said from somewhere. He couldn't see.

He tried not to sound unimpressed. It was a really nice gesture, but he had been lied to if this was what all the hype was about. "It's smaller than I thought."

"Well, this is the most I can manage." She sounded annoyed. "Sorry."

"No, it's not that." He had always read that fireworks coated the whole sky, illuminating the night with brilliant colors. She was clearly trying her best with what she had. "You want a hand?"

"What now?" She seemed confused. It was hard to see her even up close with the light source hovering so far away.

"I've been letting everyone help me for the whole summer. I want to help back." Nika held up his hand for a high five. It began crackling with necromancy. She cautiously accepted the invitation.

Contrasting the hazy green ball in the sky, the purple crackling light around the hands of the two mages on the ground was fierce and swift. It was impossible to tell how much of his soul he was using to power Morgan's summoning power-up, numbers-wise. He had come up with his own system of what 'felt' right for percentages. It was a crude scale. One hundred percent was when he passed out. Thirty percent made him need to sit down, ten percent just made him dizzy.

He let go; the damage was done. Smiling, he slumped into the grass. She panicked briefly, fearing a repeat of their last incident. He assured her everything was ok and just to push her summoning to its limit. The cloud of dozens of fireflies became thousands, if not tens of thousands. The shimmering of wings was just barely discernible against the backdrop of the sky, even without the lights. They were bright enough for the two to be able to fully see each other while flickering.

She lowered her hands like a conductor; the lights went out. With a pause and a dramatic upswing, the pathetic little stream of fireflies from before repeated itself, only on a much grander scale. A column of flickering green light shot into the air and burst near the clouds. The lights scattered, jittery and feverish, in every direction imaginable. Like before, they died down as they grew further from the center of the thing.

It matched every description he had ever read, save for one thing.

A second jet shot up. As it reached its peak, Morgan landed on the ground next to him, ready to watch, with a singular proclamation: "Boom!"

Chapter 20- End

Intermission- The Fireworks

To the surprise of nobody that knew her, Morgan managed to drum up a crowd. Nika wasn't the only one disappointed by the lack of fireworks. After the initial display, many people were wondering where the lights were coming from.

To the surprise of most people that knew her, Morgan kept a low profile. At the same time, the festival-goers returned to the park for the admittedly shorter show. Her parents returned, found the two of them sitting in the grass, and chose to sit out of earshot but very much in view. She controlled the whole show from her spot on the ground, waving her hands slowly to control the lights' flow.

The fireflies weren't moving around as much, as it turned out. They weren't faster because of Nika. She was just controlling the lights inside a gigantic cloud of bugs above them. At least, that's the answer he got when he asked.

"Happy now?" she asked. "Pop. Pop. Pop." She poked the sky in three points, causing three more 'fireworks' to go off."

"Very," Nika said. "Can't move though."

"That sounds like a problem for later."

"Agreed."

"You know." The crowd 'ooh'd' at one of her displays. "You started this with a big 'I want to help' thing."

"Yeah," he said.

"And yet here I am still doing all the work." Morgan taunted. It was nice for the conversation to get back to their usual tone. "Pchyoo!"

"Talk to me when my arms don't weigh four hundred tons," he said. "Each."

"Maybe you can help patch up my costumes." Morgan was brainstorming aloud. "Or just organize my room, sort through my cards and magazines. You know, all the pros have assistants. You look like you'd carry a clipboard well."

"I hate you."

"Nah."

Chapter 21. Worst Day, Hands Down

No one questioned why the tea shop was empty at nine in the morning, simply out of habit. In spite of the positive reception the day before, none of them were really worried about why nobody had come back. Honestly, they were happy to have the break. Catherine was running late, but it wasn't an issue. They figured she had slept in and wished they could have done the same.

When she did arrive, it was with a huge entrance. The door was flung, her footsteps were heavy. She demanded the attention of everyone in the room without having to say a single word. Her heavy winter coat also raised questions.

Daniel walked in behind her; he was also dressed for the cold. Where Catherine's face was dismayed, his was dour. They both had huge furls of paper under their arms. Karao entered from the back.

She asked over the heavy breath catching, "Catherine? What's wrong?"

"Just... come outside." Catherine dropped the cargo onto one of the tables. They were stacks of newspapers. The same newspaper, it seemed as many copies of it as they could carry. The entire staff of three followed them out the door and into the street. Nika understood the coats after a single step. It felt like a dry forty degrees like the heat was just being pulled out of his body through his sleeves.

He was expecting another kind of vandalism on the tea shop, which wasn't strictly speaking the case. The huge piles of newspapers on the table seemed to represent as many copies as the two of them could carry and made up maybe a single-digit percentage of the total newspapers he could see from the front door. They were everywhere. Tied to lampposts, posted to doors, covering windows. Nils took a few daring steps out into the cold and was assaulted by two dormant papers that had been lying in wait on the ground. They flung up into their hands.

"What's going on?" Nika asked.

"It's an emergency print," Karao and Daniel answered. Karao, who had just peeked her head out the door rather than leaving the building, spun around and grabbed one of the copies, and began reading.

A herd of newspapers rolled down the road from the east. The four-inch-tall stampede of paper drove them inside. It sounded like thunder, somehow. Karao's death grip on the edges of her copy of the paper worried them, so they all took their own copies and began reading.

There was a lot.

The entire paper was dedicated to a single story written by a reporter named Beth. It was broken down into various sections, but the gist was captured in the title: 'Necromancer Attack In Eldes; Suit Captain Cruise's Corrupt Investigation Exposed.' Every part of reading it made Nika's stomach churn.

The corruption, which took up the bulk of the paper, outlined specific examples of Cruise and Karao's relationship and how he was 'going easy' on an old friend who should have been a primary suspect. She argued that house arrest was an entirely inappropriate measure given the severity of the situation and the likeliness that Karao was involved. The proof seemed flimsy, but every detail was correct.

Morbid curiosity compelled him forward as he trudged through line after line of the damning editorial. Nils had focused on the front few pages, which were mainly about the 'potentially first of many attacks in Eldes. The story had been rumbling in the background as a growing crime spree. The investigation had been a series of dead ends. No investigator or consultant asked gave even the slightest indication that they were making progress. The article alleged that discounting a prime suspect, in the beginning, might have had a lot to do with that, and letting her onto various crime scenes tainted them beyond repair.

In the middle of page three was a small section dedicated to Karao's known history. It wasn't much. She had been a citizen of Eldes for many decades. She had garnered a modest reputation for being a powerful necromancer. At the bottom of the blurb, they named the tea shop.

"What's happening? Karao, what's happening?" Nils was panicking.

"I don't know, Nils, I need some time." She tore her current copy in half and plucked another from the stack. "I don't understand where she learned about Cruise and I. Has anyone suspicious talked to any of you? Nika?"

"No." Everyone he knew was suspicious, just not in this particular way. "I'm certain."

Daniel coughed. "Nika, you've met her." He pointed to the byline. "It's Beth; remember the reporter that bumped into us?"

Nika had forgotten Daniel was there. He had no idea what he was talking about. His memory of the time in the newspaper office was crystal clear; it was just the two dropping stuff off and leaving.

"What are you talking about?"

Daniel was in shock. "It was you." he stood up. "You did this!"

"Daniel, calm down." Karao was standing now. Catherine rapidly tapped her foot on the ground. Nils was trying to stop Daniel from saying anything reckless.

"He's lying! I swear! Why? Nika! Nika!" The desperation of his words climbed with the tension in the room. "Answer me!"

Nika was scared. He had trusted Daniel, he had trusted most people, in fact, and everything was starting to crumble around him. He sat down again. His pulse was irregular and picking up speed.

Karao took a knee next to him. "Nika, it's ok. I believe you. I want to hear your side."

What he said next was true, but that didn't make it a good idea. "I have no idea what he's talking about."

The shouting didn't stop. All five people in the room seemed to just be getting more frustrated with each and every word. Whoever was the loudest was the most heard, pretty much disqualifying Nika from participating in the conversation outright. Karao, for her part, was doing her best to put out fires and mediate, and even the stress of that was taxing.

Nika almost hated the yelling more than the content of the articles.

After an eternity and a half of shouting, the crux of things came down to this: either Nika was lying, or Daniel was. Nika seemed to have nothing to gain from secretly meeting with Beth and was the newest to the group. Nils had known Daniel for years as a close friend and trusted him a lot, but the fact that he worked at the newspaper that was now telling people to avoid their tea shop was not a point in his favor.

Catherine pointed out that Daniel was the one that brought this all to her attention in the first place. He lived in the dorms, too, and had figured it would be faster to get to Catherine than it was to run to the tea shop. She dragged him along anyway.

"Stop!" Karao commanded. She was sitting on the counter, running her fingers through her hair. "Just. Stop. None of that matters. We need to figure out what we do now. We can figure this out later."

Daniel was glaring at him. There was no trust. Nils couldn't look up from the floor. Catherine was just frustrated from not knowing how to handle the situation. Nika was trying hard to remember if he had forgotten something if this was all some huge misunderstanding. Daniel seemed so confident and betrayed.

Daniel tried to leave. In more detail, Karao asked him to leave. He had been a huge help, and he was always welcome back, but they needed time to deal with this themselves. He agreed, hugged Nils goodbye, then went to the door. He twisted the handle and pushed. Nothing. He tried again. Nothing. He shook his head and pulled, convinced he had forgotten how doors worked. That didn't work either.

"Did you lock the door?" he asked.

"No," Karao said. Her voice was as calm as ever, but her arms were gearing for a fight. "Everyone, get back in the kitchen."

"Wait, wait, that won't be necessary." A voice Nika did not know called from the kitchen. A man with curly blonde hair and a mustache to match walked through into the main room. He was wearing the same sort of suits as Cruise and the Farvues. "The door thing was us. So sorry about that. We didn't want to interrupt." He was nibbling on a bread roll from the kitchen.

"You are?" Karao had gathered everyone behind her, save for Daniel, who was dumbstruck by the door.

"Captain Monty." He folded an arm into his shoulder and bowed a bit. "Not alone, of course. Come along, everyone."

Nika had expected more people to come out of the kitchen when he said that. That wasn't wrong in and of itself. Still, he hadn't expected people to walk through each of the four walls like they weren't even there—people of every color and shape unified by steely looks and suits. One came up from under the counter. One of the ones behind him was staring him down.

One man did walk up behind Monty. Ben Farvue. He looked sick to his stomach.

To someone staring her in the eye, Karao still looked ready to fight at a moment's notice. Her deadarms had relaxed, though. Her confident and untouchable posture was back in full force. Nika was only sure of one thing: Karao was sure they were going to get out of this.

Karao spoke, unimpressed. "And the reason you're here, captain?"

"Your arrest, of course. I mean, come on." He laughed, gesturing to the stack of papers that were now scattered around the room. He twirled a chair around and sat in it. "You can't be surprised."

The moment Karao started walking, the sounds of suit sleeves rustling echoed around each corner of the room. The deadarms were intimidating to anyone who wasn't familiar with them. This was something Karao was used to. With a calm and simple hand gesture, they reassessed if she was a threat and stood down. She took another chair and sat across from him. It reminded Nika of the first time he met Cruise and a simple showdown over a cup of tea. She looked back at the three of them and behind them to the suits bordering the walls of her tea shop.

She needed to lead with a strong opening. "I didn't know rags like this passed for evidence these days. Arrest away if you want. It's your career."

"Was that a threat?" He faked an appalled look. "I know you were real cushy with the last guy, but your reign of pushing officers around ended today."

"Did you arrest him too?" She smirked. That drove him mad.

"Suspended during the investigation." One of his subordinates tapped him on the shoulder with a concerned look on her face. He brushed her off. "I've got this."

"Do you know? You've already given up quite a bit." Karao nodded towards the suit backing up to the wall. "Should have listened to her."

He pursed his lips and nodded, chuckling. "You know, I just hate a misunderstanding, don't you? I want to make sure we're all on the same page." He righted himself up in the seat. "No loose ends, you know?"

Karao glared. "As a consultant on this case-"

"Former, consultant, actually. No misunderstandings." His toothy smile seemed to irk everyone in the room.

"As a former consultant on this case, the evidence proving my family innocent was in place well before I had anything to do with it." She adjusted her posture. "You'd risk your political ambitions going after an orphanage for necromancers?"

"I thought this was a tea shop." He looked back to the woman from before.

She clarified for him, flipping through floor plans and legal documents from a slim briefcase. "Actually, sir, just the ground floor is a tea shop. The upstairs is registered as the 'Orphanage for Abandoned Necromancers.'"

"Is that legal?" he asked.

"It seems so, sir."

"It hardly matters. We're not here about the ongoing attacks. This is about the corruption investigation."

The woman behind him covered her mouth and seemed to scream silently. The other suits raised an eyebrow or looked concerned. Ben's face perked up for the first time in the entire exchange.

Karao had it. "The corruption investigation?"

"Yes."

She led him on further. "The less than three-hour old corruption investigation?"

"Yes?" He was the only one in the room wearing a suit who didn't look at least a little upset.

"You never liked Cruise, did you?"

The woman in the back ran up to her boss to stop him from putting his foot in his mouth. She was too late. "A professional can set aside those feelings, you know."

"It's just, well, you brought a fully armed invasion into a small orphanage to conduct illegal arrests connected to the investigation of a nonviolent crime allegedly committed by someone whose political position you wanted?" Her eye contact didn't let up for a second. "No misunderstandings?"

"The arrests are still totally legal. Otherwise, you could spin it that way, I suppose." For such a serious accusation, he didn't seem to mind much at all.

"Sir," the now exasperated woman in the back came up to correct her boss once again. "You specified which charge we had. Since it's nonviolent, we would have to put her under house arrest instead."

"Way ahead of you there." Karao pointed to the small red brand keeping her under house arrest.

Captain Monty laughed, catching just about everyone by surprise. "You know, they all told me to just shut up and arrest you. Sure shows me, huh. I've heard you've smooth-talked your way out of lots of things over the years. I wanted to take a crack at it for myself. I'll come clean. I had no intention of arresting you unless you said something particularly incriminating, of course."

"Thank you, captain."

"Well, I'm certainly not leaving empty-handed." He shoved the last of the bread into his mouth and ordered through stuffed cheeks, "Sweep the place, everyone. Interview them all."

"Sir!" One of the suits behind them grabbed Nika lightly by the shoulder. "This one has a charm on him." He started pushing him up towards the back. "It's pretty nasty." This seemed to be news to everyone else in the room. Nils and Catherine tried to reach out to him, but he had been pushed too far ahead by then.

"Wendy, Unta, let's set up in the kitchen. Everyone else! Investigate and question. We can't waste this valuable time with my prime suspects." He paused, then pointed to Karao. "You come too. Legal reasons."

With a total of five people in the kitchen Nika had never felt less comfortable in this home. Part of that was due to the ongoing investigation in the next room, though more directly, the man who dragged him in held him by the back of the neck.

"It looks like some kind of memory bug," he said, his eyes were swimming through some sort of blue haze. "It looks pretty fresh. We should be able to remove it here."

Monty rubbed his temple and asked Karao a question. "You're his legal guardian, right?" This was clearly not a part of his plan.

"Yes."

"Since he's a minor, we need your permission to disenchant in the field."

Karao put her hand on Nika's shoulder. "Will it hurt?"

He was worried before, now he was terrified. Monty shrugged. The suit analyzing the charm in his head made some non-committal grunting sounds. "It will only get worse the more you wait." Monty knelt down and met Nika's eye level. "Someone's been messing with your memories. The feeling of having all of them rush back at once is going to hurt for a little bit. Think you can do it?"

He hated the idea that someone was playing with him. He didn't know if he could trust the suits, but Karao didn't seem to be fighting against it either.

"Yes," he said.

The spell to remove the enchantment was simple and swift, like ripping off a bandage. He had braced himself, gripped the sides of the chair so tight that his knuckles were threatening to pop off. Nothing. The suit behind him said he was done in a matter of seconds.

The feelings of repressed memories fighting to all come back were worse than every headache he had ever had melded into one. He had been watching the clock intently the entire time; the pain only lasted for six seconds, apparently, but to him, it felt like hours. In that time, he had relived every memory.

He went to speak but was stopped by Monty. The captain commanded Wendy, the woman who repeatedly tried to save him in the other room, to take Unta's place behind him. She cast some sort of spell that made the back of his head feel really, really good. This inescapable warmth and niceness spread from the base of his skull down his spine and through the rest of his body.

"I'm going to ask you some questions, but I don't want you to answer them. Wendy, here is looking into your mind right now. She'll answer the questions honestly before you get the chance. Ok?" He glared at Karao, his prime suspect for memory tampering. "We'll find out where that bug came from, won't we?"

"He understands," Wendy said. She didn't share that he thought the captain smelled, which he appreciated.

Nika couldn't be happier that he didn't have answers for most of the questions. When asked what he knew about the investigation, the answer was nothing. When asked about Cruise and Karao's relationship, his thoughts were jumbled snippets of common information. He tried hard not to think of the fact that Cruise was a necromancer trained by Karao, but not only did the thought emerge anyways, but it also didn't seem to phase anyone in the room much at all.

Karao hated watching this, but she persevered. Nika was actually sort of relieved that he didn't need to make any choices in this. Good or bad, this was all there was to it. Whatever he knew would be shared, and that would be that.

"Have you ever committed a crime, Nika?" Monty asked. Karao stood up.

"Petty theft, it looks like," Wendy stated in the same matter-of-fact voice as all the other stuff. "He stole food between homes."

"Between homes?" Monty leaned forward a bit. "Tell me about your old home."

"Sir, I don't think-"

"The answer, Wendy."

Wendy thought before speaking each word. "I see several instances of abuse, not from the family but from townsfolk. It looks like one of those non-magic communes, and they all knew what he could do. Lots of quiet time locked in a room with books. Enough food to survive but not much beyond that. A lot of solitude. A lot."

"What's life now like?" He was trying, again and again, to 'get' Karao.

"Better." Wendy seemed relieved like she had become invested in his story and thought it had a happy ending. "No criminal activity since moving here. He's taken to this home quickly."

"I see, I see. I just needed a fuller picture. No misunderstandings, right?" Monty leaned back, smiling. "So, Nika, have a crush on anyone?"

"Sir!" Wendy cut off the magic, Nika blushed, Karao rolled her eyes.

"Only trying to lighten the mood. If you don't mind, we have one last thing to cover." The magic resumed, and Nika relaxed again. Monty began the last line of questioning. "Do you know who put the charm on you?"

He knew. He remembered it all now. Wendy's shock confirmed it. "He only knows her as Beth. She's the reporter."

Monty sat up so quickly the levity in his face fell behind. "You're certain?"

"It's definitely her. She's been talking to him regularly with a scribbler. He's been coerced into answering questions for her almost every night. That paper is currently being used as a bookmark upstairs in a book called 'The Light Below.'"

The investigation turned on a dime in that instant. Karao led some of the suits up to the upper rooms as Monty asked for more details of exactly what sorts of things Beth had asked him about. He would never have been able to remember it all himself. Luckily Wendy's magic seemed to make up for the gaps in his recollection. She stayed and scrolled through his memories a bit more, though he wasn't sure why.

When Monty burst back into the main room, every suit turned towards him. Beth's cursed paper scrap, called a scribbler, was held high in a small glass case. Nobody knew what it was.

"We are leaving," he announced to the room, "Nobody here is cleared of suspicion, just to be clear. I'll be reassigning, well, most of you all to your former cases. Wendy, Bahst, Jeorge, and Ben, you're with me."

Most of the suits left at that. Monty and his selected crew stuck around to clean and wrap things up. Karao insisted they leave it to them, but Monty was having nothing of it.

"Oh, we'll be back, Karao. Beth might have tainted this evidence, but you're not in the clear. We're just regrouping and looking into this -highly- illegal charm."

"Turn over as many rocks as you'd like. It's a good workout," she said.

"Oh, I nearly forgot." He pulled a small ring out of his pocket. Karao's neck tensed. "Surely you know what this is?"

When Cruise had informed Karao of her house arrest, she had been offered two choices. The ring was the choice she had shot down in an instant. She growled her confirmation that she did, in fact, remember what it was.

"As captain, these are fully used at my discretion. I'm sure you'll understand why I don't trust you at this point."

"Getting cozy in your new seat, Monty?" Karao spoke with more malice than at any point during the upwelling of the Pale Garden.

He invited her over to a table. "It isn't bad. Hand or foot?"

She snapped off her answer, "Hand."

He looked at her one living arm. "Are you sure? Ok." He placed the ring down on the counter. Karao placed her hand over it, covering the ring with her palm.

Monty grimaced as he smashed her hand into the ring. Karao buckled a bit from the pain but kept standing. The thing was magically embedded into her hand.

One by one, her deadarms slowed, stopped, and fell. Her demeanor changed, her liveliness cut out. Without magic, she seemed like a shell of herself. She tried to stand tall in the face of this. Her eyes gave away just how much she had lost.

She collapsed once they left. She was fully conscious, just overwhelmed. She slumped against the counter, barely managing to keep herself upright. She muttered to herself, saying that the ring was the reason he showed up in the first place; he never intended to arrest anyone.

She stared at her palm for the rest of the day.

Chapter 21- End

Intermission- Goodbye, Good Luck

Cruise was fine. Casual clothes didn't suit him, but he wasn't allowed to wear his uniform while they conducted the investigation. He had been waiting at the library waiting] for over an hour, and his schedule was remarkably still tight.

"I don't have a lot of time, kid." Cruise sat back in the comfiest-looking chair the ground floor reading section had to offer. "How is Karao doing?"

"She's surviving." It had been a few days since Monty had stripped her magic away. She sulked and dragged herself through each day, waiting for the end of all this madness. Her house arrest had been lifted, yet she didn't find excuses to go outside. He whispered his questions. "Are they going to arrest her?"

Cruise shook his head. "Monty is a jerk, but he plays by the letter of the law. There's nothing to find and a lot of documentation to prove it. I'll give him that it looks bad. I don't mind the investigation so much."

"What about what they did to Karao!" His temper was on a short fuse. He apologized for the outburst and waited for an answer.

"I would have made the same call, given the circumstances." He looked at the floor. "It's awful, but it's also the right thing to do. I'm sorry, I know that's not what you wanted to hear."

Cruise checked the clock for the third time since the two had started their conversation. As they talked about the state of things, how the necromancers and Lisa were holding up, his eyes would drift over to it again and again.

After a brief aside about how freakishly cold it was for the last day of July, he stood and threw his coat over his shoulders. He apparently didn't have time for something as silly as sleeves.

"I have to leave, but I have something very important to ask you." Cruise adjusted his hat. His hand was shaking a bit. It wasn't cold inside the library.

"What?"

"I need you to come back here tomorrow. I gave Lisa something to hold onto for me. Just in case." He bent down a bit to meet Nika's eye level. "If she gives it to you, you need to bring it to Karao immediately. Do you understand? Good. It'll be wrapped in a small box. Lisa is not allowed to know its contents under any circumstance. Heh, it's no wonder we're being investigated, huh. Say hello to Karao for me. Tell her to save me a cup."

Chapter 22. When It Snowed In August

It was beautiful in the worst sense of the word. For the first time since the article's publication, nobody stared at the necromancers as they stood outside their tea shop because there was something much weirder to stare at.

Snow was nothing new to any of them, but a week ago, it had been summer. This was unnatural. Nika's baggy deadarm sweater was finally useful again, but that was a really small victory in a bizarre and scary world. It had started sometime during the night, and a steady stream had buried the stone streets under a full two inches of snow already.

Catherine had discovered that it was the kind of snow with the satisfying crunch on her way to work. She was confused as anyone else but definitely the best at rolling with the punches. Nils seemed to flip a switch from being unable to tolerate the heat to being completely miserable in the cold. Their face was buried in their turtleneck. Almost no customers had come in the last week, and the snow day promised to be no different.

Karao had reminded them that something was behind the snowstorm, and that sort of omen never tended to end well. Catherine told her to lighten up. Karao chucked a snowball at her, the first fun act she had done in the whole week.

Nika left the three of them rolling up snowballs in the street to go do Cruise's errand. He didn't end up telling anyone about it, but he did offer to return Karao's extremely overdue library book. Gladys, the librarian, was starting to glare at Nika just by association with Karao. It was some heavy volume he had never seen her read that had been collecting dust in the basement, some history of ancient rules of law. It looked as dry as its dusty pages.

Karao had sent him with something else, too; Karao's small hourglass embedded in a coin. She had used it occasionally while running errands. Once the time ran out, he would be teleported to wherever its companion coin was. Currently, it was behind the counter in the tea shop. As much as he hated teleporting, the idea of walking through the falling snow twice was just slightly worse.

The coin hissed softly in his pocket. Being the only moving thing on the street, it was hard to focus on anything but Cruise's flighty behavior the day before. He seemed so anxious and worried about today. Nika wanted to trust him that he and Karao had done nothing wrong. Still, behavior like that would be suspicious even on a good day.

Lisa was not standing alone in front of the library. Morgan, wrapped under layers of scarves and coats, was leaning on the door, peering in. It was hard to make out anyone or anything from a distance in the copious snowfall. Still, he was happy to see them, and the feeling was mutual. He wasn't sure why they hadn't walked into the library yet. The sky rumbled.

Lightning struck Lisa Farvue.

Well, he assumed that it did. Even with his recent experience with it, the process of someone getting hit by lightning was fast and impossible to keep up with. The flash of light was familiar. The deafening sound rattled the confirmation in his brain. The way she hit the snow implied something bad had happened.

Morgan didn't have time to realize what was happening. She had pressed up against the doorway as an instinct and was shaking her head. Nika stumbled towards the two of them. He didn't know that lightning happened during a snowstorm, but that was not a concern right now. He tripped in the snow next to Lisa. She was coughing but alive. Her skin was glowing with the same faint blue glow as Ben's enchanting runes. Nika wondered if he was nearby or if this was just a precaution they set up ahead of time. Either way, She was going to be ok, probably.

It was hard to hear through the howling at first, but the distinctive crunch of footsteps in the snow was getting louder. Nika looked up.

The man's body standing before him was broken and battered. The skin had burned in intricate patterns from being struck repeatedly by lightning. The left leg dragged behind him, barely able to support any of the weight. The singed frame of a burnt umbrella served as his crutch.

Bringer's eyes hosted dancing violet lights.

Well, it was certainly the body of the man that died in the street. It was still unclear to him if that person was Bringer or the former principal, but whoever was in it at the time had almost certainly died. The shambling body stepped closer to them like it was being dragged along for the ride.

"I've been waiting to do that," he said. The voice cracked and shook, but even without those grotesque features, Nika didn't recognize it. It wasn't the man, though. He saw that she was still breathing and sneered. "You know, killing you people used to be easy." He looked up to Nika. "And you are?"

Nika stepped back. He couldn't breathe. His hearing felt muddled, and his head was still fuzzy from the snow-dampened thunder. The thing was distractingly inhuman. Nika heard some fluttering sound coming from behind him, somewhere in the library door.

Luna grazed his head as it shot past him. Morgan's conjured moth lunged at the walking demon corpse. He screamed as he was knocked into the snow, lightning forming around his arms and head as he grappled with the terrifying bug.

Morgan ran up to her mom and began pulling. She was yelling something, but Nikas's focus was on the fight in front of them. A shredded piece of wing flew by, a blood-curdling shriek of a fractured limb being bitten stuck in his mind and would likely never leave.

He shook off the mesmerizing image; he needed to help Morgan. As badly as he wanted to freeze up, this would have been a horrible time. Nika took Lisa's other arm, and the two started to lift the unconscious woman. The going was slow, but they only had a few feet to move her. They needed every second that Luna could buy them.

"Just a little more, it's ok, it's ok, it's ok," he said. He had intended to think it, but that really wasn't a concern at the moment. The only thing they could think about was getting through the doors. He honestly didn't expect to make it. He expected the moth to die and for them to be struck down just like Lisa had been. In the reflection in the door, he could see that they still had a moment as they walked up to it.

The door was locked.

"No!" Morgan rattled it, banging on the door. "Let us in!"

Nika hadn't really looked at her since this began. Her fists shook as she tried to muster the strength to keep knocking. Her voice wavered. Still, even through the fear, she seemed to have a plan. She stopped assaulting the door and grabbed her book. She needed more time, something different than the moth.

The corpse had finished the fight with Luna, skewering it with the steel tip of his umbrella. Luna dissolved into small light particles. In its own way, he took a moment to breathe a small twisted joke and looked for someone to blame for that unpleasantness.

"You little rat," it growled. "You'd dare fling filthy insects at me?

The corpse pointed its umbrella towards the sky. Morgan stopped flipping through pages and held the book as a whole up. Nika's hands began to spark with necromancy. His plan was to pour as much of his soul into Lisa as he could and hope she could get them out of this.

Lightning struck again, this time hitting the umbrella's tip. The corpse internalized the electricity, taking it in for a moment before pointing the umbrella at the three huddled in the doorway.

The door clicked. Nika and Lisa had been leaning against it and started pushing it through. Nika reached out and grabbed Morgan as he was falling out of instinct. Something was wrapped around him. That's all he could tell at the moment. He didn't dare look away from the menacing figure in the street.

Lightning was flung out from the corpse's umbrella. Nika didn't see where it connected. He was too busy trying to relearn how to breathe. Something howled like an animal releasing its final breath.

Being pulled into the library, he expected to land in the library. Instead, the three of them were falling through an endless black void. The door slipped further away from them. Nika could think of two likely explanations for this darkness.

The first was that he was dying, and this is what death felt like. The second, and only explanation for all three of them to be falling, was that the library had a magic door that detected overdue books. He had nearly fallen into this void when he first visited the library, and remembering that jarring encounter comforted him. He hadn't died yet, but they're really wasn't any sign of the fall slowing down or ending.

Like most things in life, the fall continued until it didn't.

Landing in a large copper tub of books should have hurt a lot by all accounts. If the summer in this city had taught him anything, it was that weird things like that were almost always because of some precautionary magic put in place to stop something stupid from happening. Stupid like, say, plummeting hundreds of feet from the library entrance into some sort of book collection unit.

The huge cylindrical room they were in was poorly lit. Half of the lights on the wall had long since burnt out, and what little light there was stretched itself thin, covering every inch of the empty space they found themselves in. Pipes were bolted to the walls coiling up in every direction. There was some unrecognizable shape, shifting and groaning in the middle of the room. The dim light kept it enveloped in shadow.

Something was wiggling underfoot. Nika moved, releasing a book from its place below him. It flapped like a rigid and confused bird drifting up towards the end of one of the pipes. As it approached, it was sucked in and rattled its way back into the library proper, presumably.

"Idiots," A recognized voice came from the lump in the center. It sounded like Gladys, the librarian sphinx. It made sense, but there was something off. She seemed much larger, much furrier than usual.

Nika lowered himself from the tub of books. He would like to have done it gracefully, but he was still shaken from the encounter outside. He fell onto the ground with an echoing thump.

Morgan landed next to him but on her feet without making a fool of herself. Showoff.

Morgan finally spoke, "What is happening?"

Gladys turned to face them. It wasn't the stone face they had grown used to but an ancient, organic one. Her face was as tall as Lisa's body. Her milky eyes explained why fixing the lights wasn't exactly a high priority for her. She tried to place one of her lion-like paws on the ground but winced as it connected. The seared fur and smell gave it away: she had taken the hit.

"That-" Gladys glared as Lisa clawed her way to the top of the book tub, "-is what you are supposed to tell me, Ms. Farvue, Mr. Necromancer."

"It wasn't her fault!" Nika was standing now.

"I don't care whose fault it is. I want to know why some rotting half-dead demon is currently tearing my library asunder!"

The ceiling above them rumbled as if on cue.

"This has nothing to do with the kids." Lisa stumbled her way onto the floor. The height disparity between the massive sphinx and the three of them didn't seem to phase her at all. Nika's neck was starting to hurt from some combination of whiplash and looking up at Gladys' very tall face. "He-it-whatever it was is out to get me. I can deal with this."

"You can barely stand." Gladys coughed blood. "Which makes two of us, I suppose." She laid on her side. "And here I thought I had a few good years left in me."

Morgan didn't seem to care about how things got the way they were. She just wanted to get them out of the situation. "You'll be ok! We just need to go get help."

Gladys laughed. More blood. "First, no doctor can cure an aging body. Second, there's only one way out, and it's currently being blocked by a monster who's breaking my little stone babies into pieces. You're all safer staying here and waiting out the storm."

Nika surprised everyone with his echoing shout: "No!"

Gladys was the one to finally ask for clarification. "No?"

"If we let him leave, he's going to hurt other people." Nika was thinking, specifically, of the other necromancers. Morgan's dad was also present for the fight against Bringer, so he might be a target too. "I saw him die. Why on earth is he still standing?"

"The necromancer can't figure out why a dead body might be up and walking around?" Gladys put her head down. "That's rich."

"Karao wouldn't do that!" Nika said. After taking that bold stance, he remembered that there was at least one other necromancer causing problems for the past few months. "Oh."

Lisa seemed to watch his realization unfold in real-time. "Yeah. That investigation was just a series of frustrating dead ends."

"ivest- what? What?" Morgan asked. She turned to Nika, "You know? Someone just tell me what's happening!"

"Well, barely. I don't know. I thought he-" Nika shook his head. "He was dead. I saw it. It was... it happened."

The sphinx groaned as it painstakingly moved. "Whoever that used to be is long, long gone. There's some necromancy at play, I'm sure of it. But there's something else in there now, and you let it into my library!" She stumbled and slipped down again. "If I wasn't on death's door, I would fine you into oblivion, child."

"What do we do?" Nika asked. Gladys mumbled something about irresponsible kids who didn't know how to follow orders.

"Could we sneak out a window or something?" Lisa was firmly on Nika's side on this.

Gladys gave up, unable to hold the three of them down there. "All the windows are on the second floor or higher. At that point, you might as well try to use the door."

After a few minutes of arguing and listening in on the destruction coming from above, they had come up with a flimsy plan. Lisa would go alone and try to escape the library. Gladys was counting down the stone statues that were being destroyed from above. She had direct control over them, like puppets. She could see through their eyes and feel every hit and fracture the demon corpse inflicted on them. Reluctantly, Gladys tapped a pattern into the stones on the floor, and a hole in the wall opened. The way back up was apparently a dumbwaiter embedded between two stacks labeled 'books to repair' and 'books to read.'

Lisa kissed Morgan and told her she loved her. Stay safe. Don't let Nika and the oversized cat do anything reckless.

By the time Lisa was on her way up, Gladys was down to one and a half remaining statues. One continued the fight while the other, impaled on one of the decorative knights, clung to its pseudo-life as a pair of eyes to observe.

"This is a terrible idea," Gladys commented again, wincing. "Probably the worst any of you have ever had. Including your not-so-secret hideout, Ms. Farvue."

Morgan was trying not to listen to the crashing and rumbling above them. "You knew about that?"

"Of course I knew about that. You ever meet a stupid sphinx?"

"I haven't met another sphinx. So... I'd have to think about it."

"Heh. Making fun of a dying old lady, are we? And I used to like you, too." Her smile died. It wasn't the same grimace from the pain they saw before but one filled with dread. "No. no-no-no."

Morgan demanded to know what Gladys had seen. Nika started shrinking. The idea of losing someone that he knew weighed down his lungs. His heart had the audacity to continue beating in a body otherwise frozen in fear; blood reluctant to flow.

"She's alive," Gladys started. A horrific screech rang from above, followed by a distinctive snap. The dumbwaiter fell down its chute, scraping and sparking along the walls the whole way down. It was broken beyond repair well before it crashed, but the collision with the ground did not help.

The two looked back to Gladys for answers.

"She's clever. She's staying just out of sight, but he definitely knows that she's there." Gladys frowned. "She's pinned, though. It's standing between her and the door, and the stairs are in the open. This is bad. This is very, very bad."

Morgan had gotten up partway through the explanation without either of them noticing. They would likely have continued to be completely unaware if she didn't make such a clutz of herself trying to climb back into the huge tub of books.

"What are you doing?" Gladys asked.

"I'm going to help." Morgan vaulted herself over the side and began throwing books onto the floor. The disrespect bothered the sphinx, but there were bigger issues to address at the moment.

"Help how?"

"I need my book! Where's my book!"

Nika went to help his friend. He didn't think her going was a good idea, but it wasn't like he could ever stop her before. It didn't sound like they had much time to help Lisa anyways. She didn't even notice that she had lobbed a book directly at his head, knocking him back onto the ground as he was trying to climb in.

He noticed the smell before the smoke. It was faint and hard to see under the struggling lights. Something was smoldering on the ground around the bin. The strap he grabbed was warm, which wasn't a good sign. It was Morgan's book, or it had been. The smoldering, blackened pages had burnt up around a pitch-black point in the center of the cover. Gladys wasn't the only thing struck by lightning on the way down.

"Morgan." He held it high. She wasn't happy to see it, more relieved she could move on to whatever scheme she had spent all of thirty seconds cooking up. It wasn't until she tried to pluck the book from his hands that she noticed something was wrong. He didn't let go at first. She looked him in the eye. He hadn't been able to see anyone's face in the light, but he could see hers now. She had kept herself together up until that moment.

Morgan Farvue did not have time for crying. She wiped her eyes with her sleeve as she thought aloud. "Ok. That's ok. There has to be something that still works." She flipped through page after page burned through. The lightning had punctured the book perfectly, leaving a crisp black circle that had burned out from the center of each page. The front cover broke off, and she tried to keep things together.

The soft sound of pages sliding on the stone floor resounded.

Morgan kept turning pages over, looking for something even slightly helpful. Her erratic breath suggested that she wasn't finding it.

"Morgan?" Nika tried to approach her. She didn't acknowledge him. "Morgan. It's going to be alright."

"How!" She wouldn't look up. Her screaming drowned out the rumbling. "How could it be ok?! I can't- we can't- There's nothing!" She sat up, clutching the sides of her head. "Without that, I've got nothing. No tricks, no magic, nothing." She pulled her hair. "Nothing."

Nika had nothing he could say. The loss of her book alone would have made this terrible, and it wasn't the worst part of the situation by a long shot. He went back to Gladys and asked her this question quietly: "Are you sure there's nothing we can do?"

The sphinx's breathing was strained, but she still tried her best to think. "I don't see how," she coughed. Nika had assumed that the 'dying' thing had been a joke, but it was becoming less and less of a punchline. He didn't expect anyone would act so nonchalant when things were this dire. As if the thought of death inspired an idea, Gladys lit up the slightest bit. "Well, unless."

"Unless?" Nika urged her on. He needed something to go off of.

"No. There's no way to get to the sixteenth floor." She put her head down again.

Nika frowned. Something about the lack of methods out of the room had bothered him; it was so stupid. Surely nobody would design a mystical underground cavern with only one point of entry. He looked around the room filled with books and pipes.

Pipes that books flocked into to return to their shelves, including ones on the sixteenth floor. He pointed to one of them. It took Gladys a moment to figure out what he was getting at. Her face told the whole shifting story. It started with 'impossible' progressing to 'perhaps,' restrained by 'insane,' and finishing with 'theoretically, it's possible.

She mumbled something under her breath. A massive book unlodged itself from under one of the stacks and landed by Nika's feet. "Hold onto that. You're looking for a locked book in a glass case. I don't have time to find the key. You'll have to break it open. Once you do, you'll have to make your way down to the tenth floor without being seen. The pipes are one way, but on the tenth floor, there's a book drop. You'll have a distraction. Just try not to look noticeable." She gestured to Morgan. "I'll keep her here. Hurry."

The book was the size of Nika's chest. Holding it started as a problem, but the weight magically lifted itself. Then it lifted him. The book was taking him towards one of the pipes along the far wall. Morgan watched him rise out of the room, confused and distraught. He likely looked like an idiot dangling from the spine of a book, feet flailing in the air, but it was worth it.

Nika would, after three seconds in the pipe, go on to apologize to teleportation. He had been bashing it for the entire summer for making him nearly throw up every single time it was inflicted upon him. Book-return-pipe was by far the worst method of transportation ever devised. It was just barely wider than he was, and the exit was as tight a fit as anything, but it worked. He had no time to really get acquainted with his newfound dislike of tight spaces and pressed on on the sixteenth floor.

The light was blinding, but the sound made the biggest difference. Before they listened in on the fight's muffled suggestions, he now got the full audio experience. The demon screamed and yelled for Lisa to show herself. His very footsteps dominated the air sixteen stories up. The entire room would occasionally light up from an errant lightning bolt.

Nika had no time for recon. He had a specific, non-dangerous mission that he needed to execute as flawlessly as possible. He felt like he should have been paralyzed in fear, but he pushed himself to keep going. He had read about heroes all the time. Underdog protagonists who came through, in the end, to pull off amazing feats. He definitely wasn't the main character of this story, but if he could be a sidekick that developed a bit, he'd be happy with that lot in life.

He found the glass case with the locked book. It looked more plain than he had expected. A nearby table lamp was enough to break it open. The breaking glass echoed.

Chapter 22- End

Intermission- Forty-Eight
Seconds Worth of Thoughts

'Oh no, no, no, that was louder than I thought. Agh, there's still glass everywhere.

Ok, careful. Grab the book, grab the book carefully, carefully, carefully ow ow ow ow ow.

NO!

Ok, that was also loud. At least there's- wait, it's quiet. Why is it quiet? It shouldn't be this quiet. Think, you idiot. It could be the sound. It was probably the sound. What now? It was definitely the sound. I screwed up. I need to get this book down there.

The stairs are close. I could take a peek. This library is so big. Why is it so huge?

If he heard me, he would be coming to get me now, right? I don't hear anything at all. I'll just crawl a little closer and look over the edge. Ow! Ok, I cut my hand, not a big deal. It's not so bad. Ok, it's not good either. It's a little bad. Focus! I need to see if he's there.

AGH!

Am I alive? I'm alive. Ok, the lightning didn't hit me, I think. Where did it- Oh, up there? Yikes. That's a crater. I hate this, I hate this so much.

Well, he knows I'm up here, so that's great. That's just great.

Maybe I could hug the wall, then he couldn't get a shot on me?

No, but what if he rides the stairs up? Or what if he just hits something above me?

That's a burning smell, so that's fun.

I have to move; I have to move. Ow, stupid hand. That's fine. I'll just run. The faster I get down there, the better the odds.

Wait, what's that sound?

Hm. Thanks, Gladys, I needed the time. Sorry if your statue breaks.

Ok. I have the book, I'm still breathing, and I just need both of these things to be true for about a hundred steps. Here we go.

Chapter 23. Going Down

Things went downhill in a metaphorical sense from the word go. The distraction provided by the sphinx statue was simply not enough to keep the demon's attention. It was more than able to fight off an injured stone puppet while taking potshots at Nika on his way down. The slowly moving platform 'stairs' wasn't helping him. The demon didn't know which floor he was on, it seemed, and was just wreaking havoc everywhere. It wasn't until the third bolt, fired as Nika reached the fifteenth floor's landing platform in the spiraling staircase, that he was nearly hit once again.

Things went downhill in a literal sense from that moment on. While generally well-coordinated, dazing lightning and accompanying thunder would throw anyone off their game. In this particular case, being thrown off his game also meant being thrown off the platform by a miscalculated footstep.

The stumble was fast, the fall even quicker. Had he had more time to process, he would have questioned again why the weird 'stairs' didn't have guardrails of any kind. So, the fall began. He had fallen off the platform before even realizing he was falling at all, so there was nothing to be done about it now. He would just fall.

This whole thing was stupid and awful. He had used up his ability to panic preparing for this, and now he had nothing left—no thoughts, no final plan, no clever way out, just the fall.

Slipping was a final screwup in a long, long lineup of screwups that had led him there. He didn't expect to be thinking about Daniel in his last moments, but Nils's boyfriend had a point. If Nika hadn't been there, who knows if any of this would have happened. If he hadn't run away from home, to begin with, Morgan's family wouldn't be in this mess.

He had thought acting brave would make up for all of that. The difference between him and the heroes in those books was that they all brought something to the table. They had some innate talent or boldness that he just lacked. At the very least, he had tried.

Moments of morbid self-reflection have a habit of being rudely interrupted, and this was no exception to the rule. He hadn't been paying too much attention to his surroundings and hadn't noticed the books fluttering desperately to catch him. He seemed to recall this happening before when Morgan first brought him to the library.

On a somewhat stable platform of floating books, Nika stood once again.

He was no longer upset from guilt; he was upset that he forgot something important to the moment. Maybe he had something that those characters didn't, after all; dumb luck.

Nika looked back to the spiraling rail of platforms. He had fallen too far towards the center to make the jump back to it. He was essentially in the middle of the gigantic library, vertically and laterally.

More lightning. This time almost directly behind him. He heard screaming from down below as the bolt was fired off. The message sent had been clear: move or get cooked.

At first glance, there aren't many directions to take from a floating island of hardcover dictionaries, but really there was only ever one option. Nika leaped from the island in no particular direction. The books tried to dissipate the moment his foot left them. One unfortunate encyclopedia was the demon's next victim. It collapsed as a blackened husk. Nika swore that his nerve endings would never recover from this many close shaves with that much electricity.

As he had hoped, more fail-safe books were ready to catch any poor library patron who slipped and fell. At least, that's what they were intended for. They actually made a pretty decent escape plan. He would manage to fall a few feet down and make a bit of progress back towards the wall with each jump.

It was probably the coolest thing he had ever done. He leaped like he was hopping stones across a river with complete faith the next foothold would appear.

Nika switched directions, just slightly, changing his angle in hopes of throwing the demon off. It turned out to be unnecessary; he was fighting off an increasingly broken stone sphinx with undivided attention. He thought the shift was clever, though.

When he finally arrived back on the solid floor, the first thing he thought to do was take stock of what level he was actually on. He didn't like how close to the ground floor he was.

Fifth floor. Geography and History wing. That was bad. Going down was not an option, and going up seemed just as horrid. He backed away from the stairs and into the aisles quickly. He would need time to figure this out. He held the silver volume tight and kept going.

Maybe he was too busy weighing options; maybe he was putting the finishing touches on the ultimate plan; either way, he ran headfirst into the window. The snowstorm outside had picked up, it seemed. Whirling flakes obscured the frosted glass. He could barely see the streetlight directly outside.

The streetlight was almost certainly at second-story height. The library was weird. From the outside, it looked about the size of the usual house for the area; two stories and a roomy attic at most. The transition from the outside to the inside must have caused something weird.

Something behind him on the fifth floor audibly crashed to the ground. He didn't care what it was, just that he could get as far away as possible from it. He glanced out the next window as he passed it. It was the same view then another window, the same angle as the light post. All windows inside lead to the same one outside.

It was as good an idea as any.

The locks on the windows had been installed with a lot of trust for library patrons. He assumed that as he easily pried the lock open and wedged the window open just a bit. It was heavier than he had expected. The wind seized its opportunity to break in and wreak havoc in the library. It shoved him back at first, long enough for him to notice that the window to his right was also opening and letting the snow in. The left, too.

Whatever. He wasn't the one who designed the all-for-one windows. He was too rushed to consider trivial things like consequences for his actions. The fall to the ground looked intimidating at first, but he had handled it worse. Like Karao or one of Morgan's duelists, a seasoned hero would have leaped from the window and landed with grace. His approach was more along the lines of "dangle from the window as low as possible and fall along the building to minimize the damage. It still hurt.

Trying to enter the library with an overdue or, presumably, a stolen book should have meant the door would chuck him into the void to meet back up with Gladys and Morgan. He braced himself to be disappointed and eat a bolt of electricity right to the face if he was wrong.

He wasn't, for once.

He shouted on the way down in case Gladys didn't notice his entrance. It was just as unsettling and rough as the first fall. He could have sworn he landed in the exact same spot, too. He saw his friend rise up quickly as he clawed his way out of the returns bin.

"Nika!" Morgan shouted. She was either mad to be relieved or relieved she was allowed to be mad. Order of operations wasn't super important. All that mattered at the moment was that she ran up to both hug him and slap him across the face as hard as she could.

She didn't get the chance. Gladys' tail scooped him up towards her gnarled, angered face.

"Did you just open the window?" She snarled. Terrified, he nodded.

"Wait, which window?" Morgan asked.

The librarian bared her fangs. "All of them." She let him drop to the floor, finally. "It's fine, it's fine. Morgan, my dear, add to your list of tasks to close those ghastly windows, with hammer and nails if necessary. That's priority 1."

"Yes, ma'am." Morgan jotted it down with a pen and pad. She seemed to have scrawled several pages of notes in the time span that Nika was gone. He didn't want to think about that too much.

"Boy, the book." Gladys was calm. The level of confidence in her voice was reassuring like she had everything planned out. He laid it in front of her. Her majestic roar made it stand to attention along its spine. It opened to the exact page she needed. The claw of a single massive paw covered most of the page, yet she pressed it in. "Are you ready, Ms. Farvue?"

"Yes." Morgan's resolve was as firm as the Sphinx's confidence. Nika stood back to watch whatever this was.

Gladys righted herself. Though she was lying down, her noble face was inspiring in a very bizarre sense. "I'd rather leave on my own terms than let some deity-complexed necromancer use my corpse to run this accursed library for even one more year. Or worse, if such a fate exists. Morgan, do you accept the terms?"

"Yes."

"Then I leave the protection of Eldes to you, little one. The torch is passed."

Gladys's body started burning with a soft golden light. The hairs on the tip of the tail burned away first and carved a swift path up to the body. Her feathered wings curled in the glorious heat. She was not distressed at all.

Nika assumed were ashes from the Sphinx formed spiraled in rings around her like a tornado touching down in golden sand. Small pieces formed silk, silk formed lines, lines soared around the room, searching for something.

She smiled as the consuming fire reached and enveloped her face. She was gone.

From what Nika could tell, they were now trapped in the library's creepy cellar without any sort of guide or competent figure around. He had sent her to grant her an escape, it seemed, and left them alone to fend for themselves. The tickling of outrage in the back of the throat didn't even get a chance to announce itself before the next insane magic nonsense happened. Every trace of the golden thread around the room paused. They lunged at Morgan with a speed that would have impressed Nika if he hadn't been dealing with a gung-ho lightning fanatic on the floor above.

The strings wrapped around her hands and wrists. She had been holding them high in anticipation. The final nail in the 'Morgan was in on it' coffin. She winced a bit. They probably still burned, but she stood tall and still nonetheless.

It took a full minute and a half, otherwise known as one eternity, for the weird golden magic to stop. Morgan's arms hung loosely at her sides for a minute. Her fingers twitched, formed a fist, calmed back down, all in unison with her neck and general facial expression.

She turned to him. It couldn't have been true since it wasn't how things worked, but she seemed taller. "If you ever - ever - do something that stupid again, I will kick you off our team."

"What-"

"As captain of the yet-to-be-named-greatest-duelist-doubles-team, I have decided your punishment. After all this, you're cleaning the club room." She picked up her scorched field guide off the ground and held it close. It was useless, in a sense, but she wouldn't give it up for anything. She threw the shoulder strap around her neck and dusted herself off a bit. She hit him on the head lightly.

Leaving the inane conversation about the club he wasn't even in behind, he felt now was an appropriate time to bring it up. "Are you going to tell me what that was or..."

Despite Morgan's best efforts, one smile couldn't contain smug excitement and timid nervousness. The end result was unsettling. The message was clear, though: why tell when she could show? It was a fair enough point if she could just get on with it.

She lifted her arms up together. Nika noticed now that her arms seemed permanently marked by the golden lines. They formed some sort of pattern that started at the tips of her fingers and curled around the back of her hands and up her forearms. Every form of magic had a tell. Whenever Morgan got quiet and actually focused, she was about to summon something important. The gold pattern had been hard to see, but as she dug more and more into the spell, the lines on her arm illuminated.

The entire hollow room looked better in the brilliant light.

In front of Morgan, something began to take shape. The usual green summoning magic had been replaced by the same golden lines. It was taking her longer than usual to finish the ritual, too. It was a sphynx. Gladys was coming back.

Morgan's hands started to shake, then her legs. Her breathing became heavy, and she broke into a sweat. It was too much to handle, and she was only about halfway through.

The half-finished summon dissipated into the air the moment she took a knee.

Nika walked up to her. The way he saw it, he had two options.

He could go through the motions of having the conversation where she questions if she can do it, and he would encourage her to give it another try. After a bit of banter back and forth, they would arrive at the conclusion that with his assistance, she would easily be able to handle it. This all seemed like a lot of time he didn't have, so he opted for the second.

Nika grabbed Morgan by the arm and helped lift her to her feet. They both sort of had the same gist of the aforementioned conversation play out in their own heads; it wasn't necessary. For one moment, Nika thought she was so easy to read. For another terrible moment, he realized she had read him just as easily.

"What, do I have to ask?" Morgan held her hand up.

"A please would be nice." Nika's magic coursed through his fingertips. He went back for another high five. He wondered if other people knew what a high five was or if it was specific to Morgan. He had no exact unit of measurement, but she couldn't have needed more than a third of his soul to make something impressive happen; she was most of the way there by herself.

The summoning ritual wasn't even slower than her old stuff during the second attempt. A fully formed sphinx roared to life in front of them. Its teeth gnashed, its claws scraped along with the stone floors, its wings expanded to their terrifying full span.

It didn't speak. In fact, it didn't seem much like Gladys at all. This was a younger, very different sphinx. Smaller, but being smaller than Gladys still left it being monstrously tall. It was at least two Nika's tall. He felt a slight pang. He had interacted with that Sphinx enough over the summer that her being gone felt weird. More so than the principal that he really only met once. Death was not strange to necromancers; saying goodbye is strange for anyone with a soul.

For now, they stood in awe at the obedient, shimmering beast in front of them.

Nika didn't look at Morgan. "You'll tell me-"

Morgan didn't look at him, either. "Later. Later for sure. I have something I have to do." She shook off the trance with the literal approach and ran up to the Sphinx. Nika refused to be outdone by her and followed. The creature lowered itself enough for Morgan to climb up. She initially wanted to stop Nika from following but gave up on the notion pretty quickly.

"You've already forgotten? I regret my choice already."

It was Gladys's voice. Nika, startled and still a bit hazy from using his magic, lost his grip and slid off the side of the Sphinx. The librarian was nowhere to be seen. Morgan had heard it too. It definitely came from the ground.

"Well, are you going to pick me up or not?" The silver book was speaking to them with Gladys' voice. She seemed to be inside of it now. which sat open in the middle of the floor. "I can't go splitting body and soul for a couple of nitwits to fumble my noble sacrifice."

He was cautious about lifting the book. It wasn't heavier than before, and it didn't appear marked up or changed in any meaningful way. The book yelled at him for gawking, then ordered Morgan around a bit. Morgan's conjured Sphinx spread its wings and took off, leaving Nika and the book on the ground.

It did a lap around the enormous room to gather speed, then swooped down and snagged him with one of its massive paws. Both he and Morgan screamed the entire ride up into the darkness for different reasons. They passed the door leading into the street and just kept going. At one point, the front paw of the Sphinx dropped him, only for the back paw to catch him by the back of his shirt. Morgan had a much easier ride.

They collided with something at the top. The summoned Sphinx had dug its claws into a ceiling that neither of them knew was coming. Their momentum tore them through the ground, its wings shielding them from falling stone debris.

Nika gathered himself after being tossed onto the ground. He had no idea where he was or whose desk he had slid into. Come to think of it, there weren't many desks in the library at all. The only one he could think of was the main checkout desk in the center of the ground floor, and that's exactly where they were.

There was snow, too. He looked up. The flakes were falling from every floor, cascading down the library floors' circular rims like waterfalls filling a basin. Books flapped and tried to navigate their way back to the shelves, but the wind up there was too strong for them. Opening the window invited the storm into the room, which wasn't great. In front of the largest pile of snow on the main floor stood the dark, twisted figure.

The demon was surprised, to say the least. Now, in full view and in the library's clear light, Nika could see the thing in more detail. The body was possessed, corrupted, and contorted more now than ever. Weaker limbs were reinforced with dark protruding muscles. The dreaded necromantic aura still thrived in his eyes. He recovered from the shock and wound up striking them down.

Morgan's Sphinx lunged, wings spread wide. There was a flash, though it seemed the Sphinx absorbed the blast without even flinching. He had enough sense and adrenaline to know to get out of there. Morgan was already a few steps ahead of him.

They almost left the book behind again. It was wedged under a chunk of the recently upturned floor and insisted that Nika be more careful with it as the two hid behind the far end of the desk from the action. They couldn't help but peer over the top when possible.

The thing was way stronger than when it had been Bringer. Even with a two-foot-thick paw, the demon was pushing back as the Sphinx tried to pin him to the ground. The Sphinx was winning, it seemed, but not by a lot. They broke apart, and the beast began to circle the demon, who was foaming at the mouth.

Something tapped Nika's shoulders. His yelp was stifled by a hand covering his mouth. A bolt of lightning soared over them, a reminder that the demon hadn't forgotten about the other intruders. It was Lisa.

Lisa Farvue hugged her daughter. Her hair was ragged and frizzy, her shoulder seemed hurt, and she seemed ready to cry for relief. They had only been separated by minutes, but each had dragged on much longer than the one before it. This reunion was both short and overdue.

"Now is not the time. Pull yourself together, girl. You have a job to do." Gladys said, the pages shuffling a bit as she spoke. Nika held the book open, although he didn't think it made much of a difference.

Lisa was confused, but the questioning was for later. She recognized the voice, at least, so that was a start. "What job?"

"Not you, Morgan. I need you to get me right up in that thing's face, do you understand?"

Lisa snatched the book from Nika's hands before Morgan could respond. "Absolutely not! She's just a kid. Are you a lunatic?"

"All of you are just kids in my eyes. Can you even fathom how old I am? Er, was. How old was I? What difference does it make? There's no danger with a younger sphinx around."

"I'm not taking chances." She turned to Morgan. "We're taking orders from a pamphlet now??"

Morgan shrugged. "That's how Dad describes your normal job."

Lisa ruffled her daughter's hair. "Joking at a time like this is exactly what your father would do. What a terrible influence." Lisa snapped the book shut and took stock of their position in relation to the fight happening on the other side of the room. "Proud of you, kid, now don't do anything stupid, ok?" She was about to leave, then remembered something. "Nika?"

"Yes?"

She took a small box out of her coat pocket. Cruise had mentioned it before. "I need you to bring this Karao. Cruise was right. Whatever happens, you need to get this to her however you can. Once it's safe, you need to run."

Nika nodded.

She vaulted herself over the counter and dashed straight to the target. She took cover again behind the crumbling remains of one of the many felled sphinx statues. She tore off a chunk of the wing and waited.

The demon turned away for just a second, but it was enough. She flung the stone with her still-good arm, and it hit its target upside the head. The Sphinx made use of the momentary distraction to whip its tail around and knock the demon clean across the room into a pillar.

The already damaged body broke. Through magic, it had been able to strengthen the shriveled and twisted leg, but a brittle spine dashed against the stone was too much to recover from at a moment's notice. It hollered not in pain but frustration. Nothing moved. It was trapped.

The Sphinx was starting to fade, but it wasn't finished just yet. Lisa walked up alongside it to the still fuming body. Black smoke was pouring onto the floor from every crack and fracture in it. It didn't rise. It didn't linger. It poured out and disappeared into the air.

"You can't kill me." It laughed, then coughed. "There's always the next body. I will hunt you for sport, then leave you within an inch of your life so I can do it again. Unless, of course." The head slumped down a bit, its grin grew. "You want to make a deal."

Lisa said nothing. She opened the book. The same golden threads that had tattooed Morgan's arms unfurled from the pages like the petals of a flower. One by one, the lines grappled the demon's body. Each point of contact burned gold just like the Sphinx.

"What is this? I can't die it's-"

"Would you kindly be quiet?" Gladys's face formed above the golden threads. The illusion was smaller than the real thing had been. "We'll have more than enough time to talk, but for now, a few years of rest would be nice."

The body fell over and vanished, one golden line at a time, into the pages of the book. It closed itself and refused to be reopened.

The wind stopped howling.

The snow stopped falling, save for the buildup hanging over the edges of the floors above. They revealed in the quiet. It was over.

Morgan was the first to openly celebrate. She wrapped her arms around Nika and lifted him before basically throwing him to the ground in excitement. Lisa was desperately looking for a chair that hadn't broken in the prolonged fight before settling for the back of the desecrated statue she had hidden behind.

Nika had been blaming himself for a lot of negative events recently. This was something he undoubtedly had a hand in with a positive outcome. His role was small, but he didn't run away, not again. He laughed as Morgan tried to tackle her mom.

The adrenaline of this all was still coursing through him. His hands were shaking, his feet tapping; he could even hear an imaginary buzzing sound.

Well, a sound that was less imaginary than he initially imagined, anyways. His pocket shook. He had forgotten something.

Karao's little timer was about to go off. He was about to be teleported back to the Pale Garden. He wondered how long it had been going off before he noticed it. He had completely forgotten about the thing.

Nika warped out of the library just as Morgan was about to speak.

Chapter 23- End

Intermission- Smoke

Teleporting sucked. It sucked, and he hated it, and if Nika could go the rest of his life without ever needing to do it again, he'd be a lot happier for it. He had done it enough times now to have a surefire method of not throwing up.

Step 1: stand up, find footing.

Step 2: a deep breath. Again. More. Just keep breathing.

Step 3: Think about any other thing.

Step one had gotten off without a hitch. He was back in the main room of the tea shop. This was familiar ground to him. Really, if he had fallen over the moment he teleported in, everyone would rightfully laugh at him. It wasn't until the second step of the process that things started going horribly awry.

He couldn't breathe, or rather, whatever he was breathing, his body was outright rejecting. He could barely see into the room, come to think of it. There was smoke. It was hot. Something was on fire. Most things, based on the thickness of the smoke and the temperature of the room, for that matter.

The Pale Garden was burning to the ground.

The tradeoff for having the third step of his process handled for him, fires were pretty distracting after all, was that his footing gave way a bit. He stumbled back and nearly tumbled directly into a burning pile of chairs.

Nobody else was in the room, so that was a good sign.

He was starting to cough. He needed to get out. He ran to the door, trampling some discarded rope that someone had left lying around. The front door was locked, he pulled and twisted, but nothing worked. It wasn't even moving.

It was heartbreaking looking at the room in its entirety. Karao and Nils had both put everything they had into this room alone. He had instinctively started running, likely related to the adrenaline that had just started to burn in the form of a headache.

Catherine was the one to yell at him from the kitchen doorway. He covered his mouth and ran. His eyes were stinging, his hand clutched the small box that Lisa had given him.

It was a long, long day.

Chapter 24. Burning Up

The coin in his pocket was still chirping. He couldn't find its counterpart anywhere, not that he had much time to look. If he went long enough without reuniting the two coins, he would be teleported back into the room where it was, sort of like the snooze on his alarm clock. There was a way to turn it off, but he didn't know it. He figured he would ask Catherine when he got the chance.

It would have to wait. She was barking orders with the first step he made into the kitchen. "Duck!"

He flailed out of the way with a distinctive lack of grace. She swung a metal pan full speed in front of him, hitting a man he didn't even notice was in the room through all the smog.

"Woah!" He scanned the room. Nils was sitting on the floor, staring. Besides that and the guy on the ground, they were alone. Karao was nowhere to be seen. The countertops were burning as much as the stairs leading up. "What's happening?" He had to shout over the fire.

"Doors and windows are stuck. We can't break them, either. Nils thinks it's some kind of enchantment. I say we need to hit it harder. And this guy just won't stay down!" Catherine stepped on his head on the way to the window over the running sink.

The man in question was unfamiliar, but the violet in his foggy eyes was not. More necromancy. It was more than he had seen in person before. It seemed to be polluting his veins and mind, his neck in particular pulsed purple. He didn't seem to have a thought in his mind as he tried once again to stand up. Catherine panned him again. It bought a bit of time.

She huffed and chucked the pan at the window. It bounced off without much effect other than shattering the bowl it crashed into on the countertop.

"Where's Karao?" Nika asked. The kitchen had felt cramped and restrictive before, but it had never felt small. The walls were closing in, the smoke growing thicker. He was trying his best to keep it together.

"Hey, focus on us right now, ok?" Catherine attacked her half-broken deadarm. With a few violet sparks of necromancy, she shot a small burst of wind towards some of the flames. It pushed it back a bit, then made it flare up worse than before.

"I said don't do that!" Nils yelled. "Let Nils think."

"We don't have time to think!" She grabbed a bucket of water from the sink and tossed it into the fire spreading from the staircase. It was much more effective than the wind. Nils nervously chewed on their fingertips.

Nika was tired. One can only face death so many times in a single afternoon before it loses its appeal and becomes a bit of a bore. The stairs were a no-go. The windows and doors were going to hold out longer than they would. The walls seemed firm.

Seemed. There was a knife on the table, which he grabbed and stabbed into the wall. It didn't make it far, but it did leave a mark. Catherine and Nils thought he had lost it.

They didn't have much to work with, but there was an idea. "What if-"

"That idea sucks, next." Catherine had to pull Nils further from the fire. They were refusing to budge. "What's in your hand?"

He realized what she must have thought. Carving their way out would take way too long. "No, no, it's not that." He fumbled with the box, eventually finding the clasp to open it. With stable hands, it would have been effortless. Inside was a small crystal, barely bigger than a fingernail. He poured it into his hand and threw the box aside. Why Karao needed it, he didn't know, but the box was just an obstacle. He shoved the gem into his pocket.

"Just give up," Nils said. They had reached the end of their wit. "Nils doesn't want to spend my last few minutes panicking."

Nika sat in front of them. "Nils." They cried. Nika had, less than an hour ago, staked his entire confidence on the bravery of others. He had to do the same now. It's what the hero of a book would do, and today's theme was pretending he was a hero... "I have an idea. Can you try it for me?"

Nils showed him a fresh burn running from their wrist up to their arm.

"Yes," they said. Nils took his hand, and the two stood up.

"Catherine!" Nika hadn't ever given orders before. It didn't suit him. "I need you in the front room."

"The front? That's where *she* is! She'll see us!"

The mindless zombie started lifting itself up. It was holding a rope in each hand. Nika didn't have time to ask who *she* was but plenty of time to lob a teapot at the undead. It was ineffective, so Catherine just sucker-punched it while its attention was on Nika.

He had twisted her arm, metaphorically, by taking Nils into the front. Catherine really had no choice but to follow them and give it one good shot. Nika told them to push the heaviest table that was still intact into the center of the room. While they moved Karaos's favorite table, the one with the drawers under the lip, Nika cleared everything else between that table and the front wall.

"Alright, bookworm, what you got?" Catherine was teasing him from stress, he hoped.

Nika pointed to her deadarm. "One-shot. Full force." The smoke was getting to him; he coughed. "Table, wall."

"This deadarm isn't that-" She remembered what he was getting at. Nika was already preparing to give her a boost; the purple sparks danced between his outstretched fingertips. Her eyes went wide, narrowed, and the most ambitious grin she ever hosted spread across her cheeks. "Go hide." She accepted another thirty percent boost from him. When the excitement wore off, he was going to pass out or die in the fire, whichever was more convenient.

He and Nils ducked behind the counter, the part that wasn't on fire. Nika was curious if the wind spell would even work in this small, enclosed environment. He was going to be responsible for a lot of property damage in a short period of time. That was a problem for future Nika to deal with, and that guy had it too good just for surviving.

The gale was something else. Most of the air felt like it had been sucked out of the room to fuel her one gigantic spell. It was sort of like having front row seats to a hurricane. Nika had been watching the nearby burning menu sputter out when the air was pulled away, just for the fire to come back as the room refilled with air.

Nils had the same thought as him. Neither wanted to see if it had worked or not. They needed to, but seeing a broken table and an intact wall would have been devastating.

The room got colder. Catherine cheered, briefly. Nils grabbed Nikas's shoulder and started dragging him. He could barely keep up with their speed. There was sunlight and fresh air. He could see, they had punched a clean hole through the wall.

The outside world was anything but clean. There were detritus and bits of wall and table everywhere. Nika almost tripped over one of the drawers that had flown out of the table. His first breath of fresh air was one of the best feelings he had ever had. He could almost feel his lungs healing.

There were four people in the snow beside the recently-escaped necromancers. All four had been standing, or in one case sitting, watching the tea shop burn. Two were the same sort of purple-infused undead that had tried to tie them up in the kitchen with very poor results. They didn't move much or react to anything at all. One was holding their arms up in the midst of some sort of incantation. A pattern floating around their fingertips matched a symbol that was covering the door. That was the one that had kept them locked inside.

Beth, the reporter responsible for their nightmarish situation, was another. She was dressed for the cold and reeling from the shock of watching a table fly past her at a speed notable should ever reach. Her eyes and hands glowed purple. With a wave of her sinuous arm, the zombies' necks snapped to attention, and they scrambled towards the three of them.

Beth was the necromancer. Well, they all were, but she was the unknown. Pending an actual investigation, Nika felt safe in assuming that she was the reason the tea shop was burning. She was the one that had set him up to betray everyone else. She was the one spreading the rumors of necromancy. She was desperate and ragged, focusing everything on controlling her undead servants. She was expending so much energy that the heat was boring a hole for her in the snow. They weren't particularly in the mood to hear her side of things.

The fourth person waiting for them outside was Karao. She sat in the snow, despondent. She seemed drained, completely unable to process what had been happening around her.

Catherine was too tired to fight off yet another zombie. It grappled her to the ground. Nils didn't even struggle with the other. The one that locked the door had bound Nils up with some other sort of spell. Nika had Beth's undivided attention.

"You! Where were you hiding? Huh!" The energy radiating from her grew intense and accumulated in a small sphere in the palm of her hand. She held it above her head. "You've ruined everything again, you little rat!"

"Karao!" Nika took a step back and stopped. Beth was between him and Karao. He almost didn't care about whatever useless nonsense was coming out of her mouth. He had a mission. If both Cruise and Lisa had stressed how important it was to get this to Karao, it needed to happen.

"Don't ignore me, boy!" She crushed the purple orb in her hand. A wave of crippling magic flooded down and around her in a circle. The wave struck Nika's feet. The effects were not limited to such a small area. He felt sick. A sense of lifelessness rocked his entire body... His chest felt clamped shut. This was necromancy in some form, but it was different. He could almost feel himself shutting down. This was a taste of death. Nils and Catherine were suffering the same effects somewhere to his sides.

When Beth moved, Nika could swear he saw two faces. One sneering through the cold air and a violet afterimage. It lagged slightly behind her movements. She moved her hand to her forehead; there was another afterimage there, too. That spell had put a strain on her.

"I'm doing you all a favor. This is no way to live. This is no way to live!" She gestured back to Karao. She still didn't move. "You're going to turn out as broken as I am! Or Hult!" She marched up to Karao and grabbed her hair, lifting her chin up.

"You've played god long enough, Karao. This- all of this- this is for Hult and Cruise, Bringer too. Everyone you've destroyed."

Nils was the first to connect the dots. They choked out a single word. "Liz."

This caught her attention. "Yes, but Liz died a long time ago. Chasing some fairy tale dream that this creature kept dangling in front of us like a carrot. Liz was just another victim." She approached Nils. "Or, rather, I should have died. All I wanted was to stand out. I just wanted to stand a chance against them. I did all I could to perfect it."

"You're insane." Catherine managed. Nika would never know one way or the other, but he saw it as a final act of defiance, drawing Beth's attention away from Nils and onto herself. Just talking was the last of what she had. She passed out, thankfully still breathing.

The upper floor collapsed. The monstrous fire was chewing up their home and spitting the sparks out into the street.

Beth didn't care. She responded to the unconscious Catherine anyways. "Of course I am. I've been forcibly keeping myself alive every day for decades. Have you ever tried to manually control your own heartbeat? Whatever my sins, I will pay for every last one of them just as soon as I remove this woman and her influence from this rotten planet." She snapped her fingers, and the undead dropped Catherine into the snow. Beth stepped on her shoulder, smiling. "Especially her students."

Nika had learned a lot about magic this summer. What he was about to do sounded like it violated many of the key rules and tenants of spellcasting. There was no universe where it ought to work. He was banking on a loophole he had no reason to believe existed for the physics of this trick to work. But, if she was killing him with necromancy, then...

He poured every ounce of power he had into his hand. His vision started fading, his legs fell asleep. His hand was crackling as much as Catherine's usually did. It had certainly caught Beth's attention. She braced herself to be hit by Nika's most devastating spell.

He grabbed his own chest and poured everything back into himself. Feeling returned to his legs. His chest loosened enough for him to breathe. Whatever she had done, he had undone for the time being. He shoved himself off the ground and made a dash for Karao.

His headstart was significant, but he was still working with a battered and weary body against an adult with a lifelong grudge on the line. She was gaining on him faster than he was making it to Karao. He didn't have long; he needed every second he could manage. He reached into his pocket and pulled out the cold trinket. He just needed to run a little more.

The second wave of necrotic magic was focused just on Nika. It struck him in the shoulder rather than being burst. His shoulder felt a completely different cold to the rest of his body. The snow was one thing; the loss of feeling and control from a part of his body was another. His refresh wasn't going to work a second time. He just needed to push on. He needed to take a few more steps.

Karao finally turned. Her eyes were so graven and full of despair. He could give up then and there. She was suffering from the same sort of magic that Beth had used against the three of them. Nika stayed determined with every fiber he could manage. He lifted his leg once more, now only a foot away.

He reached out to Karao, desperate to hand it to her.

Nika crumpled in the snow.

Beth laughed. "Nika, Nika. You poor, stupid kid. If you had laid low a few more months, you would have just starved in a ditch instead of going through all of this. It's tragic, really, that you got tangled up with this woman. Tell you what, hand that over and I'll let you die first. You won't have to see any more of this." She leered at him. "It's the least I can do for you."

She kicked his hand. He wasn't strong enough to keep it held tight. She plucked the small object from him and held it up. Columns of sunlight were beginning to pierce the slowly fading clouds. One narrow pillar shone down on the two of them. She inspected the golden coin with an hourglass embedded in its center. "What is this, a coin?" She asked. "Why risk your life over someth-"

Beth was teleported when the coin rang out again. Nika hoped that the coin was buried somewhere deep in the burning tea shop. He had never intended to reach Karao. That was way too optimistic for him. Being a failure was actively helpful in this case.

The zombies near Catherine and Nils collapsed, no longer taking commands of gravity's nonsense anymore. They were downed, hopefully for good. Even if Beth was alive, she had lost concentration. Nils was starting to feel better but still didn't particularly like what was happening.

Nika had held back a bit during his sprint. He needed just a bit more strength. He crawled up to Karao. She was managing the closest thing to a smile that she could. He had the crystal in his pocket. The amount of effort on both halves to put something from one person's hand into the others was unbelievable. This was the hardest single take he had ever done.

But it was done.

The crystal made contact with her palm and released the embedded ring. Karao had magic once again. Her entire body recreated Nika's stunt, shocking itself with necromancy from head to toe. Karao's triumphant return to good health was so intense he could feel himself recovering a bit just from proximity.

Karao was always tall. As she stood, she was truly towering. Even without her deadarms, she was intimidating to all that would draw her ire. At that moment, all she was concerned with was helping the three of them. She helped lift Nika to his feet and hugged him.

"I'm so sorry," she said.

Nika's thoughts were mixed. Karao had literal and metaphorical skeletons in her closet that would probably continue to haunt her and, by association, the three of them. She could do everything in her power to hide them and yet they would likely always be there. He didn't know what she used to be like, and he didn't know that she deserved the unyielding trust Nils and Catherine had for her. All of these were unknown.

He saw her for what she was: a bright and hopeful person doing her best to make the world a better place for the ones she loved. She helped those in need under the guise of favors she would rarely, if ever, cash in. She took her mistakes seriously and, even though she wasn't always upfront about her past, she never lied to him that he knew. She was the first person in this world to give him a chance. All of these were known. Strapped for time, he boiled down the thoughts as much as he could into a single sentence: "You don't need to be."

Nika hadn't noticed, but Karao had been using magic to heal his wounds. He could feel his shoulder again, and his legs were no longer numb. The after-effects of his recursive magic stunt were starting to weigh in, but there was nothing Karao could do to fix that.

Catherine cried when she saw that everyone was ok. If Nika ever mentioned it again, she was going to find a lake and throw him in it. Karao asked what Catherine had done to her deadarm, which at this point was just one chipped humerus waving frantically. It had been broken beyond repair, but that was alright for now.

Nils wanted to hug Karao for a long time, but they needed to thank Nika first.

"Ni- I - can't believe you pulled it off, Nika. Yo-" Nils sentence was severed by the crashing wooden planks and falling parts of the house. Whatever Beth had done to keep the firefighters away was apparently still in effect.

The wood continued to rumble. Beams moved. Glass shattered. The doors, no longer protected by the undead's spell, buckled under the weight they were never meant to support. The whole thing was coming down in a horrific fashion.

And through it, something stood; someone.

Beth clawed her way out of the crumbling remains of the Pale Garden. The three young necromancers stood behind Karao at her request. The lifeless face from before now seethed. Karao would put an end to this threat, and now nothing would stop her.

Whether Beth was alive or not was up to debate. Horror painted each of their faces when they saw what she had become through the fire. She stood, but barely. Her soul was fierce. The afterimage from before, the trace that followed her movement, was now the majority of her upper body. She was a violent translucent ghost from the waist up. Her features and face were blurred. Her transparent purple frame burned a brilliant orange color against the burning tea shop.

Her body was not on the same page as her half-disembodied soul. She had been broken in half. Her spine was folded backward. She had control enough over the legs to force them to walk, dragging her head and twisted arms behind them in the snow.

"I will kill you," her voice echoed through the street. There was no home for it in her throat, so the thoughts just wandered wherever they pleased. "By my dying breath, I will watch your fall."

Karao was unimpressed. "You will not." She walked towards Beth. "And you won't run."

Beth began to charge another ball of necrotic magic. Without other sources to fuel it, her soul was drained into the hand to form the attack. "Without your creepy little arms, what are you?" The projectile launched forward. Nika assumed that she had thrown the one that hit him, but this was more like the firing of a cannon. It was a deadshot aimed at Karao's face.

She caught it. "Better." It had hurt her, clearly. The projectile broke in her palm like glass and seeped into her skin. If the effects of the necrotic poisoning were what Nika had just experienced, it was a miracle Karao was standing. Karao's hand glowed with her own magic, which may have had something to do with it. She endured the first volley and stepped forward again.

Beth screamed and fired another shot. She used all the soul in her ghostly right arm to fuel it. The limb was gone. Karao caught it, the sparks of her brighter, more vibrant violet magic keeping Beth's necromancy at bay. She placed the orb in the snow, where it fizzled into the ground without effect. Karao had been hurt by this, too. She didn't care.

Beth had correctly identified that this wasn't working and shifted gears. Karao stopped in front of her. Beth's phantom was eerily calm.

Nils shouted.

One of the bodies behind them, the ones that had slumped over when Beth had been warped into the burning building, had been reanimated again and was taking swipes at Nils and Catherine. It was sluggish compared to before. It used to be able to use spells but was now resorting to non-threatening lunges and couldn't be more predictable.

Karao released a bolt from her fingertip into the zombie. It stopped moving and sat quietly. It was under her command now.

All of that to buy a moment's time.

Lacking a dominant hand, Beth made a final, rash decision. She had seen all her plans dashed before her eyes. She spread rumors of a necromantic crime spree. She had lured Bringer in to destroy her. She framed the tea shop for covering up an investigation and had, in turn, had the investigation turned back on her. There was nothing left for her, and she embraced it. Where the sphere had formed in her hand before now, it took shape in her core.

"Don't do this," Karao pleaded. She had said the same thing to Phineas, to the one she had failed earlier in the summer. She was genuine but knew how this was going. She knew that Beth could not be talked down from the edge.

Karao was correct. Beth's soul contorted and twisted into a single point. The fraying edges of her soul shimmered weakly against the fire. All she was, all that was left, was one final attempt on Karao's life.

This sphere acted differently than the others. Instead of forming one cannonball, an insidious stream of dark purple magic erupted from the core in one singular direction: Karao. It sounded like every scream, every terror-filled shriek rolled into one crashing pillar.

Karao was adamant that violence solves nothing, that fighting back would only cause more harm than good. She couldn't let her students take the hit, so she had to. Not that a mysteriously aged, aloof, and confident necromancer didn't have tricks up her one and only sleeve. While she was worried about her students, she was much less worried about the sky. This was the last that Beth had. All Karao did, with a simple trick with the palm of her hand, was to redirect the spell into the sky.

Beth was fading more and more. The beam couldn't hold out. Not even for as long as it would take Karao to reach her. The legs on the body gave out. She was nothing but the luminescent memory of a soul spitting its last foul revenge on the world. All that remained was a faint outline, a nearly invisible speck against the burning tea shop.

The beam trickled to a stop. The faucet was closed, the tank dry. She had nothing left to give and hadn't even left a scratch. Beth's soul dropped; presumably, it was hard to see. She was done. She couldn't even keep her soul together at this rate, let alone win in a fight against her old mentor.

She was hurt. Toppling over. Every step Karao took seemed twice as impossible as the last, and yet she pushed herself forward. The price of not fighting, the price of confronting someone she wronged and sought to kill her, was too much for anyone to bear, and yet there she stood.

Karao knelt down in front of her and held up a hand shrouded in the faint purple aura. It was the softer version of the usual electric necromancy. She touched Beth's face and brought color back. It was as vibrant as it was before; she still didn't have the strength to stand or the ability to fight. Beth's face lifted up. She was confused, distraught. She didn't understand what Karao was doing.

Nika remembered the day he met Karao with impeccable detail. He remembered the soft voice, the encouraging words, the sheer joy in being told by someone so confident that everything would be ok. She was the embodiment of hope.

With that same voice, Karao said, "I'm glad I got to see you again, Elizabeth."

Chapter 24- End

Intermission- Will You Forgive Me?

"Don't patronize me. I hate you. I hate you!" Beth's, or Liz's, soul strained to move but could not.

"I know. And you should." Karao kept her hand on Liz's face. The only thing keeping Liz's soul intact was Karaos interference, it seemed. "You were right about a lot of things. All of what I've done to you and the others, I know that. Liz, I thought you were dead for years. I drove you to this."

Liz said nothing.

"I'm sorry. I'm sorry for everything. For what I put you and the others through for Hult and Cruise. You were family to me, and you still are. I know you won't ever forgive what I've done. I haven't even forgiven myself, and I'm not the one which almost ended their own life to win some competition."

"You replaced us," she said. "We're all just disposable to you."

"You were never replaced, Liz." Karao was sitting now. "These three are family to me, but so are you. You all were. I love all of you dearly. Present tense. You are still my family."

They sat, staring at one another for a moment: Beth, or Liz, whatever. Nika was getting tired of Karao's enemies having multiple names. Karao's looked back at them, and her face was something new; a look, a plea. She wasn't asking for Liz to save herself. Karao wanted Liz to forgive her more than anything in the world.

One saw a face that would soon be lost forever, a final chance to make things right.

The other saw the cause of their suffering and questioned if they were in the right.

There was some commotion up the road—the sound of bells and wheels and carts. Someone had mercifully come to deal with the fires.

"Liz, I have to let you go," Karao said. She knew she'd never heard the words. "There are a million things I wish I could say to you, but I'm barely keeping it together as it is. I thought I had recovered from your passing, but it's going to hurt just as much the second time."

Liz could have cursed Karao with any number of parting words. A haunting phrase, a harrowing condemnation. She asked. "What will it be like?"

Tearing up, Karao smiled. "Like saying good-bye."

Chapter 25. With Only One Week to Go

Waiting for test scores was agony. Nika's dorm room was cleaned out just before he moved in, and already he feared he was boring a hole in the floor just with his relentless pacing. He was even reading while pacing just to walk off all the nervous energy he had compiled within himself.

He had adjusted to his new living situation relatively quickly. The school had systems in place to care for students who were in crisis, and having your home burnt down at the hands of a vengeful spirit qualified Nils and him to their own rooms in the dorm. They offered it to Catherine, too. She didn't want to accept it in the name of independence until Nils pointed out that they no longer had a source of income.

Catherine sheepishly accepted the offer from the new principal. He seemed alright, but not nearly as interesting as the last one. A little bit of boring was exactly what Nika needed right now.

The little bell by the door chimed. He had always messed this up, so he wrote a checklist by the door to remember how this thing worked.

1. Check the peephole
2. Twist the lock to the right
3. Knock twice, then open.

This would activate some sort of charm that would let his dorm door open to the street to let a guest in. Whenever he opened the door normally, he'd just end up in the dorm halls. Morgan was outside; she was whistling to herself. He didn't even know she did that. The golden tattoos on her arms were shining in the summer sun. He imagined her mom absolutely hated them.

He got it right on the first try and let her in. She hadn't seen the featureless room before, so he gave her the grand tour. There was the bed. There was the desk. There was one box of things that they managed to salvage from the fire. Morgan, as usual, cut right to the chase.

"So. Results!" she held out her hands. "Lemme see!"

"I haven't gotten them back yet," Nika said. As if on cue, the mail slot by the door clunked with a sound he had only heard once since move-in day. There was a letter.

He lost the race to the mail, and Morgan got to the letter first.

"Ok, Spooky Boy. Want to make a bet?"

He lost a considerable amount of enthusiasm. "Spooky Boy."

"If you didn't make eighth, you have to legally change your name to Spooky Boy." She held the envelope up to the window, trying to see through it. She frowned. No luck.

"And if I am?"

"Then you get invited to a celebratory lunch!" Morgan reached out for a handshake.

"So if I lose, I don't get lunch, and I have to go by 'Spooky Boy?'" When she nodded, he sighed. "Can I please just have my mail?"

"I remember when you used to be fun." She pouted and handed him the envelope.

He peeled it open and turned away from her so she wouldn't see it.

He made it. He could pick any grade up to and including ninth to join. Weeks of studying and other, larger sources of stress had finally melted off of him. For the last week of his first summer 'break', he was truly and finally free.

He put on his most distressed face and looked at Morgan, panicked.

"Hey." She was apologetic immediately. "You know I was joking about lunch too. We're already set up for it, of course, you-"

He couldn't keep his laugh suppressed.

"Oh, you're awful." Morgan was both upset and laughing. "I didn't expect Spooky Boy to get me."

"Hey, I won the bet, so quit it." Nika left out the part where he never actually accepted the bet.

There was a knock on the door. The bell meant someone from outside was visiting. A knock meant someone from the dorms. In this case, it was both Nils and Catherine. They obviously came to ask the same question, and they knew the answer as soon as he had opened the door.

Catherine gave him a painting as a housewarming present. It was a tiny canvas, about the size of his palm. It was a painting of a teacup, which seemed fitting. He needed something to put somewhere on the walls to make this feel like any kind of home.

Nils picked him up and spun him around in a hug. It was about a fifty-fifty bet whether Nils's thin frame would be able to support any amount of weight at all, but they made it work. Everyone besides him had been let in on the lunch plan. The stated purpose was to congratulate or console Nika, whichever was appropriate. In reality, it was just a good excuse to get everyone together again.

They had seen each other in the weeks since the event, but not a lot. Nika and Nils stayed at Morgan's place for a night or two. Karao had to get through the Suit's investigation and was cleared only a few days before. Daniel had a lot on his mind, but Nils had been seeing him pretty regularly and said he was doing ok. Without Nils knowing, he was the first one to visit Nika's new dorm.

Nika wasn't sure which was worse: Daniel when he was convinced Nika was some sort of traitor, or Daniel when he had to get a thousand apologies out in a single day. Nika already understood his position. He didn't need further clarification. He decided that the latter left him with another friend, and the former just meant more yelling, so annoying was better than angry.

The four of them talked for a while then left for lunch.

The city recovered from its temporary blizzard remarkably quickly. Officials weren't able to figure out exactly where it came from, but officials didn't know about the storm-toting demon locked away someplace far from Eldes.

"Oh! Did you hear about the old principal?" Morgan asked.

The three of them swallowed the lumps in their throats in unison. They all knew what happened to the principal, but nobody wanted to be the one to let the secret slip in case she didn't. In her excitement, Morgan went on to finish her thoughts without their input.

"He went missing, so they went through his house and found a bunch of stuff! Nika! He used to be a Pro Duelist!" She was so excited. "Guess which one!"

The others were surprised but didn't really have much to do with that information. Nika had a suspicion from the day of. The question was- does he use the information to get a laugh out of stumping Morgan, or does he continue to play dumb? He was in high enough spirits with low enough stakes that he went for it.

"Molten Phoenix," Nika said.

"You did hear, cheater," Morgan groaned.

Fighting her on it would mean revealing the truth that the principal would never be coming back, and they knew why. So the three let it slide. Morgan decided that the two of them needed to talk strategy for their upcoming doubles-duelist tryouts, so they did for the remainder of the walk.

Their first stop along the way was to get Daniel, whose work was along the route. He was dressed for a much fancier lunch than they were all going to, probably to impress Nils. Catherine had the honor of ribbing him for that, but Nils defended their boyfriend's attire. Daniel blushed a bit. Maybe it was the heat.

Karao was waiting for them at the trolley station. She was out in public with no deadarms, which was a new look for her; that and the sunglasses. Aside from those, she was the same old Karao. Mysterious, confident to a fault, and dominating way too much vertical space. She was happier for Nika than any of them.

Catherine sat next to him during the tram ride.

"It's been a summer, huh," she said.

"Has it?" he said. She bumped him with her elbow. He deserved it.

"What do-" She leaned back. "What do you think of the cafeteria food?"

He was taken aback by the question. "It's- it's fine?"

She groaned. Clearly, it wasn't what she wanted to say. "Look. I'm not as good as Nils with feelingsy-things. But we're all splitting up for now."

"Not too much. We're all in the dorms," Nika said.

"Not Karao," Catherine said. "I just want to tell you that just because we're not in the tea shop anymore doesn't mean you're not family. We got each other's backs, right?"

He smiled. "Of course."

The rest of the ride was uneventful. They got off at a stop well before the one Nika was familiar with near the game shop. Ben and Lisa Farvue were waiting outside a small little restaurant, both in full uniform. Lisa impatiently tapped her foot. It was her first day back full time with the Suits, and asking for a longer lunch was already a huge favor. Ben shrugged and waved to them. He would probably get yelled at, but that couldn't be too terrible.

The restaurant barely had enough room for them, though it wasn't busy. It was Lisa's favorite little hideaway, a place so far off the radar that some of the locals didn't even know it existed. The staff all knew her face and put the necessary tables together accordingly.

The food was worth the wait and the travel, but that wasn't what Nika was taking away from this. This was the most comfortable he had ever felt, eating nice food surrounded by friends and his recently discovered family.

Everyone was in high spirits. Nils was laughing, Daniel fit in pretty effortlessly, and Morgan got to explain the origin story of her arm markings while both of her parents groaned. Being bestowed the magical ritual summoning markings of Gladys Ixus Eldes - founder and protector of the city of Eldes- is sort of a big deal. Also, Gladys had apparently founded Eldes as a protective guardian of sorts. They found her autobiography tucked away under the rubble. Morgan's fake hunt had succeeded in the end, inexplicably. The world was unfair.

The library had been closed for repairs for the past few weeks. The first item on the list, likely, was finding an actual staff to replace the disappeared librarian. With all the mysterious vanishings in the city, the security was likely going to take a step up.

Everyone really felt Cruise's absence around the same time. Nika was the last person he had talked to, and he had given no sign as to where he was going. From the sounds of it, he was going to deal with Liz himself and wanted Karao to be able to back him up if things went wrong.

Things certainly went wrong that day, and Cruise hadn't been seen since. Because of that, nobody had been fully cleared of suspicion, but with a culprit found for the crime spree, they could breathe easily for the foreseeable future.

"Any updates?" Nils asked.

"Nothing. He's just completely vanished." Ben was vexed. "The worst part is that it's entirely like him to cover his tracks."

While on the topic, Lisa brought up something that had been bothering her. "What was in that box, Nika?" Lisa asked. Ben choked on a glass of water.

"He didn't tell you?" Nika weighed whether he was supposed to answer or not. Luckily, Ben interjected.

"You did not just ask that question." He pressed his fingertips into his skull like he was trying to break through.

"What?" Nika and Lisa asked.

Ben reached into his jacket and tossed a small note onto the table. It was folded and bore a wax seal with a very plain-looking C in its center. The back read: 'Give to Lisa if she asks Nika about the box.'

"Are you going to open it?" Nika asked.

Lisa, the predictable, was also annoyed with Cruise. "Nope. He can explain himself when he comes back."

If Nika was going to leave summer with a favorite memory, he would be hard-pressed to choose. This was the most fun he had condensed into a single hour, the fireflies were visually stunning, and he wouldn't miss anything the way he missed the time in the tea shop: the microscopic community, the little interactions. Even things like waiting in line for the shower in the morning felt like an endearing trait now that it was over. Picking the worst moment would probably be equally hard.

"So, Karao," Daniel asked. "What are you doing about the tea shop?"

"I sold it."

Though everyone expressed their shock with different words, yelling was a consistent theme between them all. The exception to the rule was Nika, who nearly choked on a bit of bread. Karao, for her part, reluctantly sipped some mediocre tea.

"I know, I know. Don't worry, I've found a new hookup that is completely adequate for my needs. As a customer, of course. You can all calm down now."

The questions she was bombarded with included: where she would live, where she would work, who bought a charred plot of land from necromancers, to begin with.

"We just went through a remodel. I don't think I can handle replacing all my stuff again. It's time for a new chapter, I feel. I've got my eyes on a few houses on the other side of town and some promising ventures from old contacts. Though the city did contact me about this open head librarian position, now that sounds more my speed. And if I can get a tea shop built in the library, well, then..."

They finished their food, thanked the delightful old couple that ran this hidden gem of a restaurant, and moved on with their days. Morgan's parents had left earlier than the rest, both earlier than Ben wanted and later than Lisa did. A true compromise leaves everyone annoyed.

Karao asked Nika to stay behind the rest so they could talk. She said to the rest of the group it was just about financing the year and allowances and stuff. They wouldn't be interested in what Karao had to say, anyways.

"Don't worry, we're not talking about any of that. Come on, let's go shopping for some new clothes for school."

They wandered around the different stores in the north part of town for the rest of the afternoon. Karao asked questions like 'have you figured out laundry' or 'do you have such and such thing to clean your room or the bathroom? They talked about life, about Eldes, about Catherine and Morgan and Nils. They talked about the tea shop and the end of the summer's long days.

Karao stopped in front of a bookstore. "Nika."

He was almost drooling. "Yes."

"We're going to go into this bookstore."

There was a sale on young adult fiction "Yes."

"We're going to get your texts, and you may pick one and only one book to read for pleasure. And it's only because the library is closed. And because your test results were so good."

Every shelf seemed packed tight "Yes."

"Do you understand?"

He hadn't had a new book in two weeks. "Yes."

"Ok then. After you."

The damage had been done. Karao had brought her satchel, which made whatever was in it feel lighter. Even with that, the books weighed him down a lot. The last team didn't leave until a few hours later, so they decided to have a final cup of tea together for the summer.

Karao spat it out immediately. Nika thought it was fine.

"I probably won't get to see you as much when the school year starts. I'll be busy working. Hopefully, you'll have your own work to do. Who knows how long it will be until I find the right house," she said. "In all honesty, I'm a bit jealous of you."

"It's ok. I spend a lot of time in the library anyways. You can just get me a job there."

"Are you asking me for a job, knowing full well you'd just read all day?"

"That's a mean way to put it," he said. "But yea, basically."

Karao laughed. "We'll see."

The streets always calmed down at the end of the day. Twilight was the best part of the day to sit outside and enjoy some wretched, disgusting tea with a friend. The necromancers drank up in the orange light and watched people go about their day, completely oblivious to the perils they had been through. Life was harder for them, and that was largely Karao's fault.

"You're free to decline," Karao said, staring ahead. "But I would like to continue to train you and the others in necromancy. After - that - I understand if you have reservations-"

"Karao," he said

She carried on. "-That being said, I still think the merits of proper training in necromancy outweigh the cons. So if-"

He tried again, "Karao."

"-there's anything you want to talk about. I promise you my door is always open. Even if you call off your training, I would like to continue acting as your guardian, Nika. You're part of the-"

"Karao!"

"Yes?"

Nika smiled. Truth be told, he hated necromancy. Deadarms didn't work with him, and zombies were freaky. This soul thing interested him, though. "I was going to ask to train regardless."

"Fearless, as always. No, no, that's very inaccurate. More like fearful but reckless and a small pinch of bravery. A whole swirling blend of bitter ingredients that seems to work out in the end."

The tram was pulling in, so they got up. "Are you talking about me or the tea?"

"Certainly not this tea," Karao said. As they boarded, she had one final question for him. "You've got a lot going on these next few months. Think you're ready?"

He laughed. "Not at all."

His family was displaced, scattered across the dorms, and in one case, homeless and under criminal investigation. He had gained one close friend, and if there were more like her, he couldn't handle another. He wasn't ready, and he wouldn't have it any other way.

Bitter Tea & Necromancy - End

Coda

Karao liked the desert sand just fine, so much so that she didn't mind the pun. She always tried to present herself in a larger-than-life, grandstanding fashion, and the billowing winds and blazing light allowed her to drape herself in large flowing scarves and cloth under the guise of covering her face when, in reality,,,, she just loved the way she looked.

She had brought three things with her that they had just recovered from the tea shop remains. The first was one of her deadarms, the shadow caster arm. It was extremely effective, and there weren't a lot of situations where manifesting shadows as magical limbs weren't useful, but it didn't help with the image problem that necromancers faced already. The second was her favorite teacup. It used to be her second favorite, but that one was smashed, so it moved up in the world. The last was the tagalong inside the teacup. Donut had made a home for himself, curling around the fingers of her deadarm. The lazy little snake had somehow survived the inferno, and she couldn't help but be impressed by it.

Hult was in the same place he always was, a horrific mass of bones surrounded by the amber mages who gave their lives to freeze him in time. Amber magic was terrifying and potent when used properly. At the base of the dune forming around Hult stood five recently unearthed statues. Or rather, four recently unearthed statues and one that was practically new.

"I knew I'd find you here," she whispered. She had come to talk to Hult before and had an idea of where to start her search. "And people say I'm dramatic."

Sure enough, she had found Cruise. The former suit stood permanently frozen. His fingers had just snapped in some direction. He had pulled the trigger on amber, and there was no going back.

"Rather rude of you, you're going to miss my nine-hundredth birthday, Cruise." She twirled one of her scarves around and left Donut on Cruise's head. The snake considered investigating but preferred napping.

"I'm guessing Liz told you to come here, to come alone, and to work something out, am I right?" Neither Cruise nor Donut answered. "I'll go further. You were planning to use that on me, weren't you? In case I ever slipped into old habits. It's a good trick." She looked at the hand that had frozen post-snap. It looked like the perfect place to hang her teacup; it was. "Of course, it works better if you don't miss, you idiot."

"I think it's time to turn a new leaf. Enough dwelling on the past. And now, thanks to you, my first problem is getting you out of this mess." Karao pulled her small black book out of her sleeve. She chucked it and every favor every person owed her into the sand. "Here's to a new beginning."

www.ingramcontent.com/pod-product-compliance
Lightning Source LLC
Chambersburg PA
CBHW021437240626
47153CB00001B/183